A SPLASH OF SCARLET

A FRANK HARPER MYSTERY

GREG ENSLEN

GYPSY
PUBLICATIONS

Published in 2025, by Gypsy Publications
Troy, OH 45373, U.S.A.
www.GypsyPublications.com

First Edition

Enslen, Greg
Frank Harper Mysteries Series
A Splash of Scarlet / by Greg Enslen
ISBN 978-1-955640-09-1 (paperback)

Cover by Jenn Marcano
Cover Design by Pamela Schwartz

For more information, please visit the author's website at:
www.GregEnslen.com

FORWARD

First off, welcome back, dear readers. I'm sorry this one took so long to finish. Seriously, I went down the wrong path on this one and large parts of it had to be scrapped and rewritten. But I'm certain the book is better for it.

Thank you to my folks, who poured through this book multiple times and helped immensely with plot and character suggestions, along with the bevy of typos that inevitably make their way into a manuscript that undergoes rewrites.

Thank you to my beta readers and others who read the book ahead of time and gave me valuable feedback on the characters and plot. If you're interested in being an early reader, get in touch with me through my website or on Facebook.

Four Years

As I'm writing this, it's July 2024, and things are ramping up for the election. Crazy new things are happening daily, and it's been nice to dive back into the world of Frank Harper. And I was reading through the foreword I wrote for the last Frank book, ***Green with Envy***. It's been four years since I put out a Frank Harper book? Really? Wow, sorry about that, folks. Things have been crazy. I bought a newspaper, for one thing, and I've been working on some other writing projects.

Anyway, back to the foreword—it was from late 2020, and the world was going through the insanity that was Covid-19. It's so strange to look back on those times as history, knowing everything we know now.

I've been working on this book for about four years and, like I said, this book was a lot of fun to write—so much that I almost wrote it twice! Okay, not that much, but I did have a very well-thought-out plot that I ended up replacing. I hope people like this newer and better version. It was fun to bring back some of the characters you'll be reading about.

I love a good blast from the past. The guys that write **The Expanse** are particularly good at that, resurrecting characters from five books ago that I'd completely forgotten about. If you like science fiction, I'd heartily recommend that series—I'm reading the last book, the ninth in the series, as slowly as I can to make it last as long as possible.

But the Frank Harper books are getting easier to write, I feel. I know Frank like the back of my hand and fall back into his voice without much trouble.

Upcoming

In the meantime, I promise I've been writing. I finished and published a Binge Guide to one of my favorite TV shows, the 1970's classic "Emergency!" I also wrote and released a completed Binge Guide for the whole series of "Game of Thrones" and "Mr. Robot." AND I completed and published a Binge Guide on my favorite series of films, the "Back to the Future" trilogy.

I often explain to people that when I finish writing a book, I'm wrapping up a multi-year-long process of solving a puzzle. A puzzle of my own creation, to be sure, but still a puzzle, with strange pieces that I'm trying to cram together in a way that makes sense. This book was like that, even more so, due to the fact that I had to rewrite much of the first half.

I'm working on launching another series, and I find myself describing things in longer passages that just wouldn't feel correct when writing about Frank and his breathless, take-no-prisoners style of police work. To me, Frank wouldn't be interested in long, descriptive passages. He just doesn't have time for that.

Thank You

Anyway, that's it for now. There is an extensive *Author's Note* at the end of the book with more information, but I didn't want to include it here due to spoilers. Talk soon and THANK YOU for reading!!! Stay healthy out there, and I'll see you soon,

— Greg

A SPLASH OF SCARLET

PART 1
Ready

CHAPTER 1
Gary

On a late September evening in 2012, four young men ambled randomly through a dark neighborhood, bored and looking for something to do. Trouble, or something like it.

They had been at one of the old car factories a few blocks over, breaking the remaining dirty panes of glass, and now they were bored again. It would be dark soon. They roamed the streets, mostly looking for a tourist to roll. They avoided the other gang bangers in the area—it was just easier to rob a tourist.

It was a Monday night in late September and the streets of this part of Gary, Indiana, were quiet, abandoned to the gathering dark. Most of the people who lived or worked around here were off the streets by 8 p.m., most likely for their own protection. Crime was rampant in this faded neighborhood, stuffed between huge, mostly abandoned factories to the south and a smattering of liquor shops and cheap hotels to the north.

To the uninitiated, this portion of Gary looked like it had been through a war. From a certain point of view, it had. Economics dictated that the money had gone away as soon as several of the larger factories closed in the late 1970s. Poverty and crime had swept in, covering the once-prosperous town like a tide, washing away hope and tranquility. Anyone with money had fled the area, leaving it to the criminals.

Now, the place looked like the worst neighborhood imaginable, a pit of dread in some war-torn, third-world country, a place that had long ago given up on peace or personal safety. Abandoned to squalor, the residents in this forgotten corner of America dreamed of only one thing—escape. A short drive through Gary or a hundred other similar small Midwestern towns made it abundantly clear that someone—or a whole group of people—had simply given up on this once-thriving community.

Bored, this group of young men and dozens of others like them spent their aimless nights climbing fences to gain access to places they shouldn't, or swept through dark neighborhoods, trying every car door handle in turn, searching for an easy score. In between, they drank and made fun of each other and rattled through the streets like dried leaves in a gutter, looking for easy money. Tourists were the best, if you could find them. White folks, mostly, staying at the hotels up on Bay Street, the northern edge of their gang's territory.

Money was hard to come by, and even though none of them was over 20, all of them lived on their own, long since kicked out of their respective parents' homes.

They knew that life was about taking what you could, taking it from people who didn't deserve it. In some ways, this group of four young men saw themselves as freedom fighters, recapturing some of the money that was rightfully theirs.

They had all been to the "nicer" towns in the area, tourists in their own right. They had seen the safe streets and the big, beautiful houses, the ones with wide, well-kept yards and fancy cars parked out front. It had been alien to them—the cars, just sitting there, with no one trying to steal them or at least strip them for parts. Not a single car up on blocks, the tires missing. All the wealth of the other towns they had seen, all those fancy things. All probably bought with stolen money, taken from the poor or plundered in some rich-person's scheme.

It was enough to piss anyone off.

Tonight, Trey, the group's defacto leader, was in a bad mood. It had been days since they'd had a good score, and nearly a week since he'd gotten high. It made him feel half crazy, like bugs crawling under his skin. His eyes scanned the dark streets, the hand in his pocket toying with a small, snub-nosed revolver. The gun was cheap but good—it made him feel powerful, like a god. His other hand scratched at a scab on his neck.

"What about that paint factory place again?" Nick asked. Nick was paper thin and the tallest of them. Great at getting over fences. He always looked sickly, like he was dying. "You know, where they paint those trucks?"

Trey looked at him and sneered—he couldn't help it and didn't care either. Nick was always suggesting that place, had been for nearly two years, ever since they'd gotten a fat wad of cash off a guy in the parking lot.

"They got a shift ending soon, right?" Nick said. "Maybe they gettin' paid today. Knock somebody over the head, right?"

Lacey, the smallest of their group, shook his head. He was the smart one, his eyes always moving. "Those shifts end at 6 p.m. and midnight," he said, holding up his watch. It was a fancy Apple Watch they'd taken off a dumb white woman three months ago, and Lacey had figured out how to get it to work with his cheap Walmart phone. "Nobody getting off at 9 o'clock, man."

Off to the east, Trey could hear the rumble of the highway. Trucks, cars, full of rich folks, heading somewhere important. Trey scratched at his neck and searched, desperate. There had to be people out, or a house that wasn't locked up too tight.

Nick nodded. "Maybe you're right. People get paid on Mondays?"

Lacey shook his head. "Fridays, mostly. Most get it put straight into their banks. Never see the cash."

Trey stroked the gun in his pocket again, running a finger down the barrel. His plan was to head back north. There had been nothing going on near the factories and Trey wanted one more pass through the hotel parking lots before he called it a night and sent the others home. He needed to get to work, needed to be making money. Robbing and rolling tourists and breaking into places and stealing stuff was work—it was what Trey was best at.

Trey shook his head. "We ain't going back south. Too far. We gonna hit the hotels again."

He walked north, and the others fell in line behind him.

After a minute, the fourth young man in their group, Tiny, finally spoke up. "There," he said, pointing down the street. Tiny was the quiet one, a huge guy with wide shoulders. He also had the best eyesight of all of them.

The others turned to see where he was pointing.

"Where?" Lacey asked. Trey could see him squinting in the dark.

"There," Tiny said, pointing again. "By the church. Walking north."

Trey saw him. A white guy. Old, carrying some bags. Groceries, maybe. Walking in the direction of the hotels.

"Tourist?" Nick asked. "Nice."

Lacey laughed. "Yeah, tourists are easy."

"Prolly," Trey said, nodding. He gripped the gun in his pocket, clenching and releasing. "Let's do it."

They moved in a group, hunting like a pack, following the old man with the groceries up the dark road. They passed a church and what used to be an auto parts store, falling in behind the man. He was heading straight for the hotels.

Trey and Tiny trailed the white man, and the other two boys ran ahead. They had done this dozens of times and everyone knew what to do. Trey and Tiny always followed the mark, and Nick and Lacey ran, sprinting away left and right and running up parallel streets to get ahead of them and surround their victims.

A minute later, Trey saw Nick and Lacy come out of the shadows up ahead of the white guy, who stopped when he saw them emerge from the dark. The hotel was close, but not close enough.

At least not close enough to do this old dude any good.

Trey and Tiny walked up behind the man just as he turned, looking at them. The old guy with the bag of groceries looked out of place on the dark streets of Gary. The guy stopped walking and sighed loudly, then bent and calmly set the bag of groceries down at his feet. Trey looked at it curiously—tourists didn't buy groceries, did they?

"Hey, man," Trey said. "You lost?"

The old man stood, hanging his arms at his sides. He looked at Trey and shook his head. Trey thought the man looked even older than he'd previously thought. But he was white, and therefore not local, that was for sure.

"I'm not lost," the old man said. "And you don't want to do this."

Trey looked at him. That's not what the tourists usually said first. Usually it was something like "don't hurt me" or "why are you picking on me?" Occasionally, they just dropped their stuff and started running.

"Really, man?" Trey said with a smile. "I don't wanna do this? You sure you're not lost?"

"No, I live there," the old man said, pointing. He seemed very calm for an old white guy surrounded by gang bangers. "The hotel on Bay Street," he said. "You guys know it?"

"Ain't no tourists around here, man," Nick said. He already had his knife out, waving it. Trey could see the dim light from the streetlight glistening off of it. This was going to be easy. "You seen this place? Nobody white, at least."

The old man turned and looked at Nick and stretched his shoulders in a strange way.

"I'm not a tourist," the man said to Nick. "And like I said, you don't want to do this. I don't want any trouble."

Ah, there you go. They always said that.

"Look at me, old man," Trey said quietly. The man turned back around and looked at Trey. "You out of your element, as they say. So that means troubles comin' for ya." He pulled his hand from his pocket, showing his gun but pointing it at the ground like they did in the movies. That always quieted the tourists down.

Or made them cry. One time, a guy pissed himself, standing in a puddle he'd made.

The man looked at the gun in Trey's hand but didn't react. He glanced around at the others, then back to Trey. "So, you're in charge?"

"That's right, man. Can't you see I got the gun?"

"I can see that," the old man said.

"Enough talk, Trey," Lacey said from behind the old man. Trey could see he was looking around, nervous. He always got nervous when Trey was working.

The old man put up his hands. "Listen, Trey, is it? Just let me walk out of here and nobody needs to get hurt."

Trey looked at him, confused. Tourists didn't talk like that.

"What?"

The white guy looked at him, his arms drifting down to his waist. "I said nobody needs to get hurt," the guy said slowly, like he was talking to a child. "You've got the gun, so you're in charge. Just walk away."

Trey laughed. "Man, ain't you looked around? You surrounded, and you're in the hood. Don't belong here." Trey took a step towards the old man. "And yeah, I'm in charge. And you ain't. Give me your fu—"

It all happened so fast that, for a second, Trey wasn't even sure what was happening.

The old white guy ducked away from Trey and spun around, whipping something out from beneath his own shirt. In the darkness, before anyone could even react, Trey saw it was a gun, small but with a weird, long barrel. The old man aimed it at Nick and Lacey, and the weird gun coughed twice, barking like a dog. It made an odd flat sound that sounded nothing like a real gun. Trey saw Lacey and Nick fall backwards, stiff-legged, falling like trees. Nick's knife clattered to the ground and skittered away.

It all happened in an instant. Like the man was an old gunfighter or something. Quick draw, like out of a movie.

Trey lifted his gun but again it all felt like it was happening in slow motion, like a replay from a basketball game. The old man was turning back, facing Trey and Tiny, when Trey's hand exploded in pain. He dropped his gun and tucked his burning hand into his stomach. It roared like it was on fire. Trey's gun, forgotten, slid away into the dark. Covering his hand, Trey saw blood had spattered his shirt and pants. He dropped to his knees.

Even as Trey went down, he saw the old man turn and lift the weird gun. The long barrel made the weird coughing sound again. Tiny grabbed his shoulder and fell. He didn't even have time to reach for his knife, much less pull it out.

It all took less than five seconds.

The street went silent again. And moans. His boys were moaning, making sounds Trey hadn't heard before. Then he realized he was groaning too.

"Nah, man," one of the others whimpered. "Come on, man..."

Trey looked up. The old man was walking toward Nick, the gun on him. Nearby, Lacey was writhing on the ground, crying like a girl.

"Shut up, dumbass, or I'll shoot you again," Trey heard the old man say to both of them. "I told you kids to pound sand. This is on you." The old man bent and took each of their knives. Trey hadn't realized that Lacey had pulled his.

The man turned and pointed the gun at Tiny for a moment, then looked at Trey. The man walked over to his grocery bag, dropping the knives in, then checked on Tiny, kneeling and rolling him over while keeping the gun on him. Tiny's shirt was stained deep red.

"Shit," the old man said.

He stood, taking Tiny's knife from the big man's hand. Trey couldn't tell if Tiny fought him for the knife or if the big guy was out. Tiny's knife was a good-sized one with a dark blade. It had seen a lot of use.

Then the man came over to Trey and kneeled down next to him.

"So," the old man said quietly. He sounded tired. "Like I asked before: you're in charge?"

Trey shook his head, gripping his hand and squeezing it, trying to ignore the pain. "Man, you're dead. We run with the Last Boys."

"Is that so?" He looked around. "Looks like your little army is out of commission."

"No, man. No." Trey's hand felt like it was on fire.

"Your guys are all hurt. The big one pretty bad if you don't stop that bleeding. And I could end you, right now. All of you. You still think you're in charge?"

"Yeah, man. Last Boys run this part of town. You're dead, man. Dead."

The old guy leaned into the light and Trey finally got a good look at him. Old, white, beard. The dude was smiling.

"No, I don't think so," he said. "Tell your Last Boys or Lost Boys or whatever to stay out of this area for a while. In fact, stay clear of the hotels. All of them. Tell your gang of idiots to leave them alone for the next six months. Find another source of income."

Trey didn't say anything. The old man looked away, his eyes drawn by movement, and Trey turned to look. There was a man approaching, jogging over from the nearby hotel parking lot. The old man lowered the gun, hiding the long barrel behind his leg, until the man got close. As Trey watched, the old man apparently recognized the approaching figure.

"Joe, that you?" the figure said. "You okay?"

The old man lifted his gun so the approaching man could see it. "Never better."

The other man walked up and stood next to him, looking down at Trey. "Trouble?"

"Nah," the old guy named Joe said. He popped out the magazine from his weird gun and reloaded it with a spare magazine from his pocket. "Some punks, trying out the tourists."

"Looks like they lost," the man said.

"At least I finally got some target practice," Joe said with a smile. "Been a while since I made it to the range."

The new guy bent and picked up Trey's gun from the dirt and handed it to Joe, who looked it over.

"You like guns, kid?" Joe asked.

Trey looked up at him, his mind racing. "What?"

"'What ain't no country I ever heard of'," Joe said with a smile.

"Good one, Joe," the other man said, smiling. "Or should I call you Jules?"

The old man's eyes sparkled. Trey had no idea what was even happening. He was hurt, his boys were all down, and these guys were making jokes?

Joe looked down at Trey.

"I love guns. Always have," he said. "They say a lot about the person carrying them. Take your gun, Trey. Colt .22, six shot revolver, poorly maintained." He popped it open, eyed the bullets and chambers, then flipped it to spin the barrel. "Rusty handle. Jacketed ammo, steel tips, minimal rifling. Cheap bullets for a cheap hoodlum," the man named Joe said as he waved Trey's gun at him. "Right? You ever clean it?"

Trey didn't answer.

"You ever oil it? You even know how to oil it? Anyone ever show you how to maintain it? These Last Boys folks, they give you this, or you take it off someone else?"

Trey didn't know what to say.

The old man shook his head and pocketed Trey's gun. Then he stepped closer and knelt down.

"Joe, we gotta go," the other guy said."

"In a sec," he said, then looked at Trey. "You gotta know your weapon, son." He held up his gun. It had a long, skinny barrel unlike anything Trey had ever seen.

"Now see, in an urban environment, you need to be carrying something like this."

The old man turned the gun for Trey to admire. "You want a gun like this, okay," he said. "It's a Ruger Mark II with integrated suppression. Heard of it?"

Trey shook his head, starting to feel cold. His hand was throbbing, and he was having trouble focusing on the old man and what he was saying.

"Come on, they've been making these guns since 1949," the old man said, turning the gun in the light. "Ruger Mark II? See the long skinny barrel? It's a built-in suppressor. Quiet. Not as quiet as a real suppressor, of course, but those things are huge. Like a Pringles can, really. Too big to lug around in your pocket when you're out shopping for groceries. And, with a real suppressor, you have to rifle the barrel and the suppressor and make sure they fit together really tight. You understand?"

"Yeah," Trey said quietly.

"This one is integrated into the barrel. Course it uses .22LR ammo, which is hard to come by, lately. Seems there's been a run on that caliber. Long rifle rounds. But it's worth it—the report is very quiet. Did you notice that?"

"What? Nah, man," Trey said. "Piss off."

The old man stood and lifted his gun and shot Trey in the leg.

He jumped, half from the shock of the old man's sudden ferocity and half from the instant pain that flared through his body. He reached for his leg as fire roared through it, dripping like lava.

It was the most intense pain he could imagine.

"See? Super quiet," Joe said to his friend. "Like quiet enough to shoot four dumb gang bangers and no one would hear much. Right?

They've been making the Ruger for a long time. Battle tested." He looked at the gun.

"It's nice," the other man said, glancing around. "We better go, Joe."

"Nah, cops avoid this place," Joe said. He turned back to Trey and continued the strange lesson. "But I like it, even though it makes the barrel comically long. Harder to draw, obviously, but in an urban environment, or someplace where you want to be quiet, it makes sense. Suppressors block the sound of the projectile, baffles the sound coming out of the barrel. It's 80% quieter," the old man said proudly, turning the gun in the darkness to admire it. "And it's a magazine-fed automatic pistol, so it holds 13 shots instead of the six in your revolver. Plus one in the chamber, if you keep it loaded."

He squatted back down and pushed the skinny barrel into the bloody hole in Trey's leg. The old man leaned closer, whispering.

"And Trey? I always keep it loaded."

Trey squirmed. It smelled like gunpowder and blood. Sweat ran into his eyes.

The old man sighed. "So, pretend I live here now. You and your punks stay clear of the hotels. And tell your Last Boys the same. Got it? I didn't come to this paradise on Earth to be messed with by the likes of you, son," he said, grinding the gun in. Trey felt the metal barrel push against bone. His head swooned.

"Yessir, no problem."

"I won't be around this place forever. Till then, find someone else to bother. Got it? I'm in charge. For now."

"Yessir," Trey mumbled.

The old guy kept talking, kneeled over next to Trey, but the blood was roaring in his ears and Trey couldn't hear him. His hand was throbbing and his leg burned. Trey tried to concentrate—the old man was saying something about the game of chess. Talking about a knight and a pawn and moving parts around the board, but Trey didn't understand. Did that mean the old man would let him live? What the fu—

"You listening, son?"

Trey nodded, sweat dripping off his chin. "Yessir. I hear you. No more tourists. No problem."

CHAPTER 2
Hotel

Trapper shook his head and smiled, following his boss back to the hotel. They crossed the dark parking lot, leaving the gangbangers behind. The main one had crawled over to the fat one and was trying to stop the blood.

Trapper looked around, half expecting the cops to arrive at any moment. Joe was supposed to be keeping his head down, not drawing attention—or getting into gunfights. Christ, this wasn't the wild west.

"Looks like they picked on the wrong tourist," Trapper said.

"What?"

"Only you can find a way to start a gang war all by yourself," Trapper said.

Joe Hathaway smiled and handed him the bag of groceries. Joe felt the barrel of his gun to make sure it wasn't too hot, then put it in the waistband of his loose-fitting pants. "It's not the greatest neighborhood. Thanks for that, by the way."

"Hey, you're wanted," Trapper said. "Can't exactly be putting you up at the Ritz Carlton. You're lying low, remember?"

Joe nodded. "Like I could forget in this place. You really know how to pick 'em," he said, waving at the dingy streets and sad buildings around them.

"No one will look for you here," Trapper said. "As long as you just pay cash, nobody cares."

Joe nodded. "And hopefully those kids will clear out of here soon. I don't need the cops coming, so the less crime, the better. If a tourist gets robbed or shot, the cops will be all over this place," he said, nodding ahead at the squat motel where he'd been living for the last seven months.

"I'll take a listen to the scanner when we get to the hotel," Trapper said. He'd provided his boss with a small police radio scanner unit when getting him set up in the hotel.

"But that was stupid. I should know better," Joe said, shaking his head and glancing back over his shoulder. "I don't need them looking for whoever shot four local youths. Knowing my luck, they're all honors students."

"I doubt it," Trapper said.

They walked the block back to the hotel, not seeing another soul.

"You waiting for me at the hotel? Heard the shots?"

"Yeah," Trapper said. "I know the sound of that gun. Otherwise, I would have ignored it."

Joe looked around at the dark buildings around them. "Just like everyone else around here."

They approached the hotel and Joe suddenly veered off to his right, circling around and entering the hotel parking lot from the north. It gave Trapper something to think about, and it took him a minute to figure it out—the old man wanted to be seen on the cameras as returning to the hotel from the north, not from the south, where a recent shooting had taken place.

The old man was always thinking.

Trapper crossed the pitted parking lot, puddles of rain reflecting the gaudy neon sign. Half of the words were missing. Ahead, Joe Hathaway trudged up the stairs to the second floor.

"Anyway, thanks for finding this place," Joe said. "And thanks for getting me all set up. I do appreciate it, even when I'm in a pissy mood."

"No worries, boss."

"And you know I'll pay you back once I can get access to my money again."

Trapper nodded. "Don't worry about it, boss. And it's not my money, it's yours. The Kickstarter's are still bringing in money, and the KoT faithful just want to see you safe until this whole thing blows over. We all know you're going to be fine."

The Keepers of Truth, the small cult-like organization that had sprung up around Joe Hathaway during his murder trial last year, had gone legit. They had staff now, and formed an LLC, raising funds for Joe's defense during the trial and after. The money rolled in, helping to fund "social justice" for the old man "wrongfully accused" of several murders.

Trapper was pretty sure Joe Hathaway was guilty—very guilty, in fact—but that didn't mean the old man was bad. And now Trapper ran the Keepers of Truth (KoT) organization and kept an eye on Joe.

"They still watching you," Joe asked. "The cops? Assuming you're in contact with me?"

"Every day," Trapper said. "Tails, bugs in the office, everything. It was hard to get away, but once you see why I came, it'll be worth it."

The group had recently expanded, adding a side business focused on defending the wrongly convicted. Trapper, one of the principles of the organization, thought it was a particularly clever way to bring money in, some of which making its way back to Joe.

It had been Joe's idea, of course—the old man was always thinking ahead. He'd given Trapper a bunch of money early on to secure transport out of the country during the trial, and when Joe had dropped off everyone's radar, the KoT had gone into "circling the wagons" mode, awaiting Joe's eventual reappearance.

By the time that happened, Trapper and the others were ready with updated escape plans. But Joe had told them "no"—instead, he wanted one more thing before he left the country.

A chance to take down Frank Harper.

The retired cop had testified against Joe during his trial and had also been instrumental in solving several of Joe's "crimes." Joe wanted revenge, and maybe a chance to clear his name and get his conviction overturned. In that order. Harper was a stone in Joe's shoe, and Trapper could tell Joe's obsession with the man couldn't just be brushed off.

Joe wanted blood.

So Trapper and the KoT were working hard, keeping Joe fed and housed while he was in hiding. Moving him around, funding his bare bones lifestyle, waiting for a break.

And in the last two days, there had been a very interesting development, one that had brought Trapper all the way to Gary, Indiana, and Joe's hiding spot.

"Thanks for checking in regularly," Joe said.

Trapper followed the old man through the hotel lobby and around the elevator. The lobby was abandoned, with only one clerk on duty. A small TV was on in the corner, displaying a football game to the empty room. When the elevator came, Trapper hit the "3" button for them. The old man didn't seem to relax until they were back in his room.

The inside of the rooms was worse than the outside—ratty beds, ratty carpet, stained walls.

"Welcome to paradise," Joe said with a sniff. "You wouldn't know I was rich, would ya?"

Trapper nodded and set the bag of groceries down. "The KoT is doing well, even helping out a couple of other people falsely convicted of crimes. But it's too bad all your other money is locked away." Before his arrest, Joe Hathaway had been very wealthy, but cops had seized all that money. Now, some of it was being used as a reward for Joe's capture. "You figure out a way to get it yet?"

"I'm still working on it," the old man said, straightening up and putting papers away.

Trapper watched the man tidy, wondering what was going through his mind. Trapper didn't visit a lot, but when he did, it was usually important. Like this time—Trapper had two very good pieces of news to share with his boss. One that would likely get him out of this shit hole. And the other? Even better news.

Trapper didn't say anything as the old man finished straightening, then took the bag of groceries to the tiny fridge. He watched as Hathaway took out the groceries—and three knives and a revolver—and put everything all away. The gun and knives went under the mattress along with Joe's Ruger. Finally, the man sat at the small table near the window that looked out over the rainy parking lot. Hathaway pointed at the other chair and waited for Trapper to join him.

"Okay, what you got for me?"

Trapper smiled. The guy was always the same, cutting to the chase.

"You sick of living here yet? I've got some good news on that front. Great news, actually."

"Finally," Joe said.

"But that's not why I came."

"No?" Joe said, sitting up.

"I know you have the laptop for trading stocks."

Joe nodded. "Yeah, not doing too bad. 148% return on the funds you put into the account for me."

Trapper nodded. "Nice. Have you been keeping up on the national news?"

Joe laughed. "No, I only get on for a half-hour a day just to be safe. Log in, make some trades on that new account you set up, and log off. Not really spending time surfing the net—only a search of my name once in a while. The internet sucks here."

With a smile, Trapper took out a folded newspaper, a copy of the *Wall Street Journal*, and handed it over.

"Life and Arts Section. Page 4."

Joe took the paper. "Such theatrics," he said, opening the *Journal*.

"Must be good news."

"I'll let you decide."

Trapper waited while the old man found the section he was looking for. Hathaway started reading, stopped, looked up at Trapper, then went back to reading. When he was three or four lines in, he stopped again and looked up.

"What's this about?"

"Hollywood starlet," Trapper said. "Doing time for her crimes. Keep going—and read it out loud, if you don't mind."

Hathaway rolled his eyes and continued.

"Hollywood starlet Jessica Mills was recently jailed in Los Angeles after being drunk and disorderly. She was involved in a situation that caused a minor car accident that nearly killed two people. It was reported to the press that she was serving her time in the LA county incarceration system but, in fact, she had been given a special dispensation by a Los Angeles judge. Instead of serving time in a California jail, the young woman was released into the custody of a member of the LAPD..."

He looked up at Trapper. "Who cares?"

"You do, sir."

"Really?"

Trapper nodded and smiled. "Keep reading."

Joe shook his head and went back to the paper.

"...Instead of serving time in a California jail, the young woman was released into the custody of a member of the LAPD and escorted out of town, serving her 'sentence' while vacationing in the small Ohio town of Cooper's Mill," Joe read out loud, then stopped and laughed.

Joe looked up from the newspaper at Trapper. "Cooper's Mill? This famous lady went to Cooper's Mill to serve a jail sentence?"

"Yup," Trapper replied. "Sort of. In lieu of jail, she was in the cop's custody and was getting clean. Coke, or something. They don't say. I did some reading—her lawyer convinced the judge to get her out of California to straighten her out. She was in with a bad element, blah blah blah. She got a local job in town, got clean. It's the talk of the whole state. Nobody could believe she was there. And in disguise, no less. Keep reading," he said, nodding at the paper.

Joe sighed and continued, his voice bouncing off the yellowing walls of the grungy hotel room. "Her identity was revealed during an incident at a local festival. Mills, who has over a month left on her 90-day term of incarceration, will either return to Los Angeles or remain in Cooper's Mill to serve out the remainder of 'her term' in small-town Ohio under the watchful eye of local police—and dozens of members of the press and paparazzi, who have swarmed the small town."

Joe looked up at Trapper. "Okay, that's it. Trapper, this is all very interesting, but what's the point?"

"Your hometown, all over the papers. Coast to coast."

Joe tossed Trapper the paper. "Great. I can't get the heat turned on in this place. I can only go out at night for fear of being spotted by the cops. But they're living it up in Cooper's Mill. Celebrities and celebrations and the press swarming in."

Trapper looked at him and handed the paper back. "It gets better."

"What does?"

"Keep reading."

Joe grabbed the paper and scanned the rest of the article. "It's just more about this Jessica Mills lady, some vapid actress from Hollywood. I never heard of her. She's complaining about some stalker and hired local private investigator..."

Joe stopped reading.

"No."

"Yes," Trapper said, nodding.

"It can't be."

"It is. Right there, in black and white."

"Frank Harper? The stone in my shoe? In the national news?"

Trapper nodded. "Keep going."

Joe shook his head and continued reading. "...and hired local private investigator Frank Harper and his team to provide security and..." He stopped and looked up at Trapper. "You've gotta be shitting me."

"Never, boss," Trapper said, nodding at the newspaper. "It's crazy. This famous woman turns up in Cooper's Mill, of all places—"

"And, of course, Harper shows up to help. White knight, runs in to protect her. He'll probably get her shot," Joe said.

Joe read the rest of the article again from the beginning, just as Trapper figured he would. Trapper sat, waiting. The old man was like a computer. If you were smart, you waited until he was done processing.

Trapper could see the old man calculating, computing, like one of those dusty old first-generation mainframes they showed in old movies. Brute force. Math, multiplication, division. Chess pieces on a checkerboard. The old man would run through all the permutations and variables and, at the end, he'd announce something like it was a done deal. Like he'd already seen all the other outcomes and come up with the best one and now it was just about guiding things to that best and final solution.

Joe stood, pacing around the hotel room as he read the *Journal*. Trapper waited, not wanting to interrupt. That was never a good idea. Let the man's brain compute. Trapper could see Joe's mind was turning, plotting, planning. Racing ahead, thinking out options, retreating back when they didn't work out.

After a few minutes, Joe turned and handed the paper back to Trapper.

"I have to go back."

Trapper nodded. "Yup, I know. As soon as I read this, I knew I had to come up. Figured you'd want to know right away."

"He'll be distracted with this girl, wanting to take care of her," Joe said. "It's the perfect time to take him out."

Trapper shook his head. It was never a good idea to contradict his boss, but...

"There are cops everywhere," Trapper said quietly. "State, locals, plus an LA lady cop. They are watching Mills day and night. It's VERY high profile."

Joe looked at him. "What are you saying? We can't get to him?"

"I'm just saying there's a lot of heat right now around town. Might not be the right time to make your move."

"What move? What move am I planning, Trapper?"

"Revenge, boss," Trapper said quietly. "I know you, sir. You want revenge."

Joe sat down on the edge of the bed, frustrated. "What was the second thing you wanted to tell me?"

"What?"

"When you came in, you said you had two things. If I can't go back to take care of Harper, what's the point?"

"Yes, absolutely," Trapper said, following the sudden change of subject. Joe was like that. "I've been staying in the area, Troy mostly, expecting you would want to come back." Trapper looked at him. "You've got business with Harper. Things you'd like to talk to him about, things you'd like to say."

"Yes," Joe said, his mind far away. "We have some issues to discuss."

Trapper nodded, even though Joe wasn't looking at him. "And

things didn't go well at the farmhouse."

Joe looked down at his hands. "No. No, they didn't."

"So, we figured you'd be coming back to the Dayton area soon enough." Trapper looked around at the hotel room. "When you're sick of this place."

"Happened months ago."

"Good. We've been in the area, of course, setting up a new shop. The Keepers of Truth are waiting for you to return. We've got a dozen or so folks, all working for the 'charity' that helps prisoners with appeals and such. Of course, that's the cover story. We have an office in Troy and funds are coming in. Everything is legit. We just hired a receptionist."

"Well done, Trapper."

"Thanks, boss. Between your 'donations' before you went away and the current stock trading you've been doing on our behalf, the KoT is sitting pretty. Kickstarters are going great. We rotate through several services, and I have one lady just in charge of fundraising. She's even written a few grants. And we've been reaching out, growing our base. Making new friends."

"Good."

Trapper nodded. "There is one group I think you will find particularly interesting. Our kind of friends. Preppers, getting ready for the collapse of civilization. Anyway, they have a huge spread west of Troy, off the grid. A bunch of houses and farms all connected together."

"Yes, you mentioned them last time you were up."

"I've been telling them about you—no names, of course—and they're excited to meet you. They want to host you, protect you. You'd be safe and sound on the compound—it's huge and private. They've had some run-ins with the prosecutors in the Troy office, so you have common ground."

"A cult."

"Not really," Trapper said. "Just a group of religious people who share our appreciation for freedom. Self-determination. And the compound is big, getting bigger every day. You can hide out there for months, making plans. When you're ready, you'll have the element of surprise. Harper will never know what hit him."

Joe looked at him, not saying anything for a long time. He glanced around the hotel room, then balled up one fist and punched it into the other hand.

"I hate it here," Joe said.

"I know."

"Why...why do they want to meet me?"

"Well, they're looking for a weapons instructor. Someone with lots of knowledge, lots of experience. There are about ninety of them right now, men, women and children. And they all want to become shooting experts."

Joe looked up and nodded. "Well, that I can help with."

CHAPTER 3
Airport

Three weeks later, on a Sunday night at the Dayton International Airport, ex-cop Frank Harper stood near one of the gates with his arms crossed, watching as the doors slowly closed. He breathed a sigh of relief as soon as the doors to the ramp shut.

Another job done. And well done, at that.

Personal protection was new to him, and it felt strange to watch over someone's well-being for three weeks straight, day and night. It had taken a toll on him and Monty, an amiable man that sometimes assisted Frank with his various investigations. It had been difficult for him and Monty, covering all those hours, but they'd kept her safe.

And she was leaving.

Frank hoped she would be okay. Out of the frying pan and into the fire, she'd said earlier in his car on the way to the airport. And he'd nodded, agreeing. Los Angeles was a lot crazier than Dayton, Ohio, that was certain. She was going back to her old life, old friends, the insane tumult of life in Hollywood. He hoped she'd manage to keep things together.

And, in some ways, he was very sad to see her go.

Many of the gathered throng of reporters raced from the gate doors to the nearby floor-to-ceiling windows to film the outside of the plane. As they watched, the engines of the LA-bound plane roared to life and the plane began backing slowly away from the terminal. At least three national news agencies were shooting live feeds, the on-air personalities talking and pointing at the plane outside. Cameras clicked loudly, firing off a dozen photos at a time. Flashes bathed the gate windows in flickering strobes of light. Other, less-interested reporters had already put away their cameras and started packing up, another story over.

Frank Harper looked much younger than his 56 years, with a thin body and ropey arms that betrayed his obsession with working out. He told people he worked out just for fun—and few people believed him—but he was mostly concerned about gaining weight. He'd seen it happen too many times. Cops moved to a desk job and packed on those 30 extra pounds every aging policeman seemed to accumulate once they stopped working in the field.

The reporters ignored him, mostly. They weren't here to talk to a retired cop. They had been here to see Jessica Mills, the Hollywood celebrity. She had graced the Dayton area with her presence for the past few months, popping up unexpectedly in the area and causing quite a commotion.

Now, at this very moment, she was headed back to California, and there was a palpable sense of disappointment from the local press. Frank watched the reporters doing their live shots, their backs to the glass windows that looked out onto the tarmac, wrapping up the story for the viewers at home.

"Well, that was exciting," Monty said dryly, walking over and standing next to Frank. Monty was a tall black man who, despite being a little thick around the abdomen, knew how to handle himself. "So, can things go back to normal now?"

Monty did some occasional work for Frank and had, over the last two weeks, assisted with the "personal protection" duties that Frank had been hired to carry out for Jessica.

"Yup," Frank said. "It's been weird."

"No kidding," Monty said. "Think she'll be okay?" he asked, suddenly serious. Monty nodded at the plane, backing away from the terminal, engines whining. "I'd hate to have to deal with all this insanity. Like, it would literally drive me crazy."

Frank glanced around. "Yeah, it's a whole thing, certainly. Imagine getting your picture taken everywhere you go."

"No thanks."

"But I think she'll be okay. She's got a good head on her shoulders."

"Yeah, and now that you clipped him, her stalker dude is out of the picture."

Frank nodded. Jessica had been pursued by a stalker for several years, and when he'd found out that she was in Ohio, he'd made his move. Frank had ended him.

"Maybe she can pull herself together out there in la la land," Monty said, eyeing the plane. "Or not. Who knows. Well, I'm outta here."

"Thanks, Monty," Frank said, turning and giving him a nod. "Seriously. There was no way I would've been able to cover all those hours. You did a great job, putting up with her and her schedule and those freaking photographers. I'll get a check in the mail this week for your hours."

Monty returned the nod with a casual salute, something the retired military man did with a combination of style and a sort-of "catch you on the flip side" panache.

"No problem, man. And thanks for the work."

Frank watched Monty head down the long corridor of the Dayton International Airport, passing a closed Starbucks and avoiding the few reporters who tried to ask him questions. Frank and Monty had been on every reporter's radar over the last three weeks, getting between them and Jessica on a daily basis. The paparazzi from Los Angeles had been particularly aggressive, but he and Monty had put them in their place.

Frank smiled. Monty was a good sort, with a great head on his shoulders. If Frank ever got his private investigation business to the point where he needed steady help, Monty would be his first hire.

Frank waited until the plane taxied out onto the runaway, where it sat for a few interminable minutes, waiting. A couple of the bored reporters tried to talk to him, but he brushed them off with a surly "no comment." Finally, after another ten minutes, the plane accelerated and raced up into the sky.

He'd been hired to protect Jessica, and his job wasn't really done until he saw the plane take off. Frank watched the plane get smaller and smaller in the sky until it was finally gone. He'd kept her safe here in Ohio.

As for what came next for her, Frank had no idea.

He shook his head, smiling at Mills' sassy attitude and the late nights they'd hung out together on stakeouts for his other ongoing cases. She'd been pissed when he'd told her that she would be tagging along while he worked other investigations. "I'm the only case that matters," she'd said at the time. But then she'd gotten into it, and had actually turned out to be helpful, despite all of her whining and nagging. She'd known more about Instagram than he could ever hope to learn, and it had broken one of his cases wide open.

He smiled again and turned, leaving the boarding area and heading for home.

Well, not really home—he was currently without a permanent address. Recently arrived from Birmingham, Alabama, Frank was currently crashing with his daughter Laura. So while he wanted to be heading "home," he was in fact headed back to the couch he was borrowing. A couch in Cooper's Mill, Ohio, in an apartment he didn't own, surrounded by boxes and boxes of his stuff. Stuff he'd dragged up here from Alabama.

Frank felt bad about mooching off Laura. He was eating her food and generally trying to stay out of her way. It was nice, spending so much time with her after the years when they had hardly spoken—it was great to reconnect. And spending morning, noon and night with Jackson, a grandson he'd never met up until about a year ago—that was something special.

But Frank also knew he was in the way, taking up space. He hated the idea of living off of her—it made him feel like a leech. What single mother wants her old, crotchety father crashing on her couch? Frank pitched in wherever he could and made sure to pay for groceries and the like, but he knew it was still a hassle for her.

At least there was a plan in place, now. The personal protection job for Mills had paid very well, and Frank had recently chatted with Jake Delancy, a local friend and landlord, and finally located a new place to stay. Soon, he'd be settled into the new apartment rented from Delancy and Laura could finally get back to having the place just to herself.

"Do you have anything else to add about Jessica Mills?"

Someone was shouting after him as he walked out of the secure area of the airport and toward the public exit.

He stopped and turned—it was another reporter, a skinny woman who looked like she hated food. She was waving a microphone at him.

"No, not really. I wished her luck out in Hollywood."

The place had been filled to the rafters with press and the general public, all gathered outside the security area to see Mills off. It wasn't every day a Hollywood starlet showed up in Dayton. Now the fans were heading out, chattering and sharing the photos they had taken with each other. Groups of fans were walking past him, carrying signs that read things like "Go Jessica!" and "We LOVE you!" and "Bacon Tastes Good!" Frank realized he got the reference, something he wouldn't have a month before—the bacon line was the tagline from one of her movies.

"Did her stalker say anything else before you killed him?" the skinny woman reporter asked.

"No, nothing else," Frank said quietly, eyeing the exit. He could see another smattering of reporters outside as well, clumped around a group of television vans and lights.

"What about her substance abuse issues?" another reporter asked.

He looked at the reporter, trying to keep from getting angry. "I don't really have anything to say on that, other than, in the time I spent with her, she seemed like a nice young person."

A part of the nearby crowd turned to listen to their interaction, as if craving one more conversation about the starlet and her stalker. Frank suddenly wished he were home alone, or in a bar somewhere.

Still, he continued. "She was very good at Instagram, I can tell you," he said, suddenly realizing he was smiling. Why was he making a joke for these people?

Others turned and watched, and one of the young women snapped a photo of him and started typing on her phone. Clearly, she was posting about him. He wondered if Jessica would see it.

The reporter leaned in, something they had a tendency to do. He didn't like people in his space, but reporters were clueless.

"Was she still using drugs here in Ohio?"

He looked at her and waited a second before answering. "So, do reporters think about what they're saying or just blurt out whatever comes into their minds?" The crowd giggled at that. "No, I didn't see her using. She was working hard, trying to get her life back on track," he said, his face serious. Frank looked away from the reporter and glanced at the gathered crowd. It was full of young faces. "Sometimes people get themselves into situations and don't know how to get out. I think we could all be a little more helpful to people in trouble, right? And maybe a little more forgiving. That's all. Thanks."

Frank turned and walked away, trying to blend back into the crowd leaving the airport. Unfortunately, the crowd was made up predominately of young women carrying signs and talking and he stuck out like a sore thumb. Several of them asked him questions, but he ignored them and moved on.

Outside the airport doors, three more reporters rushed him, waving microphones and cameras at him, but Frank just kept on walking, turning left and passing through the doors that led outside.

The fans chatted excitedly with each other, and some even pointed at Frank. One girl waved and snapped his picture. He was temporarily famous, a feeling he did not like at all. He was far more comfortable working his jobs, roaming the back roads in his black Camaro.

He joined the rest of the onlookers as they crossed the road to the multi-level parking lot, located across from the airport entrance. The press finally gave up and went back to their vans, and Frank just kept going, taking the stairs up to the second floor of the parking lot. There were more people in the parking structure, talking excitedly in small groups. Some carried signs, and some were dressed up as Jessica Mills from one of her movies, including a young woman wearing what looked like fake mud and carrying a stuffed pig.

Jessica had mentioned the movie she'd done called "Bacon Tastes Good!" where she'd played a rich city girl living temporarily on a pig farm. Jessica had often compared the film to her life here in Ohio— and how actually "living" in rural America, even for a short time, had altered her opinion about the vast swaths of land in the middle of the country—and the people who lived there. He'd even heard her poke fun at the idiocy of the popular term "flyover states."

Frank could see many of the young women and other fans were just thrilled to see someone famous. Dayton was a quiet town, and this kind of thing rarely happened. For one, he could use a little less excitement. It would be nice to go a month or two without getting shot at, he thought with a smile.

Walking across the expansive second floor of the parking lot, Frank found his car, a 1977 Camaro, one of his favorite possessions. It was black and looked menacing, sitting there in the airport parking lot. Even if one of the headlights was messed up, Frank loved this car, mostly because he'd always wanted a nice fast car. And he'd paid for it with the money earned from his first job as a private investigator. Actually, that case had predated him even considering a change of career—he'd solved a kidnapping case here in Ohio and earned a nice chunk of change.

Frank started up the Camaro and made his way to the exit. After paying at the booth, he pointed the car out of the lot and let it do its thing. The car purred away from the airport, headed for Cooper's Mill. The weather was still nice on this mid-October evening, and he took the opportunity to lower the windows to enjoy the breeze.

Instead of heading east through Vandalia and taking the highway north, Frank elected to take the back roads, away from the airport, enjoying the quiet and exploring a little more of the local area. As an ex-cop and current private investigator, it was always good to know the back roads—you never knew when you'd need to make a quick getaway or stake out a random home somewhere in the country. Since moving to Cooper's Mill, he'd made a point of driving the back roads, trying to learn as much as he could about the area.

And he was still looking for Joe Hathaway.

The crazy, murderous old man was never far from Frank's

thoughts. Frank's eyes scanned the area around him, studying the roads and houses and industrial areas he was passing though on the way back to Cooper's Mill.

It felt like part of him was always looking over his shoulder, looking for the old man who had killed Deputy Peters and kidnapped Frank's daughter and grandson and done a dozen other horrible things. The man was crazy—certifiable, as far as Frank was concerned—and had killed others before escaping from police custody. He'd arranged the death of a young pregnant woman. He'd killed a man and kept the man's body on ice for months, apparently pretending to converse with—and play chess with—the corpse. Who did that?

Joe had also taunted Frank relentlessly, getting inside of his head. Sending him messages and codes to decipher. And Joe had nearly taken away the only two things that really mattered to Frank: his daughter Laura and her toddler son, Jackson.

Frank felt the anger rising in the back of his mind. He slowed, recognizing the intersection of 25-A and Evanston Road. He made the turn, heading east, accelerating down the quiet country road, opening the Camaro up and letting it fly. It was quiet out here in the country, and Frank was feeling frustrated.

In the end, Hathaway had just floated away.

Literally. Frank had shot him. Shouldn't that have been enough? But the man had managed to fall backward into a river and slowly floated away. Frank could still see it, the man looking at Frank and smiling as the river moved around a corner and out of Frank's sight. After that, Joe had disappeared into thin air.

Frank and Deputy Peters, Frank's best friend in town, had finally tracked the old man and his strange little cult to a local farmhouse, a location with other bitter memories for Frank. Hathaway had managed to create a small cult around himself, the "Keepers of Truth," and had taken possession of the old farmhouse, the same one involved in the earlier kidnapping case that Frank had helped solve.

And it hadn't been by accident—Joe had sought out the farmhouse to get in Frank's mind. Apparently, Joe Hathaway was obsessed with Frank.

Awesome.

Frank and Deputy Peters and two other cops had stormed the place, and burly men with the Keepers of Truth had come out of the woodwork to protect Hathaway like linebackers defending their quarterback. Frank and the cops on site had managed to wade their way through them, but Peters died in a freak accident during the firefight.

Frank cornered Joe Hathaway near a river, shooting him at least three times. But the man refused to die. Instead, Joe fell backwards into the river and floated away.

"Sorry, Harper," the man had said with a little wave. Looking right at him, half a smirk on his face. "I gotta go."

The words still pissed Frank off. Shot in the chest, stumbling backwards into the brackish river, the man still managed to get in the last word. He'd killed Peters and shot at Frank and then Joe had just floated away. The cops searched and searched, looking for the man who had killed one of their own, but Joe Hathaway was apparently too smart to get caught.

The man was always telling people how smart he was, how his genius-level IQ was his armor. Maybe it was true.

Frank's car roared over the highway overpass, and he looked down at the I-75 below, dotted with cars and trucks. The drivers of those vehicles had no idea they should be on the lookout for a maniac, one that could be lurking anywhere.

Chief King, the head of the police department in Cooper's Mill, thought Joe Hathaway was long gone. "He's probably a thousand miles away by now, Frank," the chief had said recently when Frank had brought up the subject yet again. "You don't need to worry. And you know our police investigation turned up evidence that he was planning an escape. He had travel plans."

Frank had shaken his head. "I know."

"That man of his, Trapper, was going to drive him up to Canada," Chief King had added at the time. "Hathaway had a ticket to Iceland under a fake name, and another to Morocco. They don't extradite. He'd sent money ahead. The guy thought of everything, and this is the plan we know about. You know how he was, playing chess all the time. Three steps ahead of everyone else. He probably had ten other plans we don't know about. No way he's hanging around here in Ohio looking for you."

It didn't make Frank feel any better.

He got to South Hyatt and turned left, heading north into town. He passed the town's cemetery on his right and a large housing development on his left. Cooper's Mill was nice, a cute little town with a lot going for it. And some of the strangest people he'd ever met. Of course, maybe that was the way it was in every town—you don't see all the strange things and weird people until you've lived there for a while and started really getting to know the lay of the land.

His eyes scanned the headstones and mausoleums of the cemetery as he passed, imagining Joe Hathaway peeking out from behind one like a ghost. Of course, if it had been real, that ghost would have been carrying a sniper rifle and aiming for Frank. One ghost eye looking through a high-powered scope, tracking the Camaro. Joe was a crack shot, a man who had won awards and trophies at shooting competitions across half the country. It was crazy. A ghost with a sniper rifle? Really?

Frank shook his head and tried to smile at the dumb concept, a joke that only he would understand. But it didn't feel right, laughing it off. To Frank, it felt like he was just waiting for the other shoe to drop.

Hathaway was out there, somewhere.

CHAPTER 4
Klatch

Tuesday morning, the 16th, a couple of days after saying goodbye to Jessica Mills, Frank rose quietly from the couch, trying not to disturb Laura and Jackson. They had work and school at 9, but he was up around seven, tiptoeing around Laura's apartment. He managed to get away without disturbing anyone, heading out for early coffee and a bunch of errands.

Outside, it had turned cooler, one of those mid-October mornings that wore an angry tinge of cold, as if to say "yes, it's still fall, but winter is right around the corner." Frank pulled his thin jacket tighter and made a mental note—he would need to dig through his boxed clothing for something warmer. Of course, he might not have anything that would work.

There was certainly a taste of cold in the air as he walked to his car, rubbing his hands together. He needed gloves as well.

Soon, there would be snow and ice and he'd be experiencing his first real Ohio winter. He wondered how much different it would be—he was used to Alabama, where snow was rare. Laura had already warned him about Ohio's mercurial weather, frigid one day and sweltering the next. The standard saying was "Don't like the weather in Ohio? Just wait five minutes."

Frank started up the Camaro and headed out, making another mental note that his car would need to be prepared for the cold as well. He'd never lived up north and would have to ask around. Anti-freeze, certainly, but anything else?

He drove through her quiet neighborhood—one thing he liked about being up early was that it was like you had the planet to yourself. Everyone else was still sleeping, and there was no one up yet to bother you.

His plan for this morning involved grabbing breakfast with some friends, then running several local errands in Cooper's Mill and nearby towns. During one of his early cases here in Cooper's Mill, he'd sat down with an interesting group of old timers at the local

McDonald's to conduct an interview about a missing man. Now, he occasionally joined them for breakfast and senior coffee and chatter about local affairs.

He drove the Camaro through the downtown shopping district and headed west, looking admiringly at the large Victorian homes that lined Main Street. It was a great little town, he had to admit. Laura had done good, picking out this place north of Dayton. He'd never imagined himself moving out of Alabama—or, for that matter, moving away from New Orleans when he was younger—but if you had to pick a place to live, you could do a lot worse than Ohio.

And Cooper's Mill was a gem, the perfect small town. The weather was nice—so far—and the people were pretty chill, for the most part. Except for the psychotic murderers and kidnappers.

Frank smiled, wondering. Would the locals embrace that as their new tagline? "Welcome to Cooper's Mill – You Could Do a **LOT** Worse." Would they add those words to their marketing? Should they plaster it on billboards all over the Midwest to get folks to visit? He doubted it. "Come visit Cooper's Mill—there's only a small chance you'll be murdered."

Heading west, he passed Hyatt Street and the Dairy Queen and more homes before getting to the "uptown" part of town. "Uptown" was apparently everything near the highway, all the shops and businesses grouped near Exit 68. Gas stations, the grocery, Taco Bell, a BBQ place, more gas stations, and the McDonald's. There was a clear distinction from the "downtown" part of town, made up of the quaint shopping district and surrounded by streets lined with stately Victorian homes. One was historical and cute, and the other was gas stations and fast-food joints.

Laura had explained the uneasy truce between the two parts of town—they both needed each other. And everyone also knew that the real growth was taking place in the newest part of town, the "west side," or everything west of Interstate 75. That area held Cooper's Mills only open spaces and future potential—and more fast-food places and gas stations.

Oh goody.

But it also held the Tip Top Diner, both of the town's small hotels, and then the vast fields that were the town's promise of future expansion to the west. It was mostly open fields and empty lots all the way to County Road 25-A, which led to the airport and other points south and west. The "west side" was where all the new construction was taking place: a car dealership, a home improvement store, and, out on 25-A, a massive new factory. They had just broken ground in September, a multi-million-dollar facility and major new employer promising at least 400 jobs. It was a factory that would churn out millions of bottles of protein shakes and meal replacement shakes, along with bags of protein powder and other healthy foods.

The 400 jobs? That was the selling point. And those didn't count the 1,200 construction jobs on the new factory, or the new infrastructure that would need to be put in to support it. New roads, power lines, and water lines—all needed to support the massive factory—and all requiring workers, who would spend some of that money in Cooper's Mill. He and Laura had chatted about this potential boon to the local economy months ago when the project was announced, and now it was happening.

Frank turned left on Garber and then right into the McDonald's parking lot, parking and climbing out of his car. He saw Monty's old Mercury Montego, an ancient white boat of a car that took up the entire parking spot and more. The thing looked like an aircraft carrier, beached in Ohio, and it had a caved-in driver's side door. Shaking his head, Frank wondered if maybe he should be paying Monty more so he could afford a better car. Or, maybe, Monty preferred it.

Walking towards the door, he glanced around. Joe Hathaway was always on his mind, even at times like this. Frank would be out doing something, like crossing a parking lot, and he would suddenly feel like he was being watched. It made no sense, right? The guy was probably long gone. Of course, looking over your shoulder was an old habit for a cop. One of the first things they taught you at the academy was situational awareness.

No, Joe was dead or moved away. But where had the guy gone? Morocco? Was he still out there, biding his time? Was the old man planning something, or had he settled in Sicily and was now knee-deep in his new life? He could be playing chess in the courtyard of some small Italian village. Or plotting the murder of the next person to piss him off. Would anyone ever know?

Would Frank spend the rest of his life looking over his shoulder?

Frank entered the McDonald's and walked over, greeting the members of the coffee klatch, a group of old timers and acquaintances who got together most mornings to talk about politics and shoot the shit.

"Hey, Frank, there you are," Murphy Collins said, pointing at an empty chair. Collins was an ex-postman and retired and here every morning. "Long time no see," he said. Murphy ran the group—well, as much as anyone could "run" an informal group like this one. He always wore the same faded blue USPS windbreaker, no matter the weather. Collins mediated their discussions, making sure things didn't get too personal or political.

"Thanks," Frank said, nodding at the others around the table: Monty, Janette and Tom Duff, Murphy Collins, and Daren Malone. Frank made six.

Frank had learned the protocol was to sit first, chat for a while, and then politely excuse yourself to order coffee and food. He sat next to Monty, giving him a nod as well.

"I don't care what you say, I'm voting for him," Janette Duff continued. She was a very large woman and married to Tom Duff, the skinny man sitting next to her. Frank always thought about how interesting they probably looked walking down the street together. Well, opposites attract. "I think he's doing the best he can with what he's been given."

Frank liked that conversations just kept going when people dropped in. No one took time to "catch him up" or anything like that. You had to be smart and catch yourself up. Of course, he immediately knew what they were talking about—Election Day 2012 was three weeks away, and it was all anyone was talking about. Yard signs sprouted on every busy corner like mushrooms, shouting their slogans in silence. President Obama was very popular and running for reelection. It was looking like he would easily win a second term, beating GOP challenger Mitt Romney, not the most exciting candidate.

The group conversation tended to gravitate to whatever the big news story of the day happened to be. Earlier in the year, when he'd found time to drop in, the group had chatted regularly about the 2012 Summer Olympics, taking place in London. Collins had even kept track of a running bet they had going on the medal count and which country would win the most gold. In July they had discussed the tragic theater shooting in Colorado; Frank, as an ex-cop, had been asked repeatedly to weigh in on the topic of security and if it was easy for people to get guns, especially people with a history of mental illness. Lately, their conversations had been all about the election.

"Let's not get bogged down in that again," Murphy Collins said, putting up his hands. "I'm going to be happy when the election is over. Too many bad feelings going around."

"Yes, yes," Janette said again. She was a very portly woman and her leaning forward sometimes caused the entire table to shift suddenly. Frank saw Monty deftly reach over and lift his coffee cup off the table, just in case. He was very smooth about it, taking a sip, and then glanced at Frank and smiled.

"Man, you don't miss anything, do you?" Monty whispered.

Frank tapped the table. "Anyone need anything?" No one did, so he stood and turned, hearing Janette start up again as he walked to the counter. From what he could tell, she was the most political of the group. Every chance she got, she turned the conversation to the election or some other national story related to politics of one sort or another.

After he ordered, Frank moved to the left and waited at another area of the front counter for his food, watching the fast food workers race around. They slapped together orders, shoveling them into bags and passing them up to the front counter or over to the drive-through window. You had to admire a complex system like this, one that could crank out so much food so quickly.

"Sick of politics yet?"

Frank turned and saw Monty, who was getting a refill on his senior coffee.

"Always," Frank said. "Yeah, I guess I am. Too many other important things going on to worry about names on a ballot. As far as I can tell, every single politician is an idiot, or they answer to other idiots. Or they're power hungry."

Monty nodded. "Or both."

"You know, it would be nice to hear the folks in charge getting along. You have to figure people fighting all the time must not have any solutions up their sleeves, or they'd be working to make things better, right? Work it out with the other side, make some changes, then move on to the next problem."

Monty looked at him. "Wow, Frank. I think that's the most you've ever said at one time around me."

Frank smiled. "Sometimes I ramble."

"You really think it makes a difference, who's in charge?"

"I don't know," Frank said, nodding at the workers as one handed Frank a tray of food. "I mean, what if the government ran as efficiently as a place like this? You know, with all the bureaucracy taken out? Is that possible?"

"No clue," Monty said, shaking his head.

They headed back to the table, where the topic had moved on to the local Ohio races, also to be decided in early November. Frank tucked into his Egg McMuffin and hash brown and let the conversation roll gently over him like a warm tide. He knew next to nothing about local politics and had nothing to add. But it was great to listen to the members of the coffee klatch chat, sometimes passionately, about the local issues.

The new factory out west of town came up, and everyone except Frank weighed in on the facility, which had broken ground recently. Hundreds of jobs were coming, but a few of the folks around the table were concerned about the impacts that the facility—and the trucks that would be delivering products to and from it—would have on the local roads and infrastructure.

Finally, Murphy Collins turned to Frank. "Okay, Frank, you've made us wait long enough. Out with it!"

Frank looked up, confused. "What? Did I miss something?"

"What do you mean, 'what'," Darren Vallone said. He was a thin man and very quiet, a retired cabinet maker. "You know what."

"Jessica Mills!" Janette said, exasperated. She slapped the table with one fat hand, shaking the cups around them. "C'mon, Frank, who else?"

Darren continued. "You think anyone else at this table has spent the last three weeks protecting a young famous actress straight out of Hollywood?"

"Or running through a parade, chasing down a crazy stalker and shooting him?" Collins added with a smirk.

"Yeah, that too! Come on, Frank, spill it," Janette said, leaning forward, scooting the table. "It's driving me crazy."

"Sorry about that," Frank said.

"So, what was she like?" Janette asked, leaning forward. "Was she cool?"

"Yeah, I need all the details," Darren added. "I need to sell my story to People magazine."

Frank looked at him. "Is that still a thing? I thought people just wrote tell-all books now."

Darren shrugged. "Or maybe I'll have someone ghostwrite it for me. Come on, spill it," he said with a smile.

Frank glanced at Monty, then back at the table. "Well, she was nice."

They waited, but he didn't add anything, and it made Janette mad.

"Nice?" Janette Duff said, looking at her husband. "Can you believe this? Been waiting days and days for long, involved stories about a Hollywood starlet and all he gives me is 'nice'?"

Tom, her husband, shook his head but said nothing.

She looked back at Frank and slapped the table again. She probably thought it was a funny and cute move but all it did was make the coffee cups skitter. Monty grabbed his cup and Frank's, lifting them off the table just in time to keep them from spilling.

Janette looked at him. "Come on, man. Let's go. Spill!"

"And that crazy stalker of hers?" Collins asked. "Was it true about that house full of dead people down in New Orleans?"

Frank smiled and sighed. There was no getting around it.

"Well, I didn't really know much about her at the start," he began, and slowly recounted the whole story, starting with meeting her at the farm owned by her friend's family, west of Cooper's Mill, and wrapping up nearly a half-hour later with seeing her off at the Dayton airport. Monty nodded along, peppering Frank's lengthy tale with a few tidbits of information, including a couple interesting details Frank hadn't heard.

As he told his tale, the folks around the table peppered him with questions, and a few other people from the nearby tables pulled up their own chairs and joined the klatch. The expanded group sat—or in some cases stood—around Frank and listened as he talked about the security arrangements and taking the famous Hollywood woman out on cases. He didn't tell them anything that he wouldn't have told a newspaper reporter, and nothing they couldn't have read in any of the myriad of stories in the local papers. Frank still felt a professional level of confidentiality was called for.

Still, coming from his perspective, Frank could easily understand why the story was interesting to these folks and the others that had joined the table or stood nearby, listening in. It was a rare thing to have someone famous in their midst.

By the time he was wrapping up his story, there were at least forty people in the McDonald's dining room hovering or sitting around the klatch. Frank ended his story where most stories ended, with the finale, of course. During the Mum Festival Parade, Jessica's stalker had been waiting for an opportunity and grabbed her. He'd been disguised as one of a band of traveling clowns—you can't make this kind of stuff up, really—and was walking along with the other clowns in the parade through the downtown. He'd rushed in and thrown her over his shoulder and run away through the crowd, carrying the actress like a sack of potatoes.

Frank tried to keep it to the facts, short and sweet, but Janette kept interrupting him with more questions. Maybe she was writing a book on it or something.

"Did he look crazy?"

Frank nodded. "The clown? Well, yes. I saw someone grab her up—she was down on the street, talking to a group of kids, and I was up on a balcony. All I saw was some commotion and then she was gone."

There were a few questions Monty had to answer because he had been in a different area at the time of the incident. Frank talked about chasing the stalker along the parade route, and then following the crazy man and his unconscious prey—he had jabbed Jessica with a needle, drugging her. Frank chased the man into a furniture store on the corner of Main and Fourth Streets and then down into a strange basement parking lot located UNDER the furniture store.

"Yeah, that used to be a car dealership," Darren offered.

"What?" Janette asked. "I never heard that."

"It's true," Collins added, nodding. "That's why they've got the big windows, too, and wide doors. Used to park cars in those front windows."

"Hmm," Frank said, nodding.

"That concrete driveway goes into the building, then turns left and down the ramp into the basement. Lots of space under that building."

Darren agreed. The man rarely talked, so when he did, people turned and listened to him. "They parked the extra cars down there. Now the building owners use it for car and boat storage. Friend of mine has a car down there."

"I hope Frank didn't shoot it," Monty added with a laugh.

Frank smirked and continued. He described how he cornered the stalker and shot him, killing the man and rescuing a woozy Jessica Mills. It was the stuff of legend, apparently, although for Frank, it hadn't been that big of a deal. He was just a guy doing his job.

The questions continued for a while and finally petered out as Frank sipped the last of his coffee. Monty had refilled it for him twice during the conversation. They covered the shooting and aftermath in greater detail than in any interview he'd given out to the press. In some ways, it was a shame no one was recording this conversation—it would probably be the most comprehensive retelling of the events ever. Of course, that was assuming people cared.

Yes, it was true the stalker guy was insane and had killed before. He'd been part of a rich family in New Orleans. Frank Harper knew the type very well—old money, living in the big houses south of Bourbon Street. The sicko had managed to kill off his entire family. He'd gone the extra mile, though, and arranged them around his family's dining room table like some kind of hellish dinner party.

And, over time, the insane idiot had added more victims as well, expanding the number of "guests" at his macabre gathering. Not the kind of party Frank wanted to be invited to, that was for sure. The nutjob had killed other women and even a man delivering packages to the home, arranging them around the table as well. The stalker had big plans for Jessica, too. Apparently, he'd been saving her the empty seat at the head of the table.

She was to be the guest of honor.

Frank wrapped up the lengthy tale and answered a couple of lingering questions, but most of the coffee klatch just sat back, taking it all in.

"Well," Murphy Collins said, looking at his empty cup. "I'd say that's a wrap for today. Thanks, Frank, for sharing. I don't think any of us can top that story, at least not for a while."

Frank nodded and could tell the meeting was breaking up. Collins was their leader, and when he said it was over, people left. Collins was aware of how long they stayed and how long his group took up this table, a prime one right in the middle of the restaurant. Not that there was a bouncer or anything—he was just trying to be conscientious.

They stood, and the smattering of "new" members who had temporarily joined the coffee klatch drifted away. One woman snapped a picture of Frank and apologized. Janette's husband helped her to her feet. The klatch members mingled for another minute or two, and Frank answered a couple of more questions while they all got coffee refills for the road, and then everyone went their separate ways.

"Is that the way it usually ends?" Frank walked out with Monty. "Awkward like?"

"Yeah, it is," Monty said, holding the door open for Frank. "It's one of those situations where everyone is ready to leave but no one wants to make the first move. I'm surprised you stayed to the end."

"I've never made it to the end of one of the klatches. I always left early."

"Well, now you know how they end."

"Yup," Frank said, walking him to his car. "We square with the money from the Mills job? I feel like I missed some hours or something for you."

Monty nodded and set his coffee on the top of his car, above the passenger side door. "No, we're good. And thanks for the work. I'll take any hours you got." He pulled the passenger door behind him open, confusing Frank. The door creaked as he pulled it aside. Didn't he realize he was on the wrong side of the car?

"I'll have more work, I promise, and more hours," Frank said, looking at the car, the massive, boat like Mercury Montego. It had to be a 1977 or 1978, and they didn't make them like this anymore. There probably wasn't enough steel left in Detroit to make one of these monstrosities. "Great work on the Mills case, by the way. But this Anderson case is weird. Gonna bring in my daughter to help—I need a forensic accountant. Money went missing a bunch of times, with different employees reporting it. Someone smarter than me's gotta go through the books."

"Can't help you with that one, Frank," Monty said. "I suck with money. But if you need someone to spit out quotes from old black and white movies, I'm your man."

Frank looked at the white Montego—the thing really did look as big as a yacht. "You drive this boat on purpose?"

"Hey," Monty said with mock outrage. He climbed into the passenger side and sat down. "Don't you pick on Fiona. She's a wonder. Hey, hand me my coffee, will ya?"

"It's a wonder she drives, old as she is." Frank handed Monty his coffee. "Doesn't the driver's side door work?"

"Nope," Monty said with a laugh. "Speeding out in the country a couple years ago and slid off a gravel road. There's a lot of 'em around here. Don't take 'em too fast."

"I won't," Frank said, closing the door with a huge BANG. It felt like it weighed sixty or seventy pounds. Monty slid over into the driver's seat and started up the car, the engine roaring.

As Frank stepped back, Monty backed out and drove away with a wave.

CHAPTER 5
Fountain

In Troy, Ohio, a town located fifteen minutes north of Cooper's Mill, County Prosecutor Kevin Whitlowe was staring out the windows of his second-floor office, looking at the fountain.

Lately, Kevin had spent more than his fair share of time looking out the windows. He'd heard a rumor that the fountain would be getting an "upgrade" sometime in the next year or so, a plan to redo the pedestrian plaza and fountain area in front of the County Courthouse Building. He hoped they wouldn't change it too much—he liked the fountain the way it was. And his father had loved it. Kevin could remember standing at these same windows years ago, looking at the same fountain, when his father had held the same job that Kevin now held, county prosecutor.

But today, his mind was on something else, as it often was. Kevin Whitlowe was thinking about Joe Hathaway again. The man had simply disappeared, floating away down a river into oblivion.

Kevin had been through all the reports, over and over again. He'd had his clerks go through them as well, and Bridget, the assistant county prosecutor. They'd talked to all the cops that had been involved several times. They'd poured through the reports, reached out to anyone who might know where the old man had disappeared to—or could have helped him disappear. Bridget had even called overseas to Morocco to interface with their people, even though the country didn't have an extradition agreement with the United States. As part of their investigations, they'd found that Hathaway had made several "escape" plans, purchasing tickets to Morocco and two locations in South America. She'd tried tracking more information down, or find Hathaway's local contact, but, so far, nothing.

The whole situation had been a stain on the Prosecutor's office. He could imagine the headlines: "Psycho convicted murderer and cult leader escapes from custody, sneaking out of his hospital room when no one was looking. Criminal mastermind kills cop, escapes via simple trick of floating away." It was a mess.

Whitlowe was very worried it could impact his reelection chances, but it was worse than that—the whole thing made him look incompetent.

Joe Hathaway had been convicted of three cases of attempted murder. But he'd managed to escape their custody, sneaking out of a hospital where he'd been recovering from injuries sustained when his car had been struck by a train. Joe had had help, of course—he managed to hold sway over some folks, and a group of his merry band of idiot cult followers helped him get away. But Whitlowe blamed the cops and the guards and everyone who had underestimated the old man.

There was plenty of blame to go around.

Hathaway had disappeared, then popped up again with a group of followers. The old man staged a cat-and-mouse game with an ex-cop, Frank Harper, the man who'd helped catch Hathaway in the first place.

People were still talking about the incident at the farmhouse: civilians dead and wounded, one cop killed, and Hathaway's escape.

Whitlowe relived the whole sordid affair as he stared out at the fountain.

He assumed it had been like a keystone cops caper, people running around like idiots, shooting into the air. And bees, bees everywhere. Whenever he imagined it, the scene was always sped up, people racing around in fast motion while that theme from the old "Benny Hill" show played.

What a disaster.

The prosecution still stood, of course, and a nationwide alert for Hathaway had gone out. Supposedly cops were still looking for him now, six months later. But Whitlowe was sure he'd never be seen again. The man had been devilishly clever, evading the cops and entangling Frank Harper with a series of clues that only the ex-cop could decipher.

Whitlowe shook his head. The last six months had been rough, professionally and personally. Unrelated to the case, Whitlowe's father had taken ill, and spent the last two months of his life watching his son struggle to put the Hathaway case to bed. Even as he passed, Whitlowe imagined he could see the disappointment in his father's eyes. The elder Whitlowe had been a prosecutor for the City of Troy and then for Miami County for almost forty years.

Whitlowe stared at the fountain below. He liked the standing stones, arrayed in a circle around the fountain. He wondered how much it was going to be changed as part of these new plans he'd heard about. He hoped not. It was good, sometimes, when things stayed the same. Too much change was bad.

He heard a subtle knock on his office door.

"What?"

The door opened and his secretary entered. He didn't turn—he could tell it was Dorothy by the quick sounds of her steps. He heard her cross the room and stop at his desk.

"Sir, Bridget is here. To discuss her upcoming case."

Whitlowe looked at the fountain.

"They'll need to drain it soon, I imagine."

"It is getting colder," she said from behind him. "This is about the time of year they drain it."

He looked at the fountain and wondered what would happen if it froze over. Would ice crack the stones, or shatter the concrete? Probably. It was one of the reasons the city was planning to upgrade things—ice had damaged the fountain in the past.

"Do you think they'll change it?"

Whitlowe could hear her moving things on his desk. Tidying. She hated mess, and he had been messier lately than normal. Much messier.

"The fountain? Or the courtyard? Both, I imagine."

"I'm not sure I'm on board with this update they're planning."

"I heard they are adding more seating and tables," she said. He could hear her moving more things around. "That would be nice. Folks need a place to sit outside when it's nice. Lunchtime in summer, people like to eat by the water."

"Hmm," he said, not sure.

"I saw some of the architect renderings—they had them on easels in the next building. They're redoing the standing stones. Should be taller, I'd guess, based on the last design I saw. It's still going through the review process. But it won't change too much, I'm sure."

"Good," he said quietly, looking at the fountain. The water shot up into the air between the group of standing stones, then cascaded down into the pool. "Dad liked it the way it is."

"I know," she said quietly. "I know." Dorothy had worked for his father as well. Longer than she'd worked with Kevin. "He loved standing there, right where you're standing." She started to say something else but then grew quiet.

The room was quiet for a moment, and then she cleared her throat. "Bridget, sir?"

He sighed and turned. "Okay, show her in."

Kevin Whitlowe turned back to his father's desk—nearly everything in the office had been passed down to him. His detractors complained that the elder Whitlowe had simply arranged, through his influence and reach, to place a younger copy of himself in power. Sometimes Kevin wondered if they were right.

He sat and moved files around, finding the pile he wanted. The desk was littered with stacks of files all organized into color-coded manila folders: the ones with blue and green folders were active investigations, while those in the yellow jackets were pending prosecutions. He found the green folder he was looking for and flipped it open just as Bridget walked in.

"More trouble with the preppers?" he said without looking up. He would keep this cool. Professional. No need to make eye contact with her, not today. Not when he was already feeling emotional about his father and the Hathaway case.

No need to get into any extraneous discussions. Not today.

The red-haired woman in her mid-thirties crossed his office, straightening the front of her snappy business suit as she walked over. Bridget glanced around at his office, then sat down in one of the chairs that faced his desk, crossing her legs.

"And good morning to you."

"It's a little late for good morning," he said, still not looking up. There was no need to make eye contact.

She let out a little laugh. "Yes, that's true. But I've had a busy morning."

He looked at the file, flipping through the pages. The awkward silence began and continued. Whitlowe was aware of the fact that he should say something in response to her, something like "oh, a busy morning?" or "oh, that sounds rough." Instead, he kept his trap shut and stared at the file in his hands and waited for her to start.

"Okay," she finally said. It was all so very awkward, but nothing could be done about it now. "Yes, we won that judgment against the preppers and their compound earlier in the year. I got two of them sent to the clink on weapons violations," she said. "But it's getting worse out there. I'm telling you, they're up to some trouble."

He glanced up at her and saw that she was staring at him, a weird look on her face. Bridget Turner was very attractive. So attractive that he looked away, going back to his file.

Her looks certainly helped her in court: thin, long red hair, an attractive face and body. Juries loved her, especially when they were full of men. And she knew it, too—she knew what people thought of her. She knew how to parlay attention into action, or leverage, or favor. Bridget was no idiot.

CHAPTER 6
Errands

Leaving McDonald's after the coffee klatch, Frank shook his head as he watched Monty's ratty old Mercury Montego drive away. Frank needed to remember that if they were ever going to be in a shoot-out, Monty should drive. That car was built like a battleship. He wondered if the heavy metal doors were naturally bulletproof.

Smiling, Frank turned and walked over to his Camaro. He felt bad giving Monty shit about his car when the Camaro, while not in the best shape, was something he'd always wanted. He climbed in and started it up. The engine purred, sounding like an angry lion. The car was fast, and felt a little mean.

Frank headed east, driving through the historic downtown and passing down the hill that marked the edge of town. East of town was the flood plain, where all construction was banned in the wake of a devastating 1913 flood that damaged half of the small town. The river had also inundated other towns up and down the Great Miami Riverway, wiping out parts of many places and even flooding a large portion of downtown Dayton.

After the 1913 flood, huge dams were built in the area to control several rivers, along with large conservation districts established along the rivers that prevented most types of construction. It explained why, traveling east out of Cooper's Mill, you went suddenly from town into empty fields.

He passed Freeman's Prairie, where one time he'd almost been killed. Frank had been kidnapped, then tied up and left for dead. The local fire department regularly "burned" the fields in the area to control brush and small trees. Someone had abducted Frank, knocking him out and tying him up and leaving him unconscious in the path of the fire.

He'd awakened in the field, which was already burning. Frank would never forget that smell, waking up and panicking. Trying to figure out where he was and why he was immobilized while smelling burning grass and wood very close by. It had been a terrifying experience that he hoped to never repeat.

Frank continued east out of town, turning left onto 201 and heading north in the direction of Troy, heading for a new shooting range he wanted to try out. Ever since the final incident with Joe Hathaway, Frank had been spending a lot of time at the range. Actually, different ranges—he was trying all the local ones out, trying to find one he liked.

Back in August, Frank had gotten his own Ohio gun license, but the location where he'd taken his shooting exam had creeped him out. He'd tested for his license in the same facility where Joe was famous—the man was one of the best shots in the area and had won many local awards as proof. The range still had Hathaway's banners hanging up all over the place.

Frank had quickly decided to find a new range—he didn't like the idea of supporting a place that still revered a murderer. Hell, Hathaway had personally tried to kill Frank on two different occasions—once on a nearby lake and again at the little farmhouse where Deputy Peters had died. Frank couldn't believe that particular range was still proud of the man, but it didn't do any good to argue with some people. And he didn't think he could get the place to take down the banners, or shame them into denouncing their public devotion to Hathaway.

But what Frank COULD do was take his money elsewhere. So, he voted with his feet. He had a new mantra—don't give your money to people who hate you.

This morning, he had an appointment to shoot at a little range up in New Staunton, a tiny little town just east of Troy, Ohio.

He found the place with no trouble and headed inside. The range was nice and well-kept, and it smelled clean. Often ranges smelled like old gunpowder—the places could reek of it. Smelling like cleaning solution was preferable.

But on the flipside, the store was too small and didn't carry the ammo he was looking for. He didn't want to leave too soon, so he ended up renting a range gun and buying the appropriate ammo, then spent an hour shooting with a well-worn .357 Magnum, a huge gun he hadn't handled since he'd been back in police training at a range in the Maurepas swamps. It was a facility located west and north of New Orleans, out on that lonely stretch of 10 that ran through the darkest, greenest swamps you could imagine on the way to Baton Rouge.

The range master at the time had warned him and the other cadets to watch out for gators wandering into the firing range. Frank smiled, remembering. What a time that had been, learning to be a cop. He'd loved it.

Frank set the gun aside. It was way too heavy, and never the kind of weapon he'd be interested in carrying on a daily basis. But it was good to try out other weapons. You never knew when you'd be in a situation where you had to fire a different gun, or take a weapon off of someone and use it to defend yourself.

And it was good to get out and get some range time, nonetheless.

When he was done, Frank thanked the proprietor and headed out. He had one more meeting before heading back to Laura's.

CHAPTER 7
Satellite

County Prosecutor Kevin Whitlowe looked down at the file again, poring over the pages in a desperate attempt to avoid conversation with her. Every time Bridget was in the room, it made him uncomfortable.

Of course he was attracted to her. Who wouldn't be? Tall, thin, red hair. Confident, passionate. Took no crap from anyone. She was driven with so much passion for the law that sometimes it took his breath away. And yes, she was pretty. Too pretty to avoid trouble with the other women in any office she would ever work in.

Bridget sucked all the air out of the room—he'd seen it happen, live and in person. In court, in depositions, at a casual lunch or off-the-book plea discussions. She was so full of fire, it came across as an intimidation tactic. But he knew better—that's just who she was.

And he loved who she was.

He shook his head and concentrated on the pages in front of him. The folder on the preppers was well organized, of course. She always did her homework. You'd think someone as pretty as her would be lazy and rely on her looks to get by, but that wasn't the case. If anything, she worked harder to be taken seriously than everyone around her.

She was talking about the preppers again, and he forced himself to focus on her words without looking up at her. Bridget was talking about a large area of farms that the cops had been monitoring for over a year. Owned by a religious group in a rural area of the county a dozen miles southwest of Troy, they were slowly building up their own compound, buying up adjacent farms and stringing together lots. In the spring of this year, they had started installing long rows of barbed-wire fence along the county roads that serviced the area. And over the summer, they had apparently started building what could only be called fortified structures.

"What do you mean, they're getting up to something out there? It's a farm, Bridget. Farmers farm. They plow up the land, they put down seeds. Water, sun, plow, repeat."

She shook her head. "So, what are these buildings for? And the barbed-wire fencing? It's more than that. Lots of earth-moving equipment, bulldozers, and those cougar things."

"Cougars?"

"You know, those little bulldozers for digging and pushing dirt around."

"What? You mean bobcats?"

"Yeah," she said, undeterred by her ignorance. She never let that kind of thing stop her. "Bobcats, cougars, whatever. I've talked to the PD several times—they're always getting complaints. Loud noises, construction sounds in the middle of the night. I think they're doing something out there."

"Like what?"

"They're preppers, Kevin," she said, sitting back and shaking her head. "Don't be stupid. I have no idea what they're doing. But I'm not a prepper. You know, end-of-the-world stuff. SHTF is their favorite acronym."

"SHTF?"

"You know, when the 'shit hits the fan,'" she said with a smirk. "They're storing food, probably building a weapons stockpile. New buildings with strange purposes. Fencing in areas to control them, I guess." She leaned forward, passing him an aerial view of the compound, which was color coded. "Though we can't prove that. And they're expanding, and fast. Those three blue areas are new farms they've purchased over the last six months. They're up to nearly ninety acres, mostly contiguous. Plus, other plots of land around the county and in Darke County. The cops think they pressured and threatened neighbors into selling but couldn't prove anything."

Whitlowe looked at the map. This was new information. "Purchased legitimately?"

"As far as we can tell," she said. "Nothing shady." She had prosecuted two sketchy members of the "religion" early in the year for some firearms sales, getting convictions in both cases.

She leaned forward, but Whitlowe didn't look up. He didn't need the temptation—he already struggled mightily to keep things professional with her. She was the perfect woman.

If only she didn't work for him.

Bridget leaned over and pointed at his map. "The area highlighted on the center of the map in yellow is new. Reinforced concrete poured slabs, right in the middle of those fields," she continued. "Not near any other structures. And lots of metal shipping containers."

"The slab—foundation for a new building, maybe?"

"Yup, that's what I'm thinking." She pointed at the other farmhouses on the map. "It's nearly equidistant from all four of these."

"They look like they're preparing for World War III."

"They are."

He looked up at her to see if she was kidding, but her face said she was not. "These people are crazy, Kevin," she said, looking him in the eyes. "I really feel like we need to do something about them."

He pointed at a series of shipping containers near the central poured slab. "What are these?"

"Unknown at this point," she said. "I've been told they could be containers full of building materials." Bridget sat back, shaking her head. "It looks like another Waco compound to me."

"That's a scary thought."

She nodded. "Maybe it's WACO, maybe it's nothing. But it feels like maybe it's something. Combined with the religious aspects, the tax-free charity status, and the guns earlier this year? I don't know. They scare me, though. Cops are keeping an eye on them. Nothing we can prosecute for, not like the guns earlier this year. Those guys were idiots—the others in there are a lot smarter."

"Great."

"The Troy PD is trying to cultivate a confidential source. They're sniffing around the edges of this group, looking for someone to peel off. And the Feds are involved too—that's where the map came from, the FBI office in Cincinnati."

"And the satellite photos?"

She smiled. "I'd rather not say."

"Okay, no worries," he said, not wanting to ask. Maybe she was seeing someone. The idea filled him with relief—maybe this whole situation would blow over—and, at the same time, made him very sad.

Finally, he looked up at her. "So, FBI? This is getting serious, I guess."

She nodded, not adding anything.

He looked back at the maps. "Getting someone on the inside would be nice," he said, handing the maps and satellite photos back to her. "Maybe get some photos from ground level. Drone shots or something. It's hard to prosecute with satellite photos."

She sat back. "These are old, but I'm getting an updated batch soon. And I'm telling you, their leader has them on a path to 'get ready for an apocalypse.' I swear, Kevin, this has been going on for a while, even back before the Joe Hathaway trial. Remember when they got cited for unauthorized drilling, putting in all those wells?"

He nodded, not remembering. There were a lot of cases to keep track of. Seemed like there was an abundance of crackpot end-times folks in the county. And this group south of Pleasant Hill was not even at the top of his current list of problems.

He shook his head and handed the file back to her.

"I'm not seeing anything serious enough yet," he said. "Keep an eye on them, or, better yet, ask the TPD to keep an eye on them. You've got other cases, I know it."

She sat back and bit her lip. She probably thought it made her alluring, and more likely to get her way, but to him, it just made her look like an insolent child.

"None of my other cases are this interesting. I mean, what if they're planning a revolution out there? And why is their leader so secretive?"

"I don't know, Bridget. But it's a free country," Whitlowe reminded her. "But I understand your concern. See if you can get any purchase records on them," he said, signing the authorization for a warrant she'd already filled out. "And go check the place out. See if they're buying up guns or whatever."

"Thank you," she said quietly.

"It's fine," he said, not looking at her when he handed it back. "Just be safe. And call ATF or the State folks—someone has to be running background checks on the weapon's purchases, at least. But if they are stockpiling powdered milk and water, planning for the end-of-days, that's none of our business."

The room went quiet, and Whitlowe tapped the intercom to call Dorothy. It wasn't a good idea to be alone in here with Bridget—he might say something stupid. Or she might get too comfortable again. Maybe speak her mind. She'd made it very clear on several occasions in the past that she was interested in a relationship with him. He was trying as hard as he could to keep things professional.

Bridget started to say something just as Dorothy knocked and walked in.

"Sir?"

He waved her over and pointed at the maps. "More trouble with the preppers near Pleasant Hill," he said. "Can you get me a meeting with the county commissioner? We need to be on the same page, especially because these people are buying up lots of land, here and in Darke County." She nodded, and he looked at Bridget, who looked miffed about something. Probably because he called Dorothy in. But he didn't have time to get into it with her. Knowing his luck, she'd bring up St. Louis again, and that was the last thing he needed. "Anything else, Bridget?"

"No," she said curtly, standing and gathering her maps and papers. "I'll coordinate with the police departments and let you know what develops." She turned and left without another word.

Whitlowe's eyes followed her shape as she left the room.

"That one is trouble, sir," Dorothy said quietly after Bridget was gone.

Whitlowe nodded. "Oh, you have no idea."

CHAPTER 8
Undercover

Passing through downtown Troy, Ohio, not too far from the county courthouse, Frank slowed the Camaro and pulled into a Tim Horton's. He loved their coffee—it was so much better than Starbucks—but there wasn't one in Cooper's Mill, so he took the opportunity to stop in. Troy was much bigger, but Frank had to say he liked the smaller town better. Troy's downtown was cute, with shops and restaurants arrayed around a central traffic circle with a fountain in the middle, but the traffic could be a mess.

He passed the large courthouse on his right, where it looked like they were doing some construction on the courtyard. That building was where he'd been called in to testify against Joe Hathaway this past July.

He'd flown in from Alabama and taken the stand in the attempted murder cases, testimony that had ended up being meaningless. The convictions had happened, of course, so Frank's testimony had helped with that, at least. Over his career, he'd been on the stand for countless cases, sitting in the witness box and testifying. It was the life of a cop, or an ex-cop doing cold cases—but this case had been different.

Hathaway had tried to kill Frank—personally. Twice, actually, if you counted the rigged icehouse that sank through the surface of Trapper's Lake, nearly taking Frank and Deputy Peters down with it. He could have drowned in there.

And he could have been shot—Hathaway had set up a sniper's nest in the trunk of his car and taken shots at Frank and Peters. They had been out on the frozen lake together investigating Tom Mercato's disappearance.

Hathaway had missed, amazingly, and Frank had chased him down in a car chase through snowy streets between here and Cooper's Mill. In the end, Hathaway had tried to race the train and lost, resulting in a spectacular car wreck that nearly killed him.

Frank had come up from Alabama and testified. Hathaway got

convicted, but it hadn't really mattered. Before he could be sentenced, Hathaway had escaped police custody at the hospital and disappeared into the night, aided by a number of his cult-like followers.

Frank shook his head as he drove through Troy, sipping his "Timmy's" coffee and munching on a few of their amazing Timbits, their cutesy name for their donut holes.

Lax security was bad enough, but then, Hathaway was very smart. Too smart for his own good. And having people working for him had just made it that much easier. Frank had never heard for certain, but he guessed that Hathaway had figured out some way of communicating with his people—maybe the lawyer on the case had slipped Joe a cell phone or something.

Frank got to the highway and headed south, back towards Cooper's Mill. It was only three exits, and in just a few minutes, he was exiting the highway. He turned west, away from the downtown, passing the Wendy's and turning on Weller, taking a right and another left just before a massive home improvement store. He passed a large tennis center and slowed, turning down a narrow road that ended near one of the water towers that serviced this side of town.

There was a car waiting for him.

Frank parked and got out, walking over to the car and glancing around before getting in the passenger seat.

"Travis," Frank said, nodding. "How's it going?"

The young man waiting for him inside was nervous. Frank knew that look. The eyes were too big, and the kid's leg was vibrating. And Frank was late—that probably hadn't helped.

"Mr. Harper," the kid said. "Thanks for meeting me."

"Sure," Frank said, glancing around. There was trash on the floor of the passenger seat, and piles of junk in the back seat. "Your car is a mess."

"I know. Sorry."

"So, anything for me?"

"Not yet, sir," Travis said. "Just got on staff two days ago, but I'm working on making friends." He handed Frank a hand-written list. "Here's the people I met so far."

Frank scanned the short list of names, amused. Frank had met the kid weeks ago, bumming around the liquor store near where Frank's new apartment was located. Now, the young man was doing some undercover work for Frank.

The names on the list were all familiar to him. Employees of

Anderson Tool & Die, mostly factory floor workers and two guys in security. Next to each name, the kid had scrabbled a few words: "nice," or "keeps to himself," or "this one is a real piece of work." That last one made Frank smile.

"Great job, kid," Frank said, nodding at Travis. "This is really going to help," he lied. It wasn't. A list of names was useless, especially a list of names he already had. But cultivating undercover assets was hard, and this kid needed confidence. The kid was going to be working with these people, getting to know them.

"Thanks."

"Anything on Jill?" Frank was working for her, of course. She was the person who had hired him to look into the death of her father, the previous owner of the business. And she was paying Frank a tidy sum to figure out who had stolen money from the company on several occasions. But first Frank wanted to be sure about her. It wouldn't be the first time someone nefarious hired a private investigator—or engaged with the police—to help them cover up something illegal.

Frank wasn't going to let that happen. If Jill was at fault, she'd be going to jail the same as anyone else. Of course, he'd wait until she was all paid up on his invoices before turning her in.

"No contact with her yet," the kid said. "She's the big boss and rarely on the floor."

Frank nodded. "Who have you met?"

The kid nodded at the sheet Frank was holding. "Top of the list is HR types, the lady that did my paperwork. Next is Brad, the guy that's training me. He seems cool. I'm on a fabricator, one of the new 3D additive machines. Nice one. Very expensive."

"Additive?"

"Yeah, it lays down a bead of hot metal, very thin. Builds up components one layer at a time according to the CAD drawings in the computer. Like one of those new 3D printers, but this uses hot metal instead of plastic."

"Okay."

"Additive machines aren't as accurate as the other kind, the ones that start with a block of metal and carve away everything they don't want. They end up with a finished part that's one solid piece of metal."

"Okay," Frank said. "Anyone stand out yet?"

"Lunch was interesting. I saw a couple of guys hassling the Mexicans—there's a group of immigrant workers that stick together. They're quiet, only speak Spanish. But these other dudes, white guys, these two assholes were teasing them. Calling them names and stuff. I'd keep an eye on them."

"Which ones are they?"

Travis pointed to two names near the bottom of the list. "Real sweethearts."

Frank lowered the list and thought back, trying to place their names. Surely he hadn't been in town long enough to meet all of the idiots, right? But then Frank remembered. He did know them. These two sweethearts had been involved in a small altercation with him at Ricky's, one of the more popular downtown bars. It had been right after Frank had arrived in town, even before he'd gotten involved in the kidnapping case that had introduced Frank to the local cops.

Another great reason to recruit an undercover asset like Travis. One look at Frank on the factory floor and these two dummies would clam up.

"I do know them," Frank said, nodding. "Morons. Keep an eye on them for me. If there's something hinky going on at Anderson, those guys could be involved."

Travis nodded and glanced around at the tall corn fields that surrounded the small parking area.

"Anything else?" Frank asked.

"Nope," Travis answered. "Just meeting folks, keeping my ears open. Taking notes when I can. Watching for anything that stinks, right?"

Frank smiled. Travis had almost been a client of his earlier in the year. The young man had made an appointment to meet at Frank's "office" at the Tip Top Diner. He'd asked Frank to protect him from getting bullied at his place of employment. Frank hadn't taken the job, but he'd not forgotten the kid's name, either, jotting it down in his notebook. When Frank had decided he needed someone on the inside at Anderson's, Travis' face had popped into Frank's mind. Plus, hiring him away from his old workplace had solved the bullying issue for free.

"Good, good," Frank said. "I have another side job for you."

"What? I'm already nervous about this, Mr. Harper."

"I know. This one is easy. You can do it at home. I want you to scour the social media on all of these folks. Facebook, Instagram, whatever. Find me anything strange."

When it came to social media, Frank had learned his lesson. Jessica Mills had broken one of his cases by browsing Instagram and finding out a few things he'd never have figured out on his own, no matter how long he'd trailed the guy he'd suspected of having an affair. There was real value there—people nowadays put everything out on social media, especially stuff they shouldn't. Locations, photos of who they were with, everything. It could be a real help in his cases moving forward, especially if he could pay some kid to do it. Frank didn't know the first thing about Tik Tok or Snapchat or the other things Jessica had mentioned. But anything to get a leg up—in some cases, checking social media might be even more helpful than running a background check on someone. It could also be more up to date. Frank wondered if Chief King's men were keeping an eye on things like that yet, or if Frank was ahead of the curve.

"Oh, okay, that's easy," Travis said. "I'm on there anyway. Do you want me to check the dating sites, too? Sometimes people brag on those, say stuff they shouldn't."

"Yes, thanks," Frank said, adding another item to the list of things he wasn't up to speed on. "Just do it anonymously. Make sure you can't be traced. Don't comment or anything."

"Yup."

Frank leaned over and reached into his pocket and pulled out ten twenty dollar bills, handing them over in a wad. "You get that every other week until we wrap this case. But I need details, Travis. Get in with these folks, get me what you can. And work on that inventory I gave you. Those part numbers are important."

"Yup," Travis said. "I've already started on that, though it's hard to not draw attention. I'm using my phone, taking pictures, then pulling the serial numbers off later."

"Good idea," Frank nodded. "$200 a week, and then another $1,000 if we prosecute."

The kid took the money and nodded.

"You're doing good, Travis," Frank said, remembering what Laura had said about getting along with people. She was right—it was like back when he was a cop. If he wanted to cultivate more sources around town, people that could help him out when he needed them, Frank needed to treat them carefully. "And like we discussed, I'll put in a good word with Chief King. Like I said, he and I work together a lot. I haven't mentioned you yet, but I will, depending on how this case goes. I think he'll be interested in you for police training."

Travis wanted to be a cop, but he had a few marks on his record. He'd been denied entry into the local police academy, both because of his age and his checkered past, but Frank had told him those things could be overlooked by senior police officials. Travis needed a letter of recommendation, and Frank had implied that Chief King might be amenable to the idea. Frank was pretty certain Chief King would vouch for Travis—but only if they could crack this Anderson case.

"Thanks, Mr. Harper," Travis said. "I'll text you when I have more."

"Good," Frank replied. "And pictures. Lots of pictures, including those pieces of equipment. And group shots. We need to find out who's talking to who and why. Who is hanging out with who."

Travis nodded and Frank got out of his car, crossing to the Camaro. The kid drove away, not waving or looking back. Frank watched him go—he could tell the kid was nervous, but undercover work was difficult enough with proper police training. Without it, Frank had been forced to teach the kid the basics—keep your head down and your ears open. Write everything down, but never where anyone could see you. That made people nervous, people taking notes. Be careful taking photos—make it look casual.

And, the most important thing? Don't get killed.

CHAPTER 9
Frustration

Assistant County Prosecutor Bridget Turner stalked through the halls of the building and into her office, slamming the door behind.

"Jesus Christ!"

She threw the packet of satellite photos on her desk and glanced at the back of the now-shut door, waiting for any reaction. Most of the people on this floor, especially her secretary, knew to leave her alone when she was upset.

She paced her office, ending up at the window and looking down at the fountains. They always calmed her, much like they did for Kevin. He was always talking about them, probably because his father had been responsible for getting the fountains installed in the first place. Kevin had told her the story at some point. Apparently, the elder Whitlowe hadn't liked the coldness of the old plaza and had worked to get the fountains and courtyard installed to brighten up the area around the courthouse. The old man had overseen the design and installation, paying for it out of the prosecutor's office budget. Now, she often found Kevin standing by his windows and staring down at the fountains, lost in thought.

Or maybe he'd just been avoiding making eye contact with her.

She'd probably pushed him too fast. Or confused him with her mixed signals. And she could admit it—she'd been unsure of how to proceed after St. Louis. It was never a good idea to sleep with your co-workers. It was an even worse idea to "date" your boss, even if it had only been over one steamy weekend. That road led to all kinds of problems, just the kind that she and Whitlowe—

There was a quiet knock on the door.

"What?" Bridget shouted, louder than she'd intended.

The door opened slightly, and Norma poked her head in.

"You okay, boss?"

"Yeah, yeah," Bridget said, sitting down heavily. "Come on in—and I know what you're doing."

Norma opened the door just wide enough to enter and closed it quietly behind her. "What's that?"

"Letting me stew in here for a while alone before coming to check on me," Bridget said with a smile. "And thank you. Sorry about the door slamming."

"Oh, no one ever notices when you slam the door," Norma lied, looking at her. Bridget had been "spoken to" on several occasions about her noise level. Dorothy, Kevin's bitch of a secretary, ran the office, and had taken Bridget aside on several occasions and made not-so-subtle "suggestions" on how to keep the noise down.

But Bridget couldn't help it: she got excited. And sometimes that meant loud phone conversations, and slammed doors, and levels of cursing that probably made her co-workers wonder if she suffered from Tourette's Syndrome.

"Well, we both know that's a damn lie," Bridget said. "But I can't get Whitlowe to believe me. There is a lot of bad stuff going on out there."

"The prepper compound near P. Hill?" Norma asked. "Did he authorize a warrant?"

"Yes, but just barely," Bridget said. "Can you coordinate that with Dorothy?"

Norma nodded. "Of course. And I'll get it down to Drayton. Did you guys talk about...you guys?"

Bridget shook her head. It was no secret around the offices that she and Whitlowe had dated, off and on, a few weeks back. He had broken things off, and now it was awkward—not just for her and Kevin, but for the rest of the people in the building. Norma had told her that no one was sure who they were supposed to side with or if they were even allowed to talk about it. Just another reason not to date at work, Bridget reminded herself.

"Well, I don't have an f-ing clue where that's going, if anywhere," Bridget said quietly. "He's pissed off at me—I can tell by the way he won't make eye contact. But I don't know why. I think...I probably pushed him too hard on the dating side and he freaked out."

Norma nodded her head and didn't say anything.

Bridget looked at her. "What?"

She shook her head. "Nothing, boss. But you know how hard it is just to date in the regular world."

"Yeah, yeah, I know," Bridget said. "You sound like my mother."

"Maybe she's right. At least Mr. Whitlowe authorized the warrant."

"Yes. Those old satellite photos did the trick, and soon I'll get new ones. He seemed almost as concerned about it as I am, but not quite enough."

"Well, there you go," Norma replied. "Based on what I've seen, you've got more than enough to do a follow-up on the illegal weapons transfer from last year. And a site search for new weapons. Plus check the building permits for all that construction."

Bridget nodded. "Make me a list. And yes, it'll be good to get out there. I can get a look around."

"Whatever they are doing," Norma said, "it can't be good."

CHAPTER 10
Consultant

After his Tuesday full of errands, Frank was pleased to head back to Laura's place. He picked up Jackson from kindergarten around 2 p.m., and after Laura got home from working at the salon, the three of them made dinner and ate together around her small, beat-up dining table.

Jackson was excited, talking about his kindergarten classes. He had many more kids in his new school than he'd previously had in the downtown preschool. Frank and Laura peppered him with questions, both during dinner and afterward, while they all cleaned up.

"We still good to meet after?" Frank asked his daughter as she went off to bathe Jackson and get him to bed.

"Absolutely," she said with a smile. "Been looking forward to it all day."

An hour later, Frank had a stack of folders and files from the Anderson case spread out on the now-clean dining room table, organizing them as Laura came in. She made herself a cup of tea and sat down next to him. She put one leg up in the chair, hugging it to herself. The move reminded Frank of Jessica Mills—she'd done that as well the first time they'd met, and often sat in chairs while hugging one of her legs. Must be a young woman thing, but a thing Frank had never noticed before.

"So, how is it going?"

"Good, good," Frank said. "Actually, not so good. The Jessica Mills protection job is done, obviously. I'm still waiting for the folks in Los Angeles to pay the final invoice."

"Nice. Let me know if you want more help with all the billing—it's easy to get behind. That's a lot of what I do at the salon, just keeping up with paperwork."

"Thank you," he said, then pointed at the files. "But this other case? Anderson Tool & Die? I'm stuck."

She grabbed a folder and flipped through it, seeing page after page of accounting figures. "These their books?"

"Yes, most of them. And I'm lost. I could really use your help."

"Really?"

"I have no idea what I'm doing," Frank said. "Jill Anderson suggested I'm going to need a forensic accountant, whatever that is."

"Okay, I'm not one of those, but I can help you through some of it. At least help you get organized. Walk me through what you know."

Frank nodded and started, getting her slowly up to speed. He explained there were two separate aspects of the case, and he was working on both at the same time. They were likely related—in fact, Frank said that he couldn't see a situation where they weren't connected.

The two aspects were Jill Anderson's father and his untimely death, and the fact that large amounts of money had evaporated from the company. Jill was convinced the two were connected. She thought that her father had been investigating the missing money and someone had killed him over it.

"Do the cops think he was killed?"

"Well, it was a hit-and-run, so the case was never closed," Frank said, sitting back from the table. He explained how those types of cases just sat on the books in most jurisdictions, never to be solved unless new information appeared down the road. "They ran through the car types and interviewed witnesses, but it never went anywhere."

"So it could be," Laura asked.

"Sure. Hard to prove. He was out jogging. At night. Alone."

"Not smart if he was also actively pissing people off."

He looked at her and smiled. "Right."

"And she's convinced the money is connected."

Frank nodded as Laura borrowed one of his yellow notepads and started taking notes, asking more questions. He also wrote a few things down in his journal notebook. It was really turning out to be helpful, jotting down a running list of notes. Like, if he hadn't made a note of that Travis kid coming to see him for protection, there was no way Frank would've remembered the kid's name when he was thinking of hiring someone to go undercover into Anderson Tool & Die.

He and Laura started shuffling through the stacks of folders Jill had given him, printouts of all of the accounting for the last ten years. Jill had notated on the accounts where she thought things were hinky, but it hadn't been enough to convince the local police to get involved beyond a quick and cursory inquiry, Frank explained. The books didn't match up with revenues, but the numbers were murky and hard to follow, at least for Frank.

"Money moving from account to account for no reason," she said, pointing at an open folder. "Covering expenses, different accounts. Wow, lots of accounts," she said, pointing at another page full of numbers. "Who needs this many accounts?"

Frank shook his head.

She looked through a stack of pages, flipping between two pages seemingly at random. "And they're not using standard accounting practices."

"I'll take your word for it," Frank said. All he saw was rows and rows of numbers with dollar signs. "So, a place like this had accountants and bookkeepers and a CFO. What do they all do?"

"Well, it depends," Laura said, setting the stack of papers aside. "Bookkeepers do the day-to-day stuff, paying invoices and entering stuff into QuickBooks or whatever system they use. Bigger companies use custom software at the corporate level. Making sure that all the bills are getting paid, paying all the vendors. Checking all the deposits to make sure the company is getting paid for all the invoices they send out. That kind of stuff."

Frank nodded, making some notes of his own. "And the accountants?"

"Higher-end stuff, like taxes, estimated taxes, sales tax. Filing with the state, filing with the IRS, making sure the company stays off the government's radar at all costs. Paying local taxes, too. And all the payroll—cutting all checks or automating that process, paying into the payroll tax system monthly, sending in FICA and all that. QuickBooks Payroll takes care of a lot of that, but it looks like Anderson is doing all that in-house."

"Why?"

"Not sure," Laura said, biting her lip. Frank smiled—her mother used to do that. Back when he still spoke to her mother. "Might be they want more control, or maybe it's just the way they've always done it and haven't automated it yet. There are a bunch of payroll services out there now, but not so much ten years ago."

Frank scribbled it all down—he'd need to ask Jill Anderson about this and a dozen other things. "I'll ask the owner, see if I can find out who's making those decisions. I'm assuming doing the payroll in-house would make it easier to steal."

"Oh yeah."

Frank nodded. "So, what's the CFO do?"

"Well, they oversee all of this, of course, but mainly what they do is set policy and make company-wide decisions to maximize profit or increase sales. They're supposed to be looking at everything that's happening in the company and then make changes to put the company in a better position financially. Like, if I were the CFO, the first thing I'd do is outsource the payroll. It's an easy fix and greatly increases checks and balances. You know, more oversight. And I'd also do a full audit."

Frank wrote it all down. "They did three audits, as far as I know. Nothing came from them. So, if I were going to steal from the company, who would have the easiest time of it?"

"The CFO, certainly," Laura said. "No matter what, you could cover it up. Or one of the bookkeepers—they can syphon off money pretty easily, though I don't know if they could get to it."

"What?"

She pointed at the stack of pages. "It's easy to move money around. Anyone can do that in whatever software they're using. Especially if you have access to the main accounting setup pages. Like, if you can create new accounts and new vendors, it would be easy to move money around."

"Yup, I follow."

"But actually getting the money out? That's different. Like, if you're taking out cash, then those monies have to exist in an account that has a real-world cash balance to draw from."

Frank started to nod but then stopped. "Wait. What?"

"Look, you can have an infinite number of accounts, right?"

"Sure."

"But only some of them are actual accounts. In a bank somewhere. With money in them."

"Oh, yeah. Okay. But can't people just transfer money electronically to another account? And then pull cash out of that?"

"Not usually. Maybe. I don't know...but I could find out."

Frank pointed at the files. "But it points at the CFO, I assume. Three different ones over the past six years, plus lots of accountants and bookkeepers," Frank said, grabbing at the stack of personnel files. "They keep bringing in new people to figure out the problem."

"Yeah, but it's probably not an accident," Laura said when Frank was finished explaining. "If the books are jacked up on purpose, it would be to cover up the leakage. Whoever has access to the books is the problem."

"Well, that's another issue. Lots of staff in the finance department, and lots of admin folks, and the official books are open to them all."

"What?"

"Yeah, I know."

"They need to lock that down."

"Jill Anderson did that a while ago, limiting the number of people who have accounting access. The bleeding has stopped, and last month, the books matched. But before, lots of money went missing."

"How much?"

"North of nine million."

Laura whistled quietly.

She and Frank talked for another hour, going through all the accounts. As she got deeper and deeper into the weeds, he understood less and less of what she was trying to explain to him. The books were all messed up and had been for years, making it even harder to find the source of the problem.

"I can't do this on my own," Laura finally said. "It's too much to sift through. But I can take a crack at it and get back to you. At least pull together what I think happened."

"Anything would help."

She looked at the folders. "I could bring in some of my accounting classmates if they're available."

Frank nodded. "Give me their names first. I'll run a background on them."

"Okay," she said, making a face. "You're serious?"

"Whoever did this might have killed someone over it," Frank said. "I need to know who's involved. And you're going nowhere near the factory. I don't need anyone suspicious of you."

"This kind of financial investigation is complicated, Dad. Normally you would pay a big firm to do this, and it would take months and months of work. Plus, they would be on-site to go through the real files. Dig through all the original paperwork instead of a bunch of copies or printouts from electronic files, right? Unless they are scans, there is no guarantee any of these printouts are accurate to the originals. Jill could be playing you."

"I know. I'm working on that as well." He just had a random hilarious thought and smiled.

She looked at him funny. "What?"

"I remembered someone from a previous case who is great with finances. Like really good. And he has an...interesting background, to say the least. I could bring him in. He's had a lot of experience working with criminals—he might know some creative solutions to these problems."

She nodded slowly. "Yeah, I guess. Is he trustworthy?"

Frank thought about it for a second. "I think so. Apparently, he was a genius. Did the books for one of the biggest gangs in the area."

"Gangs? Like a biker gang?"

"No, downtown. The Northsiders, down in Dayton."

"The gang that kidnapped you? No way you're going there."

Frank thought about it. "Well, he knew his stuff. There were into everything. Drugs, gambling money, prostitution. That kind of stuff."

"And kidnapping people," Laura said, sitting back and crossing her arms. "You were missing and I was freaking out. Remember?"

Frank nodded. "I know. Sorry about that."

"Deputy Peters helped out, kept me calm," she said quietly. His name didn't come up a lot, and it was awkward when it did. He and Laura had become friends while searching together for Frank. Now Peters was gone.

She was quiet for a minute, then shook her head. "Not sure if involving a gang member is a good idea or not. The case is complicated enough without having actual criminals working on it. Jill Anderson won't like it."

"He's not a criminal anymore," Frank said, sitting back and thinking about it. "At least I don't think so. Last time I talked to him, he was getting his life back together. And the gang is gone—they relocated to Chicago, I heard."

"Great," she said. "That's very reassuring."

"I know. But he's an interesting guy. He could be very helpful."

"Maybe," she said. He could tell she wasn't buying his explanation. But he could also tell she was excited about the case—and it was a chance to use her accounting training, "And you don't need to worry about paying me—I'm just happy to help you get your PI business up and running."

"You're not fooling me for a second," he said, glancing around at the apartment and his stacks and stacks of boxes. "You just want me to make more money so I'll move out of your house."

"Yeah, that too."

CHAPTER 11
Back to Ohio

The next morning, Joe Hathaway dozed, drifting in and out of sleep, waking every once in a while. Driving always made him tired, and riding slouched down in the back seat of a moving car was even worse. The steady, quiet rhythm of the highway beneath the car made him even more tired. Trapper was driving, and Joe had nothing to do but rest and relax and, every once in a while, scooch up and look out the window.

Sometimes he slept, and sometimes he watched the landscape for a while. He'd been awake to see the sun come up and bathe the land in warmth and light, then drifted back to sleep.

At some point later, he awoke when the rhythm of the tires changed. They had been speeding along, but now they slowed, waking him. He looked around to see they were approaching an exit. Trapper had been on the I-75 for most of the trip, but now he exited the super slab and took the back ways, thin country roads the bisected overgrown corn fields. It had to be harvest season soon, right? It was mid-October, yet there were still fields and fields full of corn, most of the stalks brown and gangly and tipped over with the weight of the cobs near the top. When did they harvest? How did that work?

It was early on Wednesday morning, October 17th. They had driven through the night, leaving the hellhole that was Gary, Indiana, around midnight. Joe was glad to be rid of the place. It had felt like a ticking clock—or a bomb, waiting for the exact wrong set of conditions for it to go off.

Driving at night made it easier to avoid the cops, as long as you stayed in your lane and drove a well-maintained vehicle. Trapper had rented a car under an alias for just this trip and had picked up Joe at his shitty hotel room, packing up the two or three boxes of things Joe had managed to acquire during his time in hiding.

The drive down had been uneventful—in fact, Joe had slept most of the way. It was a straight shot over from Indiana to Ohio and then down I-75 to Dayton. Taking the highway meant they could avoid all the little towns and the aggressive police departments who depended on hassling tourists and out-of-towners with bogus violations and lame speeding tickets. Joe didn't need that kind of delay, or the kind of attention it might bring. Or, in a worst-case scenario, he and Trapper would get cornered and have to shoot it out with some hick policeman, starting the whole cycle over again.

No, Joe was tired of hiding. Tired of running.

Joe had floated down that river, lying on his back and staring up at the sky and the passing trees. He remembered breathing, in and out, the cold water splashing around his face. He'd needed to concentrate on his breathing, fearing it would just stop on its own. The gunshots had burned holes full of fire right through him. It had felt like he was leaking lava into the cold water around him.

But worse was the feeling that Frank Harper had outsmarted him. Somehow. Again.

First, the old cop had figured out the whole murder of Tom Mercato, despite Joe's weeks of meticulous planning before the murder and the careful cover up that followed. Even after the old cop had come to their coffee klatch and interviewed everyone, including Joe, who had been particularly clever with his answers during the makeshift interrogation in a McDonald's dining room.

Then the old cop had escaped Joe's attempts to kill him in that rigged icehouse. The old cop and his idiot deputy had escaped the house on the lake as it shifted and sunk into the frozen water below. And THEN Harper had hopped in his old car and chased down Joe in a stupid car chase, like something out of movie.

Joe remembered the chase. Frank Harper's car had roared up behind him, chasing Joe through the streets of Cooper's Mill. Joe had gambled on his ability to race ahead of a train at a crossing. He'd lost that bet, of course, and the train had smashed into his car, spinning it sideways and throwing it nearly thirty feet, they told him later. Joe had been lucky to survive.

And when Joe was recovering, the cops had added literal insult to injury by charging him with three attempted murders. During the subsequent trial, Harper had FLOWN IN from Alabama to testify against Joe. What kind of obsessive person does that? Travels all that way just to point at Joe and say "yup, that guy. Right there, the one in the wheelchair. He did it."

Harper was no idiot, just a stone in Joe's shoe. The knight or rook he couldn't seem to get rid of, the chess piece that swooped in from nowhere and took the checkmate. Joe always had to watch out for the bishops—they always seemed to career across the board, moving six or eight spaces, emerging from a screen of other pieces to take the game. Harper was like a bishop, swooping in from the shadows.

Harper's deputy friend—that guy had been an idiot, to be sure. At least Joe had taken him off the board. It had been luck, the whole thing with the kid's extreme allergy to yellow jacket venom. Dumb luck, getting that pawn. But taking any of Harper's pieces off the board was a win.

But now, Joe was tired of running. Months in that shitty hotel in Indiana had taught him to bide his time, of course, but now he was ready. Time to set up the board again, arrange his pieces, and then invite Harper for one final game.

Winner take all.

Joe looked out at the flat Ohio landscape, barely illuminated by the rising sun, and marveled at the fact that he was back. Cooper's Mill wasn't far from here, and Troy, and all the other haunts.

Trapper guided the rented car along back roads and narrow streets, and Joe could tell he was taking a circuitous route, doubling back on himself several times while keeping one eye on the rear view mirror.

"We being followed?"

Trapper smiled and looked back. "How long you been awake?"

"Since the highway."

Trapper looked in the mirror again. "No, we're not being followed. And I want to keep it that way."

"You're not shaking a tail?"

"Habit. And avoiding picking up one, really. Want me to tell you about Brother Xavier and the others?"

Joe shook his head and settled back down. "No, not yet. I want to get a first impression, and then we'll talk."

Trapper nodded and went back to driving without another word. Joe appreciated that—the man knew when to talk and when to be quiet. And he understood that Joe was in charge.

A half-hour later, Trapper slowed and turned onto a gravel road, then took a series of turns and stops before ending up at a large gate. Joe saw immediately that it and the surrounding fences were all topped by angry barbed wire. Shiny, like it had just been installed. No time to rust or degrade. Beyond, nothing but corn fields.

The large gate had shiny metal wheels on the bottom and looked like it either rolled out of the way or swung off to the left.

Too late, Joe noticed a pair of cameras on a tall pole—oh well, nothing he could do about that now. Joe sat up as Trapper stopped at a metal kiosk with a keypad and speaker.

"Can I help you?" a female voice said from the speaker.

"Yes, Hansel and Gretel. We're here to speak to Sampson." Trapper glanced over at Joe Hathaway and shrugged. "They love code names."

The speaker crackled. "Code word of the day?"

Trapper leaned closer to the window. "Rhubarb."

"Okay, thanks," the voice said. Ahead of the car, the gate clicked loudly and began rumbling aside, swinging out of the way. "Come on up to the main house," the woman on the speaker said. "And DO NOT deviate from the main road."

"Will do," Trapper said out the window before pulling through the open gate. Joe turned and saw the automatic gate close quickly behind them.

"I thought this was a bunch of Waco types, unorganized hicks."

"They're pretty organized."

"They're serious about security."

Trapper nodded. "You have no idea." He drove on up the narrow road. They passed a sign that said "Compound HQ" and "Matthew House." Soon the car was enveloped in corn, tall walls of the green and brown stalks encroaching both sides of the narrow road, which took several turns.

Past the corn, the farm widened out into a plain covered with cows and pasture and lots where the cows could be fed and watered. Joe and Trapper passed a half-dozen barns, apparently heading for a group of farmhouses ahead.

Joe was less than impressed.

"This is it?" he asked, looking out the window. "Some farmhouses, barns, lots of cows. And corn in all directions. What's the big deal? It looks like an episode of 'Hee Haw'."

Trapper guided the car up to another gate, this one guarded by a man in a little shack. Trapper exchanged words with the man, who nodded and disappeared back into the shack.

Trapper nodded ahead of them. "They are serious, just so you know. A lot of their compound is hidden, to tell the truth. The Church of Xavier has been growing, and—"

"Church of Xavier? Are you kidding?"

"No," Trapper said. The gate started opening, moving very slowly.

"That's the name of their church. And their leader? He's an interesting guy."

"Well, I guess I've got the Keepers of Truth," Joe said, looking around. "Sounds just as silly, when you think about it. Two cult leaders, teaming up."

Trapper smiled. "You will like him, I think. He's the smartest one out here, and he's got some very interesting ideas."

"I'm looking forward to it," Joe said, glancing around. "But it still looks like a farm."

"Four farms, actually," Trapper said. "With more on the way."

The gate rolled away, revealing another grassy area and the farmhouses.

Trapper drove up another lane, passing more fields and a barn that they were using to store vehicles, it looked like. Out front, two men were working on a rusty combine, apparently repairing something underneath.

Moments later, a large, country-style home came into view, the largest one Joe had seen. Trapper slowed and parked in a paved parking area in front of the home.

"Two hundred acres, no public roads, massive tracts of land where no one will bother you. And they're building quite a lot here, building for the future," Trapper said. "You'll be impressed, I promise. And you said you wanted privacy, right?"

Joe nodded, not answering. The man was right—hiding hadn't worked out, but being back here in Ohio made him nervous. There had been a nationwide manhunt for him over the summer, and things were finally settling down. Joe didn't want to push his luck by being back here, back in the proverbial lion's den, half a county over from the farmhouse shootout and the hospital from which he'd escaped.

But Trapper had a good point. Earlier, he had repeated part of their discussion up in Gary, Indiana, the night he'd arrived with the news about Frank Harper and the girl he was guarding. Every cop involved in tracking or hunting Joe probably expected him to flee, assuming he was in Seattle or Canada or overseas somewhere. Coming back here was a gamble, certainly, but Trapper thought it was the last place they would look.

Joe wasn't convinced, but it would give him a chance to look in on Frank Harper. He'd followed the story of the Hollywood starlet who'd visited Cooper's Mill and Frank's involvement in the tale. It had chapped Joe's hide to read about Harper, about the newspaper "journalists" gushing over his involvement, fawning over the way the old cop had shot the starlet's stalker and saved her. Whatever. Who cared? Harper was still a know-it-all busy body with a nasty habit of sticking his nose in where it didn't belong.

Joe was going to end him.

"Okay, don't forget, boss—these guys are serious," Trapper said, shutting off the car. "They don't suffer fools and REALLY don't like visitors. These people live for avoiding the spotlight, so it took a lot of track-laying to even get them to entertain meeting with someone as well-known as you."

Trapper climbed out of the car and waited for Joe to get out, which took a second. Joe could feel the years in his legs as he got out and stretched. They'd been in the car for a while, and he heard both of his knees pop as he climbed from the car.

"You okay, boss?"

"Yes, yes," Joe said, shaking his head. "Gettin' old sucks."

Trapper slammed his door and started for the house.

"It's better than the alternative, right?"

Joe made a face and nodded his head. "Yup."

CHAPTER 12
Diner

The next morning, Frank was up early. He gathered his documentation, including the reports he'd been getting from Travis, and headed out the door.

This morning was blisteringly cold, and he spent several minutes scraping the ice off the windshield of the Camaro before he could get rolling. There was not a lot of parking on the street, and he was reluctant to give up the prime spot right in front of Laura's place, but it couldn't be helped. He had a business meeting to get to.

Frank drove to the Tip Top Diner, a mom-and-pop restaurant located near the highway. It was a frequent stop for him, serving as his defacto office and primary meeting spot for clients and potential customers.

Frank had a great relationship with the cadre of waitresses and other folks who worked there, including the mom and pop owners, and they were kind enough to let him conduct his "business" out of Booth #3. Someday he'd have an actual office (and parking) where he could meet with clients, but Frank Harper wasn't there yet. Someday he'd have a place to hang his shingle, as they said, but, for now, he pulled into the parking lot of the restaurant and headed to work.

Jill Anderson wasn't there yet, so Frank got set up in a booth and ordered coffee and spread out his papers, scraping old pancake syrup from the table's brown surface. Booth #3 wasn't available—it was taken up by a sketchy-looking couple—and Frank had to make do with another booth instead of sliding into his informal "office." Maybe he should buy a little plaque or something and hang it at his booth: "Reserved – For Frank Harper Investigations Use Only." The thought brought a little smile to his face.

Someday he'd have an actual office, with visiting hours and filing cabinets full of papers. And maybe a receptionist who answered the phones and did her nails all day long like they did in the movies.

For now, this place would have to do. And you could do worse: the coffee was great, and the girls knew to leave him alone when he was working, head down in a stack of folders or speaking quietly on his phone. And they knew that, when he was with a client, keep bringing the coffee.

It was like that joke from "Back to School." Except here it was "bring coffee every five minutes until someone passes out, then bring coffee every ten minutes."

Frank met almost all of his clients here, so far, and it had worked well. It was a neutral location, public but not too public. And a few of his guests had loved it. He'd even brought in the Hollywood starlet when she'd been tagging along in his life. That had caused quite a stir, obviously. Booths full of onlookers, with paparazzi outside, photographing everyone entering and leaving like it was some trendy LA club.

The Tip Top Diner, but with bouncers and a velvet rope. The whole thing had been a dose of crazy. Frank was sure that the waitresses were more impressed with him after all that.

Of course, Jessica Mills had been on her best behavior on her visits to the Tip Top Diner—she'd talked up the staff and taken selfies with everyone and done all the other things that a visiting celebrity would be expected to do. She'd even gone in the back and pulled on a hair net and cooked eggs as the staff snapped pictures. And now, a large color photo of her and the staff hung on the wall behind the front counter for every customer to see.

He smiled, thinking about her. She was a trip, certainly, and self-absorbed, and entitled. Frank had dismissed her crazy talk about her "stalker" as just more of her self-absorbed, delusional attitude. Frank had written it all off as exaggeration, of course, right up to the moment the man had materialized on the road and snatched Jessica up right in the middle of a parade. Who does that? He'd been dressed as a clown and walked right up to her—Jessica Mills, one of the most famous people in the world—and grabbed her, throwing her over his shoulder like she weighed nothing. Frank had chased, as one does. Gunshots, knives, down into a creepy basement full of cars. And the guy had died.

Now, a month later, Frank wondered at his attitude. She'd been right, of course, and he'd assumed she was an idiot. He'd never believed her until it was nearly too late, and it had almost cost her her life. And Frank could have died as well—the man had been crazy. And crazed. Who knows how it could've turned out.

He shook his head and organized his papers on the brown table, scooting the bowl of creamers out of the way. That case, protecting her, was over. Solved, invoiced, waiting to be paid the final installment.

But this case, the Anderson Tool & Die case, was still taking up space on his plate—and in his head. It was turning out to be much more complicated than he had imagined. He'd been working on it for months, doing interviews, pouring through the personnel files, even bringing in Laura to help with the financial aspect.

It was Frank's only case right now, and it seemed like it was going nowhere.

He'd poured over all of the financials too, of course, but it was Greek to him. He felt better, knowing his daughter was looking over the stacks of printed reports to see if she could tease out a clue. Or, better yet, peak behind the wall of numbers and find the $9 million needle in that financial haystack.

His client, Jill Anderson, was convinced. Someone had stolen from her father's company, even though her internal investigations had yielded nothing. The CMPD couldn't find anything either. And there was the death of her father. Before Jill had inherited the company, it had been her father's. Royce Anderson had run the company for nearly twenty years, but in the final years, he'd taken to questioning his employees regularly, double-checking deposits and expenditures, and getting very in the weeds as to the company's finances. He'd grilled Brad Billingsly, the company's CFO at the time, trying to pinpoint where the money was going. He'd told his daughter as much three nights before he'd been killed in a jogging accident.

They found Royce's body in the woods near the canal out on Canal Road. He'd been thrown nearly forty feet before impacting a tree.

Jill had inherited the company and came in like a hurricane, with a very skeptical notion of what the company did and how she thought she could improve it. She cleaned house, vowing to improve the company. She'd had the books done over again, fired Billingsly, and locked down all the finances. But it didn't help. Money kept evaporating from Anderson like dew on a sunny morning. Finally, desperate, she'd hired Frank. So far, he'd had no luck either.

Still, it didn't seem to matter to Jill Anderson. She was willing to foot his bills for the foreseeable future. Jill wanted him to kick over every stone in the company, and Frank was happy to oblige. He'd work until he got to the bottom of it and figure out if her father's death was an accident—or something else.

A few minutes later, she arrived, and, for a second, he didn't recognize her—she was wearing a big floppy hat and sunglasses, just as she did every time they met here. She'd said she didn't want to be recognized, and on some level, it made sense. Of course, if he thought it could impact the case, Frank would have suggested they meet up at a place up in Troy or even down in Dayton, where few people knew either of them. Besides, it didn't really matter if people knew Jill was having Frank investigate her company; anyone who knew her situation wouldn't have been too surprised.

She saw him and nodded, walking over. He stood, more out of habit than any bit of chivalry, and shook her hand.

"I don't know if your disguise is going to fool anyone, Ms. Anderson."

"It's Jill, Frank," she said, sitting down and looking around. "I've told you before."

"Yes, ma'am."

A cup of coffee appeared in front of her, as if by magic. Frank nodded at Doris, one of the waitresses, as she walked away. Jill added way too much cream and sugar into the cup and sipped.

"It's cold out there," she said with a smile. "Too early to be this cold. Okay, what you got?"

He nodded and started, going over the last two weeks of his investigation. There had been several developments since their last meeting: hiring the undercover kid now working on the floor of her factory, updates on some of the background checks, and Frank bringing in his daughter to go over the books. Frank himself had started a second review of every current employee's file, looking for people who might be working together.

Jill listened respectfully for a few minutes, sipping her coffee and adding cream and sugar to a refill before interrupting him.

"So, nothing new?"

He looked up at her, then sat back.

"No, not really. Making good progress, of course, but nothing new for you. We called it 'eliminating variables' when I was on the force. It really just means closing loops, answering questions on cases where we can. Locking stuff down to get to the truth."

Jill Anderson nodded and started to say something, then waited as Doris topped off the coffee for both of them. When the waitress was gone, Jill continued.

"Good speech. I bet you say that to all the clients."

"Wait, no, that's not—"

"It's okay, Frank. I don't mind. You're actively investigating, which means I don't have to. 'Things are happening,' as they say, right? And while you're working on this," she said, tapping the papers between them, "I can relax. You're going to do a better job at this than I ever could. Even if you don't figure out what happened to the money, or who killed my father, it makes me happy knowing you're on it."

Frank wasn't sure what to say. "Um...well, thanks. But we're early on this, and I feel confident that we'll figure some of it out—"

"Oh, I know you're confident," Jill said. "That's good. Keep working."

He sat back, curious at her demeanor. Was she orchestrating some kind of elaborate coverup? It might explain why she wasn't demanding results. What if she was behind the thefts—and the death of her father? He didn't think so. She was always the first one to bring it up, and he could tell that it still upset her. If Jill had arranged for her father's death, she was a better actress than he was giving her credit for. Maybe she should relocate to Hollywood and join Jessica Mills' new production company.

Frank, on a whim, decided to test that theory.

"I just brought in someone else to go through all the forensic accounting," Frank said.

"You said that—your daughter? She has a background in accounting."

"Yes, but I hired another person. He's actually got a background in criminal accounting—it's a very special field. He's an expert in working with criminal organizations, tracking how money is moved around to avoid detection."

Frank watched her eyes for the reaction, but she was cool as usual. She seemed to be confused by the notice, and asked several smart questions, but none of them seemed to indicate guilt on her part.

"And you think they will help?"

"I hope so."

"Good."

Her reaction was that of someone happy to get one step closer to the truth. Not that of a person engaged in a years-long coverup involving murder and malfeasance. Of course, time will tell. As it always did.

CHAPTER 13
Arrow Slits

Arriving at the location, the first thing that struck Joe was the silence.

Closing the car door and stepping away from the rented car, he was taken by the absolute quiet out here in the country.

There were no sounds but the wind and an occasional lowing sound from a distant group of cows nestled against a split-wood fence railing that separated a nearby field from the parking lot and the homes. Joe stood for a moment, listening to the lack of noise. So different from the sirens and gunshots and hustle and bustle of Gary, Indiana. Here there was nothing but a few buildings and some cows—and miles and miles of nothing. Just the blue sky and green and brown fields and a few stands of trees, stretching to the horizon.

"Wow, it's quiet."

Trapper turned and looked at him.

"You know it."

Maybe Trapper was onto something with this place. Here, a person could certainly get lost. Or avoid the prying eyes of civilization.

Out here, no one could see you.

"Come on, boss," Trapper said, nodding at the nearby home, lit up from the inside. Smoke drifted from the chimney, and Joe got the sense that the place would be cozy. "You're going to love it, I promise."

Joe looked around at the cows again and, after a moment, shrugged his shoulders.

"Where else am I gonna go?" With a smile, he followed Trapper in the direction of the large farmhouse. It was impressive in size, surrounded by flat farmland and a half-dozen outbuildings. But, as they approached, Joe slowly realized the scope of what these "preppers" were building out here. Two of the buildings were tall and skinny and rose on either side of the farmhouse. In each, the windows at the top were tall and narrow, almost like arrow slits on old castles.

They were guard towers.

Now, upon closer inspection, Joe Hathaway discerned more

details, like the metal doors at the bottom, likely heavily reinforced from the inside to prevent breach. The tops of the towers were flat and looked like they could be accessed from inside—if he had to bet, he'd guess that there were low railings on all four sides to provide a good, secure place for cover.

Trapper slowed as they approached the house, and two men were waiting for them, standing on either side of the wide set of steps that led up to a front porch and the home's main entrance.

"Okay, don't forget, boss—these guys are serious," Trapper said quietly.

Hathaway started to say something snarky—Trapper had already mentioned this several times—but then paused and simply nodded. Trapper was nervous, and got talky when he was nervous. But he was also smart. And one of the few friends Joe had left in the world. Joe was starting to learn—finally, after decades—that he needed to keep a few good people close to him. He'd had enough of being out in the world on his own. Even if he was the smartest person most of these people would ever meet, Hathaway didn't have to flaunt it.

"Ready?" Trapper was looking at him from the top step, and Joe realized Trapper had been talking but Joe hadn't been listening. He'd been woolgathering, planning, thinking. Distracted, as usual, trying to take the information in front of him and extrapolate every single possible outcome.

But this was different. He had no idea what was coming next, or who these people were or how they would react to him. Joe couldn't predict anything about this Xavier person, the supposed cult leader. He knew nothing about the man other than what Trapper had told him. He was apparently very talkative, very charismatic, and held his people under his sway. But it made it nearly impossible for Joe to predict. This whole thing could be a disaster, but it was something different, and better than moldering away in a dirty hotel, hiding from the world. Shrugging, Joe followed Trapper up the steps of the farmhouse and headed inside.

PART 2
Aim

CHAPTER 14
Shaving

A few days later, Joe stood by the mirror in the bathroom, shaving. He could hear Trapper snoring in the adjacent room. The preppers had set them up in a nice little suite on the second floor of the main farmhouse, with two bedrooms and a shared bathroom. Joe didn't really like the arrangement, but there was nothing he could do about it right now. He was a guest of the Church of Xavier, and they were keeping him away from prying eyes. Joe knew he had a bad habit of biting the hand that feeds. Trapper was here to keep things smooth.

So far, things had worked out. Xavier, the leader of this particular bunch of ultra-religious nutjobs, was no worse than other people Joe had met in his life. Joe was good at reading people, and picked up on the man's rampant narcissism the moment he met him.

Upon arrival, Joe and Trapper had been shown into the main house, the Matthew House. It sat in the middle of the Matthew Farm—and yes, there were four main farms (and four main houses), and they were named Mathew, Mark, Luke and John. No surprise there. Trapper had mentioned the Church owned quite a bit of land in the area, and not all of it contiguous. He had also said something about Xavier trying to stitch together properties to create large areas of land he controlled. So far, it sounded like it was working.

They met Xavier in an expansive living room, and the man rose and greeted Joe and Trapper as if they were old friends. Xavier looked Mexican, wizened, his face wrinkled from the sun. The knuckles on his hands were rough, calloused. He'd seen a lot of hours outside, if Joe had to guess, and had worked his whole life.

Sitting, Trapper formally introduced them, and Xavier greeted them warmly. "I am glad your journey was uneventful," Xavier said, nodding to Trapper. "I heard you would be taking many of the back roads."

"Yes," Joe said. "Thank you for asking, and thank you for your hospitality."

Xavier shook his head and waved over a woman, who passed out drinks. Some kind of lemonade, but it was cloudy and had the bite of a splash of agave or something. "We have made a home here, and now I welcome you to it."

They drank, and Xavier spoke about his church and their travels before coming together to establish this "garden of peace" in central Ohio. From his accent and word choice, Joe knew immediately that English was not his first language. It was always interesting to hear English filtered through the mind of a person who had learned it later in life.

"What brought your group here?" Joe had asked.

"Land," Xavier said, standing and going to a large picture window that looked out onto the rolling corn fields. "And violence." The corn was high, the stalks bent over from the weight. "We needed land, first. Both for our purposes and to be self-sufficient. We needed privacy, of course, and a place to build what we are building—literally and figuratively."

He turned to look at Joe.

"Tell me, Mr. Hathaway, do you believe in self-sufficiency? Do you believe that people have the inherent right to fend for themselves, to take care of themselves?"

"I do, Xavier. More than you can know, really. And call me Joe."

Brother Xavier smiled at that, and Joe felt the level of tension in the room go down. Trapper, who had been leaning forward up to this point in the conversation, finally sat back and smiled and relaxed. Apparently, self-sufficiency was a big deal to these folks. That and corn. And guns.

The conversation continued in earnest, and Xavier finished explaining the history of his church before turning to Joe. Xavier wanted to know all about him, how he'd come to be on the run, and why he was seeking sanctuary.

Joe glanced at Trapper. "Well, sir, I'm here to teach your people to shoot."

"Yes, and I am grateful for it," Xavier said with a smile. Two of the other church members in the room, seated near but not next to Xavier, shifted uncomfortably in their seats, and Xavier glanced at them before turning back to Joe. "From what I hear, my men and women will soon be expert marksmen. But what brings you here?"

Joe looked at the man. "Revenge."

"Ah, that is good," Xavier said, sitting back and pointing at Trapper. "Your friend here—and now my friend—tells me you have a particular stone in your shoe."

"I do."

"And you would like help getting rid of the stone."

Joe shook his head. "No, I can handle it. I just need a place to work from."

Xavier smiled. "Ah, yes. Self-sufficiency. This is good."

"Yes."

"So, how can I help?"

Now, three days later and standing in front of the bathroom mirror, Joe smiled at his reflection. It had been a good conversation. Wonderful, in fact. Full of plans and agreements. He'd watched the smile slowly grow on Xavier's face. At the end, without a moment's hesitation, Xavier had agreed to provide exactly 100% of the things that Joe needed, in exchange for teaching Xavier's people how to shoot.

Joe remembered how calm the church leader had remained throughout the conversation. That was one thing that Joe had never mastered, the ability to stay calm in the face of stress. Joe always got caught up in the moment. While he usually came out on top, he would have preferred to keep a calm head at the same time.

Oh well, just another skill for him to work on acquiring. Maybe if he spent enough time with Xavier and his people, Joe would develop some kind of Zen-like approach to the world.

Or not.

Joe remembered something that had always calmed him in the past—calculating percentages and odds. Joe looked at his face and began doing the math on how long it would take for him to shave his face. It didn't really matter—he didn't have anywhere to be—but Joe liked to keep his mind sharp.

After a moment, he fell back into the old habit, one he'd routinely used during his time as a Wall Street guy:

- THREE DAYS STUBBLE
- 50 SQUARE INCHES OF FACE
- TWO PASSES
- ELECTRIC RAZOR
- SEVEN MINUTES

"It's okay, it's okay," he said quietly, over and over. "Seven minutes to finish. No worries." He leaned over, arranging his tools.

Of course, doing something like shaving didn't slow him from his favorite hobby, talking out loud to himself.

"And you have a plan," he said to the mirror. "Well, part of a plan. It will be great. The Great Game, as they say in the old books. Holmes did it. There have been movies about it. Entice the prey into the trap. Yes. Xavier loved what I told him."

A cool breeze parted the curtains and filled the bathroom with a dash of chilly air. It was that time in Ohio when the late fall, Halloween-style weather was starting to compete with the occasional chilly breezes that signaled the approach of winter.

He started a timer on his watch and began shaving, doing so in a slow, methodical fashion to cut down on the areas he would need to repeat during the second pass. You could shave fully in one pass, he knew, but people inevitably missed some areas when they hurried. Joe did not hurry. He kept to the task at hand, focusing.

When he was done, he stopped the timer and then washed up, rinsing the tiny hairs from his face. When he was done cleaning his face and the sink area, he picked up the phone and looked at his elapsed shaving time: seven minutes and 33 seconds.

"Not bad."

He walked out into his bedroom, pulling clothes from the small closet and getting dressed. Outside, he could hear one of the church members yelling at a group of animals—it was likely pigs, as the farms also seemed to house an inordinate number of the beasts. The guy yelled, sounding like an idiot, shouting and making pig noises.

Joe shook his head. The Church had a great leader, but he was learning that it, as with the rest of society, held members of the Idiot Brigade. He liked being around smart people. Over the last week of knocking around the compound, he'd met a bunch of smart folks, people that were capable of carrying out a normal conversation.

But the rest of the members of the "Church of Xavier" seemed like extras in some movie where the entire planet had been dumbed down to levels not seen since medieval times. American and Hispanic men and women working together, heads down, doing their jobs and the business of running the farms and related industries.

Xavier had mentioned that the harvest had just started in earnest, apparently, and the men were working 18 hours a day riding their rusty, second-hand John Deere combines, shaving the stalks from the earth as he'd just shaved his face. They called it "bringing in the corn," but as far as Joe could tell, they didn't really bring it in—they carted it up and immediately sold most of it to the local processors. The rest seemed to disappear into the farm's buildings and unseen storage.

The people struck him as very simple. Religious, studious, committed to doing the work. Cut off from the outside world, they just went about their business, herding pigs or feeding the other people who lived here or working on the construction projects that dotted the compound.

Maybe they weren't dumb. Maybe they were just focused.

None of them were yammering away about President Obama or Mitt Romney or the national election being held in two weeks. None of them had an opinion on politics or climate change, as far as he could tell.

None of them cared enough about any of it to even ask him—and everyone knew he and Trapper had just come from the "outside world." Xavier didn't allow TVs or newspapers or the Internet in his domain. Just by limiting the amount of information these people had, it seemed to make them happier. More focused. They seem less obsessed than other people with that state of the world—or the rising amount of turmoil that seemed to plague the modern world.

And they were utterly devoted to Xavier.

They hung on every word and the words of his lieutenants, carrying out his commands as if their entire world depended on it. And, on some level, Joe supposed that it did. These morons had thrown in their lot with Xavier, and he was looking out for them, planning his future and theirs.

And wow, did the man have some plans. A few of them were ridiculous, and some of them complete pie in the sky. But you had to admire the man for thinking outside of the box. Some plans had even managed to surprise Joe, and that was saying something. This place had serious potential.

But the people around the farm, harvesting the corn or canning the vegetables or fixing the group meals that were provided for everyone at precisely 6 p.m. every evening? These people were not the brightest. Joe was convinced that some of them were not capable of feeding themselves. And the kids were worse! Dumb as posts, as far as Joe could tell. The kids scampered about, going to the little one-room school Xavier had built for them, then playing in the fields afterward. Playing chase, throwing things at each other, the boys teasing the girls and the girls teasing the boys.

But it was a free country, and people were free to be dumb, right? People were free to do what they needed to do to get ahead. He'd tried doing that. He'd gotten along, paid his dues, made his money on Wall Street. He'd had friends, a home, a life in Ohio. And yes, he'd broken the law. Killed a few people. Whatever. They had been dumb enough to get in his way. Joe had been smarter than all of them. Everywhere he went, Joe was the smartest person in the room.

He dressed and thought about his own plans. He wanted a great big—and very exciting—reunion with Frank Harper. One neither of them would ever forget. It was a good plan, if derivative. It had been done to death in movies and on TV shows, but rarely in real life. He'd have a hunt, and Frank would tag along.

While he dressed, he looked out the window at the corn. The farm's operations were all meticulously planned. Xavier and the Church of Exodus were preparing for "The Tragedy," their word for the end times. Instead of worrying about it, they got busy, making detailed plans and progressing on their projects. Xavier had shown him maps of the farms, with areas marked with the particular crops.

In the middle of the map, strange circular areas were drawn, and other lines, thin traceries connecting the circular area with the farmhouses. Xavier didn't answer Joe's questions about the circular new construction, but instead pointed out areas for Joe to use in his plans for Frank Harper. Joe had explained the rough outline of his plan, one he hoped to execute with Trapper. Xavier had been delighted and had volunteered a few of his own people to assist Joe.

"Can they shoot?"

"Better than most of our people," Xavier had said with a smile. "Of course, you're here to help with that."

Last night, Xavier had invited Joe to share a drink on the front porch of the main house. Xavier had talked about the future, of an American government that was power hungry, out of control. Joe had let him wax on at length, taking the opportunity to enjoy some truly great Scotch while the man rambled. Finally, he'd turned to Joe.

"When you've finished your plan for Harper, I invite you to stay. Help my people. Stay as long as you wish," Xavier looked at him, then out at the land. "This is a good place. You will be safe here, and, with your help, so will my people."

Joe had nodded. "I will consider it."

"But we must do more. Each of my people must be a warrior for peace, and that means being deadly accurate with the weapons I will be providing them."

"Now that, I can help with. You'll have an army of sharpshooter when I'm done."

"Good," Xavier had said, his eyes far away. "We must be prepared. The Tragedy is coming, and we must be ready."

As he finished getting dressed, he shook his head. Xavier had a lot going on. And Joe had enough to worry about with his own plans and schemes. He wasn't certain he wanted to get caught up in Xavier's approaching apocalypse.

CHAPTER 15
Lock and Load

"We ready?"

Tom Drayton looked up from his desk to see Bridget Turner standing over him. She was the sassy Assistant Prosecutor and technically outranked him, but Drayton was a member of the Troy Police Department and really only answered to one person, his boss, the Chief of Police.

He already knew what she was talking about without any introduction. She was investigating the Church of Xavier, a religious cult of preppers located southwest of Troy. They'd been buying up land and were building their own paradise on earth, as one of Tom's men had dubbed the collection of farms.

Tom had been studying it for years, the prepper compound in the middle of nowhere. They had bought their initial farm near the Stillwater River, securing a permanent source of fresh water. A small amount of water from the river had been diverted into a series of underground culverts and storage tanks. It was all above board, approved by the county. And the preppers had also built a tiny water treatment plant. And the latest photos passed around the office had shown more construction. They were planning for the long haul, that was for certain. But what did it mean?

Tom had spent an hour this morning reviewing the roads and paths in and out of the location. It was rare he got to scout such a large area—usually, on the rare occasion when the TPD's SWAT team was called up, they were busting into a house or maybe a business. This was completely different. But he'd made a plan, and now the raid was approved. He'd shared the maps with his team, a good group of guys. A few of them had had some great suggestions, and he'd incorporated it into the plan. Now, after yesterday's review, they were ready.

"Yes, ma'am. We've got a good team, and they understand the location."

"It's not a raid, you know," she said, pointing. "We need all that?"

He turned. She was pointing at two stacks of heavy Kevlar vests piled on the empty desk next to Drayton's.

"We always prep like it's a raid, ma'am," he said. "You have no idea how many domestic situations turn into shoot-outs. Serving a warrant or searching a property? That shit can get crazy. Go south in an instant."

He wondered how ready she was for this. The judge was allowing them to inspect the property for more illegal weapons, but there was a lot of property, nearly an infinite number of places for the Church to hide a cache of weapons. And that didn't count the other thirty or so smaller properties they had bought in the stretch of land between Pleasant Hill and Ludlow Falls.

She frowned and sat in the chair next to his desk without being invited. She was a beautiful woman—it was not a secret around the police station—and carried herself with the air of a woman who was used to getting her way. Drayton smiled. She was the kind of person who probably always got doors held open for her and extra fries with her takeout. She lived in a "bubble," where the pretty people just got better treatment than the rest of humanity. There had been a 30 Rock episode about that, where some hot guy who was used to special treatment got his face injured or something and had to temporarily experience life outside the "bubble" of his own awesomeness. It had been funny but also more than a little true. Pretty people took things for granted. He wondered for a moment if she was going to get them all killed.

"So, we're good to go?" She pointed at the calendar on the wall behind him. "First thing in the morning?"

"Yes, ma'am. I've got three vehicles, nine men including me. You'll be in charge of the paperwork and warrant, and I'll make sure we get in and out of there in one piece."

She nodded, looking at his desk, which was a complete mess. He wasn't sure if he was supposed to keep talking or not, so he went on.

"We've done a lot of these, ma'am, so no need to worry."

"I know, Officer Drayton."

"Tom, ma'am."

"Tom. I know. But what I've read about these people, they're especially crazy. And there are a lot of them, men, women, and children, all living it up out there on their compound. I hope things don't get ugly."

"They won't, ma'am."

She looked up at him and he saw there was real concern in her eyes. Like actual worry. He realized her concerns weren't about her career, or her being used to getting her way because she was skinny and blonde. She was genuinely worried about her safety and the safety of their team.

"I don't want this turning into another Waco. Promise me."

"I promise you."

She seemed to think about that for a moment and then stood, nodded at him, and walked away. Several of the other cops in the station glanced at her and her backside as she left, but Tom was only thinking about the visit to the prepper compound. Now he was a little more concerned. She was right—there was no way to predict how things were going to go down.

CHAPTER 16
Tour

Later on Monday, Joe was planning to spend the day scouting the portions of land the preppers—sorry, the Church of Xavier—had offered him to use for his plans. Apparently, most of the land had been purchased straight up, while other local landowners were "encouraged" to sell. Joe didn't have a problem with intimidation techniques, per se. But Xavier had mentioned several times that he had studiously avoided any kind of illegality, and intimidating regular folks into selling seemed fraught with hazards.

Trapper was in Pittsburgh for the day, running an important errand for Xavier. Joe worried also Trapper was getting a little too friendly with these church types, so he'd sent him on an errand. Trapper was a smart guy, and Joe's right hand man. Joe needed him 100% loyal to him and the Keepers of Truth organization. Joe needed to get back to work with them. He needed to get on the phone and get back up to speed on the organization's status and fundraising efforts. And Joe needed Trapper focused, not caught up in their "shit hits the fan" plans. Some might be credible and prescient, depending on how bad one thought things were going to get in America over the next twenty years. But Xavier might also be cuckoo for cocoa puffs.

And Joe had only one focus: Frank Harper. He was going to get what was coming to him.

Without Trapper to show him around, Joe was stuck with one of Xavier's acolytes for the tour, a young kid named James.

"You ready, Mr. Hathaway?"

Joe turned around—where he had been waiting, there had only been a little shade—and saw a young man pulling up in an electric golf cart. At least they wouldn't be walking the whole time, he thought, relieved. He was getting older and didn't need to be soaking his feet tonight.

"Ready," Joe said. He stepped off the covered porch attached to the Matthew House and climbed aboard the golf cart. "So, how many big farmhouses are there?" Joe knew, of course, but wanted to give this kid something specific to talk about.

"Four main ones, so far," the kid said. "I'm James, by the way. James Marshan. You're staying in the Matthew House, of course," he said, nodding. "You probably already knew that."

Joe didn't say anything, but he glanced up at the large sign on the front of the building: "Matthew House."

James followed his gaze. "Oh, yeah. Of course. Sorry."

The kid lifted his foot off the brake and they headed off, taking one of the many gravel paths that seemed to connect all of the properties. "So, as you know, the church has purchased much of the land around the original farm," James began saying, launching into a presentation that Joe could tell had been given many times. "The Matthew House is the center of our compound, and this and the other three houses are named for the four books of the Bible: Matthew, Mark, Luke and John."

Joe nodded, following along and holding on to the handle that hung from the roof of the golf cart. James took a corner quickly, and Joe gripped the handle tighter.

"There are also nine other houses on the property, one named for Mary and one for Joseph," James said, pointing in the direction of two distant buildings. The layout was clear, even from far away. James also pointed at a laminated map attached to the dashboard of the cart. It showed the various buildings forming the rough shape of a cross. Clever.

"Is he buying more land?"

James glanced over at Joe. "Not at this time—he has a more pressing initiative. We'll head to the Mary House first," he said, pointing in the distance. On either side of the gravel path, tall corn stood, and in some places, it leaned out over the path, creating ominous shadows.

"I'd like to see the central area as well," Joe said, pointing at the laminated map on the dash and the weird circles.

"Sorry, sir, that's off limits," James said, not turning to look at Joe. "There is always a lot of construction there."

"Can I see it in the future?"

"Umm, well," James said, unsure of himself. "I think...that's something you would have to ask Brother Xavier."

Joe nodded, not saying anything else. He had always enjoyed making people uncomfortable, and it was nice to see he still had it, even after months of cooling his heels in a dingy hotel in Indiana.

They passed another stack of metal shipping containers, taller than a stack he'd seen behind Matthew House. "What's with all the shipping containers?"

"Construction supplies, mostly."

They rode in silence through thick fields, the corn at least ten feet high as it leaned over the cart. Joe could see the corn on the stalks, or he would've had no idea what they were growing. "Isn't it time to harvest?"

James nodded, slowing and turning onto another gravel path. "Almost. In the next three weeks, all of this will be gone. "

CHAPTER 17
Textbook

Tavon Walker turned up his headphones, trying to concentrate on his homework.

It was nearly impossible with the constant barking and braying and other dog sounds coming from the next room. Tavon was huddled in the back room of his sisters' grooming business, using the only free space in the building to study.

He stared at the accounting textbook, concentrating on the formulas on the page and the booming bass of the song he was listening to. He had stuff he HAD to get done today, no questions.

Tavon took off his headphones and sighed. He was a thin young black man in his mid-twenties, just trying to keep his head down in life and make something of himself. And the barking got louder than ever and part of him wondered if he should just move away from Dayton and start fresh. He could hear two of his three sisters, Shawnda and Minnie, out in the main part of the store, yelling at each other to be heard over the sounds of the dogs. Why were they trying to have a conversation?

All they did was scream.

He looked around at the table in front of him, covered with his books and papers and his cheap-ass phone and a sketchy, second-hand laptop. And the ratty bookbag he carried everything in. He shook his head. Tavon used to be rich. It was so frustrating. Back when he ran with the Northsiders. More than ran with them, he'd been an important part of the business of the gang.

Now, all he had was his car and the cheap bag of stuff laid out on the table in front of him.

Two of his sisters, Shawnda and Minnie, ran the place with their mom Lucinda. He tried to stay out of the way as much as possible. Back when he'd been rich, he'd funded the startup of their dog grooming business, using some of his ill-gotten gains to diversify. They always say, invest invest invest, right? His mom helped them out. Tavon had also paid to have his youngest sister, Talisa, relocate to

South Carolina, where they had extended family. She'd been through enough and wanted to get out.

But he'd had more money than he knew what to do with, and it had made sense to pay for her to get away. And it had made sense to put a chunk of the gang money into something outside of the sphere of drugs and prostitution and bookmaking that the Northsiders had overseen. Opening the grooming salon had been a good call, in hindsight.

And it had come just before the Northsiders decided to pick a disastrous fight with the Dayton cops and their anti-gang task force. It was what happened when you started killing civilians, burning them out of their homes. Tavon had seen it, firsthand.

Once the Northsiders had started down that road, they were bound to attract too much attention. The Dragon, the woman leader of the gang, was a genius at keeping the Northsiders in the shadows—and it had helped that she worked in the office of the Mayor of Dayton. She'd known about every law enforcement decision the Mayor was involved in.

But once the cops had gotten involved, things had escalated quickly. They raided a strip club—but the Dragon had set it up as a trap and blew up the building, killing a bunch of cops. Maybe she'd thought the cops would just drop their investigation and go away. But killing cops seemed to piss the rest of them off even more.

Tavon had been smart enough to keep his head down, but he'd still ended up in a gunfight in a local hospital, trying to stop the Northsiders from literally executing some cops injured in the strip club explosion. Tavon hadn't thought the gang would sink that low, but the Dragon had gone off the rails by then. She would stop at nothing to get clear. Even if that meant sending two dozen armed gang members into a heavily guarded hospital, where the group of injured cops had been recovering.

By then, Tavon had met an ex-cop named Frank Harper who was looking into the gang's dealings. That was how Tavon and Harper and another cop, a Deputy Peters, had arrived at the hospital during the gunfight. It had only been by dumb luck they had managed to infiltrate the place and put a stop to the killing.

Later that year, Tavon had read in the paper that Deputy Peters had been killed up in Cooper's Mill. He'd been trying to arrest some old guy who had escaped custody. Peters had apparently been stung to death by bees or something. Sounded like a bad way to go. Tavon had been shocked to read that. You just assumed cops had an easy gig, right? They had nice cop cars and radios and state-of-the-art weapons. AND they had each other. They could call in backup at any moment. Even helicopters.

It was harder for gang members and drug dealers to eke out a living on the street, right? They were on their own, using junky cars and guns they'd bought off the street or taken off someone else. No backup, no communications other than cell phones. And it was each man for themselves. The Dragon had changed that for a while, getting the gang members to work together, but even that had ended. The Dragon and some of her crew had given up and relocated to Chicago. And Tavon and not been invited to tag along.

Tavon shook his head and went back to his books and tried to ignore the yapping dogs in the next room. He was taking classes at Sinclair, a local Dayton community college, and was getting his accounting degree as quickly as he could. Tavon had gone legit. And it sucked.

Tavon had been good for the Dragon and her men. He'd spent years sorting piles of cash and typing up reports. He'd tried to keep it all organized, fighting the chaos. At the time, the Northsiders had worked out of the old Salem Mall, and Tavon had worked in their "vault." He'd worked to streamline and improve their drug manufacturing and selling processes, making them more efficient. The Northsiders had relied on him to streamline their operation as much as possible. Truth be told, Tavon had been great at it. Tavon could "see" the holes in the operation and suggested ways to improve the output. He'd come up with novel ways to make the distribution more secure and, therefore, less vulnerable to "shrinkage," the term for stuff that went missing.

Now, it was all gone. All he had managed to keep was the money he'd stashed away—and now it was gone too. At least the dog grooming business was still here, and doing well.

Tavon shook his head and put his headphones back on to block out the barking. Turning up the music again, he concentrated on the complicated accounting formula he was trying to memorize.

Chapter 18
Back to It

It was a quiet evening, and Frank was alone. He was sitting at Laura's dining table, papers spread out all around him again. It seemed like he'd been going over these same stupid stacks of papers and personnel files for months. Maybe it was because he felt like he wasn't making any progress. And he hated taking up space at Laura's. He was working on getting his own place, and things were coming together on that front, but he was impatient.

And he was impatient with the case.

Frank Harper stared at the stacks of papers and folders and sighed. This was the kind of case he hated the most: cold, with very little new information.

Of course, when he'd been with the Alabama Bureau of Investigation, he'd had cases like this all the time. He'd lived for them. Frank would dig them out of storage, even on his own time, just for the challenge. He'd work on them for a while, try to dig up some new leads or updated information. And, at the end of all of that, if he didn't have anything new, the files and photos and bits of evidence, along with his latest notes, would go back into the box and back into storage. They rotated the cold cases out on a regular basis, revisiting them to see if anything new had happened that might help.

He hadn't been around for it, but he'd heard about how a new DNA profile database, set up by the FBI, had finally closed out hundreds of cases across the country. The DNA had been collected from thousands of criminals and suspects, categorized, and then uploaded for police departments and other law enforcement agencies to use.

But no tech breakthroughs were going to solve the Anderson Tool & Die case for him. Nothing but good, old fashioned—and boring—grunt work.

Sometimes he loved the grunt work. But now that he was out on his own, paying his own bills, Frank couldn't just cram these files in a box, seal it up, and mark it for reexamination in 2017, five years from now. No, there were people out there counting on him to crack this case. And not in years, but now. People like Jill Anderson.

Maybe he was getting cocky. He'd waded into this case, and others lately, assuming he'd knock it out of the park. Hell, he hadn't even solved the last case he'd closed—the divorce case. That had been Jessica, leaning into her knowledge of social media. If she hadn't known how to research stuff on Twitter, or wherever she'd found those photos, he'd still be struggling to solve that case.

Frank shook his head and wished again that he had something strong to drink. He wasn't comfortable bringing alcohol into Laura's place—all the more reason to look forward to his new place.

He looked at the pile of papers on the table and shook his head. Instead of digging in, Frank glanced at his notebook, flipping to his current list of cases. "Anderson Tool & Die" was at the top, under several other cases that were crossed out.

The only other open case consisted of two words: "Joe Hathaway." There was nothing to be done about that case either. Only endlessly driving the back roads around Cooper's Mill. It accomplished nothing, but it made him feel better. The guy was out there somewhere. Or maybe he was dead. Maybe his body would turn up someday and Frank could finally cross his name off his list.

It was those kinds of cases that were the worst, the ones with no resolution. They never went away. They just drifted in the background, like a ghost in an old mansion.

Like Ben Stone's murder, unsolved. The details flickered through Frank's mind. Coral Gables, Florida. Stone was a crack shot and better at the range than Frank would ever be, but it hadn't mattered. He'd been looking into child trafficking and worked a lead on his own. Dumb idea. Stone never even got a chance to draw—they'd found him with his gun still in his holster. Shot in the back. Fat lot of good his range rating had mattered.

Sometimes, Frank thought the bad guys were just destined to win. In the end, they would always stoop a little lower. They had no class, no rules. No morality to follow, no conscience to bother them in the quiet hours of the night. They killed whoever they wanted. Like Hathaway, traveling over to Indianapolis to kill that poor pregnant girl and her unborn child. Or that serial killer they had caught in Virginia. Frank had read out that insanity—the guy with the white van full of body parts. Killed by the son of one of his earliest victims.

Or Jessica Mills' stalker, and his dinner party of death.

So many sickos, doing sick things to people. Sometimes, it seemed like too much.

Or that child trafficker in Atlanta.

Frank and Stone had found a little kid, dead. Suffocated, stuffed in a buried cardboard box in the middle of an industrial area of Atlanta. A little boy, six years old. The coroner said he'd only been dead a few minutes when they found him.

Who did that? What did it gain? That case was messed up, hard to move past. They'd investigated, getting nowhere. The kid was identified but didn't seem to connect to anything else. Frank had taken some time off after that case, but Stone had been haunted by it. He'd bring it up after they'd moved on. He'd talk about it obsessively.

Frank should have known the man was still working it. Still digging for clues on the side. One clue had apparently taken him to Florida. And then the grave.

There were cases that never ended. Cases that you could never put away, no matter how much you tried.

Add Joe Hathaway to the list, Frank thought. He could be out there somewhere, right now. Frank stood, shaking his head. There was no point in fretting about it. But Frank felt restless, aimless. He needed to be working on something, even though there was nothing to work on.

He needed a drink. Bad. It would fix things, help straighten his mind out. Let him concentrate on the Anderson case—he needed to be making progress. And a beer or three would calm him. His fingers itched. They needed to be cradling a bottle of something. Anything. It didn't really matter what...

Frank tried to distract himself. He needed to get an office.

As much as he'd hated his old job down in Birmingham, at least they had had plenty of workspace. He'd had his choice of places to work: his desk, empty rooms, an abundance of conference rooms. He'd often find himself alone at a big table in one of those conference rooms, three dozen pieces of paper spread out in a particular arrangement as he worked to crack one of the cold cases he'd been assigned. The others in his office had known to leave Frank's piles of papers alone.

He needed something like that for this case.

Shaking his head, Frank grabbed the pile of folders and arranged them carefully, reading the titles quietly out loud that he'd written on each one. He pulled the one out for Jill Anderson, flipped it open, and started reading. Pretty soon he'd have all of these files memorized.

CHAPTER 19
Site Visit

Bridget sat in the back of the Ford Explorer, organizing her files and the stack of satellite photos.

The prepper compound was located about twenty miles west of Troy, Ohio, out in the middle of nowhere, south of Pleasant Hill and near the Stillwater River. Like she had told Whitlowe, these people were planners. And they were planning for the long haul, that was for certain. Or the SHTF date, whichever came first.

She was lucky to have a source that could get her these photos and at this level of clarity. Far more up-to-date than anything on Google Maps, these showed changes as of this summer, only a few months ago.

Okay, it wasn't really luck. She was pretty, and she knew it, and it had helped her in nearly every aspect of her career and her personal life. She wasn't afraid to wear a low-cut top when the situation called for it. Bridget was also pragmatic enough to admit she wasn't above using her looks to get her way in most situations. Some people were super smart, and some people were physically intimidating. Other people were good at memorizing case law or passages from the law books, reciting them at the perfect time and for the perfect scenario.

She was pretty. So sometimes she used that to her advantage. Whatever.

This packet of satellite photos was a great recent example of her using her looks to get ahead. She knew a guy who worked at First Terra, a Dayton subcontractor that was employed by a defense contractor down near Wright Patt. His company was in the remote sensors field, meaning they watched the planet from satellites in space. There were two dozen of these companies, nationwide, and she knew she was lucky to have access to a local office here in Dayton.

So they had a mutual agreement. He was trying to get into her pants, and had been for years, and she let him think he had a chance. He did not, really, but it would take him a while longer to figure that out.

In the meantime, she played off that to get what she wanted. Most times, it was access to the base, or a trip here and there to some conference. Last time, it had been a nice set of free tickets to the annual Dayton Air Show. All she'd had to do was show up in something cute and tag along with him for the day—and, in exchange, she'd gotten great seats and a pass to all the free food and massage chairs in the air conditioned VIP tent.

But in this case, it was for something more important, and she'd decided to play the cards she had. They'd gone out on a date, their first actual date in two years, and he'd dropped a pretty penny at Nest, a fancy Italian place in the Oregon District downtown. She'd enjoyed the best raviolis of her life and talked about her case and wished out loud that she could have up-to-date satellite photography—or at least something newer than the generic Google Maps shots available to the public. And a few days later, he had come through.

He wasn't horrible looking, and he was nice to her. She might sleep with him, or not. She hadn't decided yet. Women might have disadvantages in many aspects of life, but this was one place where she was glad to be a woman. You got to decide who you slept with and when.

Most of the time.

"Five minutes, ma'am," one of the cops up front said.

"Thanks," she answered, absorbed in her thoughts. She wasn't above sleeping with someone to get her way—it was the way of the world. But you had to be smart about it. Picky.

Whitlowe had made it clear that was a non-starter. She'd had her eye on him for a long time, and it looked like it was a done deal, but then he let her know he wasn't interested. Something had happened in his head when his father, the old prosecutor, had passed away. He was dealing with the repercussions of his father's death, and the estate, and a dozen other things, all on top of his 80-hour-a-week job.

He'd acknowledged her obvious advances and they had slept together, a few times. But then something had happened in his mind and he'd started pushing back, asking for distance. She hadn't been pushing, either, so it was weird. It was like he needed time to make a decision, but Bridget wasn't sure what the decision was about.

Maybe he really liked her, and he was having trouble figuring out how to make it work.

The thought made her smile. He was nice to her, and together, their careers would be unstoppable. It was always a minefield, dating where you worked, but she'd managed to avoid any serious mess-ups. St. Louis was the closest she'd come to throwing herself at someone in a long time. But the last time they'd finally discussed the situation, his face had gotten all serious, and he'd reminded her that they couldn't date while they worked in the same office.

She didn't care and let him know in no uncertain terms. It was up to them, she said, and not the rules. But still, he'd said no.

Was it because he didn't like her enough to risk his career? Or was he really following the regulations? He was a lawyer, for the record, and one who seemed to honor the whole concept of "don't shit where you eat." Now it was weird, seeing him every day. Walking past him in the hallways, heading to court. Or being in his office. Maybe she shouldn't have slept with him in the first place. The heart wants what the heart wants.

God, what a cliché, she thought.

She looked up and out the window at the passing farms, the fields towering with corn and wheat. Fields of gold and green. The two cops up front were concentrating on the road, watching for the turn. The guy in the passenger seat was loading a rifle.

"There it is," she said, even though she knew they could see the turn for themselves. Assertiveness was a muscle—you had to exercise it every day or you forgot how to use it. Or, more accurately, other people forgot that you knew how to exercise it.

The heavy Ford Explorer slowed and took the turn from the paved road and onto the gravel. She glanced behind her and saw the other two black Ford Explorers that followed close behind.

A minute later, they were approaching the edge of the Church of Xavier compound. Bridget and the cops were approaching the main houses, the center of the compound and the location of most of the construction activity.

"Okay, that's not on the satellite photos," one of the cops said, and the truck slowed.

Ahead of them, stretched across the public road, was a new gate of wood topped with barbed wire. Off to each side was a stretch of chain link and barbed wire fencing that ran off and disappeared into the fields on either side. It was impossible to see how far the fences went into the corn. Next to the road—and inside the fenced area—was a short tower built of wooden pallets. It was ten or twelve feet tall, with a ladder up the back, and topped with an enclosed room with a window and a peaked roof.

It was an honest-to-God guard tower, like something out of "Lord of the Rings."

"Great," she said, setting aside her files carefully and climbing from the vehicle. "I don't have time for this horseshit. What are they doing, building their own country?"

She walked around the front of the Explorer and could hear the engine ticking as she passed the hood. Bridget walked up to the closed gate and banged on the wood.

"HEY!"

A face appeared in the window of the "guard tower" and looked down at her, the dusty face of an Hispanic kid in his early twenties. She could see he was holding a shotgun.

"What you want?" He yelled out. "Go away. I'm armed up here, lady."

"I can see that. Don't point it at me, or these guys in the car behind me will just get out and shoot you—and your little house—full of bullets."

The kid eyed the trucks suspiciously, then looked down at her.

She held up her badge and the sheet of paper. "You need to let us through," she yelled, pointing at the gate. "I have a search warrant. Plus, this is a public road."

"Can't read it from here lady," the kid said. "How I know it's a real thing—"

"It's the real thing, alright," Bridget said. "A search warrant for the main farmhouse and surrounding structures. Church of Xavier. And this public road is maintained by public funds, so I'll send out a crew tomorrow to tear it down. Anyway, open up the gate."

He nodded but didn't say anything.

She shook her head. "The road between here and Brennan farm must be open to the public, except of course for the driveway leading up to the property. You can't just fence it off and declare it yours. Now, let us in—"

"Matthew House."

She looked up at him, the sun in her eyes. She heard the other cops in her vehicle climb out and walk up behind her, taking up defensive positions.

"What?" she asked.

"Matthew House," the kid yelled down. "Old name was Brennan farm. But we changed the name."

"Great," she said. "I'll alert the media. Now let us in."

"Nope," the kid yelled. "No trespassin'. Boss said so."

She put her hands on her hips. "Kid, you're pissing me off. Let us in, or these fine members of the Miami County Sheriff's Department will shoot you," she said, turning and stepping aside for the two bulky men behind her. "Let me get out of the way. They are excellent shots, I assure you. And they look bored. You guys bored?"

Both cops nodded at her. One of them smiled. "You know, I could use a little target practice."

The kid thought about it for a minute, then climbed out the back of the little room at the top and down a ladder she couldn't see. Without saying a word, he leaned the shotgun against the tower and walked over, unlatching the gate, and pulling it open.

"Gonna get me in trouble, lady," the kid grumbled under his breath.

"Thank you," she said and got back in the car.

"Idiots," one of the cops up front said after they were back in the vehicle and past the gate. "That right there is how you get yourself shot. Or some truck is gonna come along and take it out." He reached for his radio and called in a public works truck to start removal of the "gate."

They drove on, and the paved road led another half-mile to the south before the driver turned into a long driveway that branched off the main road.

Thirty feet in, they pulled up to a much larger gate. Above the gate was a sign that said, "Welcome to the Church." There was another guard tower, this one made of concrete. This fence and gate were much more serious, she could see, and would be able to withstand an assault for at least enough time for the people inside to get ready. Inexplicably, the wide gate stood open, with armed men on either side. One of them waved the cars through and pointed at the main house.

"Not sure if I like this any better," the driver said. "I guess they have comms. That kid probably called it in."

"Boxing us in?" the other cop asked him.

"Not sure," the driver said, shaking his head. "But I'd rather have them in front of me then behind."

The road led directly to a large farmhouse, the Brennan farm. Or whatever it was called now. It was a massive home, with what looked like sizable additions tacked onto the original structure. She had seen pictures of it from two years ago, and it had been an unassuming farmhouse, standard in size, with a wraparound front porch. It had been just like every other farmhouse in this state or the next.

Now, it looked more like a building than a home—if she had to guess, Bridget assumed this building was the headquarters of the cult.

Once the truck came to a stop in the large, paved parking lot in front of the home, Bridget got out of the truck and looked in the window to adjust her hair. If you've got it, use it. Behind her, the other two trucks pulled up and parked, and several cops got out. She could see the reflection of Tom Drayton in the window as she finished straightening her hair.

"We ready?" he asked from behind her.

"Yeah," she said. She pulled the door open again and retrieved the folder of paperwork she was delivering, along with her purse and a sizeable camera, which she handed to the cop who had been driving her vehicle.

"We're taking six people," Tom said, nodding around them. "That includes you and me. The other five are staying with the vehicles for now," he said. She glanced around and saw several cops staying in the Explorers.

"Okay, your call," she said. Bridget straightened her outfit and turned to see the four men with Tom—they were all armed and wearing body armor. They gathered around her.

"Okay, I'm chatting with Xavier, their leader," she said, raising her voice so it was clear she was addressing the group of cops. "I do not want this to go south, though I would like a look at their construction areas. If we get into a confrontation, I want an orderly retreat. This is not turning into another Waco, do you hear me? I'm not dying—"

Before she could finish, the front door opened, and Xavier Castillo walked out of the building with several others following him. He was an attractive middle-aged Hispanic man, dressed nicely and sporting a very expensive pair of shoes. His belt matched, she noticed, and he had a twinkle in his eye as he stopped at the top of the stairs. Xavier waved and smiled like a man attending his own parade.

She stopped talking. He was still fifty feet away, atop the steps, but she could already see his wide smile and relaxed demeanor.

"There he is," one of the cops said.

"Yup," she said.

Xavier headed down the steps, followed by ten of his followers. He strode with the confidence of a man who commanded many. He looked like a president—or a general, coming to negotiate. Bridget felt the cops around her tense up. Several moved their arms, placing their hands on the butts of their guns.

"Relax guys," she said with a dazzling smile. "I've got this."

"Ah, Ms. Turner," the church leader yelled, smiling his toothy grin. "You have come to take a stroll with me, yes?"

She stepped towards him, and extended her hand when they were close enough. She had forgotten how attractive he was—and charismatic. "Hello, sir."

He smiled and took her hand. "I remember you. Bridgette, right?"

"ACP Turner is fine, thank you," she said, but felt herself blush.

"ACP? What is this? Are we not friends, *chica?*"

She felt herself smiling. It was a response she regretted immediately but couldn't help. The man carried himself with so much confidence that it was difficult to take your eyes off him.

"Assistant County Prosecutor Bridget Turner, if you don't mind."

"Oh, okay," he said, dropping her hand and pretending to frown. "So, we are being formal today?"

She nodded. "Yes, sir," she said. "We're here to inspect your compound."

"'Inspect?' you say?" He looked around. "Compound? *Dios mia.* It is our humble church, *chica.* Surely you don't think we're doing anything wrong out here?"

"I have no idea, Xavier. Last year you had gun runners. That's why I have to—"

He put up his hand, his face suddenly very serious. "Sorry, it's Mr. Castillo. We're being formal today, yes? Don't forget." He gave her a look for a second, then smiled.

"Okay," she said. She turned to the cops that were standing around her. "Tom, where do you want people?"

"You two with ACP Turner, the rest with me." Tom turned to look at her. "We are doing walkthroughs, inspections, right?"

She nodded. "And photos, please." They'd done this six months before but at two of the other farmhouses, ostensibly to check on "building violations and other failures to adhere to building codes. Of course, everyone knew it was just a fishing expedition to find anything out of the ordinary. Unfortunately, this whole compound—and the people living on it—were the epitome of "out of the ordinary."

Bridget looked at the men. "We're walking through the property, being respectful," she said, loud enough for all of her men—and all of Xavier's—to hear. "We're just looking for any building code violations or anything illegal—drugs, firearms, etc."

She turned and smiled up at Xavier Castillo who stood, waiting patiently. He seemed amused at her, and that angered her on some level. She shook her head.

"Okay, let's get started."

CHAPTER 20
Breakfast Interrupted

It had been a quiet morning. Joe Hathaway was enjoying the morning paper while eating breakfast in one of the common rooms of Matthew House. It was a nice treat, now, to read the paper the same day it came out. He was flipping to the next section of the *Wall Street Journal* when Trapper walked in with a very serious look on his face.

"Morning," Joe said with a smile. "Back from Pittsburgh?"

"Yes, boss. I'll tell you all about it, but we have to go."

Joe looked up from his oatmeal. "What?"

"The police are here," Trapper said, picking up the newspaper that Joe had spread out on the table in front of him. "They do occasional inspections of the compound. Do you remember that woman prosecutor from Troy?"

Joe nodded, thinking. "Bridget...something. Pretty. Seemed like a pain in the ass."

"Well, they're heading up the driveway now. I need to get you out the back door while the cops come in the front. We need to go."

Hector, one of Xavier's more senior people, walked into the common room and looked around, concerned. He spotted Trapper and Joe and hurried over.

"Here you are. We need to move you to a secure location," he said to Joe. "The local police are here. Please come with me."

Trapper nodded. "We know. I overheard some of the men talking. Out the rear entrance?"

Hector nodded. "I have a cart waiting. Please leave your breakfast," he said. "We must hurry."

Joe glanced at Trapper and followed. Hector led them through the main floor of Matthew House. Xavier's men took their security seriously. They followed Hector to a waiting golf cart and climbed in. It also had a map of the compound on the dashboard.

Hector turned the key in the ignition and they were off, driving away from the house and heading out at a brisk pace. Soon they were speeding down a crushed gravel path that connected the main house with other buildings to the east.

"Where are we going?" Joe asked Hector as they sped away.

Hector looked around and pointed. "There were at least three vehicles worth of cops arriving. Xavier asked me to move you to the Bunker."

Trapper pointed, and Joe saw several Ford Explorers driving up the main road. They came to a stop in front of Matthew House. Just before the golf cart rounded a corner, Joe saw a blonde woman climb out of the lead car.

"That's the prosecutor lady," Trapper said. "Good thing we're not there."

Joe nodded. "I heard someone else mention something called 'the bunker.' What is that?"

Trapper looked at the back of Hector's head, then leaned in close to talk to Joe. "I've been here for a while and heard little about it. They are building something here, but I haven't figured out what yet."

"This bunker?"

"Yeah, that's what they call it. On the rare times someone mentions it. It's a big part of their plans here. If we get to see it, we'll be among the few that aren't directly involved with the project."

Joe spoke up. "Hector, what is this about a bunker?"

Hector turned, his eyes still on the path leading away from Matthew House.

"Brother Xavier wanted to show you himself, but there wasn't time. It's...dammit." He swerved the golf cart to go around a group of church members walking on the path. "He will explain it further at a future time. Perhaps today, if he can break away from his other obligations."

Joe didn't know what else to say and sat back, nodding. Sometimes, if you didn't know what was going on, it was better to seem unperturbed, as if being kept in the dark didn't bother you. He'd seen all the construction equipment. And his mind was always working. He had some notions about what was going on, but kept his questions to himself and sat back and waited, watching as they approached.

As they headed in the direction of another farmhouse, Joseph House, if the map on the dashboard was to be believed, they passed through the central area that was equidistant from the four central farmhouses. Joe saw a smattering of shapes grow closer and soon he realized they were shipping containers, stacked on top of each other, eight pairs in a circle. The boxes were arrayed in a tight circle around a large square concrete foundation in the middle. Off to the sides, more stacks of metal shipping containers. He also saw at least two small forklifts, along with two short cranes.

Hector slowed the vehicle and turned. "The foundation was poured this summer. It will hold a new, larger HQ building," Jason said with a smile. "Much larger than Matthew House, and more modern. Seven stories. It will be the largest building on our campus."

Joe smiled. He had a guess, the size of the pour and the way the containers were arranged...

"But that's not the point, right?"

Without answering, Hector slowed and turned the golf cart toward the nearest shipping container and pulled up next to the end. Climbing out, he walked over and unlocked the handle, then pulled the doors open. They shrieked with rust and age, pivoting on pistons.

Hector leaned down and flipped over some pieces of wood on hinges attached to the base of the container, and Joe realized they were small wedges to use as ramps to drive up and over the thick lip of the container. They matched another set of tiny ramps that led down from the lip onto the floor of the container.

"In we go," Hector said as he climbed back inside and put the cart in gear. "Just wait, my friends."

"What the hell?" Trapper said next to him.

He drove the cart into the dark shipping container, cutting off the sunlight. The inside was wide, more than enough to accommodate the vehicle. Hector stopped as a pair of lights—probably motion activated—came on, illuminating the inside of the container, which looked unremarkable. Four metal walls, a metal roof, and a metal floor. The only thing that broke up the monotony was the bank of bright shop lights hanging from mounts in the ceiling.

Hector reached up underneath a metal protrusion on one wall of the container, then appeared to slide something sideways. He then moved something up and back again, all hidden from view.

Behind them, the two doors on the end of the shipping container—where they had just entered—slowly swung shut on their own. It took a few seconds and then they closed with a thud. Joe heard them lock.

"Well, now we're stuck in here," Trapper said.

"Look," Hector said, pointing.

Ahead of them, the metal floor of the shipping container moved, slowly hinging down. A thin light appeared at the bottom, a line of whiteness that got thicker as the floor tilted downward. It looked like the floor was tipping downwards, creating a wide metal ramp down into the light.

"What is going on here?" Trapper asked.

"One moment," Hector said, waiting.

The ramp's downward movement stopped with a thud from below, echoing in the enclosed metal space. Below, lights ringed a curved wall, revealing an open space surrounded by concrete walls.

Hector eased his foot off the brake and the cart proceeded across the floor of the shipping container and then down the slope into the space below.

CHAPTER 21
Xavier

Back at Matthew House, Bridget stepped up onto the porch and paused at the doors. Xavier, holding the door open for her, also hesitated.

"How did you know we were coming?" Bridget asked. "You guys were ready for us. The kid at the guard gate?"

"No," Xavier said, shaking his head. He pointed behind her.

She turned and looked at the smattering of low buildings and barns that circled the parking area next to Matthew House. Bridget was looking for cameras or a monitor, one which might show the county roads or maybe a camera feed of the long driveway. But there was nothing out of the ordinary, just a dusty farm road.

"I don't get it."

Xavier walked over, letting the front porch door swing closed. The others waited for them. He walked up behind her, and she could feel him near her back. Too close for comfort. He was a presence, not touching her but near enough she could feel his breath on her neck.

"Look closer," he said, pointing at the fields. "Most people are too trapped in their technology. Most of my people don't even carry cell phones. Too many electronic fields. Do you see it now?"

She could see the fields of corn and wheat. Beyond them, small plumes of gray dust drifted up from the horizon. She saw a car moving through the parking lot and the gray cloud that followed it.

Bridget nodded, trying not to think about his closeness, or the fact that she could smell his cologne. She was here to investigate him and his cohort, not get swept up in his presence. Finally, she saw it.

"The dust. Dusty roads. Right?"

"Yes, *chica*," he said. She could tell by his tone he was smiling. "The dusty roads send up a warning. Well, at least to those who pay attention," Xavier said. "We can detect any approach."

"Clever," she said. "And lucky for you."

"No, not really," Xavier said. "We don't pave anything we don't have to. The dust is helpful. And it's one of the reasons we prefer gravel roads," he said. "That and the government isn't out here all the time, maintaining it. I'm assuming that's real, that they are truly spending time and money keeping the paved roads up to code. But it doesn't mean they're not also using their proximity as an excuse to monitor us."

Together, they walked to the front door, and he again held it open for her. She saw the looks on Tom Drayton and the other cops' faces. Clearly, she wasn't the only one who thought Xavier was being too familiar. But maybe she could use that to her advantage.

Inside, the home had been made over to look more like a hacienda instead of the old Ohio farmhouse it had started out as. Colorful paint covered the walls, and some had been knocked down to make the rooms bigger. The interior space had been expanded, as well, with several new additions that didn't show up on any plans.

"You've enlarged the living space—do you have permits for those changes?"

"Of course," Xavier said, walking them through the living room. "Everything is completely legal. We are a growing church, and we need more space."

She could see it—as they made their way through the main part of what was now called the "Matthew House," there were several large rooms and hallways branching off of them. Two of the larger rooms had been converted into a group of offices, and a third was a large conference room, complete with an expansive table. In the offices, she could hear people talking on phones—it looked like a call center, actually.

"Making money? Isn't that too 'earthly' for your church?"

Xavier smiled. "Someone must pay for our extravagant lifestyle, no?" As he spoke, she heard a woman in a nearby cubicle explaining how to fix a printer.

"Tech support? From a church that hates technology?"

"We don't hate it, ACP Sharp," he said. "We just don't trust it as much as you people. But yes, we have several tech support contracts. Over there, we have a department that builds websites, and at one of our other farmhouses, a call center for a toy manufacturer, *si*? As you can see, it is all completely legal. My people work hard and are paid for their labors."

They continued through the house and the tour led them to a huge kitchen and dining area, taking up another large addition off the back of the house. The kitchen and dining room looked like it could serve two dozen people at a time. Four large, industrial refrigerators ran along one wall, opposite a bank of stoves, ovens, and a wide flat-top griddle like you would see in a restaurant.

"Shall we sit? I can have them make you something."

Unsure of what to do, Bridget nodded. But before she sat, she looked at Tom Drayton.

"Tom, take the rest of the team and start your search," she said, one eye on Xavier. "I'll go over the warrant with Mr. Castillo. And please have your team take photos," she said, her eyes lingering on Tom, who nodded and had the good sense to not smile.

He understood what she was doing—keeping Xavier here would be a distraction, and his men (or at least some of them) would have to go with Drayton and the other cops as they started the search in earnest.

Xavier looked curious, then turned to his men and nodded. Drayton and the other three men moved off and Xavier's men followed.

"Divide and conquer, no?" Xavier said as they sat.

"Whatever works, right? Have you read Sun Tzu?"

"Of course."

"I had a case last year," Bridget said, taking out the search warrant and laying it on the table between them. "The man I was prosecuting was obsessed with Sun Tzu, The Art of War. Joe Hathaway was the defendant's name—he had killed at least three people and tried to kill two cops. A real piece of work."

Xavier nodded, his face tinged with a hint of a smile. "I know the type."

His response was confusing, but she pressed on. "But he loved Sun Tzu. Like, this guy was really obsessed. He quoted the 'Art of War' in open court on at least two occasions, so I had to read it."

Xavier waived over one of the kitchen staff and turned to Bridget. "And what did you think of this book?"

"Interesting, I thought. 'Ancient wisdom' sounds like a joke, but it had a savage attitude, I found. A brutal take on what it means to be at war. Winning at all costs, that sort of thing."

"You like omelets?"

Bridget smiled at the sudden change of direction in the conversation. "Yes." This guy was great at keeping people on their toes.

A woman in a brown apron arrived at the table. She didn't make eye contact with Bridget or Xavier—instead, she stared at the floor. Bridget was immediately angered at the submissive posture, and the tone that followed.

"Something for you, Brother Xavier? And your guest?"

Xavier nodded. "Two Western omelets, please. And can we have sour cream and some of that salsa from last night? It was excellent."

The woman scurried away without even acknowledging his words.

Xavier turned back to Bridget.

"You know, it's difficult to teach you *gringos* how to make a proper *pico de gallo*, but they are learning, I have to say," he said, sitting back and pointing at the kitchen. "It is good she is teaching them. She knows the ways. And it is an efficient kitchen. We can feed thirty people at a time."

"Why do they treat you like that? It's disgusting."

He sat up and frowned. "What do you mean?"

"Like a god," she said, trying to keep the tone of distaste out of her mouth. "It's a gross violation of your power over them."

He sat back. "I apologize. I can see how, from your perspective, that was too subservient. I can speak to the woman—"

"What's her name?"

"Who?"

"The woman. You probably don't even know her name—"

"Triana Avillar. She came from Guadeloupe, with me, in our first group of pilgrims to come to America. Her husband was killed before we left."

Bridget nodded and sat back, crossing her arms. "I understand what you're doing here, Xavier. Your own private kingdom. But the government can't allow you to just do whatever you like. You can't just build bigger houses and buy property and build your own city out here. Not without some oversight."

"Why not?" he asked quietly.

She shook her head. "Because we live in a society. It's made up of all of us, working together. Do you know what that means? Earlier this year, some of your people were running guns. Now, you and your cohort are building something in the fields south of here, something that requires large amounts of construction equipment," she said with a scowl.

"We follow all the rules, *chica*," he snapped, and for a moment, she saw the man behind the Xavier Castillo mask. THAT man was a hot head, impulsive, angry.

"And your 'flock' is growing so fast, we have no idea how many people are living out here. I get reports of busloads of people arriving in downtown Troy, asking for directions to this place. Do you know how many you have here?"

"Yes, roughly."

The food appeared, brought by another person who was apparently mute, and Bridget held her tongue, digging into the omelet. They ate in silence for several minutes, and, to her dismay, she found the food to be excellent. She had eaten half of the omelet before he laughed.

"What?" she asked.

"I guess you were hungry," he said, nodding at her plate. "Too busy to eat before your big raid?"

"Yes, actually," she said, nodding at the warrant that she'd put on the table between them. "I put a lot of time and thought into that."

"It wasn't necessary," he said, eating. "*Dios mia*, this *pico* is as good as any I could get in Guadeloupe." Xavier looked at her. "And what if we didn't?"

She looked at him. "Didn't what?"

"You said we 'live in a society.' That assumes things will continue on as they have into the future."

"They won't?"

He sat back and shook his head. "I hope so. Truly, I do. But don't you watch the news? Read the papers? Things have spiraled out of control, like a sinking ship. The whole world. People jump off to save themselves and are only pulled down with the rest of the flotsam."

She nodded. "Yup, gloom and doom. I've heard it all before."

"No, you haven't," he said quietly. Xavier stared at the table and, for a moment, Bridget thought maybe she was going to get another moment of genuine honesty out of him.

"I have already seen it in Mexico, society breaking apart," he said quietly. "Death everywhere. Trianna's husband and a thousand more. In vast parts of Mexico, life holds no meaning, no honor. I have stepped over more dead than I can count."

Bridget said nothing.

"People die on the streets over a loaf of bread," Xavier continued, his voice growing louder. "Or having the wrong kind of car. Do you know what it is like to drive past a mother, slumped by the side of the road, holding her own dead child?"

"No."

"What would you do if you saw that, here in Ohio? You would drive—"

"Of course not," she interrupted. "That's absurd. I would stop and help. I would always stop and—"

"No, you would not," he said. "Not in Tampico, or Culiacan. Not in the gang-controlled areas where you race from one safe place to another. Society is crumbling south of the border, and the gangs and gang lords have taken control. Fleeing over the border was our only choice."

"Well, welcome to America," she said with a sneer. "We're doing all right here. And you're welcome—we have a stable society. Just be glad you had somewhere to run to, a safe place to hide."

"But you don't, don't you see that? America is not safe."

"It is."

"No, it is not. Corruption, murder, Mexico is only further along on the road to destruction. There is a Tragedy coming. It is the only word for it, and our word for it: Tragedy. And America will soon follow. Governments always fall, and there will be chaos in the streets. Every man and woman and child for themselves. Fighting, beating, killing for their next meal. And then, after the Tragedy, there is only one thing that can save you. Community. Like what I am building here."

She didn't answer, and a quiet settled over the table. She finished her omelet but had the self-control to resist complimenting him and his staff on what might have been the best omelet she'd ever had in her life. Bridget certainly wasn't going to give him the satisfaction.

"All we can do is prepare for the future," he said quietly, as if he were unhappy to be sharing such sad news. "There is only that. A New World is coming." Xavier tapped the search warrant with one finger. "Your papers mean nothing, not in the face of the Tragedy. Not in a society that is teetering on the edge of failure. I am out here building."

"Building what?"

"Building for the future. Digging, planting, using my own hands and the hands of my people. Preparing for a better future. Can you not see that?"

Unsure of how to reply, Bridget held her tongue.

CHAPTER 22
Golf Cart

Joe grabbed onto the side of the golf cart and held on as Hector directed the vehicle down the metal ramp that was still slowly descending down. The metal floor was bumpy and the slope sharp, so the golf cart picked up speed. They passed a curved wall of reinforced concrete on their right and moved down into a wide open area. In the center, the concrete foundation was held up by wide columns.

The ramp curved around the edge of the large circular area. Joe saw other ramps, three more, and realized they must come down out of the bottom of three of the other containers.

Hector finally spoke up. "We dug out this large pit, then poured the floor and built the columns. Scaffolding and several of the Comex shipping containers held up the wooden forms we used to pour the roof, which will also be the foundation of the building that will be built above."

Trapper and Joe looked around, and Joe saw that Trapper's mouth was hanging open.

At the bottom of the ramp, Hector slowed and parked the cart next to several others, all arrayed in the middle of the large open space along with two shipping containers and two Bobcat earth moving machines. The large lights around the perimeter and more suspended from the concrete ceiling illuminated the central area.

"We just finished removing all the scaffolding and finally have the center cleared."

"It's an underground parking lot, out in the middle of a corn field," Trapper said, shaking his head. "Why? What's this all for?"

Hector smiled. "It is much more than a parking lot. This is the central core, which will be widened in the future. Above, we'll construct a building and use it to obscure our operations down here."

"Why?" Trapper asked again.

"Spy satellites," Joe offered. "The authorities are monitoring your activities, so you've gone underground?"

Hector nodded. "Yes. Partially. The Americans have eyes

everywhere, to be sure. But we also need more space, more buildings, for our growing church. Moving some of our operations below ground will help us conceal our numbers."

"Ants in an ant hill," Joe said.

"Yes, something like that," Hector agreed. "This central area is just the start. Follow me." He walked over to one wall and Joe saw the doors of one of the large shipping containers—the doors were, somehow, embedded in the middle of the concrete wall.

"This might look like part of the wall, but it's not." Hector pulled on the handle and swung the door open. Beyond, a dark square tunnel ran off into the darkness. It looked like it could be nothing but a dirt hole, but Joe saw immediately from the square shape and the ribbed metal walls that it was a buried shipping container.

Hector walked to the wall and flicked a switch, and lights came on in the tunnel. Buried metal containers, lined up end-to-end, stretching away into the distance.

"What the shit?" Trapper was shaking his head. "Where does that go?"

"South," Hector said. "We are on one end of the tunnel."

Joe looked at him. "I assume this connects to another building, or the basement of another building, to be more accurate. One of your other farmhouses?"

"Yes, to Luke House," he said, then turned and pointed. There were three other tunnels. "Those lead to the other houses."

All buried under farmland, a warren of connected buildings. Very impressive, Joe thought.

Hector continued. "We can move people and materials—or vehicles or weapons, if needed—from one location to another."

"You're building an underground city," Joe said.

"We are," Hector said with a toothy smile.

Trapper was shaking his head again. "How?"

Hector smiled. "Actually, it was not that difficult, once we had the central chamber dug out. Then we dig a trench leading out from the center and placed a stack of containers into the trench. From above, it looks like a stack sitting on the ground."

"But it's in a trench," Trapper said.

"Yes," Hector continued. "Then we go into the bottom container and start digging sideways, shoring up the walls as we go, creating a tunnel. Then we lifted the other containers in the stack just a few inches, all except for the bottom one. We slide that down the tunnel and lower the others into place where the bottom container used to be."

"And add another to the top of the stack," Joe said with a smile. "From the surface, it just looks like you have the container stack, even though some are underground."

"Yes," Hector said. "We must use the same color containers in case we're being observed. As you can see from today's raid, the authorities are paying close attention."

"Then what?" Trapper asked.

"More digging," Hector said. "Always from inside the container. It is strong enough to hold up the dirt. We dig to the south, then slide the container into the space when we are done. The one above is lowered into place. As we build the tunnels, all the containers are moved one position to the south."

"That could go on forever," Joe asked. "And no one would know."

Hector nodded. "All we have to do is stack another on top. There was a mechanism to control the containers and how they were lowered into place. And we have made these pushing arms—they move one container by pushing off the others. It slides them down the open tunnel. We have just figured out how to make curves in the path. Pits are dug to create wider areas and junctions, though those are done sparingly, for obvious reasons."

"Those can be observed from above," Joe said.

"You can't just keep sliding these along the whole way, can you?" Trapper asked.

"So far, yes, but we're looking at branching off from the tunnels. That would require a pit and lowering more containers at the point of the branch."

Joe was doing the calculations in his head. This place could hold hundreds of people and be nearly impossible to seize—short of calling in the National Guard or a small army. The Miami County Sheriff's Department was going to have their work cut out for them if they ever came down here.

"Brother Xavier has a vision—and with this land, and farms, and fresh water, and these underground spaces, we can welcome as many people to the church as possible," Hector said. "They will be safe, away from the eyes of the authorities. Our church in Mexico had a few similar structures, but here, we have much more room. And freedom."

"It's insane," Trapper said.

"We are branching off, building other underground rooms," Hector continued. "Common rooms, armories, power generation, water storage, bunk rooms. Right now, we can handle 200 people down here, or will be able to once the power systems are complete. Right now, we're working off 'city' power. But a new bank of solar is coming online next month."

Joe whistled. He couldn't help himself. "Impressive."

Hector nodded. "Thank you. Brother Xavier wanted to give you both the tour himself but, unfortunately, the authorities surprised us with a visit this morning. Here, let me show you around."

CHAPTER 23
Lookout

Back at Matthew House, Bridget was getting more of the tour, although Xavier's mood seemed dampened after their breakfast. He showed her the second floor, which was mostly guest rooms and bathrooms. There was a small room on the third floor with four windows, one on each wall. The windows looked out over the surrounding farmland.

Near each window, there were small tables that held cameras, paperwork, and a pair of binoculars. At the south window stood a small telescope. In the center of the room, near the stairs that led back down, was a desk piled with papers.

"Keeping an eye on the neighbors?"

"Yes, *chica*," Xavier said. "Trust but verify, yes? Your President Reagan said that. I want you to know what we are good neighbors, but it still makes sense to keep up our lookout. And we watch for signs."

Seeing nothing that made her curious, they headed back downstairs and finally back out onto the front porch. Tom Drayton and his men were already outside in the parking lot, milling about and discussing something amongst themselves. Bridget saw Xavier's men standing off to the side.

"Hang on, I need a minute," she said to Xavier and left him on the front porch. She walked over to the knot of cops.

"Anything?"

Tom Drayton turned and glanced at Xavier on the porch. "No, nothing, really. A few construction issues, but they have permits." One of the other cops held up a stack of papers. Drayton continued. "We searched it all, top to bottom."

"There a basement?"

"Yes, nothing down there either," Drayton said. "Bunch of mechanicals, huge new HVAC system. They also have an interesting grow operation down there, harvesting microgreens. Lots of mouths to feed, I guess."

"I'm assuming we didn't get lucky and catch them growing pot." Bridget glanced around at the other cops. "Nothing out of the ordinary?"

The group shook their heads.

"I don't see any violations," Drayton said. "We were especially looking for weapons, but only found six, and they were all on Xavier's men. All the serials check out."

"Well, we need to check those barns," she said, pointing. "That's where we found the others earlier this—"

"Everything okay, *chica*?"

She turned to see Xavier coming down the steps. He was joined by his men, who fell in line behind him.

"Yes, the main house checks out," she said. Turning south, Bridget pointed. "Next I need to see the circular area."

"Of course," Xavier said. He waved and a young man drove up in a golf cart and hopped out, leaving it running. Xavier directed her into it. "I will show you myself."

After she climbed in, the cart sped away from the house, Xavier at the wheel. Bridget turned to see the other cops and Xavier's men following in several other carts. She tried not to smile at the awkward way the people were paired up, with skinny religious zealots acting as chaperones and drivers to scowling cops in Kevlar vests.

She and Xavier drove along a path of crushed gravel, not going too fast. Xavier seemed to be enjoying his role as tour guide, pointing out new gardens going in between the existing buildings. "We're building between the farmhouses, creating a small town of our own. The gardens will help. And we have a robust canning operation every fall, to put away food for the winter."

They passed a sizable herd of sheep. Did sheep move in herds? What did you call a large group of sheep?

"It's hard to guess how many rules you could be violating out here," she said. "Just because you don't like rules, it doesn't mean you can ignore them. There are rules for caring for animals, and open burning, and a dozen other things you might be doing wrong—"

"Of course, *chica*," he said, his tone less pleasant than at breakfast. "We follow all the rules. Our animal husbandry folks are familiar with the space requirements, feeding requirements. County and state. Federal rules don't apply yet with the numbers we have, but they will soon. And everything we build is inspected. Don't your record show that?"

It was true, she thought as she watched him drive. Technically they were not breaking any rules—but it was very likely more was going on out here than what they were showing her on today's tour.

"Preparing for the end of the world?" she yelled over the wind from the moving vehicle.

Xavier glanced at her. "It was like I said before. We are preparing, that is all. The church is not interested in bringing about any kind of change, *si*? I do not want a role in hastening the inevitable."

"You really think this "Tragedy" is inevitable?"

He nodded, steering the golf cart around a stack of standard Comex metal shipping containers, the kind used by the shipping industry to carry things on large cargo ships.

"I do, sadly. I read yesterday a summary of some of the things that have happened worldwide just in the last few months. Assassinations, war, famine. North Koreans are testing missiles. 600 million people without power in India. Protests in the Middle East. And this election coming up soon, *chica*? Americans are at each other's throats."

She looked at him. "Summer Olympics."

"What?"

"It's not all bad," she said. "We just had the Summer Olympics in London. The world coming together in friendly competition."

"Friendly competition? Then why do they drug test? And why are some countries not invited?"

She didn't have an answer.

"And what about Africa? This group, Boko Haram? Bombings, killing nearly 200 people. Not a month ago. That's the same group kidnapping and raping young women, taking them as wives like it's the 1700's. The world is going mad, ACP Sharp. It's happening all around you. To not see that is willful blindness. You must admit it."

"Maybe," she said. "Things are getting crazier every year," she admitted. She turned and looked at him. "And your church is going to fix things?"

"No, no, of course not," he said, slowing and turning onto another path. "We have no power to stop it. We cannot hold back the tide—no one can." She could see they were approaching the area that, on her map, had made her so curious. "But for our people, we are a comfort in the storm. A *castillo*, a place of solace."

She nodded, and wondered if he noticed her nodding. She couldn't be sure, but the man didn't seem to miss much. She said nothing but got the reference, of course. Castillo, his last name, meant 'castle' in

Spanish. A safe place, sure, but also a battlement from which to wage a war. It could be neither, or both, at the same time.

"After the Tragedy, we will be on our own," he said sadly. "Before that happens, we must re-learn the old ways. Farming, feeding ourselves. Growing our own food, making clothes. Protecting ourselves."

"What else?"

"Well, generating power, for one thing. After the Tragedy, it will be impossible to buy solar power panels or electrical equipment or batteries to store the power. We must set these things up ahead of time. We must have foresight and plan for the future."

"Guns?"

"Of course. And other weapons. It is crucial that we be able to protect ourselves. Guns, knives, bows and arrows: all will be helpful. And we are learning how to make our own ammunition for the inevitable time when it runs out."

She said nothing, disheartened by the news. These people were serious, even more serious than she'd guessed. Not only were they planning for the SHTF moment, but they were also planning for the days and months that would follow.

"And walls," he added. "We need to protect ourselves, and that means walls. To hold back the horde."

"You make it sound like a zombie movie."

He nodded, not disagreeing with her suggestion. "When we are the only ones with food and shelter, others will seek to take it from us."

She looked over at him and his eyes were distant.

"What about those gates? You built a gate on what is a public road. That cannot stand—"

"You are correct. And that was unfortunate," he agreed. "Some of my people can be...overzealous. I will correct that and have it removed immediately. Thank you for mentioning it. But the guard towers are going to multiply. We have had some...difficulties with a few of the nearby farmers. They are unhappy with us."

"Runoff from the fields?"

He looked at her. "You know about the complaints?"

She nodded. "There have been complaints of the church overgrazing your lands, causing too much runoff into the local streams."

He went back to driving. "Yes, it was an issue. And we had some people...visit us in the night. Burned down one of our barns, killed twelve head of cattle. Hence the gates and guards and more fences."

She looked over at him. "This is the first I've heard of it."

He nodded, not looking at her. "We don't like to bring attention to ourselves if we can avoid it. But we follow all the rules, and we're working on the small amount of runoff that occurred. It was a one-time event, I assure you."

"I can investigate the barn incident. If it was arson—"

"Thank you, Bridget," he said quietly. "We will turn the other cheek. I follow the rules of God.

For the first time in their conversation, she chose not to correct his use of her name.

"He says to bring in the needy and care for them," Xavier continued. "We need room to do this, and we expand as needed. We pool our resources and purchase more property. It's all legal."

They approached a group of shipping containers that appeared to be arrayed in no particular fashion. They sat near a large square concrete pad that looked like the foundation of a new building. She had seen it and the containers on the latest satellite photos, but things had been moved around since those were taken. And the concrete pad was now complete, turning a bright shade of white in the sunlight.

Xavier slowed the golf cart and drove between the containers, then up a short wooden ramp right up onto the pad, stopping the cart in the middle and getting out. Xavier spread out his arms, showing off the wide concrete pad.

"What do you think?"

"What are you doing out here?"

"Another building, *chica*," he said. "Our largest yet. And, before you complain, of course we will get it approved," he said, putting up one hand. "I have seen the drawings. It will be our new headquarters, a center for pilgrimage. Our own Mecca. Seven stories, surrounded by smaller buildings. We will gather here and share our faith and prepare for the coming of the end times. It will be like one of those old tent revivals. Do you know those?"

"Yes," she said, climbing from the cart and looking around. As far as she could tell, it was nothing but a building foundation. Nearby there was construction equipment, stacks of wood and pallets of other construction materials. Several metal shipping containers sat open nearby, and she could see inside of them even more construction materials.

"People are already coming here from all over the world," he said with a smile. "So many that I can't remember all of their names."

She looked at him. "Funny."

"But it is true. And we need more room—all of the farmhouses are full. We are doubling up, living like we had to back in Mexico. And we have built more barns and the like. But we need more space for the pilgrims that have arrived. So many that, without a larger building, we won't be able to accommodate them all."

The other policemen arrived with their "drivers" and joined Bridget. Tom Drayton walked over.

"You alright, ma'am? You got way ahead of us," he said, looking at Xavier, who grinned. The other cops spread out, walking around the foundation and taking pictures. Two of the cops began searching the nearby containers.

"I'm fine, Tom," Bridget said. She turned to Xavier. "So, what are you really building out here?"

Xavier smiled. "The future."

"I'm serious."

"But I have just told you," he said, confused. "My English is not as good as I like. You understand? We're building for the future."

Drayton nodded. "And the shipping containers?"

"We try to buy in bulk when we can," Xavier said. "And then we tear down the containers and reuse the metal in our buildings and barns to strengthen them."

She let that one go—it didn't make sense, but she'd ask the cops more about it later. Bridget nodded and looked at Drayton.

"Anything else?"

He shook his head. "Once my guys look through these containers, we're good."

She turned back to Xavier.

"When we're done here, I'd like to see the large barns near the Matthew House, please. I'm worried more of those guns have turned up," she said. The two large red barns next to the Matthew House apparently housed their armory, and this was where she discovered several unlicensed weapons earlier this year. She'd gotten convictions on two of Xavier's men at the time, the first prosecution of anyone connect to the prepper compound.

"Of course," Xavier said, pointing to their golf cart. "I will drive you."

Moments later they were headed back to the main house. Bridget couldn't shake the idea that something else was going on with the foundation, but there was nothing to go on. When it came to judges, she had to deal in facts, not hunches.

"You are worried about more guns?" Xavier said, interrupting her train of thought.

She nodded even though his eyes were on the path as he drove. "Always. I don't know why you need so many weapons out here. It makes people nervous. You ever heard of Waco, Texas?"

"Of course," he said quietly. "You think that's what we are, yes? Some kind of cult, bent on our own destruction?"

"I don't know."

"Well, if you don't know, then you haven't been listening," he said sharply. "You must know we want nothing from the world. Nothing."

"Well, you do want construction equipment. And shipping containers. And power generation equipment, and access to the local power grid while you're getting set up. And water. Lots of water. Is that about it?"

"Yes," he said with a hint of a smile. "You understand what I mean. But we also just want to be left alone. We will not be coming into any kind of conflict with you or the police or anyone else. There will be no fiery confrontation with you and the other authorities. No *fuego*, I can assure you."

"I hope not."

"Well, I can assure you, that's not what I want," he said, his voice barely audible over the sound of the golf cart. "We want to live in peace. I want to preach the word of God, see to my followers, give people a *castillo* in this world."

She thought about that for a moment. "And the guns?"

"We must be ready to defend ourselves, Bridget," he said quietly. "No? But war? This I do not want."

"Some of your people do not follow the rules—"

"That was unfortunate," he said, cutting her off. "Sometimes the lambs stray too far from the flock. Sometimes they can get themselves into trouble, despite how much the shepherd watches."

"And you're the shepherd?"

Xavier looked over at her and smiled. "They could do worse."

CHAPTER 24
The Whole Enchilada

Joe and Trapper spent the next hour underground with Hector as he drove through the maze of tunnels the Church of Xavier had constructed so far. They called it "The Garden" for reasons that were lost on Joe. The facility was larger and more impressive than anything Joe could have guessed. He was free with his compliments and suggestions, although Joe would have preferred to take the tour with the church leader.

There were kitchens, food storage areas, dining rooms and sleeping areas. They had at least three larger common rooms that were surrounded with branched rooms containing bunk beds. Clearly, they had been building out here in secret for a while, putting all of these rooms into the ground long before starting on the central hub.

One common room sported an adjoining game room with three ping pong tables. And Joe lost count of the number of underground grow rooms, each decked out with full spectrum grow lights and a micro-irrigation system. One of them featured a crop of cabbage that was nearly ready to harvest.

It was obvious the church was preparing for a long siege, if necessary, with redundant areas where they could monitor and control the whole facility. He saw two armories and three different areas for making ammunition.

Even though Joe doubted that Hector was showing them everything, Joe could see from the maps and electronic controls that they had built the place to hold a large number of people for an extended amount of time. He also saw three separate command centers, redundant rooms with live camera feeds showing everything going on above and below ground. Everything was powered and up and running already, telling Joe that they were nearly ready to start moving some of their people down here.

And there were exits, plenty of them, concealed on the surface to ensure that no one got trapped down here if the facility was even breached.

From the command rooms, the church could control a whole series of metal doors, cutting off sections of the tunnels. To Joe, it was clear that they wanted to be able to block out intruders, sealing them off. If you could trap a group in one of those metal containers, twenty feet under the ground with no way out, it would serve as a tomb.

Joe was impressed. It didn't help him much, not with his particular situation and the plans that he had for Frank Harper. But it was impressive, what they were doing down here.

If things worked out, Joe had planned to stay on here and teach some shooting lessons before moving on. This was an excellent place to hide from the world, even if things went poorly with the hunt. There were a lot worse places for Joe and Trapper to spend some time year in hiding. And the underground city made it even easier to hide away from the authorities.

During the tour, Joe was pleased to see that Hector felt comfortable answering nearly all of their questions. Hector also made notes and wrote down all of Joe's suggestions, taking the time to ask follow-up questions and getting Joe to elaborate on his thinking. Joe brainstormed a number of improvements and sketched them out on some papers he'd taken from one of the command rooms.

The tunnels that branched out from the central core were only one "container" wide, so Joe suggested widening the tunnels at regular intervals to allow multiple golf carts to pass each other. This could be accommodated during a "slide", their term for when the containers were being moved lengthwise into the hand-dug tunnels to take up their next position. Before sliding the container lengthwise, they could also dig sideways in both directions out from the metal box, widening the tunnel to three containers and removing the metal sides of those containers before sliding them into place. This would create a wider area and, using the same idea, containers could be dug in sideways to create junctions that would allow new dirt tunnels perpendicular to the main tunnel.

After an hour, Hector's phone rang, and he answered it, speaking in quiet Spanish for a moment. "Okay, we're all clear," Hector said. "The police have gone, and Xavier would like to speak with you."

Joe nodded, and they drove back to the central core. It looked even more impressive now to Joe, knowing what it led to. Hector drove up the ramp and into a different container, stopping the cart and climbing out to push the hidden buttons again. The ramp lifted up behind them and became the floor again. Even now when he knew what he was looking for, Joe could not see where the ramp stopped and the container floor started. It was seamless.

The doors at the end of the container opened and Hector drove outside. Joe shielded his eyes—it was very bright. Blue sky arched over their heads.

Hector drove the golf cart down the path and around to the concrete foundation and up a small ramp onto it. Joe found it difficult to believe the area below it was a massive open space. Hector slowed and parked near another cart which sat empty in the middle of the wide foundation.

"Please wait here," Hector said, nodding at a man who was standing on the far side. "I will be right back."

Joe watched Hector walk over to the man and greet him and Joe realized it was Brother Xavier. He looked different outside, smaller somehow. Hector gestured back at the golf carts and handed Xavier something, probably the notes Hector had taken while talking to Joe.

"That was crazy," Trapper said quietly. "They're ready for war."

Joe nodded. "Their own *castillo*, designed for a siege."

"Except it's invisible," Trapper said. "An invisible castle, an invisible town. I have half a mind to sign on with these folks permanently. When the shit hits the fan, I can't think of a better place to be," he said, looking around. "Food, water, shelter—and guns. Lots of guns."

"It's impressive," Joe said. He leaned closer. "Find out everything you can, and get us a map of the underground. Find out what they need and see if the Keepers of Truth can help. You need to make this a solid, long-term partnership."

Trapper nodded.

"Oh, and Trapper? Good job."

"Thanks, boss."

Hector said something else to Xavier, and the shorter man slapped Hector on the shoulder. Hector turned and returned to the golf carts.

"Brother Xavier is waiting for you, sir," Hector said,

"Thanks," Joe said, climbing out. "And thanks for the tour."

"It was nothing," Hector said. "And thank you for your suggestions. If it's okay, I'll take Mr. Trapper back to Matthew House."

Trapper nodded and gave Joe one of those mock salutes he gave, and the golf cart started up and raced away. Joe turned and walked over to Xavier, who had his back to the golf carts.

"Mr. Castillo, that is a very impressive facility," Joe said. "Hard to believe it's all under our feet."

"Mr. Hathaway," Xavier said, turning and extending his hand.

"Your tunnel system is amazing."

"Ah, yes, you like it? We are expanding, always expanding. Moving forward, like the shark."

"And it looks siege-proof, as far as I can see."

"It sounds like you got the full tour, my friend," Xavier said to Joe, looking him in the eyes. "And I like your ideas," he said, waving the papers Hector had given him. "I will study them in full, believe me. Widening the tunnels to allow carts to pass? Smart. And using the stored water to flood select tunnels in case of invasion? Very clever."

"You have the water pipes anyway. It makes sense to release the water for defense. Perhaps you could put drains under the containers and recapture that water."

Xavier smiled and looked at Joe. "Trapper was right—he said you were the smartest person I would ever meet."

"Perhaps," Joe said, and the humble word felt strange in his mouth. He wasn't used to compliments. "So, the local police are curious?"

"Yes," Xavier said, turning and looking back at Matthew House. "Search warrants, looking for drugs and guns, the usual harassment. This one was different, the county prosecutor's office. More serious, si? Normally it's zoning people or the USDA. We cooperate as we must. But they are stupid."

"They can be, yes," Joe said, nodding. "Most of the time, they're a crowd of idiots, racing around in their cars and playing at enforcing the law. But sometimes they can be clever. Too clever by far," he said quietly.

Xavier nodded. "Ah, yes. Trapper told me something of your troubles. You have been hounded by the law, forced into hiding. But now, your plan. It is progressing?"

"Yes."

"And after your success, you will help train my people in the shooting. Yes?"

"Certainly."

"Then we will help you in any way that we can."

Joe nodded. "Like I said before, I'm planning a game, and I need a field of play. Far from your sensitive areas, of course," Joe said, nodding at their feet. "There is no need to compromise what you're doing here."

Brother Xavier looked around and then back at Joe. "I'm certain we can get you some land. We will find the perfect place for your game."

CHAPTER 25
Sandwiches

Jake Delancy was cleaning up yet another mess. At least, this time, it was a mess of his own making.

Jake was a thin man in his mid-thirties, skinny likely from his constant need to be in at least two places at the same time. It might have explained why the hair on his head was thinning prematurely. Jake had so many businesses, sometimes it was difficult for him to keep track of what he was supposed to be working on at any moment. He had so many to do lists, lately he'd started keeping a list of all of his lists.

On any given day of the week, he might be pulled in ten different directions, and usually sorted his daily "to do" list based on priority and urgency. He wrote dates and times in the margins to track it all. When one of his tenants' hot water heaters stopped working, that went to the top of the list. Or, when the fall the weather turned nasty, he needed to run out and winterize his beehives.

Most of his work—and income—came from the smattering of rental properties he owned and managed around Cooper's Mill and the surrounding towns. And those came with a lot of messes. Even the best tenants, the ones that paid on time and moved out when they said they were moving out, left behind stuff that needed to be cleaned up. Most of the time, he could clean it all out himself, loading up the bed of his red truck with the discarded bits of someone else's life.

Of course, worse things happened.

Worse things HAD happened, like that time the Robinson family, one of his tenants, had nearly died down in Dayton when one of his properties had burned. Thank goodness they had escaped.

Jake couldn't even begin to contemplate what it would have been like to have a family die, burn to death, in one of his properties.

The whole incident, them disappearing and then turning up again and Jake putting them up in a hotel in Columbus for their own safety, the whole series of events had almost convinced him to get out of the rental business for good. It was all just too stressful. But things had turned around, and the Robinsons were alive and well.

The fire? Turned out it had been arson, carried out by one of the Dayton gangs.

At least the insurance company had paid up with no fuss.

Yes, Jake would much prefer the act of cleaning up someone else's trash than dealing with a property burning down, or the potential deaths of an entire family of tenants.

Shaking his head, he got back to work. The local farmer's market season had just wrapped up a week before—usually it wrapped when the weather turned colder. Sometimes some of the farmers insisted on adding on more dates into the end of October so they could sell hay bales and pumpkins and the like, but this year, the downtown organization that held the market ended it October 13. It was held on Saturday mornings and was usually his favorite part of the fall season.

Today he was breaking down all the stuff he had gathered for his booth. He'd dragged all the booth-related stuff into his living room a week ago and it was still sitting here. Jake had a quiet afternoon planned—it was a Tuesday, a quiet one—and started tackling the stack of stuff.

First, he found the cash box and counted out all the money he'd made at the last three weeks of market. He hadn't had time to go to the bank between markets, and he'd let the money build up in the metal case box that he made change out of.

Jake went through the box, pulling out the cash and counting it out. The box had started out with $100 in small bills to make change with, and now the total in the box was $440, so a good haul. Over $100 a week, and that didn't even include the three checks he had taken as well. He'd need to remember to put it all into his accounting software.

Jake counted out $100 in change and put it back in the box to be used next season. If he didn't do it now, he'd forget. He used the same cash box for other occasional markets and outside events that he got involved in, so it was good to keep change in there and keep it ready for use. He put the cash box aside, then made up a deposit envelope and slip for the cash and checks.

Next, he broke down the folding table and collapsible tent he'd used in his market booth. He took both out to the garage, locking them up for the winter along with the signs he'd had made up.

He headed back inside, one eye on the weather. It was getting cloudy again, and to his practiced eye it looked like cold weather was incoming. It made sense—it was that time of year, when cold and snow lurked around every corner. It was similar in the early spring here in Ohio, when cold could be interrupted at any moment by the warm rains that drew new plants from the ground.

Lastly, he needed to work on his honey, the impetus of his sales and the point of his booth at the market. He had used some of the bottles for samples and he wanted to consolidate them into full bottles for sale over the winter. Also, some of the labels had gotten messed up during the season. Jake grabbed all of his material, including a stack of new labels, and sat down at the dining room table.

Jake maintained several large beehives out on a farm east of town—the farmer liked him and liked his bees—and let Jake use the land for free. Like much of what he did, Jake had taught himself to raise and tend bees, learning most of it from YouTube and a bee farmer in the area. He took care of the beehives and gathered the honey, which he packaged in glass jars for sale at the market and a few other locations around Cooper's Mill. It was just another one of his side jobs.

Of course, at this point, sometimes it felt like his whole life was about side jobs.

He heard someone stir upstairs and looked up, surprised. Jake had forgotten that Rosie had slept over. The sudden noise had given him a start. Shaking his head, he went back to work on the honey, consolidating the jars and replacing the damaged labels.

Rosie, his girlfriend, had been sleeping here less and less over the last few months. For some reason, things had been rocky between them. Last night, they'd had a bad fight. Jake had assumed she'd left, either heading home or dropping in at her bar Ricky's and picking up a shift.

Her bar was going gangbusters, and Rosie was flush. It shouldn't have been a problem for a progressive man like Jake, but, for some reason, it really bothered him. He liked the idea of providing for Rosie, but that was difficult when she was far more successful than he was. Her bar was packed most nights, and alcohol was a lucrative and popular balm for people's anxiety.

And people seemed to be so anxious lately. Between the upcoming election and that theater shooting out in Colorado, people were on edge. A nice evening at Ricky's, preferably one that involved a beer or five, was a great way to alleviate that frustration and stress.

And it meant Rosie was raking in the dollars.

So why did that bother him so much? Who cared if she was making money hand over fist? Or making more money than him and all of his businesses combined? If they were a couple, and sharing resources, then that just made his life that much easier, right?

Jake shook his head and finished consolidating and relabeling the honey jars, then put them into a laundry basket on the table. When he was done, he picked up the laundry basket and headed downstairs. The honey would keep fine over the winter, and then he'd show up at the first market in the spring with bottles ready for sale.

Actually, was that true? Would there be a farmers' market downtown in 2013?

Jake didn't know yet. Normally they took place every year—or had since 2007, when the Downtown Cooper's Mill Partnership had started it up.

But Jake also knew there was a massive construction project going on next spring. They were ripping up all of Main Street through the whole downtown and replacing all the underground systems. At the same time, the city was taking advantage of the chaos and replacing and reconfiguring the sidewalks and curbs to make it more appealing and "walkable."

They were calling it "Streetscape," but to the downtown residents and businesses, it sounded like a nightmare. The sidewalks would be widened, sure, and the utilities would be updated. He'd seen some mockup concept drawings. It looked like a great update, or would be after it was done.

But what about the businesses downtown? Would they survive? Main Street would be closed for months, and the businesses would surely be impacted by the road closure and construction equipment, right? How many of the side streets would have to be closed as well?

And would they even hold the market? He knew of several farms and other local mini-businesses that counted on displaying their wares each year. Where would they hold it, with half the downtown off limits? He had no idea.

Jake would need to ask about that the next time he saw one of the folks from the Downtown Cooper's Mill Partnership, the small local group that oversaw most of the promotions and events that took place downtown. He was happy to know there was a group of people out there dedicated to that mission, but he was also happy to stay out of their way. He had plenty of stuff on his plate already without getting involved.

Jake already had so many "open loops" to keep track of, he couldn't write them all down. The folks who ran the Partnership—and the market—could figure out all those issues without him getting involved.

In the basement, he'd lined the walls with wooden and metal bookshelves that held a bewildering array of items: half-finished projects, painting supplies, jars and jars of jams and jellies and preserves, and various equipment and supplies for his rental properties. A large stainless steel table stood in the middle of the basement, itself covered with other projects in various states of completion.

There were more piles of items on the concrete floor of the garage, some items sitting on blue plastic tarps that he'd laid down to keep them clean. Most of the "protected" pieces were furniture, chairs and bookcases and tables that he'd bought for one of his properties or "acquired" after tenants had moved out and left them behind.

He set down the basket on an open folding table and started stacking the honey jars on an empty shelf above the jars of jelly. He'd also put up thirty bottles of pickles this summer, and those looked like they were aging and darkening nicely. Jake organized the honey and moved more glass jars around to make room on the shelf for all the honey.

When he was done, he made a mental note to winterize the beehives before it got much colder. Jake headed upstairs and was walking toward the kitchen when he heard a knock on the front door.

"Coming!"

He jogged down the hallway, hoping the knocking wouldn't wake Rosie. He wasn't in the mood to finish their fight from the night before, and he didn't need a visitor waking her up with his knocking.

On his front porch was Frank Harper, one of Cooper's Mill's newest residents.

"Frank! Glad you stopped by."

"No problem."

"Come on in. I was just getting ready to make a sandwich in the kitchen," Jake said, walking through the house as Frank followed. "You want one?"

"I'm okay," Harper said, looking around at the interior of the house. Harper was an ex-cop, and Jake noticed how the guy's eyes were always moving. Searching, studying, looking for something or someone that was out of place. Maybe looking for threats around every corner. Jake had no idea what it was like to be a cop, but it sounded exhausting.

"I know, I know. The place is a mess," Jake said as they passed through the old home and out into the kitchen, which had been added onto the back of the house at some point. "These old houses, they're a lot to keep up with. I've been working on that fireplace restoration for years."

Harper nodded and sat down on a chair next to the kitchen island. "Yeah, I bet it's a lot of work keeping these places going. I don't know if I would ever want to own one."

"It's not that bad," Jake said. "A lot of systems that you have to keep up with: roof, heating, cooling. If you let them get away from you, the house can get out of whack pretty quickly. So, you here for your keys?"

"Yeah, I think Laura's getting pretty sick of me," Harper said with a smile. "Plus, it'll be good for me to have my own place again. I like to come and go without having to check in. Laura and Jackson are on completely different schedules. Plus, you know how it is. You get used to living on your own. When you're living with somebody else, it can get complicated very fast."

"Yes, that's true," Jake said. He glanced at the ceiling, wondering about Rosie. "I know what it's like. Rosie crashes here sometimes. It can get frustrating."

Jake got to work making himself a sandwich while Frank watched, apparently mused, passing along a few pointers while Jake put some bread in the toaster. Jake had learned a long time ago that when someone was giving you advice, especially someone older than you, the best path was to just let them go ahead. Why stop them or interrupt them? And they often had great insight—they'd been on the earth a little longer.

Taking a break, Jake went and got the keys to Frank's new place. Jake kept all the keys for all his properties in one place, in a lockbox near the front door. He kept that box locked with a small key on his own key ring. Every once in a while, a tenant would get locked out or someone would drop by and need a key to something, and he didn't want to have to keep track of where he put them. It was just much easier to just keep them all by the door. He walked back into the kitchen and handed Frank the keys to his new apartment.

"Here you go, man," Jake said. "I hope you like it. It's all cleaned out from the last guy, and I went ahead and had my painter's paint.

Everything should be fresh, but if you find anything weird, let me know. Or if you find anything from the last tenant, feel free to keep it. If not, put it out by the curb for the trash people to take. In that neighborhood, the trash truck comes on Wednesdays."

"Thanks, Jake," Frank said. "I really appreciate it."

"No problem. Let me know how it still smells. The paint usually does a great job of freshening things up, but the last people in there were smokers. Let me know if it's bad and I'll have it painted again. And thanks for renting the place. Lots of people passed on it because it's behind that strip mall with the Dominoes."

"It's not a problem," Frank said. "I'm looking forward to having my own place again. Well, if that's all, I'm gonna head out. Got some errands to run. You got the check? I mailed it last week."

"Yeah, thanks. That covered your first month and the security deposit, so you don't owe me anything until December."

"Thanks again!" Frank said as he stood and walked out of the kitchen, showing himself out.

Jake watched him go, then heard the front door close behind him.

"What an odd bird," he said to himself. Frank Harper was a man of few words, that was for certain. Fortunately, Jake had met Frank at just the right time. Frank had helped Jake out with a couple of sticky situations.

Jake went back to finishing his sandwich. He considered himself somewhat of an expert in the sandwich-making arena, so he took his time. Maybe Harper had got tired of watching the process. Jake loved making sandwiches. He loved pulling together just the right mix of foods to make it awesome, kicking it up to the next level.

Lately, he's really been into it, and was even toying with the idea of maybe opening up a sandwich shop in downtown Cooper's Mill. The town desperately needed some kind of cute, casual cafe as opposed to the several upscale, fancy restaurants located in the downtown. There used to be a great little sandwich shop and deli located right across the street from O'Shaunessys, but that had closed several years before. Now it was an editing company of some sort.

Of course, opening a downtown restaurant was probably a horrible idea right now. The economy was already rough, and the downtown construction was going to kill even more traffic. But maybe he could be on the lookout for a place. If a place closed during the construction, he could scoop it up for a song. He'd never run a retail establishment or a restaurant, but Rosie had lots of experience in that area. Maybe they could go in on it together.

As if summoned by his thoughts, he heard her feet on the back staircase, the narrow second stairs that ran from the back part of the second floor straight down into the kitchen. He didn't like to call it the "servant's stairs," but that was the technical term for it.

She came down the last two steps and padded barefoot into the kitchen, wearing only a long t-shirt, her hair a mess. He smiled at her.

"Was somebody here? I thought I heard voices."

"Yeah, Frank Harper came by to get his keys."

"Why are you smiling?"

"I like this look," he said, pointing at what she was wearing. "And your hair? Very sexy."

"Oh, this little number?" she said, adjusting her shirt and pushing her hair up on top of her head. It stayed for only a second before cascading back down, this time flopping in her face. "There, that's better, right?" she asked, blowing it out of her face.

"Looks great to me," Jake said.

"Well, the 'no bra' look is in, right?"

"I'm a big fan."

She looked at him. "Hey, sorry about last night," she started to say, but he put his hands up.

"No, it's me that needs to apologize. You're just too darn successful. It's very intimidating."

Rosie smiled. "It doesn't have to be."

"I know. It just is. I'll get over it."

"You will?" she asked, sidling closer. "You promise to try to get over the fact that I'm raking in the cash at Ricky's? What if I spend it on you?"

"Sure," Jake said with a smile. "Take me on a vacation or two and we'll be square."

She sat down at the island, taking the seat that Frank had been in just minutes before. She put her head in her hands. "My head is killing me. Start me some coffee, will you? I need to stop with the tequila."

He went over and started a pod for her in the Keurig.

"And Frank got his keys?"

"Yes," Jake said. "He took that place uptown, behind the Dominoes."

"Oh, that's good," she said. "No one wanted it, right? Location, or the cigarette smell?"

"The smell, mostly. I had it painted, and it's much better."

"Good. And I'm glad he's got a place of his own now. He was living with his daughter, right?"

"Yup." Jake waited for the coffee maker to finish and handed her the cup, then sat down to his own sandwich.

"That's nice," Rosie said, sipping at the coffee. "Thanks. And he seems like a nice guy. Kind of intense, but nice. And good to have around. Maybe I should pay him to do security at Ricky's."

"Yeah, he really helped out with that whole situation with the Washington family."

"How they doing?" Rosie asked.

"They're doing good, Jake said. "So, do we need to talk about last night?

Rosie leaned over the island and rested her head on the cold marble. "I'd rather not."

"Me neither."

"It's that new daquiri machine we got at Ricky's. It's killing me."

"Too powerful?"

"Too easy to make strong drinks. Plus, I was in a really bad mood," she said. "I think one of our serving staff is stealing. I can't catch whichever lady that's doing it, but I need to. It's either that or suddenly we're making less money on beer than we used to."

"Sorry to hear that. I was just thinking about asking you for advice on opening a sandwich shop. Now that I know you're getting fleeced by someone, I won't."

"Shut up," she said with a smile. "It's just frustrating, you know? I mean, it's someone I work with every day. It has to be."

"Well, you could always ask Frank. I know he's working on a case right now where he's looking into a bunch of money going missing from a local business. He might look into for you."

She sat up and looked at him. "That's a good idea. I will. But what did you say earlier? About a sandwich shop?"

Jake pointed at his plate. "I'm getting better at these."

"Oh, I know it," she said. She grabbed part of his sandwich and ate it, making a face. "Oh my GOD that is good. I've been telling you for months now, this is your thing, Jake. I'm serious. These are so much better than any you can get anywhere in town."

"Oh, I don't know about that."

"Where did you learn to make these?"

"Trial and error. You really think they're good?"

"I do," she said, then sat back, thinking. "You know, we have that

VIP/party room on the front of the building that just sits empty half the time. We could…it would make a great little sandwich shop."

He looked at her to see if she was teasing him, but her face looked serious. Businesslike.

"What? What are you saying?"

"You, Jake Delancy, make great food. Can you crank these out a few at a time?"

"Maybe," he said, thinking about it while he ate. "Yeah, probably, if I had a proper kitchen. And some staff."

"Scaling up to a lunch service—that's a lot different than making a sandwich here and there."

"Yup. The hardest part is arranging all the ingredients. Why, thinking of having a party and you want me to cater?"

"No, but that's not a bad idea. You could do a few catering jobs from here, see if you like it."

"And if it makes money."

"No, not really," she said. "Ricky's is doing fine. But you don't want to start something you hate and get sucked into it."

"That's true."

She punched him lightly on the shoulder. "I'm trying to figure out which one I like the best. Those BBOTs you made the other day? Bacon, basil, onion, and tomato? Those were stupid good."

"I like those too. Fresh basil is the key."

She made a face. "Oh, and the steak sandwich, with the white cheddar. That was so good. Like Panera but better."

"Thanks. That's the one with pickled red onion."

"Is that what it is?" Rosie asked.

"Yeah, the acid gives the sandwich a little bite."

"It's great. They're all great. You should do it. Open a shop. Sandwiches, soups, etc. I'm serious."

Jake shook his head and finished chewing. "Not a good idea, opening a place during construction next year."

"Oh, that won't be a problem, at least for Ricky's and the other places on that end of town. The construction starts at First and Main, so we're lucky. Parking all along First will stay open, so we'll only lose the spots in the front. And close when there's no water or power."

"They're cutting power?"

"Here and there," she said, snacking on the part of the sandwich she'd stolen. "And we'll be back up and open by May, if they stick to plan. The other places further down Main? They'll be closed the whole summer."

"Yikes," Jake said. "Hope everyone stays afloat. Some of the businesses are already just barely getting by."

"It's going to get ugly."

"Bad if they can't get foot or car traffic. I wonder how many will close," he said, nodding. "I'm glad you like my sandwiches."

"I do," she said. "And this could be fun. You opening a shop. Something we could do together. That space is the perfect size. Counter, four tables, maybe some shelves—oh, honey, you could sell your jams and honeys year round, if you want!"

He could tell she was getting happy with the idea. And, while he hated to admit, the whole thing was starting to sound pretty exciting.

"I can't afford to open a store."

"Ricky's is doing great—you know that. So, I can loan you the money for the whole thing, if you like. Or we'll go 50/50 on the net until the loan's paid back. Or you can work for me, and I'll open it myself. Think about it."

Jake nodded, not sure what to say. "It's a lot to think about."

"Well, there's no hurry," she said, eating the last bite. "And for the record, damn."

"What?"

"You make great sandwiches."

CHAPTER 26
For the Prosecution

"I'm not sure, but I think we can get them on at least eight charges," ACP Bridget Sharp said, leaning over the table of folders and notes.

It was later in the day on Tuesday, and they were back in Whitlowe's office. She was checking in, having just returned from serving the search warrant and getting the grand tour from Xavier Castillo. She was still mad about the whole visit—it had started out like a raid and ended up feeling like she'd been taken on a relaxed tour of some new farmland she was thinking about buying. And half of the "raid" had felt as casual—and personal—as a first date. It was frustrating.

Xavier had a way of getting in people's heads, that was for certain. But there was more going on out there at Matthew House, she was certain of it.

"I just know they're not following code on some of those buildings," she said, grabbing the largest folder, a yellow jacket, which held all of her notes on the various construction projects the preppers were carrying out. Whitlowe liked to have all the current filings in a folder of a particular color, yellow, to keep it from being confused with the rest of the case files and background, usually relegated to beige or green hanging folders or the larger, thicker black notebooks.

"And there's something funky with that new building he's started. That foundation is strange. He said it's a new building, a prayer center or something. Who builds in the middle of nowhere? That doesn't make sense, does it?"

She looked up at Whitlowe. He was just looking out the window.

"Kevin, are you even listening?"

He turned around and looked at her. "Dad always said he loved this view the best."

She looked at him. The old man was dead, and Whitlowe still wasn't handling it well. He was confused, sullen. And alternately angry at the world. He'd been suggesting charges on some cases that were well outside of the Federal recommendations, and, in other cases, he was considering dropping entire prosecutions.

And last week he'd brought up the weekend in St. Louis.

If she hadn't known better, Bridget would have thought he was hitting on her. She would have let it go without much comment—it was par for the course, unfortunately, and she got hit on by everyone from the criminals to the barman across the street—but Whitlowe wasn't even entertaining getting back together. It was one of the things she liked most about him—his complicated nature. She would have jumped at the chance for another roll in the sack with the man.

But today, no mention of St. Louis or their fun weekend, the last fun weekend for her in a while. His mind was all over the place lately.

"What?"

"My dad," he said, pointing. "He loved this view."

She walked over, biting back the snarky comment she was about to deliver. She looked out the wide windows at the stone courtyard in front of the building. To the left was Main Street and a smattering of bars and shops, but the real view was to the right—the huge Miami County Building, standing nearly eight stories high. In this part of Ohio, it was the biggest building around.

"I know, Kevin," she said quietly. "And I know you miss him."

He stared at the large fountain as it threw water into the air.

"Thanks for going out there, Bridget," Whitlowe said. "I'm sorry...I just can't think about anything clearly right now. Not the cases, not you and me, nothing."

She looked at him, curious.

"It's okay."

"I don't...I just...I just miss him," Whitlowe said. She saw his eyes were shiny. Normally, when she thought of seeing a man cry, it made her think less of him. But now, here, seeing Whitlowe nearly in tears after losing his dad...she swallowed, grasping for something to say.

Bridget leaned over slightly and put her head on his shoulder.

"We all miss him."

She felt Whitlowe move his head—it felt like he was nodding, agreeing with her.

"Thank you. And thank you for tolerating my mood shifts." He sniffled and she stood up to see him wiping his eyes on his sleeve. He stepped to one side, moving away from her and back to his desk. "You're doing great work. Can you...can you pull together a report? Write up your recommendations?"

"Of course," she said, looking out at the fountains. For some reason, she didn't like fountains. They gave her the creeps.

Last year, she'd seen a documentary on a serial killer they had caught back in the mid-1990s. He'd traveled the country in a dirty white van, killing people, mostly women. He was known as a collector, keeping parts of his victims, and this had been part of what had helped the cops afterward track his victims' families.

Of course, the man had gotten away with it by constantly staying on the move. This was in the time before inter-department communication and criminal databases, and the man had ravaged from one side of the country to the other before finally being caught. Anyway, in the end, the serial killer had been trapped in a shopping mall. He'd been shot and fallen into a large water fountain located at the center of the mall. The documentary described the water turning red from the blood in the water.

Ever since, she'd disliked the concept of fountains—she could only see a replay of that image from the documentary, a fountain of blood shooting into the air and cascading down. From that day, she'd always wondered. How much blood did it take to make a fountain turn crimson?

CHAPTER 27
Shop Visit

Barking, endless barking. It was enough to drive a person crazy.

Tavon turned up his headphones, leaning over his accounting textbooks and concentrating as hard as he could to block out the sounds.

In his class, they were doing a unit on statistical analysis and, while it came pretty naturally to Tavon, he still needed to get the formulas memorized.

For some reason, numbers and calculations all just seemed logical to him—as long as he could remember, he could visualize numbers and do additions and subtractions and even some long division in his head. It was just the way his brain worked. Some people were good with words, writers or whatever. And some people could get other people to do things for them, like the Dragon. She was like a witch in that way, getting people under her spell. She could get her boys to do just about anything—even kill cops, if that was what she needed.

He was glad that was all over. But he didn't miss the violence, or the panic of trying to decide what to do while you watched a house full of people burn. He remembered everything from that night: the smell of smoke, the fire licking around the base of the house, catching the dry scrub alight. The doors had been chained from the outside until he intervened.

No, Tavon didn't need that kind of stress in his life.

But he missed some of it. The camaraderie, always having something to do. He had always stayed busy, counting money or working on a better to increase profits—

The door burst open and his mom walked in at full speed. She was carrying a wet dog that proceeded to leap out of her arms and scamper around the small storeroom.

"Oh, sorry, I forgot you were here," she said loud enough for him to hear over his headphones. He pulled them off.

"Mom! I'm trying to work!" he said. The dog started shaking, spraying water everywhere. Tavon threw his arms over his books to keep them dry.

"I know, I know," his mom said, exasperated. "Sorry!"

She chased down the dog, a small Rottweiler, and he kicked out his legs to direct the dog in her direction. "Precious, get over here!" Finally, she cornered the dog and scooped it up. "Sorry about that—I was going to lock him in here for a second while I waited for the sink to be free."

"What about a cage?"

"They're all full. We're crazy busy."

Tavon took off his headphones and set them on his books, sighing. The barking continued, louder than ever, and now he could hear his sisters too, both of them talking loudly over the sound of the dogs. It sounded like they were screaming, trying to have a conversation.

"I'm trying to get some homework done, Mom," he said. It was pointless to have this argument again, but it was better than doing homework.

"I know, Tavon," she said. "And like I've asked before, wouldn't you be happier at the library or something?"

He shrugged.

"It's just...I want somewhere private."

"What about that coffee shop? Ghost something?"

He made a face, and she shook her head.

"Okay, well, I'll remind your sisters to leave you alone." His mom pulled the door shut behind her, and he went back to his books.

At least the dog grooming business was doing good. They had more work than they could handle. His sisters had been discussing hiring more people—it was a great problem to have. And it would let him cut down his hours—he volunteered at least twenty hours a week, washing dogs and pulling shifts for his sisters.

Tavon was also doing the books for free and filing all their taxes. But he stayed away from all the decision making—that was up to his sisters and his mom. Let them figure it out. He'd made enough bad decisions in his life—and now he was back to living with his mom and sisters, sharing their mom's small house in Vandalia/North Dayton. It was too small for the four of them, but his sisters and mother never said anything. With Talisa moving to Charleston, it had helped. And they knew him leaving the gang had been hard, and not just because the money had dried up.

He'd been accepted, valued, by the other gang members. But

neighborhood folks hated him and had hated the gang. He'd been a traitor to his neighborhood, helping the Northsiders sling their drugs. Tavon had worked hard to keep the gang thriving.

Now that they were gone, Tavon was all on his own. It was the reason he didn't want to be seen at a coffee shop or hanging out at the library. Tavon assumed everyone hated him.

The dogs started up again, barking and barking. He cursed, slamming the accounting book closed. It was too loud here, too crazy. He couldn't get anything done.

Tavon stood and gathered up his books, stuffing them into his backpack. He pulled on his jacket and went out into the store. Along one wall was a series of stations for grooming dogs and other animals, and the back portion was taken up by three washing stations where the dogs could be washed and dried.

Up front, chairs for waiting customers and a front counter with the cash register and a small retail area, where they sold dog shampoo and collars and dog treats.

"What you doing?"

Tavon turned—it was Shawnda, one of his three sisters. She was the skinny one and was always vibrating with energy, unlike Minnie, who was always trying to figure out how to work while sitting down. They worked well together, though, divvying up the important work of the "pet salon." It was just a dog grooming place called "Tips and Toes," but his sisters were always looking for ways to make the place more "classy." They were thinking of adding "pet salon" to the name of the place to elevate the status of the grooming location.

"I can't work back there," Tavon said, nodding at the closed door to the supply room. "Too many barking dogs," he said, nodding at the wall of cages, which held six or eight agitated dogs, all of them barking in his general direction. "Can't concentrate."

"Sorry about that, Tavon, but we can't do anything about it, really," Shawnda said. They all had matching nametags, another new addition to make the place classier. "We are absolutely slammed."

"We need to be hiring another girl," Minnie said from across the room, even though she wasn't part of the conversation. "Or three. That wall of cages is always full."

"Customers are gonna start leaving, going somewhere else to get their dogs groomed," his mother Lucinda chimed in.

"What about the library?" Shawnda asked. "I'm sure it's quieter there."

"I don't like the way they look at me there," he said quietly. "They know...I'm an ex-gangbanger. They hate me. I can tell."

"It's fine. People change."

"No, it's not fine," he said, and it came out sharper than he wanted. "I was rich and sorta famous and now I'm nothing. People are laughing about it."

This had been a point of contention between the two of them for a while, ever since the Northsiders had left.

"Don't worry about that," Shawnda said. "We're making it work on our own, with no outside help. And we're doing fine."

"Maybe," he conceded. She was the smartest one of his sisters.

"AND you don't know what the hell you're talking about. You got a good life, and you're makin' it better," his mom yelled over, nodding at his book bag. "We need your help, believe me."

Minnie chimed in. "This place is doing good, and it's paying us salaries. Good money, enough to hire some girls."

"I help out, you know," he said, feeling himself get defensive.

"That ain't what I mean," she said. "We need you making things better. More efficient," she said with a smile. That was one of his favorite sentences, and he smiled as well.

"I know what you mean," he said. "I guess...I guess I'll head to the library."

"Good," she said. "Get that homework done so you're all caught up for class. Don't worry about what other people are thinking."

Shawnda started to say something else but the little bell on the door rang again as someone came in. The dogs who weren't already barking started up again, filling the shop with noise.

Tavon turned to look at the person, who was backlit by the light coming in from outside, and noticed two things immediately.

One, the person wasn't carrying an animal. That was rare in and of itself. No one came in here empty handed.

The second was that the person was white, a rarity in this part of Dayton. Their clientele was almost exclusively black. Not that there was anything wrong with old skinny white dudes coming in here, but usually they had a pet—

—and then Tavon recognized the white guy.

It was the old cop. The one from the Salem Mall, and from the hospital shootout. Harper.

"Shit," Tavon said quietly, backing away.

The old man hadn't spotted him yet, his eyes scanning the inside of the pet grooming facility like some time-traveling robot seeking his target.

"I gotta go," Tavon said quietly, backing toward the back door.

"Who is it?" Shawnda was squinting, trying to see who it was standing near the front doors. The light from the street made it hard to see.

"Frank Harper."

She looked confused for a second as he backed toward the door, then nodded. "Oh, that old cop from before. Thought you said he was a good guy?"

"Yeah, sorta," Tavon said. "He kept that family safe, but he's a cop. And he drinks. A lot."

"Oh," his sister said. "Okay, I'll distract him."

Tavon laughed at that. "Yeah, thanks," he said with a smile. "Distract him."

He left, heading out the back door.

The shop was located in a strip mall on North Dixie Drive, a run-down portion of North Dayton. Next door was a bail bondsman, and on the other side, some college kids had just opened a store that sold "vaping" stuff, some kind of new alternative to smoking. A few blocks to the south had been Riley's, the old strip club the Northsiders had used as a headquarters. Of course, that was before it had been blown to smithereens with a bunch of cops inside.

Tavon hurried along the back of the vape store, pulling out his phone to check his messages before heading to his car and the library. He hated the idea of going there, but he didn't have many options. He needed a table and power for his laptop and didn't feel like plopping down in some yuppie coffee shop.

Tavon turned the corner, heading for his car. At least he still had it. The Northsiders took off so fast, they hadn't had time to demand he return it.

"Not happy to see me?"

Tavon stopped. Mr. Harper was leaning against the corner of the vape store with a bemused smile on his face. Up close, the old man still looked like he could rip a phone book in half—how did the old guy stay jacked? Tennis? Golf? Some other fancy white sport Tavon had never heard of?

"Nah," Tavon said, stopping. He might as well talk to the man. "You're bad for my rep."

"What, talking to cops? People think you're a narc?"

"Nah," Tavon said. "Kidding. It's just that...well, after the Northsiders left, I'm trying to make a new start."

"Good, good for you," Harper said, walking over. Tavon looked for a weapon but didn't see one—of course, that didn't mean he didn't have one. Maybe a gun under his shirt, or maybe in his sock. Or a knife, or something else.

Tavon suddenly realized he was scared.

"So, what do you want?"

Harper smiled and stopped, putting his hands up. "Whoa, it's okay, Tavon. You're not in trouble. That's not any way to treat a friend."

"Oh, we friends? I had no idea."

"Course we're friends, Tavon," Harper said, strolling over and leaning on Tavon's car. Just like a cop would do. Like when they wanted to have a "casual" conversation with someone but also subtly keep them from leaving.

Tavon didn't like cops. He'd had too many bad interactions with them over the years. Getting pulled over, hassled because of his skin color, handcuffed, questioned for no reason. Too much bullshit. They had their power and loved to wave it around, rub it in people's faces.

Tavon realized that Harper had stopped talking and was just staring at him. The silence was uncomfortable, but Tavon did his best to avoid talking. It was usually the best policy with cops, or even ex-cops.

Keep your mouth shut, Gig had always said. Don't give them nothing. Don't give them an excuse to shoot you. Plus, Tavon had no idea what Harper wanted or why he had shown up at Tavon's family business.

Harper smiled. "I get it. You think you're in trouble or something?"

"No clue, man," Tavon said, hugging his bag to his chest. "Just trying to get on with my day."

Harper stood up and put up his hands. "Sorry, man. I have no idea why you're mad at me, but it's fine. I'm not trying to hassle you or anything. I'll be on my way."

Tavon nodded. "Good. Thanks," he said, unlocking his car with the remote in his pocket. "Have a good one, man."

Harper looked at him across the hood of the car, his arms crossed. "Sure, no problem. Just had a job for you."

Tavon was pulling his door open but stopped and looked at the old man.

"What?"

"A job. Maybe."

He looked at Harper. "What kind of job?"

"Something you'd be good at, I'd hazard to guess. Very good."

Tavon shook his head.

"I don't go out for any more gang stuff, sorry. Trying to get right. If you're looking for some kind of enforcer or someone to kicking people's asses, I'm not your—"

"Oh, no, nothing like that," Harper said, puttin up his hands again like Tavon was the one doing the arresting. "You think I'd come all the way down here and talk to you for something like that?"

"I got no idea," Tavon said. "Since the Northsiders left, it's been hard to make money." Tavon nodded behind Harper at the dog grooming place. "My sisters and mom run that place."

"Yeah, you mentioned that a few times when we worked together before," Harper said with a smile. "Going well?"

"Yeah, pretty good," Tavon said. "Busy. Lots of dogs needing grooming."

"That's good."

"I'm helping them out."

"Well, then they're lucky," Frank said. "Actually, I need some accounting help. Thought it might be something you'd be good at."

Tavon was confused by the odd change in the conversation.

"What?"

"Accounting. Actually, I need some forensic accounting, specifically. Kinda what you did for the Northsiders, but this is legit. I can pay you by the hour, if you like, or a lump sum."

Tavon was still confused. "You want me to do your accounting? For like a business or something?"

Harper laughed. "No. Sorry, let me back up. I'm living here now, in Ohio, up in Cooper's Mill. I started a private investigation company. It's going pretty good."

Tavon nodded, not saying anything. Was the guy bragging?

"Anyway, I've had several cases," Harper continued.

"I saw the one lady you were protecting, from Hollywood?"

Harper nodded. "Yeah, she was a sassy one. But I'm working on a bigger case. Involves a company up in Cooper's Mill. Someone has been stealing money from them for years. The owner died mysteriously, and now I'm working for his daughter, the new owner. She's convinced the lost money and her father's death are connected, somehow, but the cops don't agree. They looked into it but came up with nothing."

"The dude's death or the missing money?"

"Both, actually," Harper said with a smile. "Cops couldn't find anything to go on and dropped the case. That's why the daughter came to me, to go through the books and figure out what happened to her father."

Tavon nodded.

"One of those I'm good at, but accounting? Nope," Harper continued. "Not my bag, as they say."

Tavon nodded—it felt like all he was doing was nodding, but he wanted to hear more.

"My daughter has an accounting degree, and she's looking at the current books," Frank continued. "I'm checking all the personnel, past and present. But the lady owner, Jill Anderson, gave me digital copies of all their books going back eight years. I remembered that's some of the stuff you did for the Northsiders. Am I remembering that wrong?"

"No, that's right," Tavon said. "You said you'd pay me?"

"Yeah, flat rate or by the hour. The client's paying me, and I can pay you."

Tavon nodded. "That might be interesting."

"Good," Harper said. "I'm not kidding around here, either. This is a complicated case. The murder? I can investigate that all day long. But accounting? No. I could really use your help on this."

The two of them, a young black kid and an old white guy, spent a few more minutes in front of the vape store, discussing the particulars of the case, with Harper getting Tavon up to speed.

It was a little strange, because Tavon had lots of questions and wanted more details, but he had nothing to write on and didn't want to get out his laptop or paper to take notes on the hood of his car. He and Harper talked about the general parameters of the case, and Harper's impressions of the people involved. At one point they discussed Tavon's fee, a flat rate of $1,000 that he literally just made up, and the old man agreed without hesitation.

A few people drove by, and Tavon wondered if he'd hear about it later. Would people be suspicious of him talking to someone who clearly looked like a cop? Did people even care?

Maybe Tavon was overly concerned about what other people thought of him.

At some point during the conversation, Harper handed over a USB drive, like this was some kind of secret meet-up in a movie.

"That's their books for eight years. The owner died two years ago, in 2010, and his daughter took over. I'd like you to dig through everything, see what you find. You're looking for patterns, money moving around in strange ways. Anything, really, that jumps out at you."

"Okay," Tavon said. "Thanks." He put the thumb drive in his pocket but kept fiddling with it as he talked to Harper, who must've assumed Tavon would help. Why else would he bring the files? "Anything on the murder?"

Harper nodded and relaxed, smiling. "Yeah. Background checks, employee interviews. Trying to find someone with a bunch of money. And I've got a person on the inside. New employee. I'm hoping they dig around, get me a list of people—and equipment. This place buys a lot of expensive equipment."

"I'll get digging," Tavon said. "And we'll talk. Text okay?"

Harper nodded at Tavon's pocket. "My numbers and email are on the USB drive. Let me know what you find," Harper said. "And thank you, Tavon. I really appreciate it."

Tavon nodded and started to get into his car when he had one more question. He stood back up and shouted after Harper, who had already turned away. "One more question."

Harper turned and looked at him. "Shoot."

"What if we follow the money and find out your client is involved? This Anderson lady? How is that going to work out?"

"I don't care," Harper said with a smile. "I'll call the cops myself. But after she's caught up on the invoices. Right?"

"Okay," Tavon said and, in spite of himself, laughed.

Chapter 28
Search For It

Two days after Joe got the big tour of the Church of Xavier property, he was out in the wilds of Ohio again. It was Thursday, October 25, and he and Trapper were off the big compound, driving around and winding through another patch of beautiful country somewhere north of the compound. It had been raining off and on for the last two days, and there were patches of standing water on the narrow country roads.

Most of the land they were investigating was taken up with fields, all burdened with heavy concentrations of tall corn and wheat. Some of the stalks were so heavy with grain, they were starting to bend and sag.

Trapper asked some of the locals about the corn, and they said that the harvest was already starting in parts of the county. Apparently, harvest was running late this year, with most farmers were looking at clearing their fields around the week of November 10, depending on the temperature and how much rain they got over the next three weeks.

How they picked that week, Joe had no idea, but he liked the way the tall crops leaned over the roads. He marveled at the acres and acres of rippling fields of gold and green and brown. Joe hoped they would hold off until mid-November, as the fields of tall corn and wheat could serve as camouflage.

Joe scanned the country on both sides of the road, searching. He was looking for something in particular, even though he was having trouble defining exactly what that was. He had been thinking about how this game would work for a long time, but it was difficult to describe. Trapper had come along to help, but Joe could tell that he was getting frustrated.

Joe would know it when he saw it. Firstly, it had to be accessible by public roads, something that eliminated a large portion of the prepper's territory. But not anything that was too public, nothing along a highway or major road.

And it needed to be a place that he could completely control. It would be a game of cat and mouse, yes, but none of it could blow back on Xavier or his church.

Joe had taken a liking to the guy, even though he was half off his rocker. But they had things in common, personalities that attracted followers.

Joe had discovered that peculiar talent by accident when he'd shared information about his trial earlier in the year online. Doing so had been a desperate attempt to sway the jury or maybe influence the judge—but, instead, Joe had somehow "gathered unto him" a flock of crazy followers.

They started showing up at the courthouse and chanting and sneaking into the courtroom and disrupting the proceedings with chants of "Freedom for Joe" or "The Truth will Set You Free!" From that, the "Keepers of Truth" movement had begun, evolving into an organization that now helped those wrongly convicted of major crimes.

It had been a trip, to be sure. And another great example of how powerful leaders could control groups of dimwitted plebs.

"That's three fields and two small forests so far today," Trapper said, not doing a great job of disguising his annoyance. "Plus, that abandoned farmhouse the church owns south of West Milton. And those ruins of that town near the Stillwater River. We getting any closer?"

"Yes, we are," Joe said, equally impatient. "I know you're tired of driving me around, but there aren't that many places to look," he said, nodding at the map Trapper was holding as he drove. Xavier's people had given Joe a map of their holdings, a smattering of properties sprinkled around three counties.

"I know," Trapper said. "I'm nervous, having you out in public."

"Me too, trust me," Joe said. "Just mind the speed limits and we'll be fine. And you know what I want—trees. Lots of them."

"And you want a field near a stand of trees," Trapper said, repeating something Joe had said earlier. "The tree area needs to be at least a quarter acre, and you would prefer some natural borders, like hills or cliffs. Right?"

"Yes," Joe said. "Where are we going next?"

"Well, I had an idea, so we're heading there now."

They continued along the country road and Trapper slowed to take a sharp turn. There were plenty of small country roads in the area, but this one didn't even look like a road: it wasn't striped and humped in the middle. It was barely wide enough to allow another car to pass if they came upon one.

"At least it's paved," Trapper quipped.

"Barely."

The road emerged into a large flat area, and Joe could see a line of low hills running along the far side of the fields. A small stand of trees stood near what looked like a fenced area. Trapper took two more turns and slowed, parking next to a small forest. An area under the trees was fenced with delicate metal fencing.

"What's that?"

"A family cemetery," Trapper said, climbing out and stretching. "They have these all over, little private plots of land with headstones."

Joe walked over and looked. He could see only five ancient gravestones, barely legible, inside a small, overgrown plot of fenced land. There were three other headstones that had, at some point, toppled over into the scrub. Now they were nearly impossible to see. There was a gate, but when he tried to open it, Joe found it rusted shut.

"'Hagar,' I think it says," Trapper pointed out.

"What?"

"To the left. The sign, by that tree," Trapper said.

Joe turned and found it, an old sign that read "Hagar Cemetery." The sign had long ago fallen over and now had been partially reclaimed by nature. Roots from a nearby tree nearly covered it. How long did it take for tree roots to grow?

"What's the land look like around here?"

Joe heard Trapper rattle the map. "Nothing but fields. And none of it church property."

Joe turned. "Then why are we here?"

Trapper nodded at the cemetery. "You said you needed a landmark, right? Somewhere to send Harper."

Joe looked around at the cemetery again, his mind whirring like an engine. It could work, yes, if he could come up with something clever. Something to draw him in, something with just enough mystery for him to take the bait. Harper was a smart guy, or at least he thought he was smart. This puzzle would need to be subtle, clever.

Another game of chess.

This location, no, but something like it. And Joe would come up with something. Something to entice the old cop and finally put an end to him.

"Okay, maybe," Joe said, walking back to the car. "Not this one, but maybe another. We're getting closer, narrowing things down. You see any cemeteries on that map? Any on church property?"

"Yup. I marked them in red," he said, handing the map to Joe. There were several in the area, tiny spots of red in a field of green and white. "How 'bout you navigate for me?"

Chapter 29
St. Louis

A couple days later, Bridget sat across the desk from Whitlowe, scowling at him and the rest of the world. She was peeved, he could see, and the further he got into the report that she had whipped together out of pure anger—the more questions he had.

Bridget wanted these guys to be breaking the law. And, when they didn't comply, it pissed her off. It had been two days since her tour of the prepper facility, and he could see in her eyes that she was still seething.

"Oh, you have NO idea," she'd said at the top of the meeting, storming in and handing him a copy of her report to review. Now, fifteen minutes later, he was only on page three and every answer back to him had a knife edge. "He was...there was no respect!"

Now they were alone in his office, the wide windows showing the inclement weather outside. Being late October in the Midwest, the weather had lately been alternating between cold rain and occasional blasts of heat that made Ohio feel like it was basking in the middle of summer. Indian Summer, they called it, a name that didn't feel politically correct for today's times, but people went with it for now. He wondered how long it would be before someone insisted on changing that phrase to make it less "racist."

Oh well. Rain pattered to the ground outside, coating the steps around the fountains and painting the concrete a dark gray to match the cloudy, forbidding sky above.

Whitlowe was going through Bridget's report. He'd asked her to send it ahead of the meeting, so he'd have time to review it, but she said she'd rather be there for his first read to answer any questions immediately. Bridget was thorough, of course, and brought up a lot of good points, but, in the end, she'd found literally nothing to be concerned about.

He glanced up at her, mentally preparing himself for what he knew would be a harsh response.

"So, nothing? Nothing we can indict on, or even investigate further?"

She shook her head. She seemed to have calmed down and now even seemed a little sad. "No, not really. I thought I had them on that runoff, but he was right—the mitigation steps they took with the county passed muster. They've expanded in size and scope, and have lots more people running around, but Xavier has all the permits in place. Except for that business with the gate across the road, and it's already gone."

Whitlowe smiled, suddenly nervous.

"From the report, it sounds like he was practically hitting on you. Maybe we can charge him with harassment."

"And pandering," she said. "He kept calling me *chica*."

"He sounds very magnetic," Whitlowe said, fishing for more information. Was she interested in this Castillo guy? That would be a conflict of interest, of course. As bad as screwing your boss in St. Louis? Or screwing your employee? Whitlowe couldn't figure out which one was worse.

He concentrated on the picture of Castillo — the guy was "dreamy," as the kids said nowadays. He held up the photo. "I can see why he has such a following."

She nodded but didn't say anything.

"Would you consider him a cult leader?" he said, continuing down a line of questioning he wouldn't be able to sustain much longer. "Do we have any recourse to send in social workers, make sure everyone is being treated well? Make sure everyone is there of their own free will? Lots of the people at his compound are women, right? Kids?"

Bridget continued frustrating him by not saying anything.

He gave up and moved on.

"And the firearms? Any more issues with those?"

She shook her head. "No, he's got the guns locked down tight. They worked up an inventory system, and he showed me the rooms in the barn next to Matthew House where they store the guns and all associated ammo when they're not being carried by his men. He gave us a copy of the inventory, which included all the serial numbers. Drayton ran them all through the NCIC while we were on site. Everything checked out. But I'm sure they're up to no good out there," Bridget said, looking at him. "I can feel it."

"Sadly, we can't prosecute based on that," Whitlowe said. "Or even bring them up on any charges. So, nothing shady?"

"No," she said.

He set the report down. "I know you think they're up to no good.

But we can't look like we're targeting people who are just doing their thing out there and following the law."

Whitlowe scanned through the section on the recent construction, including new additions to existing properties, and the facility for water purification and storage near the closest river. And two new, large barns topped with solar panels.

"Are they generating their own power? Maybe the county will be buying from them someday."

"Or they won't sell back to the grid," she answered. "They claim to be 50% self-powered, but I didn't see any proof. They have added some battery packages to use for power storage."

She sat back and waited for him to ask more questions. He didn't like being alone with her, and considered calling in Dorothy for the last part of the meeting, but then decided not to. He could handle crazed murderers and arsonists and child molesters—surely, he could handle one sassy ex-girlfriend.

Ex-girlfriend? Was that what she was?

Had they been that close, technically? That made him stop and think. What was the nature of their relationship? What HAD been the nature of it, technically?

What had happened between them had been quick, completely consensual and amazing. Amazing. He found himself looking at her and thinking about the conference in St. Louis and Union Station, where they had stayed. The entire interior of the old train station had been converted into one massive interior space filled with shops and restaurants—and a hotel. They were staying there while attending a conference nearby. After the day session, they had returned to Union Station, changed clothes, then gone out for drinks. She had looked so nice in that dress she'd been wearing—

"Kevin, are you listening?"

He looked at her and cleared his throat.

"Sorry. Can you say that again?"

"I said there is nothing we can get them on, and we both know it."

He nodded, tearing his mind away from St. Louis. A whirlwind weekend, for certain. But those days ranked right up there in his life experience. And he couldn't stop thinking about it. Could she? Was she flirty with him because she wanted a repeat of that crazy weekend? Or was she past it and had moved on and now things were only ever going to be awkward between them?

He should have controlled himself better, not let himself get pulled into the situation. But they had been out of town. Did that change the rules? A nice meal together, two friends in a strange town where they knew nobody. Dinner at a fancy steak place in Union Station, which lead naturally, casually, to getting some drinks at a nearby bar. Some fun karaoke, more drinks, then stumbling back to their respective rooms.

Why had he gotten them adjoining rooms? Some part of him could remember him asking Dorothy to set that up. Had he been hoping something would happen? Looking back on it, the whole thing felt almost inevitable. Or destined, as cheesy as that sounded.

She'd come to his room, ostensively to "check on him" after he'd stumbled in the lobby of the hotel. He'd laughed it off, and she'd held his shoulder, and he'd gotten a long, heady whiff of her hair as she scrunched up close to him. It was intoxicating, certainly, but he was an adult. He could handle it. She'd come to his room and the loudest voice in his head reminded him that they were friends and coworkers, and he was her boss.

But another voice in his head had disagreed.

And then one thing had led to another, has they had a tendency to do when you took a single man and single a woman and mixed them together with alcohol and isolation and a long-term flirty relationship. It really only had two directions it could go: sex or a falling out. Good times or bad times. The middle could not hold. At some point, the scales would tip in one direction or the other.

Bridget coughed and Whitlowe realized how long it had been since anyone had said anything. He'd completely spaced out, thinking about that weekend. Thinking about the smell of her hair, and what she'd been wearing that night in St. Louis—or what she'd worn until she wasn't wearing anything at all.

He felt his face flush and tapped the report.

"Good, good, it looks good," was all he could muster. It sounded stupid the moment it passed his lips. But he was too flustered to think of anything else to say.

"Good? What do you mean 'good?' It's a disaster," she said.

He looked at her—really looked at her—for the first time since she had sat down.

"It's not a disaster, Bridget," he said quietly. "It's just a bunch of people keeping their noses clean. Nothing you can do about it, other than monitor the situation."

She looked at him and didn't say anything. He could hear his dad's tall grandfather clock ticking away loudly in the corner of the office. It was a massive old thing that Dorothy had insisted he keep even during the phase where he was remodeling the office and keeping only a few things that had been distinctly his father's. He'd tried to put his own stamp on the room but had failed. Would he ever think of it as his own?

He shook his head and focused.

"You're a good prosecutor, Bridget," he said. "And I'm sorry about what happened in St. Louis. I messed up. I apologize for that, and I should have been stronger," he said.

She looked up and shook her head. "No, it was my fault," she said. "I've always liked you."

He couldn't help but snicker. "Bullshit."

"No, it's true," she said, sitting up and nodding. "It's totally true. I just...things are so weird now, with work relationships. You know? How do two people who work together date? How do they let each other know they are interested?"

He knew it was his imagination, but it suddenly felt ten degrees warmer in his office. Had the heat come on? He glanced out the window at the fountains, then back to her.

"You mean without HR getting involved? I have no idea."

She smiled. "It's impossible to date at work anymore. Too many eyes watching. But that's where people spend most of their time, right? If you can't date your coworkers, how do you meet other people?"

He just shook his head.

"I had a co-worker one time, a woman editor," Bridget continued. "She told me the greatest story about how her and her husband got together."

He smiled, just happy to listen to her talk when she wasn't mad at him.

"Go on."

"Oh, you know, she and her husband worked at the same place, this big computer company," Bridget said, sitting back in her chair and relaxing. "She did editing, technical documents, and he was some kind of document manager, whatever that is. Anyway, they both worked for the same person, so technically they were allowed to date, but it was a small office, and it would have been very awkward, especially if things didn't work out."

"I know the feeling," he said.

She gave him a look. "Okay. So, when they started seeing each other, they just kept it a secret."

"Makes sense."

"Anyway, they dated for a while and never told anyone. People at work knew both of them were dating someone, but nobody guessed it was someone in the office. After eight or nine months, she moved in with him, and they started driving to work together, and they had to take turns pausing in the parking lot so they weren't seen walking in together. But then they got engaged. Once they knew it was the real thing, they knew they had to tell everyone. My friend wanted to find a way to announce it to all of their coworkers at the same time."

"That's ballsy."

"Yeah. But you don't know the half of it. She did it at the company Christmas party."

"No."

"Yup. In front of their bosses and everything. So everyone's at the party, the whole company, including her fiancé. The boss gathers everyone together to talk about the year and how things were going and such. You know, 'you're all doing a great job,' yada yada. She thanked them for coming to the party, and then my friend says she has an announcement to make: she's getting married."

"No."

"Yeah. Well, obviously, everyone is excited for her, and people congratulate her and start peppering her with questions. She says 'there's more to it than that. The guy I'm engaged to? You all know him.'"

Whitlowe smiled and leaned forward. "That's good. I like that."

"Everyone is looking around, including the fiancé, who's pretending to not know anything. Then my friend says 'not only do you all know him, he works in our division. In fact, he's here in the room with us. Right now.' People are freaking out and her fiancé is pointing at other guys to keep up the ruse."

"Normally I don't like it when people draw stuff out, but that's good."

Bridget nodded. "THEN she says 'okay, I'd like you all to meet him' and asks him to step forward and the fiancé waits an extra ten seconds before stepping forward. The people all freak out. Obviously, everyone is excited for them both—and it makes a great story, right? If you're going to announce your engagement, that's how you do it."

"But they dated for a while on the side," he added, sitting back.

"You know, to see if was actually 'a thing' or not, as you put it."

She nodded and looked at him. "Yup. That's okay. And that's how I'd do it. Keep it a secret for a while. There are too many eyes watching people nowadays, I think."

"Says the woman who can't wait to prosecute a bunch of religious people for absolutely nothing," he said with a smile.

"Shut up, Kevin," she said with her own smile. "Don't be an asshole."

"Thanks."

"But you know. You can't even date to see if things are serious. But I did have feelings for you. I did want to pursue something with you. At the time."

He wasn't sure what to say next. Keep pushing? Get sued? Get fired? It was a gamble—but then, life was a gamble, wasn't it? Getting out of bed in the morning was a gamble. Getting on a bus with a bunch of strangers, or going to a concert, or driving on a Friday night when the drunks are out. Life was a gamble. He could die tomorrow. He could be struck by lightning or killed by a bear.

Kevin rolled the dice.

"And now? Do you still feel that way?"

She looked at him and bit her lip. She probably thought it made her look cute, but he always thought it made her look like a predator. A hungry animal searching for prey. It was alluring and terrifying, all at the same time.

"Yeah," she said. "I think so."

"Wow, so romantic."

"No, that's not what I mean," she said, standing up and putting her hands on his desk. Leaning over him, she looked even more intimidating, except for her red hair, which cascaded down around her shoulders and nearly took his breath away. He could smell her shampoo from five feet away.

"I mean, yeah. Yes. Definitely yes."

"Me too," he said, glancing at the door. "But how?"

"Keep it a secret? Like my friend?"

"Only tell people when we get engaged, you mean?"

"Sure. Why? Are you asking?"

He put up his hands. "Whoa there. I'd like to do all the fun dating stuff first before we have to have that conversation. Maybe you'll hate being around me," he said, serious. "Maybe we won't work out, and then how can we work together?"

"I don't know."

"We should know these things. You work for me."

"I'm not aware of this."

"And it's not like with your friend and her situation. The two of them worked for the same person. If this gets out, we'll both be finished. Well, me at least."

"Then it doesn't get out."

He shook his head. "If it doesn't work out, or it gets awkward again..."

Bridget sat back down and smiled at him.

"It won't," she said.

"How do you know?"

"Because I love you. I've been hot for you since before I even worked here. It's why I came to work here."

He looked at her, trying to decide if she was kidding. "What? Are you joking?"

"No," she said quietly. "I'd been following your career. And I hoped on that first day I started that we'd end up together. Good to see you're finally on board."

"Wait, you're the one that said we should take some time."

"I know. But a woman likes to be pursued. You know, wanted."

"Please. No means no, right? Make up your mind. And it sounds like harassment, no matter how you say it. And not very modern."

"Whatever. And no amount of flirting or wearing cute outfits or cozying up to you seemed to matter. I just assumed you didn't like me after what happened in St. Louis. Or you had turned gay," she said with a smirk.

"No, not gay," he said, leaning forward. "Not that there's anything wrong with that," he smiled, quoting Seinfeld. "I'm careful. Reserved. There's a big difference."

"Tell me about it."

"Just trying to keep it professional. And failing, miserably. I tell you, I can't stop thinking about that trip to St. Louis. I can't believe how unprofessional I was, and then, at the same time, I wonder how I resisted you as long as I did."

"Nice to know you've been thinking about it."

"It's difficult to be around you, sometimes."

"The guy at the deli says the same thing."

Kevin smiled. "Funny. But do you feel it too, or was that like a one-time thing, caught up in the drinking and singing and the fact that we were out of town and alone?"

She glanced behind her to make sure the door was closed. Bridget walked around to his side of the desk and, again, he felt the air in the room warm. Or maybe it was just his face.

Bridget put a hand on his chair and slowly spun it around until he was facing her, then leaned over.

"You 'were' trying to keep it professional? As in past tense?"

Her face was close to his and he could smell her and it was pointless to lie to her for even another second.

"Yes," he said.

"And are we done with all that now?"

"Yes," he said.

She leaned in and kissed him hard on the mouth. It was the kind of kiss that had been building up for months. Moments later, Whitlowe had forgotten all about Dorothy or the fountains or the rest of the world.

CHAPTER 30
Found It

On Saturday, a few days later, Joe and Trapper were out again, searching. They'd spent too much of the last week together, and Hathaway was starting to get tired of both Trapper's company and the endless riding in the borrowed car.

And it seemed like they had already covered every single back road and rutted-out farm path in this part of the county. Trapper assured him there were "plenty more" places to see. They were getting down to the end of it. Joe could feel it in his bones, something that went against his calculating, efficient nature. They were almost done searching.

"That's three fields, two farms, and another three small family cemeteries, so far today," Trapper said. "We getting any closer?"

"Yes, we are," Joe said, impatient. "Show me these two cemeteries here," he said, pointing at the map. "And I don't need your sass."

"Sorry, boss."

Joe could tell that Trapper was scowling but he didn't care. This had to go perfectly and would require more planning than anything Joe had pulled off since setting up that ice cabin to sink last winter. That had taken more planning than killing Mercato or his stupid girlfriend.

But this plan? It had to go like clockwork.

They drove on, searching. The first cemetery was too close to a busy road, so that would not do. But they parked and got out anyway and walked through the copse of trees and between the lonely tombstones. They had seen quite a few over the past week, and Joe had taken to writing down the names of some of the people who had been put to rest in these lonely locations. Even though the cemeteries were nearly always surrounded by beautiful countryside, the plots themselves seemed sad, cold. An air of death hung over each patch of land.

He wondered, was that just his imagination running wild or did each of these cemeteries actually create some kind of "zone of unpleasantness" around them? If someone was brought here, blindfolded, would they too feel a sense of dread surrounding the place, or was it all in his head? He'd have to remember to ask Harper when they were wrapping things up.

"Okay, let's go," Joe said, heading back to the car. He didn't like to linger out in public—and he preferred to not linger in cemeteries.

They drove on, checking out another Church of Xavier property on the way. It was yet another small farmhouse, bought with the piles of tax-free money that flowed steadily into the church's coffers. Joe had thought he'd been smart, coming up with the whole "Keepers of Truth" organization to rally his supporters and keep them donating money to his defense, back when he'd been on trial.

But his scheme paled in comparison to religions and their ability to take in money tax free. And spend it, buying up property and other businesses and anything else they wanted. It might make sense for the big religions, but why did the federal government extend those protections to all "churches," no matter how legitimate? The Church of Xavier brought in piles of money, so much so that they struggled to move it all around. You know your church is doing well when you have to hire a big-name New York accountancy just to keep track of it.

And that didn't count the local money they were using for construction purposes. And moving that money through different accounts to hide the purchases. It was all like a beautiful dance.

"What do you think?"

Joe wasn't listening and looked up, drawing his attention back to what they were doing. The car was stopped, and Trapper was pointing.

"You wanted a field near a stand of trees," Trapper said, repeating something Joe had said days before. "The cemetery butts up into the tree area."

Joe turned and looked as Trapper was climbing out of the car. Joe saw a small cemetery, this one with a black fence and an arched sign over the only gate. The sign read "Donnelly" in rusted letters. Inside the fence was a small cemetery with several headstones in an overgrown plot.

"Ah, yes," Joe said with a smile as he got out of the car. This was perfect. It was a great little plot of land, and he could see legible names on the headstones. Several others were toppled over, face down in the scrub.

Joe heard Trapper rattle the map. "Beyond this, it's about a half an acre, all church property. The forest to the west is on the land, and there's a creek on the east side. There's also a hilly area to the north."

"A natural barrier."

Trapper nodded, putting one leg up on a tree stump and looking around. "It's got pretty good road access on this side, but it looks like it gets very wild back in there," he said, pointing at the forest beyond. "That's what you want, right?"

Joe walked slowly between the gravestones, nodding, taking it all in. There were several names on them, legible. Clues that could be meted out. Real names on headstones, real people. Better than anything he could have made up—but he would have to provide a back story. One huge piece of bait.

He turned and looked at Trapper.

"This part is perfect. Can we walk the forest?"

"I'll see if there's a trail."

Trapper walked around the fence and disappeared into the trees. While he was gone, Joe snapped photos of the headstones in the small plot.

When he came back, Trapper had good news.

"There's a game trail into the woods, heading east. Could lead all the way to the creek," he said, pointing at the map. "There are breaks in the trees so you can see north, up to this area, with a low hill that blocks access to the north. Not sure about this area to the south."

Joe followed the map and nodded. "This will do nicely, I think. Can we get golf carts through there?"

"No, I don't think so," Trapper said, making a face. "But I saw the church has some of those off-road utility vehicles. I think they're called Gators. John Deere makes them. They hold two people. Big tires, so they should work."

Joe thought about it for a moment and then smiled. "Good. And I need a good map of the whole area, including any issues."

"I can get a couple other guys to help clear brush, make some paths," Trapper nodded. "One thing I did notice is that it's not as thick as this photo," he said, waving the picture. "This is probably from the summer, and a lot of the trees back in there have lost most of their leaves."

This location could work. In a day or two, Joe would know for sure, but this was the closest he'd come to finding the perfect location. Now, he needed a plan. One that would get Frank Harper out here. Not yet, of course—Joe wasn't ready yet.

Then they needed to prep the area. And Joe couldn't underestimate

Harper. The guy was like a rat—he could escape nearly anything.

And after Frank was dead, Joe would need to make sure things didn't come back on him or Trapper or the church. Depending on the situation—and the amount of damage Harper displayed—they could dispose of the body in one of many ways.

Then there was Harper's car. Joe couldn't forget that. He wanted it bad—Harper had chased him in that car, causing Joe's nearly fatal accident. Joe wanted it as a prize. A trophy, like one of his shooting awards, or Mercato's body in his garage freezer. Trapper could change the plates, and then Joe could take Harper's car out west. Finally get away from everything. And the car would be his trophy, the ultimate proof that Joe had won.

Yeah, that sounded perfect.

CHAPTER 31
HarvestFest 2012

Frank was starting to think he'd never solve this stupid case.

It was Saturday, late afternoon, October 25. It had turned colder outside, and he was at the Tip Top Diner, going through the latest set of notes he'd gotten from the kid he had working undercover at the Tool and Die shop. Nothing interesting, and nothing that moved the ball down the field.

He sighed and closed his notebook, rubbing his eyes.

"You okay, Frank?"

He looked up to see Rosa, one of the newer waitresses. She lived on some large farm commune north-east of Cooper's Mill and always talked his leg off. She had come from Mexico last year and was affiliated with something called the Church of Xavier. Frank wasn't in the mood for a long conversation with her tonight, plus he had another appointment to keep.

"Yeah, Rosa, I'm fine. This case is killing me."

"More coffee?"

"No, that's okay," he said. "Can you cash me out?" He'd stopped in to enjoy a late lunch—which had turned out to be breakfast food, with coffee—on his way home.

Home. It wasn't really home, was it?

"*Si*, I'll cash you right out."

"Thanks," he said, handing her the check and his cash. "Just keep it."

"Thanks, Frank," she said. Her accent said northern Mexico, and it made him smile. He remembered back in the day in the New Orleans Police Department (NOPD), when he heard dozens of different accents on every shift.

But he'd come to Tip Top Diner to give Laura some space on this busy Saturday. She'd said the downtown was hopping ahead of the HarvestFest 2012 event tonight, and he'd gotten the sense that she would enjoy a few hours at home alone with Jackson, her son.

It was good Frank would only be living there a few more days. Now that he had his key, he kept driving by the new apartment. Technically he wasn't supposed to move in until November 1, but Jake Delancy had given him permission to start moving things over early. Frank had already taken over three loads of boxes and was looking forward to more trips.

Standing, he gathered his items and headed outside, getting waves from half of the staff. They loved him here. God forbid they ever tore this place down. Where would he work?

Frank drove downtown, watching carefully for kids out walking. It was Beggar's Night, the weird name that Ohioans used for the night when kids (and a few adults) went out in costume and did the whole "trick or treat" thing. Apparently, all the towns around here called it that.

When he'd asked why, someone had mentioned that it had a religious connotation, as if calling it "Halloween" or "trick or treat" was somehow evil. He knew the name came from "All Hallow's Eve," but he didn't see the point of trying to pretend it wasn't Halloween by calling it something else.

Carefully, he navigated the streets of Cooper's Mill, heading slowly across the tracks and into the historic downtown. The streets were packed with kids and adults in a dizzying array of costumes, visiting the shops and homes that were handing out candy. He drove slowly through the historic downtown shopping district and passed Second Street, which was closed south of Main. He saw cops loitering in front of a set of tents in the road that read HARVESTFEST 2012. Driving on, he circled the downtown streets until he found a place to park.

Walking through downtown, Frank was starting to get used to living here and was finally able to recognize some of the people. A few nodded and waved, and one pair of young women shrieked as they ran past him, hurrying off on some adventure.

He got to the HarvestFest location and smiled as both of the cops nodded at him. Frank got in line with a bunch of people in costumes and wondered if he should've dressed up. Off the top of his head, he couldn't even guess at what kind of costume he'd be interested in. The thought had never occurred to him. Frank was only here for the music and to support the downtown.

Plus, he'd made a point of remembering. Last year, on this very night, he'd been investigating a nearby property and had been jumped and knocked out. He remembered hearing the sounds of distant music. This year, he wanted to relax and just enjoy the show.

Frank got to the front of the line and handed over his $10.

"No costume?" The young woman looked at him with a smile.

"Not this time."

"That's okay," she said. "You've brought your own costume."

He looked at her. "What?"

"Oh, you're dressed as Jessica Mills' bodyguard. Right?"

He smiled at being recognized. "Sure."

She smiled as he moved down the line to the next tent, where they were checking IDs. The people behind the counter—it was just a folding table decorated with beakers and bubbling science equipment—carded him as they were carding everyone. A young woman in a scientist costume wrapped his wrist in a red band.

"Now, don't take that off if you want to drink."

"I won't."

It was weird, being recognized like that. Most people treated him normally, and then, every once in a while, someone would act strangely starstruck. It was strange.

He bought beer tickets from the "scientist girl"—she giggled and whispered something to her friend, who looked at Frank and her eyes went wide. He scurried away with his tickets—they had been 3 for $20, a little steep but well worth it to support the local community group that was putting on the shindig. They were the Downtown Cooper's Mill Partnership, a group that, according to the brochure he'd been handed, were dedicated to "preserving and promoting" the historic downtown area.

Well, as far as Frank could tell, they were doing a good job.

The HarvestFest 2012 concert and party tent took up the entire block of Second Street from Main all the way down to Dow Street, running in front of several shops and a pizza place and some homes. The stage bisected the street at the alley halfway between Main and Dow, the huge stage facing north. Behind it, Frank could see several food trucks and some smaller tents, probably for the bands.

The whole area was fenced off by orange plastic hurricane fencing. They had decorated all the light poles in the downtown with corn shocks, and on this stretch of road, they'd done them up with big spiders and fake webbing. There were three booths along one brick wall, one for beer and, at another, a man dressed as a mad scientist was giving out shots of some kind of alcohol in what looked like plastic test tubes.

The whole scene was festive, electric. It was great to see adults out on the town, drinking and having fun together. The band on the stage launched into another cover of some 1980s song, getting the crowd dancing. Frank got a beer and stood off to the side. Dancing was a young person's hobby, and he was happy to sit back and admire all the young ladies in their costumes.

"Harper? What are you doing here?"

He turned to see Chief King, who was dressed as Jack Skellington, that weird gangly skeleton from the kid's movie. It was hard to even tell who it was inside the large round costume head, but Frank knew the voice and nodded.

"Chief!" he yelled over the music. "Here for fun or keeping an eye on things?"

"Both, really," Chief King said, leaning closer. "Thanks again for what you did with Jessica Mills. That's really upped our profile. I've heard about it from every other police chief in the area. People are taking me out to lunch to hear the stories."

Frank nodded, knowing it was better than speaking. The band wrapped up a song and there was a momentary respite.

"Remember last year? Wasn't this the night you got kidnapped?"

"Don't remind me," Frank said, as if it weren't fresh in his mind. "If I drink too much, you might find me out at Freeman's Prairie again."

King shook his head. "Not funny, Frank. Besides, I thought you were off the stuff," he said, nodding his giant head at Frank's glass.

"Just celebrating your cute little town."

Chief King started to say something when a woman dressed as Sally, also from *The Nightmare Before Christmas*," squealed and ran up and threw her arms around Chief King. It took a second for Frank to recognize Lola, the dispatcher who worked at the police station. She started to kiss the giant white head the chief was wearing but then realized who Frank was and stopped.

"Frank, you know Lola, right?"

Frank nodded and smiled. "Matching costumes?"

"Oh, we just worked it out at work," she said, looking away. Frank looked at the chief, who also happened to be looking away at the moment. It took Frank about a half of a second to figure out the situation. They were dating, though why they were out here risking being caught, he had no idea. Of course, King hadn't taken off his head—maybe he was counting on staying anonymous. Frank didn't really care—to each his own.

"Okay, Frank, we're gonna circulate," the chief said, grabbing

Lola's elbow. "See you around!"

Frank nodded at him and Lola and turned to see the band launch into another song. Frank smiled and wondered how long the chief and his employee had been dating. What were the rules on all of that nowadays? He had no idea.

It was nice to be thinking about something else, nice to take a night off from both of his cases, each of which nagged at him in a different way. The Anderson Tool & Die case was going nowhere, and Joe Hathaway had floated away down a river and disappeared.

Nothing could be done on either of them tonight.

Frank stayed for two more hours, watching all three bands and enjoying all three beers. He was tempted to have more but decided against it. Nothing would make Laura angrier then having to come bail him out of jail. Plus, a DUI would threaten his private investigator's license.

But he was sure looking forward to having his own place. Soon, he'd be able to sit back with a beer—or something stronger—and relax after a hard day's work. Laura wouldn't be there to scowl at him. And his new place was located near a liquor store, so he could just walk over and buy a single beer if he wanted to.

Frank was pretty sure he could handle having his own place now and handle the ability to manage his drinking at home. Living with Laura had really helped him keep it in check, and now he planned to apply that same "slow and steady" approach at his new apartment.

CHAPTER 32
Prep It

Over the next few days, Joe and his posse got to work, scouting out the area that was apparently known as Donnelly Woods. It had been part of a larger farm area, but the agricultural land had been sold off to another farmer and the Donnelly home torn down. It had stood facing the road, with a large, fenced backyard that encompassed a small area of the woods. A trail had led from the back of the fence to the cemetery and larger wooded area.

All that remained was the small forest and the tiny cemetery. The gravel parking area was what was left of the home—apparently, after it was torn down, the previous landowner had poured gravel to cover the remains of the home's foundation. Everyone in the graveyard had been a member of the Donnelly clan or married into it or related in some way. Back in the "olden days," families and small towns operated their own small private graveyards. And now, a hundred years later, it was all that was left of their legacy—some fallen stones and a rusty fence.

Joe and Trapper got to work, recruiting four of Xavier's men (with his permission, of course) and three John Deere Gator vehicles. They transported the Gators on a borrowed flatbed trailer to Donnelly Woods and offloaded them, then began mapping out the woods.

After a day of driving around in the rain, they had a good idea of the layout: north side was the cliff face, where Joe had identified a few great sniper positions; west was the road and the graveyard; the east side was edged by a stream—not a large river, like he would have preferred, but it would work; and then, to the south, the forest got thicker and thicker before ending at a large blue body of water, an old quarry. Inside the perimeter, the forest itself was perfect, sizable but cut through with animal paths and numerous clearings.

Driving one of the Gators, Joe was alone now, scouting the central path. He'd had some of it cleared back and hopped out every once in a while to wield one of the large machetes they were using to cut down brush and clear the trails.

Now, the central path had been widened and it connected the two largest clearings—he'd named the western one "King" and the easterly one "Queen." There was a sizable clearing to the south, which he had dubbed "Knight," which overlooked the weird white/blue water in the empty quarry. Another small clearing to the north was named "Bishop." Trapper had drawn a map that displayed the various locations along with the connecting trails. Trapper had duplicated the map and placed laminated copies in all of the Gators.

But it was the "Rooks" that would require the most planning. Those were Joe's three spots, all aligned along the north edge of the forest and elevated so he could get a good view down into the forest—and would be free to line up a great shot with a sniper's rifle. They were numbered left to right on the map, with Rook 1 closest to the cemetery. Rooks 2 and 3 were on the cliff face to the east. All of them needed to be set up ahead of time, and he was counting on them to be perfect.

He'd already visited Rook 1 this Monday morning, taking pictures, and now he was headed to Rooks 2 and 3 to continue clearing brush around them and scout out areas around them. Those two had the best views down into the forest, and he'd need guns for both.

He'd asked Trapper and the two church men helping him to set the Rooks up as blinds, camouflaged hunting spots with clear views of the terrain, along with food and water. The Rook positions would afford Joe the ability to hunker down and wait things out in hiding, just in case something went wrong.

Just in case Harper escaped or somehow turned the tables on Joe.

Driving the Gator, Joe reminded himself that he needed to plan this out to the tiniest detail. There could be no wiggle room. Joe had already had a few discussions with Trapper along those lines, and he was already hard at work coming up with some solutions that might involve the church and some of their commercial operations. Things were already moving in the right direction.

But Harper was good at making things up as he went. The old cop could take any bad situation and somehow turn it to his advantage. Of course, that was probably part of being a cop—they learned how to read a situation and react in real-time. It kept them alive.

Joe had some ideas percolating in his mind. He wanted to make this a real hunt, with real consequences, but he wasn't stupid enough to give Harper any chance of escaping with his life. No, Joe was getting ready for the biggest hunt of his life. And, this time, his success would be complete.

CHAPTER 33
New Case

At the same time Joe was driving around on his Gator, making plans and getting things all set up for his great game, Frank Harper was back in his "office" at the Tip Top Diner. While Joe crawled around in the dirt, setting up his blind, Frank was enjoying coffee and a Western omelet.

Frank was meeting with Travis again, this time for breakfast. The kid had yet to come up with anything from his time at Anderson Tool & Die company.

Travis sat back from his plate of pancakes—well, it wasn't anything but an empty plate now. The kid ate like he'd never had food in his life, and was skinny as a rail. He reminded Frank of Tavon—of course, at their age, it was easier for kids to stay skinny.

"Wow, that was good, Mr. Harper," Travis said with a smile. "And thanks again. I don't usually pig out like that," he said as Doris, the waitress, stopped, dropping off two more fresh cups of coffee.

"Fresh cups," she said.

"Thanks," Frank said. Frank knew that most times, the staff here at the diner brought around the coffee pot, but every once in a while, they brought fresh cups full of coffee. If there was a particular pattern to it, Frank hadn't figured it out yet.

"Glad you liked it."

"But I don't feel like I deserve it, really. I'm not getting you anything good at Anderson, am I? Nothing but routine, back-office gossip."

"You never know...gossip can be very helpful."

Travis shrugged, something he did a lot. "I guess. But I want to be a cop, right? I figured there would be files to go through, or a group of workers I'd need to cozy up to. So far, I'm just doing my job and keeping my ears open."

"Not exciting enough for you?" Frank asked, adding cream and then sipping from his fresh cup.

"Yeah, yeah," Travis said, looking at the table. "I don't mean to me ungrateful."

"Well, the next time I have a foot chase through downtown Cooper's Mill, I'll call you."

"Really?"

"No."

Travis smiled. "What you're doing is pretty cool, too. Being a P.I. Do you like it?"

Frank made a face and put his coffee down. It was rare anyone asked him that, and he thought about it for a second.

"Yeah, I think I do. It's like being a cop, but without all the drudge work. You know? Reports, filing stuff with the state and Feds, and answering to a boss that sits in the office all day long playing SimCity 2000."

"You've got a concealed carry, obviously," Travis said, nodding at the gun in its holster that Joe kept on the seat next to him. "But is it hard getting cases? Paying the bills?"

"We'll see. I'm just getting started. Anything else from Anderson?"

Travis shook his head and finished his coffee in two big sips. He might be a young kid, but he was smart enough to know the meeting was over.

"No, just those three guys that I'm pretty sure are running some kind of racket with the 3D printers. I think they're using them for outside work."

"I'll look into that," Frank said. "And remember: just doing your job and keeping your head down? That IS the job. You don't have a weapon, and we have no idea who at Anderson is involved in the larger theft that Jill—Ms. Anderson—has us investigating. You need to get out of this in one piece. You do that, I'll talk to Chief King."

Travis looked at him and nodded. "Thank you. That would be great."

The kid slid out of the booth, heading out the doors without even looking back. He was smart and seemed to enjoy the undercover work.

Of course, you could never tell when things were going to turn exciting. That was part of the job. One minute you're walking through a parking lot after touring a condo under construction, and the next, you were waking up in a field on fire. And you are tied up, and luck out by finding a box of paperwork that happens to contain a pair of scissors.

Sometimes, you just got lucky.

Frank spent a few minutes checking his email and was just packing up his things when the little bell that hung in front of the front door of the restaurant rang. Frank looked up instinctually. He probably couldn't avoid looking up, even if he tried. It was just part of his DNA, like always sitting facing the door. It just came naturally. Why would anyone sit with their back to the door anyway?

He was surprised to see Chief King walking into the Tip Top Diner. He'd never seen the chief—or any other cops, for that matter—in the diner, except for the one whose wife worked here. Frank and that cop had gotten into a little scrape and Frank had put the cop on his ass. That had been one of Frank's first encounters with the CMPD, and didn't go well for the cop. They say you only get one chance to make a first impression, and that one was a doozy.

The chief looked out of place in the restaurant, decked in his uniform and far too official for a place with wallpaper from the 1970s.

King walked in and took off his sunglasses and looked around slowly, taking in the whole space with one practiced glance. Situational awareness, they called it, something cops naturally did when they entered a new space. Identify the people inside, any exits, any threats. He'd probably counted the number of cars parked outside to get a sense of how many people were inside eating.

That's what Frank did—without even really thinking about it.

Frank's stomach sank. He knew what this conversation would be about, and it wouldn't be good. He'd been expecting the call from the chief. "Hi, Frank, yeah, can you not mention that you saw me and Lola at HarvestFest? See, we're keeping it quiet..."

Might as well get the awkward conversation over with.

"Hey, Chief," Frank said, waving him over.

King looked over the low wall that separated the waiting area from the first row of booths. Seeing Frank, he nodded, and then nodded at the waitress as well. It came naturally, knowing where everyone was located. Checking the exits. Doing a quick scan of the interior. After a few seconds, Chief King slid into the booth across from Frank. Before either of them could even say anything, Doris appeared as if by magic.

"Need something?"

"Just coffee, thanks," Chief King said, nodding at the cup in front of Frank.

The waitress disappeared and Frank looked at the chief.

"So, what do I owe the pleasure?" Frank asked, sure of the answer. "I never see you in here."

Chief King looked around and leaned back. "I heard this is your office. Booth #3, right?"

"Yup, most of the time."

"You gettin' your mail here yet?"

"Just about. They're cool," Frank said, nodding at the waitress delivering a coffee for the chief. "They let me hang out all day, and the coffee is great."

"Heard you're getting your own place?"

Frank smiled. "Word gets around, huh?"

"Welcome to Cooper's Mill," King said.

"I thought you might be checking in with me on the Anderson Tool & Die case."

"How's that going?"

"Good, good. All right, it's not going anywhere," Frank said, shaking his head. Chief King and his department had been involved in earlier versions of the same investigations, of course. Frank had already sat down with King and his men, reviewing things. There had been nothing to investigate with the man's death—it was a simple hit and run. No one came through with any leads, and after checking the vehicles of everyone who worked at Anderson—and coming up with nothing—the CMPD had ended their investigation.

Their pursuit of the missing money actually took longer, and the case had stayed on the CMPD books for several months before being closed.

"Well, we couldn't find anything there, as you know," Chief King said. "You're looking into the CFOs, right? Something about the one we investigated didn't sit right."

"Oh?"

"Yeah. I mean, we looked into him, of course. Billingsly, I think his name was. Money was going missing on his watch, but it wasn't him, that was certain. And he didn't have a new Porsche."

Frank smiled. "Too bad. I love it when they're dumb."

"It does make them easier to catch," the chief agreed.

He looked at the chief. "Why can't we just investigate the stupid ones?"

King nodded. "That would make my job a little easier."

"I don't know what Jill Anderson wants more—the money back, or answers about what happened to her father."

"Nothing happened to her father, I'd wager," King said, sitting back. "Hit and run. Nothing exotic about it. Nothing ever came back on forensics, or the paint transfer to the body."

"Yeah, white car."

"Really narrows it down, right? Anyway, glad you're looking into it. I hope you prove us wrong."

"We'll, we'll see," Frank said. "I've got a couple of accountants going through all the books now. Laura, my daughter, and a guy I know."

"Laura—she was friends with Peters, right?"

Frank nodded. He knew enough not to say anything else. Chief King was still smarting over the death of his cousin, a young man named Peters that the chief had personally brought onto the CMPD. The deputy had paired up with Frank on a couple of cases, and, unfortunately, tragically died in the line of duty during their last run-in with the infamous Joe Hathaway.

An awkward silence descended over the table. Not wanting to seem callous, or cruel, or insufficiently honoring Peters' memory, Frank decided to drink more coffee and wait out the man across the table. When the next words out of his mouth weren't about his relationship with Lola, it was a surprise.

"Look, I might have a case for you," Chief King finally said. "It's an old one, but I've been hearing rumblings about it," King said. "We looked at it in 1997, back when it happened. Huge case in the area, with a couple of local connections. Came up with nothing. And we got a couple of tips over the last day or so. Not just us—social media stuff, too."

Frank was intrigued. "Cold case?"

"Yup, your specialty," King said with a smile as the waitress set a new coffee and some creamers down in front on him. "Thank you. Yeah, we don't really have the manpower to do a deep dive. I was going to call in the Ohio Investigative Bureau, a branch of the State Patrol, but I figured I'd give you a crack at it first."

Chief King began recounting the details of the case, and Frank grabbed his notebook and started taking notes.

It was a missing person's case, a woman and her young daughter, both named Masterson. They went missing on the same evening back in 1997, disappearing from a home in Cooper's Mill. The husband was out of town at the time and later cleared of any involvement.

"The mother and daughter just up and disappeared," King said, sipping at his coffee. "I called a couple of the old timers who worked the Masterson case—both are long retired, of course, but they remembered it well. I pulled our files for you," King said, pushing a file across the table. "It's a copy of the original case file from Columbus—that's where they go to get stored. It was on microfiche—remember that stuff?"

"All too well," Frank answered, flipping through the file. "So, what brought it back up?"

"Calls to the library downtown two days ago, if you can believe it," King said. He leaned back so the waitress could refill his coffee. "Someone apparently read up on the case and contacted Mrs. Havers, one of the librarians. The guy on the phone was some writer, doing research for a book on the Masterson case. He faxed her photos from a cemetery down north of Cincinnati—this person thought they found two unmarked graves that matched the case. But we had the Cinci locals check them yesterday. They didn't match—police records show the graves are from 1989."

"So, a bust?"

"So far. But it got the librarian thinking, and now she's hot on the case. You should talk to her—she's scouring the internet for more potential graves in cemeteries around the state and even over in Indiana. She's convinced that, given the unique nature of the case, finding a grave or at least a headstone might give people closure."

Frank glanced through the file—it was a standard missing person's file from fifteen years ago. He'd seen a thousand files just like this one during his time working cold cases in Alabama.

"I'll go through it and get back to you with any questions," Frank said. "And I'll chat with the librarian."

"Be careful—I think she might be sweet on you."

"What? How? I've never been in there."

"Haven't you heard? You're famous, my friend. We good?"

Frank nodded and patted the file. "And thanks for the case."

"No problem. And, for the record, there's no reward or anything. Just you, donating your time."

"Got it."

Frank watched as King stood, dropped a couple of dollars on the table, and walked out the door, waving at Doris as he left.

"Have a good one," he said to her.

Frank saw the few other people in the restaurant watch as the chief left—it was always amazing how nervous people got around cops. Or maybe it wasn't amazing—more likely it was just sad. There were a lot of good cops out there, but there were a few bad apples running around as well. People were wary of the cops and the power they wielded.

Frank needed to head home, but instead got another cup of coffee and tucked into the folder on the Masterson case. Frank sorted the old, thin papers into stacks as he'd done on a thousand cases before this one. Witness reports, information on the missing women, location maps from the home where the women were abducted. It was a new puzzle, the kind Frank loved. He stayed at the Tip Top Diner for nearly another hour, scouring the documents and scribbling notes in his journal.

CHAPTER 34
Tavon Does the Books

Tavon ignored the looks he was getting from the rest of the people in the library and concentrated on his work. Or maybe he was just imagining it. People knew he used to run with the Northsiders. If you were looking for drugs or girls or wanted to lay some money on a b-ball game, you loved the gangs. They satisfied the needs of the locals. But they weren't for everyone.

It had been a week since he'd seen the old cop, Frank Harper, and Tavon had spent the time digging through the files on the USB flash drive he'd gotten.

It was mostly the years' worth of financials on the company up in Cooper's Mill, a place called Anderson Tool & Die. Just a regular company, making metal parts and fabricating a hundred different kinds of metal products. They'd recently gotten into 3D milling and CNC machines, using Computer Numerical Control or computer-guided equipment to carve parts out of blocks of aluminum, parts for aerospace, automotive, railroad and other industries.

It was all fascinating.

Tavon sat at a computer in the library on North Dixie, a few blocks from his sister's grooming place, going over screen after screen of accounting entries from Anderson Tool & Die. He had another spreadsheet of his own open on his laptop in front of the computer screen, going back and forth between the two screens. The need for multiple screens—and the increase in efficiency that they provided—had been the incentive he'd needed to finally swallow his pride and set up at the library. Two screens meant he could compare data without switching back and forth or making separate notes. Plus, the screens at the library were huge.

Harper had given him an interesting puzzle to solve, and Tavon was digging in. He'd been through all the financial documents already, twice, making notes on the various accounts and where money was coming from and going to. It was all similar to the Northsiders books, except that nearly all of the gang's transactions had been in cash.

For Anderson Tool & Die, all their money was tied up in inventory, as it had been to some extent with the Northsiders. But Anderson had lots of equipment, as well, and some of it was being replaced on a very aggressive schedule. Too aggressive, as far as Tavon could tell, to be explained logically. After his first night of research, he'd emailed Harper with a list of questions, to which the old man had responded "I have no idea. And there's no one I can ask without tipping our hand that we're investigating. Can you research online?"

Sure, I can research online, man, Tavon had thought at the time. I can do all the research you want on the industry and pricing and contracts.

"Sure, I can do that," he'd written. "But that won't help with specific decisions that were made at Anderson. Or get me part numbers or the equipment specs."

"No kidding," Harper had emailed back. "Assume we won't get those answers."

So now, Tavon was making his own list of separate questions for a later investigation. Questions that a forensic auditor—or the IRS— would want answers to.

It was a big deal, Harper bringing Tavon in to help. The ex-cop surely had all kinds of people he could call on, right? Why reach out and help a young black kid? Was it charity? Or did Harper really think Tavon could offer a unique insight, or bring something new to the table that any old regular forensic accountant would not?

The more Tavon thought about it, the more he liked working for Harper.

And it also made sense. Tavon was used to working with criminals. Since Harper was looking for evidence of theft, or possibly even murder, it made sense to bring in people who could help him spot criminal intent. Or at least people who wouldn't immediately discount a particular accounting idea because it wasn't legal. No, Harper needed ex-criminals if he had a chance in hell of catching actual criminals.

Another reason Tavon was at the library was because he had a bunch of stuff to print out. They didn't have a printer at home or one at the grooming place, so he'd paid for a card that allowed him to use the printer and got started.

On his screen, Tavon had the tabulated entries for all the equipment that Anderson Tool & Die had purchased over the last eight years. Unfortunately, they didn't use logical "names" for the equipment.

Instead, as if to make it as confusing as possible, all the equipment at the facility was referred to only by part number. Those numbers, long strings of letters and numbers, sometimes didn't match up with the equipment purchased or the invoices that were being submitted by the companies from which the items were purchased.

He'd texted Harper more questions, but the old man told him to hold his inquiries until they could get together. Harper also said he had his daughter working on the books as well. Instantly, that had put Tavon into a funk—he assumed the daughter was doing the "real" work and Tavon was just doing backup or unimportant work. But then Harper had continued, saying that Laura, Harper's daughter, was going through all the background financial checks on all employees and their available finances, looking for weirdness.

"You're doing the accounts and equipment side of things," Harper had typed in their text conversation.

So, Tavon had lots of work to do. He'd completed the inventory and was now nearly finished with the day-to-day books of the place, meaning the last few years of sales and purchase numbers. Those were easy to follow, and easy to track. Order comes in, items are collected or built or created from raw materials. Finally, the finished products are shipped out the door with a piece of paper that says what it is, what it cost, and who is paying for it.

All very straightforward.

Those were easy to follow. It was like the drugs side of the Northsiders business: incoming ingredients, manufacturing, outgoing product. Easy to follow, and easy to find "shrinkage," the industry terminology for "losses" that occurred during any manufacturing or sales process. Other companies called it "breakage" or some different term, but they all meant the same thing: stuff going missing, either from waste or theft.

And it seemed like Anderson had way too much shrinkage.

Tavon was still searching for some industry-wide numbers on the amount of loss expected from something like design, automation, and assembly of appliance parts, but it felt like Anderson's numbers were all out of whack.

When he was done reviewing the losses, Tavon needed to compare those to the information he'd been provided on the physical inventories of the Anderson facilities, including purchased and sold equipment. He needed to get it all out on paper and organize it so it made sense. How could companies like this have so much inventory and then not use a logical, easy-to-follow system to track it? It was almost like modern inventory systems were designed to encourage theft.

Tavon still needed to mark up his printouts of all the inventories, and then search for duplicate entries or copies of other entries with minor changes. And he'd already started creating separate spreadsheet files with what all the inventory items were called—and which ones he suspected could be duplicates.

He'd also started making a list of names. There were employees connected to each purchase, of course, and some of the same names kept popping up over and over. He crosschecked those names with a list the old man had passed along, and it started to make sense: some names were past CFOs, so they were probably signing off on big purchases. It was logical.

Of course, there was no way to prove any of the duplicate pieces of inventory actually existed without a physical inventory of the equipment on the factory floor. And even that might not tell the whole story—some of the equipment had been removed or replaced over the last few years, so those numbers and pieces of equipment were long gone.

"Hey, man, whatcha doing?"

Tavon turned and saw Wasson, a guy from the neighborhood. Wasson had managed to stay clear of the Northsiders and other gangs and worked as a roofer for a company over in Union, Ohio.

"Working," Tavon said, turning from the library PC. He had the spreadsheets up on his screens but didn't bother covering them up or anything. He doubted Wasson would know what they were, or care.

"Workin, huh? Accounting stuff?" he said, nodding at the columns of numbers on Tavon's screens. "I heard you ran the numbers for the Northsiders."

"No, didn't run numbers with their gambling arm, or anything like that—"

"Sorry, man," Wasson said, putting his hands up. "I don't know what it's called when you do accounting for someone. No clue."

"Oh," Tavon said, relaxing. "Doing their books, usually."

"That ain't the same as running numbers?"

Tavon smiled, shaking his head. "No."

"Oh, okay. Gotcha. So you an accountant now? Doing books for people?"

He glanced around as two other people walked past, then looked back at Wasson. "Yeah, I guess I am. A friend asked me to help with his company. They're thinking someone is stealing."

"What? That sounds cool. Good to see you, man," Wasson said, and they did a fist bump thing that felt weird and awkward.

"Yeah, good," Tavon said.

Wasson went off into the library with a wave. He was always in a great mood despite the fact that he had a horrible job that forced him to work outside in the hot Dayton summers. Or maybe that was why he was in a good mood all the time. There were worse things than putting in a real day's work.

It reminded Tavon of what he'd been thinking about a few days ago, about how everyone is so busy doing their own thing that he doubted they were spending a lot of time thinking about him or what he was working on. Wasson couldn't care less, other than he'd figured out that Tavon was doing accounting for someone. No judgements, no questions, just pleased to see Tavon busy with work.

It was the same with his mother and sisters. They had been very excited to hear about Tavon working on something to do with accounting, and that he was helping on a new "job," especially one that paid. But that was their interest pretty much ended. He'd been asked about the case a few other times in the days since Harper had showed up at the groomers, but after that, they didn't press him for more information.

And it was fun, he had to admit. Getting back to doing accounting, even for a different client and a wholly different purpose, felt good.

CHAPTER 35
Sandy

Late Tuesday, Frank was back at Laura's place, taking a break from packing and taking carloads of boxes and other stuff over to his new place. He also had a bunch of furniture in storage—all the stuff he'd brought up from Birmingham—but none of that could go into his new place until he was "officially" moved in.

For now, just clearing out all his clothes and the dozens of boxes he'd been storing around her place was enough. Her apartment was starting to look bigger, and his stress levels were going down. He hated being a burden.

The two of them were also supposed to be getting together to talk about the Anderson case, but Laura was spending her time watching the television. Hurricane Sandy, a late-season storm, had been barreling up the East Coast, threatening coastal cities over the last week. Today the storm had taken a sharp left turn in the Atlantic and now was headed directly for the New York City and New Jersey coastline.

All the television stations were doing round-the-clock coverage of the storm, the first hurricane to approach New York City proper in decades. Hurricane-force winds were battering Long Island, and storm surges were flooding parts of the battery and other coastal areas in New York City. At one point, JFK airport reported a wind gust of 79 miles per hour.

Obviously, all eyes were glued on the storm and the forecasters tracking it.

Frank was keeping his head down. He scribbled notes, updating the Anderson case first in case Laura wanted to take a break from the storm coverage and talk about it.

But Frank's mind kept being pulled back to the disappearance of that woman and her daughter, the new case that Chief King had approached him with. Even as he was noting down the new and completely useless information he'd gotten from his informant, Travis, Frank kept thinking about the other case.

He made a note in his journal to go speak to Mrs. Havers, the librarian at the Coopers Mill library downtown. She might know more about the case, and she could tell him more about this author who had contacted her. Supposedly, he'd uncovered some new facts.

In Frank's experience, that's the way most cold cases worked: nobody knew anything for the longest time, and then suddenly there was a weird change, or a break, or someone found something in an old family bible or an ancestry website. And, with that one tiny, seemingly insignificant change, a cold case that had sat for decades would end up being solved.

Laura got up from the couch and walked over.

"Hey Dad, what are you doing?"

"Going over some of the numbers on the Anderson case. Do you have any interest in sitting down and talking about that, or do you wanna keep watching the coverage."

"Actually, I could use the distraction." She pointed at the TV. "Now they're getting reports of damage up as far north as Canada. Ontario and Quebec are getting ready."

Frank shook his head. "Landfall?"

"They're not sure yet, but they're thinking New Jersey. Sometime overnight or in the morning? So, do you want to talk about the case?"

"Yeah, if you do."

"Let me make a tea first," she said, disappearing into the kitchen. Jackson had already had his bath and was in bed, and Frank noticed how much she always seemed to relax after he was asleep. It was understandable, of course—and it had been that way with him and Trudy, he suddenly remembered. Having little kids was exhausting.

Frank suddenly remembered an area of investigation that he'd completely forgotten: Chief King's case files for their original Anderson investigations. Of course, Frank had been through all the files. He'd met with King after accepting the case, and Frank had interviewed everyone who was still around who had any kind of involvement in the original investigation. King had brought it up again today, making small talk at the Tip Top Diner. But there was something else that he'd said, something that seemed to not line up with—.

Laura came back in and he moved the papers around to makemade some room on the table for her drink, some kind of tea. It smelled sweet.

"So, what did you find out about the employees?"

"Not a lot, really," she said, sitting down. "But I did notice there were some patterns in the way they interacted with each other."

"What do you mean?"

She started to explain, and he sat back and listened, occasionally asking questions or jotting things down in his notebook. She had gone through the available finances of all of the employees that he could gather through his background checks.

"Nothing out of the ordinary, really. Of course, you said all of these accounts were from the background checks. But if someone was hiding something, would it show up in the normal accounts?"

"Only if the people are idiots," Frank said, smiling. "Most criminals are smart enough to create separate accounts or hide them in some way. But some people are stupid and get caught when they steal money and then drop it into their regular, day-to-day checking accounts."

"Hmm," Laura said. She continued, explaining how some of the people at work were more frugal while others seemed to spend money like it was going out of style. "I'm assuming that's just how people are, right? Savers and spenders."

Frank nodded, jotting down the names she had mentioned.

"Have you met with your other accountant friend again?"

He shook his head. "Tavon? No, we've been texting back and forth, and he's already asking questions that are too complicated for me. If you're okay with it, I'm gonna have all of us get together. We need some quiet space to work in, uninterrupted." He had a thought. "Does the library downtown have meeting rooms you can borrow?"

"I think so," she said.

He rummaged into his pocket and took out a USB flash drive, handing it over.

"Okay, that's an updated copy of all the files I gave Tavon. It's the same as the one I gave you last week, but with some updated tables on the employees' compensation packages. I'd like you to look through them as well, and BEFORE you and he talk. Two sets of eyes, digging for anything that looks hinky, okay?"

She took the USB and nodded. "Glad to help."

Frank really hoped that between the two of them, Laura and Tavon would find something to break this case, because he wasn't having any luck.

"What's that," Laura asked, pointing at the printouts of the Masterson missing person's case.

"Oh, Chief King came to see me today. Might have another case. I haven't decided officially yet, but it's interesting."

"He came to your 'office?'" Laura asked, smiling and making air quotes.

"Yup. Hey, it's either the diner or a borrowed conference room at the library. Or I bring people back here. By the way, I need to stop in there anyway tomorrow to meet with a woman about this case," he said, tapping the Masterson files. "I'll get us a room and text Tavon."

She nodded, telling him what times she was available over the next few days.

"You know, it's going to be very weird, not having you around here," she said, glancing around her place. "I'll have to make an appointment to see you."

"Never," he said, grabbing her hand. "And thank you. Thank you for letting me crash here, for sure, but also thank you for letting me spend some time with you and Jackson. It's been...really, it's been nice."

She smiled and squeezed his hand. "No problem. Okay, I'll leave you to it." She stood and went back to the television, switching channels to find the latest update, and Frank went back to his files.

The Masterson case was somewhat famous, based on a few quick internet searches. It was no wonder the author was looking into it. In fact, the case was famous enough to be listed on several cold case websites, including a slick-looking website called "Ohio's Greatest Unsolved Mysteries." It wasn't related to the old TV show, but it was similar. It looked like a fan site, one that could be edited by anyone, but it contained a lot of interesting information that Frank could use for his investigation. There were maps and graphics and photos of this and several other big unsolved cases, just the sorts of things that had always fascinated Frank.

Working quietly, Frank pulled up the website again and reviewed the details there to see how they matched up with what Chief King had passed along in his files. A couple of popup ads appeared, and he clicked "yes" and closed them out to get to the details of the case.

It all checked out. The mother and daughter had disappeared in 1997, and it had made regional news at the time. For some reason, there had been some local interest in it lately, according to his web searches and this "unsolved mysteries" website.

Frank jotted down some relevant facts in his notebook, deciding how to approach the librarian. Most people just blurted out all the information they had, and rarely in an order that was helpful, but he hoped the librarian would be able to shine some light on what Frank had learned so far.

CHAPTER 36
Scouting

"That's it?"

Trapper was in the front seat, driving. It was dark and cold outside the car, and Joe was hunkered down in the back, making him feel like a child. They had been driving for about a half-hour, sticking to the back roads and avoiding any kind of attention. It was exciting, though.

He was back in Cooper's Mill. For the first time in a long time.

"Yeah, that's it," Trapper said, slowing the car and stopping. "His daughter lives there. That's his Camaro, right?"

Joe scooted up a little just to see. The duplex was small, cheap looking. Two small homes, one on each side. Frank Harper's Camaro was parked not ten feet away from where Trapper had pulled over.

"Yeah, that's it. Can you see him inside?"

rapper squinted, then shook his head. "No, too late, I guess. I can't see anyone, not him or the daughter or that annoying little kid."

"The daughter was pretty annoying as well," Joe said from the back seat as he stared at the house, taking it all in. Frank Harper was inside that scummy little apartment, not fifty feet away. Joe's old house wasn't too far away, either—although that had been seized by the county and sold long ago. No chance of dropping by his old haunt. But Harper was there. Right now, in that little apartment. And not living in Alabama anymore, not a casual infrequent guest. Now, Frank Harper was a resident. And this apartment would be the last place Harper ever called home. Joe would see to that.

"She was annoying," Trapper said, looking around. "Remember how she figured out how to get out of that rusty old car in the garage? That was crazy. She wasn't bad looking, though."

"See anything?"

"The curtains are all closed. Want me...want me to slash his tires or something?"

"No, no," Joe said, shaking his head. It was habit, even in the dark and where no one could see him. "I don't want him suspicious of anything. I need Harper relaxed. Overconfident. Let's go."

Trapper put the car in drive, accelerating away from the quiet neighborhood.

"Anyplace else?"

"Yes," he said. "Drive me through the downtown, if you don't mind. Then we can head back."

Trapper nodded and turned the car back onto Main Street, heading east. Joe sat up as much as he could and took in the sights. The town was all decorated for Halloween, and there were lights and pumpkins and fake cobwebs everywhere. Some of the yards sported large, inflatable monsters, gyrating slowly in the cold night. Downtown, the houses looked as large and grandly decorated as he remembered. The light poles along Main Street were decorated with corn shocks, a nice festive addition they did every year. Joe had forgotten about those.

"It's good to be home," he said to no one in particular.

CHAPTER 37
Library

Two days later, Frank was fully up-to-speed on the Masterson case. He hadn't really decided if he was going to "take" it or not, but who was he kidding? Frank was excited about the details of the 1997 disappearance. It was just his kind of case, with decades' worth of files to dig through and maybe a sudden breakthrough. One that he could exploit to move the case from "cold" to "solved."

That would suit him just fine.

It was colder today, and rainy. He was happy that the real cold had held off until after the big downtown HarvestFest party last Saturday night. It had been nice to see people out and about, dancing and singing along to the music. The upcoming presidential election, now only a week away, was making everyone cross and paranoid, or at least that's how it felt to Frank. Everyone he ran into seemed to be on edge. Or maybe they were saddened by the news out of New York and New Jersey—Hurricane Sandy had caused devastating coastal flooding. Several bridges were out, and people were stranded or without power.

Just the idea of being in a hurricane sent shivers up his spine. He'd been through Katrina in 2005, and he'd ended up trapped inside the flooded St. Bart's Hospital in New Orleans.

Even though he'd managed to get past all the horrible memories of floating bodies and his near drowning, all the coverage of Hurricane Sandy was driving him nuts. Just the word "hurricane" set him on edge, and the name "Katrina" was getting dropped with frightening regularity. Every time the television newscasters mentioned the largest hurricane to ever hit the United States, it forced his mind to flash back to those bodies, floating in the hospital corridors. He could still remember the smell. The experience had also given him crippling claustrophobia for years—maybe it was a good idea to avoid enclosed spaces for the time being.

This morning, his next-to-last at Laura's house, he'd gotten up early and gotten back onto his computer, digging and digging for more information on the Masterson mother and daughter. They had disappeared from a local mall—in fact, it was the old Salem Mall, a popular old shopping center in the area until it fell on hard times. Frank had been there, too—it was now abandoned, but not long ago, the entire mall had been taken over by the Northsiders, a local Dayton gang. They had kidnapped him and held him inside the old mall until he managed to escape.

Crazy times.

Anyway, the news reports from the time said the women had gone missing from the expansive parking lot that stood on the southern side of the mall near a weird theater with an odd Asian theme. Frank pored through what he could find on the internet—he almost always preferred going back to the original newspaper articles, if he could, before checking for later updates. But sometimes those original articles held great information. The old pictures from the scene could be very helpful, too, often more helpful than the police photos.

He'd continued researching the Masterson women, including a side-jaunt to Ancestry.com, where he could do some preliminary searches. He paid the $30 required to run a full report on the mother, assuming all the DNA and family information would be nearly identical for the daughter. It showed the Masterson woman had descended from a long line of a family named Donnelly, many of whom were located in Ohio. He'd made a note to research that further and ordered a print copy of the $30 report, so he'd have it for his files.

When he was done, he'd gathered his things and left, and now he was on his way to the local downtown library.

Frank pulled his jacket tighter around him and walked out to the old Camaro, the one indulgence he had in his life. The left front light cover might get stuck closed sometimes, and there were no seatbelts, but it was his and he'd always wanted a mean-looking car. His first case here in Cooper's Mill had paid for it, and Frank hoped that the Anderson case would at least get him set up with a few months' rent in his new apartment.

He started up the Camaro and headed downtown, parking in the secret parking lot located behind the library and going in the back door. Deputy Peters had pointed out the hidden lot, and Frank felt a pang of sadness. He'd been a good kid, and an avid learner. Peters had even taken to jotting down some of the things Frank had said, as if he was some kind of wizened mystic. He was nothing but an old, tired, cop, but the kid had taken a liking to him when no one else in town seemed to care.

Frank missed him.

Inside the library, he looked around to get a sense of the interior. It was a standard library, with a front counter to the left and shelves of books ahead and to his right. Several carts of books stood waiting to be put away and, on the wall directly ahead of him, rows and rows of DVDs and VHS tapes, presumably available for checkout.

Frank walked over to the front counter and asked for Mrs. Havers. The woman on duty pointed him in the direction of some stairs that led down into the basement, and Frank took them down, finding the basement held kid's section, some computer stations, and a woman who looked old enough to be Frank's mother.

"Mrs. Havers?"

She looked up and gave Frank a warm smile. For some reason, her smile reminded him of a clown—maybe it was the wide set of her jaw, or the historic levels of makeup she'd chosen to apply today. Either way, she almost looked like a young person in old person makeup. The woman stood and almost shrieked.

"Frank Harper? Oh, my goodness. I CAN'T BELIEVE IT!" She waved him over and nearly pushed him down into an empty chair next to her basement desk, which was piled with stacks of books and the remains of a half-eaten sandwich. "Just sit right here, if you please. I've seen your picture in all the papers."

"Thank you," Frank said, settling into the chair and wondering just how long he was going to be here.

"The *Cooper's Mill Gazette* just did another story on you. Did you know that?"

"No, ma'am, I didn't."

"Oh, they love you. Me too. So, Chief King called you? Let you know about what happened? The phone call?"

"Yes, ma'am," Frank said. "Actually, he came and chatted with me, brought me the files. He said you had a phone call on the old Masterson case?"

"Yes. Oh, what a dreadful time that was. They were from here, of course, but got kidnapped over at that old mall in Trotwood. You know the one? Well, it really went downhill..."

Before he could stop her, she launched into the case, going over everything he'd just spent the last two days figuring out and reviewing. He took out his notebook and started jotting down notes as she spoke.

The Trotwood police had led the investigation, she said, interviewing the husband, workers at the mall, and any other pertinent local people. They found nothing out of the ordinary. In fact, she said, the case had dropped out of the local news quickly. This matched up with what he'd read, but it was nice to hear it from someone besides Chief King, someone who remembered it from when it happened.

"Thank goodness it didn't happen here, you know. In Cooper's Mill. It was all anyone could talk about for the next two weeks. The media moved on, as they do, but people were scared, you know. People I knew stopped going to that mall, I can tell you. Might have been the beginning of the end for it. Do you know the place?"

"I do," Frank said with a smile. "I've spent some time there," he said, not elaborating.

"Well, it used to be much nicer," she said, and he had to hold his tongue. "You can believe me on that one. Looking back on it, all they really needed to do was hire some security. People need to feel safe. I've got a book of pictures from the mall around here somewhere—someone did a retrospective on it before the mall closed. Do you want me to find it for you?"

"Maybe later."

"Okay. But it was dreadful. Just dreadful. The disappearance, I mean."

Frank nodded. "I've reviewed as much of the case history as I can find. Can you tell me what this author told you? When he called?"

"Oh, yes, of course," she said. Her eyes flickered over his shoulder and went wide.

"NO RUNNING!" she screamed, standing suddenly.

Frank jumped in his chair, and turned to see a pack of young kids, now standing perfectly still and holding library books and looking at the old woman.

"I said NO running," she said, looking at the kids with a serious look that would chill anyone's heart. "If you have to run, go outside. Now move along."

He smiled. "You would make a great cop."

"Thanks," she said, turning back to him and sitting. "Can you tell me about Jessica Mills? She seemed so nice. And that stalker—how did you catch him the basement of that furniture store?"

Frank smiled and launched into a brief description of Jessica and all of the things that had happened at this year's Mum Festival parade that had led to Frank shooting and killing a stalker who had been targeting the Hollywood starlet. Mrs. Havers had the good sense not to interrupt him more than thirty or forty times with questions.

When he was finally done and her thirst for Jessica-Mills-related knowledge was finally sated, a half-hour had passed. He glanced at his watch and she got the hint.

"Oh, so so sorry to make you tell me that whole story," she said, giving him a smile that, on anyone else, might have been alluring. What had King said, that the woman might be "sweet" on Frank? Someone she'd never even met?

"It's okay. But if you have anything on the author who called, it would be helpful."

"Yes, certainly," she said, launching into the story of the phone call.

It turned out the caller had called twice. He'd not given his name, citing confidentiality, but said that he was writing a book on the Masterson case. The man was trying to track down more of the Masterson and Donnelly families, some of whom were located in Cooper's Mill and up in the Troy area. He was apparently calling around to all the local libraries and faxing them photos of the local cemeteries, including the one he'd shared with Mrs. Havers.

"Why did he send you those photos?"

She shook her head. "Said he thought the graves were somewhere in the area. I couldn't find them—there were several—and passed them along to the chief. His people found one north of Cincinnati."

She went on, explaining that the man was working from a theory—one with disturbing implications.

"He said he thought the family did it. He's writing a book on the case and can, of course, say whatever he wants. But I don't believe it, not for a second. Her family were all over the TV back in 1997. Seemed like a nice bunch. And it was a shame they never found anything. People need closure, you know."

"They do," Frank said. "When I worked in Alabama, I specialized in cold cases," he said, bending the truth. Of course, he specialized in the only thing they would let him work on.

"That sounds so dangerous," she said, balling up one hand in front of neck and chest. It looked like something a woman would do in an old movie involving the Deep South, where a woman who say "oh my" and put her hand up near her neck, ostensibly to protect herself.

"Oh, no, cold cases are rarely exciting," he said. "This one, if we can solve it, will be bloody dull. But it would be great to solve it, right? Tell me anything else you can remember about the man on the phone. His voice, his speech patterns, anything. Did he have an accent?"

"Well, there's really nothing to tell," she said. "Only that Chief King said they found the one grave, but there were more in the photos. At least six or eight, I thought. They didn't find them all, did they?"

They chatted for another ten minutes, him taking notes in his journal, but she had little else to offer. That was the way it was with personal interviews—twenty minutes of chatting to get to the one or two pieces of actual, critical information.

"Well, thank you, Mrs. Havers. You've been very—"

"Dottie," she said. Her eyes sparkled.

"Dottie."

"Yes. And please drop by anytime. Anytime at all. We're open... well, the hours are strange, but when we're open, I'm usually here. If you have questions. For me."

"Thank you," Frank said.

"And can I get your card? In case I have any more information."

"Oh, I don't have cards. That's actually a great idea."

She laughed out loud. "Oh, I did forget something. I forgot to show you the cemeteries," she said, standing and clapping her hands. "How would that be if I forgot to show you those? Oh, I'm so forgetful," she said with another big, clownish grin.

Dottie turned and sat back down at her computer and started pulling up photos that she had apparently saved.

"There are a lot of old family cemeteries in the area," she said. "It's surprising how many are left, considering how people today don't really care much about history. Anyway, after I talked to the young man on the phone, I did some research and found about sixty of the small plots. Some of those graves could be in these locations, I was thinking. It's the perfect place."

Frank looked at the photos, which she started printing out, one at a time. This was going to take forever. He saw page after page of small, old-looking cemeteries, all with fallen signs and eroded tombstones he couldn't read. Below each was a physical address or directions to the nearest cross-street if the cemetery didn't have an actual address.

"Thank you for these," Frank said.

"Oh, I've got a bunch more coming," she said, adding more to the stack in his hand.

"What do you mean the 'perfect place'? Place for what?"

"To bury a body."

Frank looked at her. That was not what he was expecting her to say.

"What?"

She smiled. "Oh, Frank. I've read more mystery novels than there are in print, probably. Many more than once. I know the hardest part of a case is always getting rid of the body, right?"

Frank nodded, not wanting to stop her.

"Putting a murder victim in a little cemetery like these guarantees the body will never be found—it's just in there with the rest of them."

"Why not just bury the body in a real cemetery? Those things have plenty of space and—"

"No, they register all those. I used to have a mortician friend. He used to tell that same old joke over and over. You know the one. 'Why are there fences around cemeteries?'"

He waited, but then he realized she wanted him to ask her even though he knew the punchline.

"Why do they have fences around cemeteries?"

"People are dying to get in," she said, her eyes sparkling again. She might be getting up there in years, but at least she still had her sense of humor. "Anyway, my friend told me that real cemeteries have to track all the details of who is buried there. Federal rules of some kind, I think."

"Why not get rid of the bodies? Burn them, or some other way?"

She handed him more photos. "Ha, that sounds like your department, not mine. Like I said, I just got to thinking. After that author guy sent me the first set of photos. It's a smart place to hide a body."

He had give this woman some respect. It actually was a great place to hide the inconvenient dead—in a little, nondescript location where the land would likely never be disturbed again. And, even if it were, finding a body would not be a surprise to anyone—and would require them to track down who was supposed to be buried in the little cemetery and who was not.

Twenty minutes later, Frank finally left the library, carrying the sheaf of photos and a piece of pumpkin pie she'd stuff into his hands. She'd insisted on going next door and getting him a piece after he'd mentioned in passing that he'd never had any from the local restaurant.

On his way out, he passed Tina Armstrong, the editor of the local newspaper. She had an eye thing, photophobia, so she always wore sunglasses, inside or outside. He'd stopped to chat with her for a few minutes before leaving.

Now, in his car, Frank set the pie on the dashboard and opened up his journal, taking more notes. He made a list of next steps to follow, jotting down that he needed to visit the Salem Mall area again.

And he still needed to decide if he was going to take the case. But who was he kidding—the thing was fascinating.

CHAPTER 38
Travis

Travis was back at work in the main building at Anderson Tool & Die. He was excited to be involved—all he needed to remember was to keep his head down and come out of the other end of this investigation alive.

He had always wanted to be a cop, but things in his past, including his complete lack of academic ability, had kept him from getting the grades that he had needed to be able to qualify for the Police Academy in Dayton. That, combined with the fact that his family was not at all supportive of him, had held him back. But now, working with Frank Harper on this investigation, Travis could see a way forward. Harper was famous, and a good teacher. For Travis, it was as if he could see all the possibilities branching out in front of him, and in one of those possibilities, he might actually—

"Hey, watch it!"

Travis turned and realized he'd almost walked straight into the path of a forklift, the two metal tines coming right at him, threatening to decapitate him. He ducked out of the way as the operator scowled at him. There were thick yellow lines painted on the factory floor, making it obvious where you were supposed to walk. Step into the areas marked "FORKLIFT ONLY" and you could expect to get shouted at.

Travis continued on his way, heading to his workstation, a huge, water-cooled router that could drill through thick sheets of aluminum in seconds. Once he got to his post, he chatted with the other employee, a nice guy named Scott, and then got to work feeding sheets into the router and press assembly. It was a two-man job, Scott working the computer controls and Travis feeding the sheets in and then taking them out when the stamping and routing routine was complete.

He hoped the case would go well—being a cop had always been a dream of his, as far back as he could remember. Of course, he might just end up staying here. He enjoyed the folks at Anderson, and he'd had a conversation or three with Jill, the owner. She was nicer than you would expect the owner of a multi-million dollar company to be, and it never hurt to be friends with the richy rich folks of Cooper's Mill.

He was keeping his eyes open, that was for sure, and one thing that he had noticed was that Jill Anderson definitely needed more security. There were a lot of expensive things on the factory floor, and it was a wonder stuff didn't go disappearing more often.

But for now, he would just keep his head down, and keep an eye out for anything strange. He hoped to have more to report back to Frank Harper soon, but he wasn't holding his breath.

CHAPTER 39
Moving Day

It was the last day of October, moving day, and Frank was up early. He ran to McDonalds for coffee and to check in on the coffee klatch, but he didn't stay long, excusing himself and passing along the news that he was getting his own place. Everyone at the klatch already knew—he'd been talking about it for weeks—and everyone congratulated him.

Taking his coffee to go, he climbed into the Camaro and drove off. The sky was scuddy and gray and it started snowing, slowly at first and then picking up speed. It was coming down at a good clip when he arrived at the storage place, finding two burly guys loading the meager contents of Frank's unit into a white panel van. The lead mover, a guy named Derrick, greeted Frank and walked him through the moving process. It took Frank a minute to place where he'd met Derrick before—and then it hit him.

Frank had hit him.

"You remember me?"

Derrick nodded. "Of course, Mr. Harper. Me and some mates got into a bar fight at Ricky's last year. You stepped in."

"Put you down on your ass if I remember correctly."

Derrick looked embarrassed. "I was making an ass of myself."

"It happens," Frank said. He pointed up at his stuff, which didn't even look like it would fill half of the truck. "You gonna be nice to my things?"

"Oh, yes, sir," Derrick said, suddenly worried. "We'll take great care of it."

"How are you doing?"

"Better, much better," Derrick said. "Thanks for asking."

Frank watched the guys load his couch, a TV, some chairs, his old round dining room table. The bed and dresser, plus about ten boxes of various sizes and shapes, stuff he hadn't seen since Birmingham. When they were done, Frank asked Derrick to read off the address of Frank's new place, and then he left them to it, heading to Laura's.

He let himself in, trying to keep the noise down, but it didn't matter—Laura and Jackson were both up and dressed and ready to help.

"Wow. Good morning. Can't wait to get rid of me?" Frank asked.

"You know it," Laura grinned. "I've got big plans for this couch." She had grubby clothes on and was making herself a big metal thermos of coffee.

"That's a great idea," he said, nodding at the coffee. "It's brisk out there."

"And only going to get colder. Why'd you have to move on a day when it's snowing?"

Jackson scampered into the living room, decked out in a snowsuit and hat. He looked like a little ball of fabric, trying to pull on thick gloves and having little success. Frank knelt down beside his grandson and helped him pull the gloves on.

"There you go. You ready, champ?"

"Yes, grandpa," Jackson shouted, excited. "But why do you have to move?"

"Your mom is getting sick of me."

"Hey," Laura said from the kitchen. "Don't listen to him, Jackson. This is all your grandfather's idea."

Frank looked at Jackson. "I've got too much stuff. You know how you have collected all those different leaves from all the different trees?" His kindergarten class had recently done a week on trees and Jackson was suddenly fascinated with leaves and leaf shapes. "You know how it's hard to find room for all those leaves? Well, I'm like that. I'm old, and I've been collecting stuff for so long, it takes up a lot of room. Too much room for me to keep staying here with you mom."

The little kid made a face, processing what Frank had said. Then he looked up and smiled.

"You should collect smaller stuff."

"That's a great idea," Frank said. "But I need my own place. Will you come visit?"

"Every day!" Jackson smiled, hugging Frank.

His mother came over and pulled Jackson away. "That might be a little too much, Jax, but we're going to help him move in today, so you'll get to see it."

Frank stood, feeling one knee pop. Getting older wasn't fun, but it was better than the alternative.

He started stacking stuff by the door and walking it out to the

Camaro. Between trips, he directed Laura on what she could load into her own car.

Frank thought Laura might be a little bit upset—she had told him on more than one occasion that he could stay in her apartment as long as he wanted, but he needed his own place. Jackson thought the whole thing was very exciting, and eager to help carry small items and boxes out to Laura's car.

Between the three of them, they soon had the rest of his things loaded up. It was a tight fit, and he had to shove to get the Camaro's trunk to close. Soon, Frank stood by the door, giving a wave goodbye to Laura's place.

"You gonna miss it?" Laura asked.

"Yeah," Frank said, suddenly sad. "I am, actually." Laura's place looked weirdly empty.

"Well, we'll miss you too," she said, pulling on her hat. "And I'm gonna miss you doing the dishes. It's been a big help."

They headed out and Frank gave the place one more wistful look before pulling the door shut behind him. It was snowing again, light flurries, and Jackson was trying to catch the flakes that fell from the sky. They climbed in their vehicles and began the drive over to Frank's new place, Jackson riding shotgun.

"Is it a house?"

"No, it's an apartment, like your mom's. But there's lots of space."

"Is there a room to play in?"

Frank nodded. "Of course, there's a living room. Do you want to play there?"

"Yes," he said, looking out the window. He was tied in with one of Frank's leather belts—Laura wouldn't let Jackson ride in Frank's seat-belt-free car without some kind of restraint. Frank had MacGyvered a makeshift seatbelt for just these occasions.

Pulling up in front of his new place, he was surprised the truck wasn't here yet. His new house had a garage, so he went in and through the kitchen and opened it from the inside. Jackson followed along and mimicked what Frank was doing.

Once the door was open, Frank started taking items from his car and piling them in the garage. Laura arrived and he directed her to park in the driveway, having her back in. They unloaded all of Frank's stuff into the garage, and then he gave Jackson and Laura the tour.

She seemed impressed with his new digs, making faces and nodding along as he walked them through the place, which was larger than hers. It had a kitchen and living room and a bedroom and bathroom in the back. There was a smaller half-bath up front, near the front doors, and a short hallway off the kitchen led to the small garage. And the price was right—he wasn't sure, but Frank thought maybe Delancy had given him a break on the price. Maybe he liked the idea of renting to an ex-cop.

"I like it," Laura said as they were wrapping up the tour. There was a small patio off the back of the house, and Jackson was doing laps around the inside of the chain link fence that ran along the perimeter. It had snowed enough to cover the ground, and Jackson was running like a dog, digging a path in the snow. Frank and Laura stood on the patio, both of them crossing their arms in very similar fashions.

"Thanks," Frank said. "It's more space than I need."

She looked out over the fence and across a small creek that ran behind the property. There was a short path that led up to the backside of a small strip mall. "That's convenient."

"Pizza and a nails place," Frank said. "I'll be eating a lot of Dominoes in the very near future, I think."

"And getting your nails done?"

"Sure, why not?"

Her face grew serious. "And the only liquor store in town," she said, pointing. As they both watched, a man came out of the back of the shop carrying a stack of broken-down cardboard boxes. They looked like boxes for wine, but flattened. "You think that's a good idea?"

He heard a honk out front and shrugged. "I can handle it."

"I hope so," she said and turned, heading inside.

Leaving Jackson to his yard laps, she and Frank walked out front. Laura moved her car so the truck could back into the driveway, and then the two men started unloading his furniture. The bed and dresser went into the bedroom, and the rest into the living room. The boxes got distributed to the rooms marked on the outside of the boxes. Frank had put Post-it notes up on the doors of each room to mark which room was which. It was done in twenty minutes, and Frank gave Derrick and his friend a tip as they headed out.

Back inside, they sat on Frank's couch. No one had sat on it since Birmingham. Jackson was inside now—he'd gotten wet and cold outside—and was running laps in the rest of the house, running from the bedroom and into the kitchen and back, giggling as he ran.

"He's gonna be tired," Frank said.

"That's the plan. Did I ever have that much energy?"

Frank nodded. "Actually, yes. Trudy used to call you our little "dynamo." I always thought you were more like a tornado. Always causing messes, wherever you went."

"That sounds like you, now," Laura said with a laugh, slapping him on the leg. "Everywhere you go, you find trouble. Or it finds you."

"No kidding. I'm a magnet. I can't even go to a parade without getting nearly killed."

"Or killing someone," she said under her breath.

"Funny. You're a real comedian. But seriously, thanks for helping me move in."

"No problem. I like your place."

"Thanks." He tried to think of another topic they could discuss. Suddenly, he didn't want her to leave. He didn't want her and Jackson gone and him to have the place to himself. He didn't want to be alone.

But she stood and went to gather up Jackson and the moment was over. Jackson resisted his mother's efforts to get him dressed again in the wet coat and shoes that he'd just shedded. Jackson ran up and threw his arms around Frank's leg, ignoring her. Finally, she gave up and carried him to the car, but not after a big hug from his grandfather.

"I'm gonna miss you, grandpa," Jackson said, suddenly serious.

"Don't worry about it," Frank said. "You'll be over here all the time. Why don't you bring some toys over the next time you visit? That way there will be something for you to play with."

"Okay, I can do that. Maybe those dinosaurs you got me. And you'll still visit?"

"We're still going to see just as much of each other as we did before," Frank said. The only thing is, now you'll have two different places to play."

"Okay bye!"

"See you soon, Jackson," he said before walking them out to her car and helping strap Jackson into the car seat in the back seat of her car. Laura hugged him and it lasted longer than he'd expected—maybe she was already missing him. Frank invited Laura and Jackson over for dinner the next night.

"I don't know if you'll be ready for us or not," Laura said. "But we'd be happy to come over if you're ready."

"I will be. And I'd love to cook for you."

She looked up at the flurries, then gave him another quick peck on the cheek. "Take care."

"You too," he said.

Frank gave her another hug and then she left, driving away.

Chapter 40
Ready It

The board was almost ready.

Joe was walking the central path again, treading back and forth between the clearings he'd named King and Queen, counting his steps. He'd spent the night, bunked down in Rook 2, so he could get a sense of what the natural sounds were like without anyone else around.

Trapper and their posse would be here soon—they had nearly completed prepping Donnelly Woods, but there were a few things left to do. Not much, but a few things.

Joe counted his steps and came up with the same number for the fifth time: 209. There were 209 steps between the edges of the two large clearings. And there were great sightlines into both clearings from Rook 2 and 3. Rook 1 had okay sightlines to the road and cemetery, and Trapper's men were spending today clearing more brush to fix that situation. Joe would need a clear view of the cemetery to monitor Harper's arrival.

He nodded and noted the step count on the map in his pocket. Joe needed to know this place like the back of his hand. He needed to know it as well as he'd ever known any other place in the world.

This place would determine his freedom—and his vengeance.

But after all his visits over the last week, Joe was getting a good feel for the stretch of land, which he had taken to calling the Board. It was yet another game of chess, but this Board had a different shape. And the pieces—Joe, Harper, Trapper, his men—all had different moves. Some could be relied upon, and others not so much.

What would the church men do when the shots started flying? How would they react when and if Frank Harper confronted one of them?

But, with enough planning, this Board would be the scene of Joe's finest game, a most dangerous kind of game, he thought with a smile.

Joe headed north, walking along the animal path from King to Rook 2. He had a pair of binoculars around his neck, and he used them to peer in the direction of Rook 2. He could see it clearly—he'd placed an orange traffic cone on top of it to make it easy to check the sightlines from down in the forest.

The plan in his head was solid, and now he was iterating it, over and over again, playing it out in his mind, looking for issues or problems. He ran through the steps in his mind even as his eyes wandered over the forest floor, looking for anything out of the ordinary. Even a sharp stone in the wrong place could upset the balance.

As he walked, scouring the ground, Joe reviewed his plan:

1. <u>Prepare</u> - *Board ready, rooks prepped, gravestone, Gator staged at Rook 1, people staged where needed for first positions*

2. <u>Arrival </u> - *Harper arrives, looking for the gravestone. He will be alone.*

3. <u>Set</u> - *Test walkie talkies, all in locations, ready? Me and Trapper in Rook 1, two men in Bishop, two men in Knight.*

4. <u>Confusion at Cemetery</u> - *It's not there. What? Harper can't believe it. Wait, was this whole thing just a setup to get me alone out here in the middle of nowhere—.*

5. <u>Go</u> - *Spring trap. Harper incapacitated (method TBD Trapper working on it). Bind Harper, disarm, move to Queen clearing*

6. <u>Harper Wakes</u> - *He's bound and gagged. I'm there to explain the rules to him. It's a hunt and he's the prey and that's that. Trapper ungags him and Harper and I chat. When we're done, I signal Trapper who hits him on the head, knocking him out.*

7. <u>Free</u> - *I move to Rook 2 while Harper recovers. He awakes and gets himself free by undoing ropes on the nearby sharp rock we left for him to find - make sure no one moves it. He needs confidence.*

8. <u>Sacrifice 1</u> - *Send in two men from Knight to Queen to "get Harper." They are of course defeated by Harper, and he takes a gun off of one of them. Guns were modified and will not fire. They are marked with white tape on handles.*

9. <u>Hunt Part 1</u> - *Harper moves on, probably heading east in the direction of the river, which is loud. I take shots at him. This should drive him to King.*

10. <u>Helper</u> - *Trapper is set up in the woods to the north and also shoots at Harper, confusing him. I take Gator and set up at Rook 3.*

11. <u>Hunt Part 2</u> - *More hunting and shooting from a distance. No need to get close. Keep everyone else back. Trapper recovers injured men from Queen.*

12. <u>False Hope of Survival</u> - *Gun he took off the kid is designed to misfire re: dirt in the barrel. Useless as a defensive weapon*

13. <u>Sacrifice 2</u> - *Send in two men from Bishop to King to "get Harper." They are of course defeated by Harper.*

14. <u>Wounded</u> - *During step 13, Trapper shoots Harper in the leg and Harper is injured. He crawls across King clearing toward river.*

15. <u>Checkmate</u> - *I'm set up in Rook 3 and take Harper out from a good distance. DO NOT APPROACH. Three shots: legs, chest, and then head after a few minutes. Let him suffer.*

16. <u>Clean Up</u> - *Meet Trapper and any survivors at the King clearing to confirm kill. Approach with caution and be ready to finish Harper if he's down. Be careful—he's played dead before. Trapper to dispose of body (method TBD) or bodies.*

17. <u>Leave</u> - *Trapper and I take the Camaro back to the prepper compound, swap out the plates, and leave for the west coast. DO NOT LINGER. Need to be on the road within the hour and into Illinois by sundown.*

The plan was all there, in his head, floating around and coming together. It wasn't written down anywhere, but that wasn't necessary. Joe could see it clearly, like a printed piece of paper in his mind, as clearly as if he were holding up a copy of the plan. Joe needed a scaffolding upon which to attach all of his ideas and permutations, and then he could walk around the idea virtually, observing it from all sides and looking for problems. It was the same as chess, really—you had to know the board, backwards and forwards. He would write it down at some point, but that was more the others than for him.

As he walked through the woods, Joe found several broken pieces of glass and an old, rusting pole, just the sorts of things that Harper would somehow stumble across and use to turn the tables. Harper was a clever one, and his daughter was too. She'd kicked her way out of that rusty old car and managed to get her stupid brat back and get away. He wasn't involving her in this situation. Harpers were trouble, wild cards. He didn't need the two of them together. Knowing the universe, their weird random permutations would surface together to somehow tip the scales in their favor.

Joe walked the Board, surveying the area, heading for Rook 2. This was where it would happen—he would finally put a bullet in the man who had been plaguing him ever since he'd shown up to "interview" the coffee klatch. Joe remembered sitting there in the McDonald's, watching, answering slowly and quietly as the ex-cop reeled off a series of questions about Tom Mercato who, at the time, was simply missing. Joe hadn't told the cop anything helpful, of course, and had neglected to mention that Joe knew exactly where Tom Mercato was. That conversation would have been fun:

"Why, of course I know where Tom Mercato is. He's at my house."

"Um, I don't understand. Forgive me, but I'm a simpleton. What do you mean?"

"He's my guest."

"Huh?"

"He's dead. I killed him. And now he's in my garage, you idiot. In a freezer in my garage."

Joe could imagine the gasps around the table, especially from that obese woman and her simpering husband. Joe would have loved it, basking in their stunned disapproval.

"Yes, I know where he is. Sometimes I walk out to the garage and open the freezer and Tom and I have conversations. They are a tad one-sided, of course, but it's still nice to have a friend. A friend who really knows how to listen."

Joe heard some birds rise into the trees and take flight, and turned and concentrated, listening. There, a car. It was approaching from the west, and he could hear the crunching of a vehicle pulling into the gravel parking lot by the graveyard. It sounded like a truck, and he hoped it was Trapper and the other men. They had a lot of work to do.

Joe turned and hurried back through the King clearing, reviewing the plan again, over and over in his mind as he went to meet the men. The plan wasn't foolproof, not yet, but it was getting there. He could lose parts of the plan and add new ones in, but it was getting close, he thought.

Approaching the edge of the forest, he slowed and used the binoculars. Yup, Trapper and four men, working near the flatbed truck they'd been using for a week now to transport the Gators and other supplies from the Church of Xavier compound to this location.

Joe walked toward the cemetery, passing his own Gator. He'd

left it parked inside the tree line so as to not attract any unwanted attention from the road. Joe rounded a corner on the western-most trail heading toward the gated cemetery. Trapper and the other men were unloading the back of the truck. He passed the cemetery and glanced over. It was old, or at least as old as things got in the United States. It looked ancient, even though it had been established in 1867 and the final grave was interred in 1933. The cemetery only sported eleven headstones, but Joe knew the names on each and the stories therein contained. He'd done his homework, as usual. Joe knew them all. They were his ambassadors to the world, the party of greeters that would draw Harper here.

"There he is," one of the young men said to Trapper as Joe approached. Trapper turned and greeted him.

"Morning, boss. We've got the last few things for the overwatch positions. The second Gator, obviously. And those trimmers you wanted."

Joe nodded and helped them unload the rest of the stuff off the back of the truck. Among today's volunteers were Hector and James, the young kid who had given Joe and Trapper their arrival tour. Once it was all down off the truck and organized on the ground, Joe started divvying them up. Hector lowered a ramp and unloaded the second Gator while Joe worked.

"Okay, we're almost done. James, I'll take you with me in my Gator, just inside the tree line," he said, pointing over his shoulder. "These two piles need to go with us," he said, indicating two piles of supplies.

James nodded and picked up an armload of supplies before heading off into the woods.

"This big pile here goes to Rook 2," he said to Trapper and Hector and the others. "Can you drive it over and set it up? On the way, drop these guys off at that area I wanted cleared." Joe had picked out a couple of places where he wanted the underbrush cleared away. He didn't want to give Harper too many places to hide.

Trapper nodded. "Yup, and after they're done, I'll call you," he said, tossing Joe a walkie talkie. "This is the equipment for the big day, so we should test it," Trapper said. "What else?"

Joe looked at the walkie talkie. "Not sure if we should test it until the game starts," Joe said. "What if someone catches the frequency?"

"We can test it if we keep it short, boss," Trapper offered. "I'd hate to have them not work on game day."

Joe nodded. "Okay, but no names. And use—use channel 13. It's unlucky, so people are more unlikely to use it. And Hector, don't forget to have your guys gather up all the brush you cut yesterday," Joe said to the others. "We're going to use it by the river."

Trapper and his men left on the second Gator, and Joe and James headed north to Rook 1, circling around the cemetery and up the small rise. When they arrived, they unloaded the Gator, and James finished setting up the rest of the blind, a large, camouflaged tent-like structure. It was shorter than a tent, with camouflaged openings and a green and brown covering that blended expertly into the surroundings. It was designed to be used lying down, so James had faced the "shooting end" towards the forest.

While he worked, Joe unloaded some food and water packages and stowed them inside the tent, along with other supplies and the extra ammo, stored in water-proof containers. He'd bring his guns out on game day, of course—there was no way he'd be leaving weapons out in the weather, even if they were protected inside a tent. You never knew what could get inside the tent, or how the weather might affect the weapons.

Earlier in the week, Joe had picked out three matching sniper rifles, and Trapper had driven through Indiana and into Illinois to buy them. He'd used a fake ID and bought them in a shady, less-than-reputable gun store in central Illinois, just east of St. Louis. It had been located near a large riverboat casino, in a part of East St. Louis along the river where the cops feared to go. Trapper had described it as the kind of gun store where they barely even looked at your paperwork and ID. And he'd been propositioned to purchase drugs in the parking lot, so there was little chance the cops were hanging around this particular gun shop.

But the weapons were perfect, top of the line. Joe had already stripped them and modified the guns to add distance. He'd also cleaned and resealed the upgraded scopes that had come with the weapons. He still needed to get in a bit of range practice with them to calibrate the sights and make sure they all fired perfectly and smoothly.

Fortunately, the preppers had built at three underground ranges as part of their extensive tunneling efforts. Shooting in an enclosed space could damage your ears, as Joe was well aware, but it also meant no one else could hear you practicing. He didn't need some member of the public calling the cops, who might want to know why he was practicing with three identical weapons—guns that weren't even his. Or legal.

"We done?"

Joe looked over at James, who was wrapping up the setup.

"Yup, let's head out."

They drove to Rook 2, skirting the top of the cliff face that overlooked the forest below, and passed Trapper and the others unloading. With a wave, Joe continued along the rise, heading for Rook 3. When the golf cart came to a rest down the hill from the spot, James climbed out and started unloading.

"I like the name 'Rook' for the sniper spots," James said as he unloaded supplies into the blind. "Can you have three rooks in a chess game?"

"No, not technically."

"Still, Rook 1, 2 and 3 sounds cool."

This guy was an idiot. Any misgivings evaporated that Joe might have had about sacrificing this "piece" in his game of chess with Harper.

They continued unloading and setting up. In the distance, Joe heard people cutting down saplings with a mini-chainsaw and removing undergrowth with a weed eater. Once they were done setting up Rook 3, Joe and James climbed back in the Gator and headed in the direction of the sounds of the chainsaw.

They arrived shortly after the men were finishing up. Joe got out of the golf cart and asked them to clear a few more things out, including a small stand of saplings and short trees that blocked the view to the north. Joe didn't think it would matter, but it was better to be safe than sorry.

When they were all done, Joe helped the others gather up all the cut brush and small trees and toss them onto a large plastic tarp that Hector had spread out on the ground behind the Gator. He attached it to the back of the cart with a chain, and, when they were ready, Hector got in and slowly drove the cart, towing the large blue tarp in an easterly direction toward the creek. Joe and the others walked behind the tarp, freeing it when it became caught on a branch or threatened to tip over and spill its contents.

A few minutes later, they approached the river. At this point, it was a small span of water, maybe thirty feet across, but it could still be a place that Harper might be able to reach and use to escape or hide or further complicate the situation. Joe needed everything under his control, or at least as many things as he could foresee.

At the river's edge, Joe and the others grabbed up branches and logs from the load on top of the tarp, throwing them over the edge and blocking the view of the river. It wouldn't be enough to stop a driven person from making their way to the river, but it might slow them down. Joe stood back and directed them, arranging the logs and bushes and small trees in such a way as to screen the river as much as possible.

Joe's walkie talkie beeped, and he fiddled with the handle until he got it to work.

"Mic check."

"Coming in clear," Trapper said. "Two is all set up."

"Copy that," Joe said, feeling silly.

"I moved some more brush, loading it up," Trapper added. "Where are you guys?"

"River," Joe said. There were plenty of places he could be along the "river," but there was only one place like this, where they were actively working to disrupt the view and interrupt the terrain. "Head here."

"Copy that."

When he arrived, Trapper helped them finish unloading the tarp. Joe helped where he could, but moving all that wood and other kinds of physical exertions were a young man's game.

After another half hour they were done, and it looked good. Great, actually. The river could barely be seen. If Harper did make it this far, he'd have to go around this blockage to get to the water. He'd be visible from either Rook 2 or Rook 3, depending on which direction he went. Joe had verified the view of each with his binoculars—it was a clear shot into this clearing from either location. If he made it this far, he'd be dead.

"Okay, I think we're nearly done," Joe said. "I'm staying overnight again."

"You sure? Want to keep Gator 1?"

"No, take them both home this time. Come pick me up in the morning."

Trapper nodded. "You guys take Gator 2 back to the truck and load it up. I'll meet you there in a few."

The men nodded and loaded up, heading away down the path through Donnelly Woods that would lead them to Queen and King clearings and finally the cemetery.

"Thanks, Trapper," Joe said.

"Not a problem, boss. "I'm still working on ways to incapacitate Harper. Any ideas?"

"I'll leave that to you, if you don't mind," Joe said. "Go with a Taser, if you must, but I'd rather you decide."

"Can I ask why you want me to come up with something? I mean, this whole plan is yours, boss. Down to the kind of food you want in the blinds. So why am I in charge of this part?"

Joe smiled at him as they walked over to the remaining Gator. Trapper climbed in, but Joe didn't join him. "Just say I'm a little worried that I might be too predictable."

"What do you mean?"

"Harper, that's what I mean. I'm concerned that if I come up with something, he might be able to anticipate it."

Trapper nodded, following along.

"I'm thinking you've got access to things I don't know about," Joe said. "Or might come up with something strange I wouldn't have thought of, right? Your history is different from mine. It's the easiest way to mix things up. It's like playing chess against two different opponents at the same time—if they're both professionals, they're easier to predict. But play a pro and a novice? Or a pro and a middle-of-the-road or hobby player? They can surprise you."

"You're saying I'm a novice," Trapper said.

"No, of course not," Joe said, shaking his head. "It's just we're using two brains instead of one. You head on home and come get me in the morning."

"Ride to King?"

"No, I want to walk it all again."

Trapper looked at the sky, which had been darkening. "Just watch out for rain. See you in the morning. Xavier wants to have dinner with you tomorrow night, check on your progress, so I'll tell him we'll be there. And don't worry, boss. We've thought of everything."

Joe nodded as Trapper drove away. Dinner—the preppers loved to get together for group dinners. Maybe it was a Mexican thing, or a family thing. Most times they were in the common rooms in the various houses, but a few of the dinners had been held among the higher ups in the organization—and a few had been held in the underground complex. Dinner with Xavier likely meant dinner in one of the underground dining rooms. Joe was still amazed that these people had managed to build that kind of underground city without outside help.

It was like finding out the ancient Egyptians hadn't needed the assistance of aliens to build the great pyramids, Joe thought with a smile.

Turning, he checked the river view one more time, then started up the path to Queen, counting his steps while simultaneously pondering his plan. It had a few areas he still needed to finalize, but it was getting there. Getting to Queen, he walked the perimeter of the clearing for what had to be the twentieth time, checking for debris or anything that could assist Harper.

Joe looked down at the clearing, visualizing it all. This is where Harper would die. This was where it would happen—if things went to plan, Harper would have a gun and make his last stand here. Talking to Trapper, likely. Harper would wave his useless gun and fire it and find it wasn't loaded—

No, that wouldn't work. Frank was smart enough to check the gun to see if it was loaded. Okay, we need another option, Joe thought. It can have bullets and look like it's good to fire but it has to fail.

Or he could give Harper a loaded gun and let him kill Trapper. Pawn for King. It was a trade Joe could stomach if it got Joe a clean shot at Harper.

No, that wouldn't work either—Joe couldn't drive himself to California. He'd get spotted on every traffic camera from here to Los Angeles.

Okay, so Trapper has to live. So Frank can't kill him. So the guns can't be operational.

Joe pondered this for a few minutes, standing there in the Queen clearing, oblivious to the rain that started to fall in the clearing around him. He was a statue, thinking, his brain working through an array of possibilities. He stood there in the rain until he came up with a solution he could live with. Joe iterated the new solution a few more times, trying multiple options and testing outcomes. Finally, he nodded and brought his attention back to the clearing. He realized it was raining and hurried the 209 steps to the King clearing.

There, Joe walked the perimeter again, searching. The spot where Harper would wake was marked with a traffic cone, and another smaller cone stood off to the side. Under it, unseen, was a half-buried broken bottle. Harper would see it and get free of his bindings.

It was all planned out.

Joe walked, heading north. He crossed through Bishop and then climbed the slope up to Rook 2. It should be a clean shot, Joe thought as he climbed. It was a clear view from here to both clearings. Joe had plenty of practice, shooting both still and moving targets.

At the top, Joe looked over every aspect of Rook 2 again, checking each box again. This would be Joe's primary location for most of the game, and Trapper had done a great job. It was ready. Joe stood next to the camouflaged tent, looking down at the clearing far below. He visualized exactly how it would go—Harper, struggling after being shot by Trapper in the leg. Bleeding, desperate, armed. He might stand, but Joe thought it more likely that he'd take cover behind a set of trees on the eastern side of the clearing. Trapper was supposed to shoot at Harper until Joe had a clear shot.

Harper would fall to the ground, injured. A few minutes later—Joe wanted to bask in his victory—two more shots, and Harper would be dead.

Finally.

Joe had shot at Harper from the trunk of his old car, but Harper had escaped him. Joe had shot at Frank and several people in a field north of Troy, firing from a second-floor window and aiming to take out Harper or his daughter. He'd watched them scatter, panicked, but his shots had gone wide, and he'd only hit a few of the fleeing idiots.

Joe had missed killing Frank Harper on two occasions: on that frozen lake, and then near the river. Now, Joe was getting another chance.

No, he was not "getting" another chance. Joe was "making" another chance. Creating it. Manifesting it out of thin air. Fashioning another chance to kill Frank Harper with sheer willpower. He was literally "willing" it into existence, this Game and all of the pieces, the very Board itself.

Joe was creating a final opportunity to kill Frank Harper.

And, this time, he wouldn't miss.

Chapter 41
Homework

Laura sat at her little dining room table, working on the Anderson files again. The house was so quiet, much quieter than she was used to. She found herself looking around occasionally to see if something was wrong.

She had the television on, watching the election night returns coming in. The commentators were adding up the numbers, making predictions, calling states for Obama or Mitt Romney, the GOP challenger. It was all coming to an end, the contentious and ugly 2012 presidential election. Soon, the country would have a winner and everyone could stop talking about it. Laura wouldn't miss all the hard feelings and tense conversations that seemed to erupt daily at the salon or at the coffee shops.

Of course it was important. But everyone took it so personally. At times, it felt like this whole election process was tearing families apart, making people pick sides and calling each other horrible names. She also wouldn't miss the ugly words, or the forest of yard signs that seemed to spring up in every yard and on every corner in town.

She looked over at the couch, thinking about her father. He had his own place now, which was great, but now he was on his own. That wasn't great. His drinking had been under control for months, and him being here let her keep an eye on him. He'd gotten completely sober over that time when he'd been kidnapped by the street gang. Before they'd taken him, her dad had been dealing with an Oxy addiction, but he'd gotten clean.

Laura shook her head. She had to be the only woman in town who had a vicious criminal gang to thank for getting her father off of Oxy. It sounded crazy. It sounded made up.

But it had happened, and he'd been clean there for a while. At some point, he'd even joked about the Northsider gang opening their own string of rehab centers.

But he was drinking again, now, and she thought he was getting worse.

Of course, she was sad to see him move out—he'd been good to her and Jackson. It had been nice, better than she could have predicted, really. And he'd done a good share of the chores, freeing her up.

And he'd cooked some evenings, a nice change from her regular rotation of meals that probably bored Jackson to tears.

But there was another reason she was sad to see him move out— she'd been keeping an eye on him and his alcohol intake. Out on his own, he could backslide. Especially with his new place being located literally next to a liquor store. It was just asking for trouble.

Shaking her head, she stood and went over to the kitchen counter and made another cup of tea. Laura had been really into tea lately, and it was nice to fluctuate between the caffeinated and non-caffeinated versions depending on how her day was going. Tonight, she needed caffeine. She and her father and this Tavon guy were getting together on Sunday to talk about their forensic accounting of the Anderson books, and she still had several things she wanted to resolve.

Unable to put it off any longer, Laura walked back over and sat, folding one leg under her. She rearranged the stacks of papers she'd printed out at work today, spreadsheets from Anderson Tool & Die. There was something hinky going on with the books, of course, and it felt like she was getting tantalizingly close to coming up with a breakthrough.

She sipped her tea and dug back into the files, trying to ignore the nagging suspicions running through her mind that her father. Was he drinking, now? Like right now, alone and in his own place? If so, there was no one to help him.

Chapter 42
Settled

Frank Harper sat in his new apartment, watching TV and fiddling with his new camera. Over the last three weeks, he'd gotten all of his stuff out of Laura's apartment. He'd moved the last of it yesterday, and last night was the first night he'd been able to relax in his new place.

Moving was difficult business, and it felt like he'd been moving for months. His last day in his old apartment in Birmingham had been July 20th. In a sense, he'd been "moving" ever since. It was nice to finally be settled in a new place—one that he was paying for—even if it had taken three months.

And he was paying for it. Between the jobs he was doing and the windfall from providing personal protection for Jessica Mills, the money in his checking account was starting to pile up. He'd paid Jake Delancy for first and last month's rent on this place, and there was still plenty of money in the account, even after he'd paid Monty Robinson and his other expenses. It occurred to him that the Robinsons, the couple from his divorce case, shared a last name with Monty. He doubted they were related, he thought with a smile.

No, things were looking up. He was in a new place, and all of his furniture fit fine, along with a new TV he'd splurged on. Laura and Jackson had visited earlier today and complimented him on his choices. Jackson had run around like a crazed monkey, getting into everything. Frank reminded himself to "kid-proof" the place as much as possible before he started having Jackson over regularly.

Nodding, Frank dug out his notebook and added "kid-proof the apartment" to his list of things to do. He was knocking things off at a pretty good clip.

His phone dinged, and he grabbed it off the side table, muting the TV. It was an email from Jessica Mills. He'd followed her return to Los Angeles on the news. The judge had waived the last days of her house arrest, and Jessica was settling back into her life. Her email was just her touching base. She was doing fine, was starting to look for work. Wanted to know if she should try to get him cast in her next movie as some kind of tough guy. He smiled. She was still feeling indebted to him, obviously. But he'd just been doing his job, a job he'd been hired to do.

That wasn't exactly true. He had taken a liking to her, after a few days. Frank tapped at the tiny keyboard on his phone, emailing her back. He told her to be careful, have fun, and not to take life too seriously.

Frank put the phone down and went back to the TV, unmuting it. It was yet another episode of "Forensic Files," probably his favorite show. They were always using new technology to crack cold cases. Of course, some of these episodes were fifteen years old, and the "new" technology they were using was positively quaint.

Frank felt restless. The move was done, his two biggest cases had wrapped up, and there was nothing more to do on the Anderson Tool & Die case this late at night. He was still looking into the missing money and running backgrounds on the employees. He would start redoing the personal interviews soon, try to shake something loose. People didn't like being interviewed if they were under suspicion, and they would hate being interviewed by Frank. He could sit there all day with his arms crossed, waiting for people to talk.

He glanced at his list of cases. The only other open case consisted of two words: "Joe Hathaway." There was nothing to be done about that case either, other than endlessly driving the back roads around Cooper's Mill. It accomplished nothing, but it made him feel better. The guy was out there somewhere. Or maybe he was dead. Maybe his body would turn up someday and Frank could finally cross that case off his list.

Or not. Maybe he'd reappear to haunt Frank some more.

He shook his head. It was those kinds of cases that were the worst, the ones with no resolution. Like Ben Stone's murder, or that little kid who suffocated in a cardboard box in the middle of an industrial area of Atlanta. Cases that you could never put away, cases that haunted you.

Add Joe Hathaway to the list, Frank thought. He could be out there somewhere, right now. Frank stood, shaking his head. There was no point in fretting about it. But Frank felt restless, aimless. He needed to be working on something, even though there was nothing to work on.

He heard a noise outside and looked out the windows, the ones off his living room that looked out on the neighboring strip mall. He could see the back of a pizza place and the local liquor store. A guy was standing out behind the strip mall, smoking and sipping a beer.

The thought of having a drink drifted into Frank's mind with no hesitation.

He was riding high, on a roll, and deserved to celebrate. Money was coming in, and he had a place of his own now, so he didn't need to worry about drinking in front of Laura or Jackson. Or listen to her complain, if she didn't like him drinking.

No, there was nothing wrong with it, really. He was celebrating his new place, and his new town, and his new life.

A few drinks wouldn't kill him.

Frank nodded, making up his mind. He grabbed his keys and his wallet and left the house, heading through the thin strip of woods that separated his duplex from the liquor store.

CHAPTER 43
Anderson Tool & Die

In the end, it only took five hours to solve the Anderson Tool & Die case.

Endless hours of work, of course, and piles of paperwork. And an undercover asset, working inside the facility, watching people and taking notes. And two amateur forensic accountants pouring over all the books for the last eight years. And scores of phone calls and interviews and at least two hundred hours of research between the people involved. Oh, and thousands and thousands of dollars of the client's money, spent on background checks and financial inquiries and a hundred other things.

But it was five hours in the basement of the Cooper's Mill library that did the trick.

Frank had arrived early, securing a conference room for two hours on the lower floor of the building. Sundays were busy at the library, and he was happy to get one of the rooms as he'd been told they were hard to secure.

Mrs. Havers had seen him checking in and taken him downstairs with glee. Playing with her hair, she showed him to the conference room, one of several located in the library basement. While she was talking, he wondered if she wore the same amount of makeup every day, and how anyone could afford that.

She showed him how to work the controls on the large screen that hung on the wall in front of the conference room table, and during that demonstration, he got the distinct feeling she was drawing it out, making the discussion last as long as she could.

"I don't really need this much space," Frank had said. "There are only three of us. We just need space to spread out our files and—"

"Oh, don't worry, dear," she'd said. He wondered if she called everyone 'dear' or if that was something special. She touched his hand while she said it, and Frank thought that answered his question. "All the conference rooms are the same size. And they're available a lot of the time. This one is the best, the most private. If you ever want to just come down here and hang out and work, I'm sure they'd be available."

She showed him how to get onto the internet and how to connect his laptop to the large screen on the wall so he could show files. At one point, she was clearly leaning in, getting very close to him, before she stood and slid away with a smile. She smelled like rosewater, or whatever that old kind of perfume was called. It was thick, cloying. Was she hitting on him? It had been so long since someone had hit on him, he wasn't sure if he'd even recognize the act if it did occur.

It also made him glad to be a man. He couldn't imagine how annoying it would be to be an attractive woman and have men hitting on you all the time. How did they ever get any work done—or enjoy a quiet evening—when no one would leave them alone?

Finally, she left the room and headed back to her desk, but not before offering to run and get pie and coffee from next door for his meeting. He thanked her but passed, and when she was gone, Frank got to work, spreading out the printouts and arranging them in a manner that he could follow. He pulled up the list of employees on the screen from his laptop—he hoped to start the meeting by reviewing all of the "major" employees and their files at this meeting.

Laura arrived right before the appointed meeting time of 2 p.m., lugging her own laptop and a large bag of papers.

"Hi," he said. "How have you been?"

"Good, good," she said, struggling with the bag. She plopped it down on the table. "Busy, you know."

"Oh, yeah?"

"Yeah. Between the salon and Jackson and this crazy case of yours."

"Well, thank you for working on it with me," he said, pointing at the piles of papers on the table. "It's a lot. And I'll pay you for your time." He chuckled. "It's weird—I'm so used to just seeing you every day. It feels weird to ask you how your day is going. Used to be, I could just tell by what you were making for dinner."

"I know. It's weird, not having you around either."

"Same. How's Jackson?"

"Good. How's the new place?"

"Good. Quiet." He started to say something else when Tavon walked in, breaking the mood in the room. He was carrying a bag and his laptop but seemed harried and rushed.

"Hey, sorry I'm late," Tavon said. "Took longer than I thought to get up here. It's been a while since I've been in Cooper's Mill. I think

I'm the only black person in this whole town. People were staring."

"Really? That's weird."

"Oh, you get used to it. Couldn't find parking, either."

Frank walked over and shook his hand. "Sorry about that—I forgot to tell you. There's a secret parking lot behind the library. Lots of spots, and you can come in the back door off the alley."

Tavon smiled. "That would have been helpful. I'm parked like five blocks down, past the train tracks. Parked in front of a little train station or something—green building right next to the tracks. Nice town, though. Cute houses. Huge."

"Thanks," Frank said, like he had anything to do with the houses or keeping the small town tidy and cute. "This is Laura, my daughter. Laura, this is Tavon."

They shook hands and chatted for a minute, then Tavon got to work, digging stuff out of his bag and setting his things on the table.

"Watch out, he's a dangerous gang member," Frank said with a smile as he passed out copies of his reports. "Used to run heroin for the Northsiders. Did their books on the side."

Tavon shook his head when he saw the shocked look on Laura's face. "As usual, your dad has it wrong. I did the books. Helped them be efficient. I only ran drugs on the side, when they were short-handed."

"Oh, sorry," Frank said, grinning.

"No problem, boss," Tavon said. "And we ran pot and coke, usually, not horse. The Dragon frowned on the really hard stuff."

Laura was looking at them funny.

"Okay, get your stuff arranged," Frank said with a laugh. "We only have this room until 4 p.m. I might be able extend it if we're making progress."

Laura and Tavon sat, each arranging their own stacks of papers and getting their laptops arranged.

"What do you mean 'efficient?" Laura asked as they were getting ready.

"Oh, making drugs takes a lot of steps," Tavon said as he booted up his laptop and looked for a place to plug it in. Frank pointed out a series of recessed plugs in the top of the table. "Meth and coke, mostly. Helped them make the process more efficient, organize the materials, that sort of thing."

"Sounds like 'Breaking Bad' to me."

Tavon shook his head. "Never seen it. Good show?"

"Oh, it's a great show," Laura said. "Chemistry teacher goes bad, starts making meth. Actually, it would be interesting to hear your perspective on it, how much they got right or wrong with the whole meth production process.

Tavon started to ask something else, but Frank cleared his throat.

"Okay, let's get started." He launched into the introductory talk that he'd prepared, going into the background of the case. "Anderson Tool & Die, located here in Cooper's Mill, had been established back in 1988 and currently employs nearly 60 people. A few years ago, the owner at the time had started noticing what he believed to be money missing from the accounts. He started an investigation but could find nothing out of the ordinary. After that owner suddenly died—a hit-and-run accident—his daughter Jill took over the company. She too suspected that money was going missing, and she also feared that her father had been killed due to his curiosity over the money. She went to the police at the time and—"

Laura interrupted him. "What are you doing?"

He looked at her. "What?"

"What are you doing? Giving a seminar? We already know all this stuff."

"I just wanted to give an overview of—"

"Don't need it, boss," Tavon said. "Let's skip ahead to the questions."

"Um, okay," Frank said, miffed at being thrown off his presentation. "I worked on this for hours last night. Wanted to do a nice summary, get everyone up to speed."

"And we appreciate it," Laura said, nodding at Tavon. "Right?"

"Oh, yeah," Tavon said, nodding enthusiastically. "Totally appreciate it."

"But we're already up to speed. And I've got questions," Laura said. "Tavon has questions. And Dad, I'm sure you've got stuff you were hoping we dug into, right? Areas where you wanted us to tear the books apart?"

"Yes," he said without hesitation.

"Good," Tavon said, nodding. "Let's get going on that. We don't need background."

"Okay," Frank said, a little miffed but ready to make progress. "Who's first?"

They started out slowly, talking back and forth and discussing various parts of the case. The first thing they covered—and the first thing Frank was going to suggest they cover during his prepared statement—was the information on, and background checks of, all the Anderson employees.

Laura went first, covering everything she had found out about each employee. Frank pulled up the employee list on the big screen in front of them, and they went through each person, starting with Jill Anderson. Laura had found some strange connections between some of the employees, but nothing criminal.

"And no money that can't be accounted for," she said, sitting back after talking for ten minutes straight about what she'd found in her study of the current and past employees. "None of them are driving around in Ferraris or anything, that's for sure," she said. "If they did steal money, they're not spending on themselves or hiding it from their wives."

"Could be hidden," Frank said. "Lots of people set up accounts in Switzerland or the Caymans to launder money." Tavon was nodding along. "We just can't see them because we only did a surface background check," Frank continued. "I only have that kind of access."

"Need a court order for anything more, right?" Tavon asked. "Gig used to say the cops could dig into anything if they got suspicious enough."

Frank nodded. "But convincing a judge is the hard part. You can't just be suspicious—you have to have proof that something hinky is going on, or at least a suspicion you can back up with a paper trail." He turned to Laura. "Then, with a search warrant, you can do a global search for any accounts connected to the person's name or social. Still doesn't mean you find everything—people are smart enough to create shell companies and the like. Sometimes you never find the money."

It was an hour in and they were just scratching the surface. When it was Tavon's turn to ask questions, he moved on to the equipment inventories. He had identified a list of equipment where invoiced items didn't match the serial numbers of the equipment, so Frank pulled up the floor inventory numbers on his laptop and projected them onto the screen. He had forgotten that Jill Anderson had given them over.

"Here we go," Frank said. "Jill gave me these, plus some of these are from my guy on the inside. He's been quietly doing a physical inventory."

Tavon made a face. "It would have been nice to have these ahead of this meeting, boss," the young man said.

"Would you have had time to go through this whole list?" Frank said, searching and scrolling for a particular set of purchases that Tavon had highlighted.

"Maybe," Tavon said. "Maybe not."

Once they got into the weeds on the inventory finances, it became a long and tedious conversation that had to be restarted several times at Frank's behest, because he couldn't follow what the two of them were talking about half the time.

But he knew enough to know that they had something, something to go on. It was like a fish on a hook. Frank could tell, based on the hundreds of cases he'd worked on in the past, that they were making progress. Solving the case? Maybe. Maybe not.

But they were getting closer.

When the two hours were nearly up, Frank left and asked Mrs. Havers to extend their reservation. She scampered off, assuring him that she would block out the room for the rest of the day if necessary. He wondered how a woman that old could get around like that.

Back in the room, Laura and Tavon were still talking.

"It's like there are three different people stealing," Tavon said. Tavon pointed at a stack of papers and ran his fingers down the list of numbers printed on them. "Stuff goes missing, or stuff gets ordered but never shows up. Or it's showing up somewhere else. Either way, it goes on the books and then comes off the books." He pointed at Frank's list. "And it's not on this new list, either."

"How does a two-ton CNC router go missing?" Laura asked. "I mean, that begs the question if it ever even arrived."

"Or if it existed in the first place," Frank added.

Tavon was shaking his head. "And it happened over and over. And under different people. Same shit, different day," he said, then glanced up at Laura. "Sorry."

"No worries," she said. "They went through several CFOs and accountants. Could that have something to do with it?"

Frank nodded. "Jill said they had people in to look at things, but none of them could get to the bottom of it."

"I don't know," Tavon said after they continued the same discussion for another half hour. "It's like three different people got the idea to steal money, and each one of them did it separately, but then, each one of them managed to cover up for the other ones. That's the only way I can figure it."

Laura shook her head. "There's no way all three of them got the same idea at the different times to steal money. Who did you say it was?"

They spent the forty-five minutes going over the list of people who worked there again, this time going slowly. They narrowed the list down to the people who were in charge of purchasing equipment and paying those invoices. Tavon and Laura kept pulling up new lists, cross-checking them against the inventory. Some of the inventory sheets were just long lists of hand-written numbers, scans of physical pages.

"Easy to mess those up," Frank said, pulling them up on the big screen. "Handwriting inventories? Doesn't make sense."

"Does if it makes fraud easier," Laura said. Tavon nodded along with her.

"And these are the accounting managers?" Frank asked.

"Yes. Actually, three different positions: CFO, Controller, and Purchasing Manager. But it's the same three people, over and over," Laura finally said. "If it was them, they hid their tracks very well, right?"

Frank sat back, crossing his arms. "No, I don't think so. There were too many checks and balances on these people. Maybe that's when the money went missing, but it couldn't have been these three, could it?"

Laura was looking up the names. "Weird—look, these three people all held those positions. Over time, they've all been the CFO, Purchasing Manager, and Controller. These are the people overseeing purchasing?"

Frank nodded, thinking about it. If she hired from within, it was possible that people had multiple positions within the company. But the same people? "I don't know. Jill was watching them like a hawk. And then the independent accounting firms she brought in checked their work as well. There has to be another explanation for the missing equipment."

Tavon shook his head. "There's not, though, boss. Look at this list here," he said, pulling up another list he'd created on his laptop. "The serial numbers don't match—but they're only off by one number. See there," he said, pointing. "You have to have the actual serial numbers to do that, right? You order the parts, get the serial numbers, then change them by one digit. People think it's a mistake and assume the parts arrive, right? Then the order gets canceled, but the money arrives and is moved out into a fake account. When the parts inventory is finally done later, the one-digit difference is chalked up to user error or something," he said. "Folks assume the parts came in and the inventory is just off because someone read the part number wrong."

"But over and over again?" Laura asked. "You make the mistake once, sure, but consistently? That's a lot of reading errors."

Tavon stood his ground and verbally sparred with her, making his best argument. For a minute, Frank just sat back and was suddenly proud of this young man, using his accounting knowledge for something good. It was nice to see him defending his supposition and backing it up with numbers and theories that he'd developed on his own after studying the available data.

This kid was smart.

"No, that's wrong," Laura said, arguing the other side of his supposition. Frank could tell she was enjoying herself, too. And it was interesting to see the two of them doing what Frank did when he was really deep into investigating a case. They were on the chase, digging and digging and trying to solve a mystery.

It was intoxicating.

After another twenty minutes of back and forth, Frank sat up and put up his hands to calm them down.

"I don't know," Laura said. "These three managers? They have some of the best attendance records at Anderson."

"That doesn't prove anything," Frank said. "One characteristic of embezzlement cases is the employees appear very dedicated and attentive to their duties. Often times, they don't want to miss work, even for vacations. It can mean they want to be there to cover up their misdeeds."

"Okay, okay," Tavon said. "So, these three CFOs or ex-CFOs or manager people. Could they have been working together?"

Laura nodded, pointing at the sheet in front of her. "Their employment dates all overlap. Several times, in fact. They knew each other, did some of the same jobs."

"That would work," Tavon said. "Covering for each other, reporting to each other?"

"Maybe, if they kept it quiet. You ran their backgrounds—do they socialize together? Are they always at each other's houses?"

Frank shook his head and pulled out their personnel files. "No way to know that, really. But I didn't see much overlap in their lives. Any shared bank accounts?"

"No, nothing like that," she said, biting her lip. "But they might have hidden accounts, like you were saying."

"Hidden accounts," Tavon said quietly. "That's interesting."

"What?" Frank asked.

"Hidden accounts," Tavon repeated. "You're assuming the accounts are somewhere else. What if they're still in the company?"

Frank and Laura both looked at him.

"What?" Laura asked. "What are you talking about?"

Tavon grabbed his laptop and pulled up some of the files Frank had sent over. "Here, these accounts. Right here," he said, pointing at a short list. "Foreign accounts, used to fund overseas purchases. There's money in a bunch of accounts. Thailand, Qatar, other places."

Laura shook her head. "I know about those, Tavon," she said. She looked tired, and Frank could tell they were all getting antsy. They would need to end this meeting and regroup to talk again soon. "But that money is all accounted for. Look at the exchange rates."

"What if they're wrong?"

Frank looked at him again. "Tavon, my brain hurts. Out with it."

"Look, we said there are lots of checks and balances on the purchasing managers, right? Well, no, that ain't true. Lots of people were involved in those purchases. But I had come up with that list of weird equipment that couldn't be accounted for or had somehow been purchased and then sold immediately at a much lower price. Right?"

They both nodded. Frank hoped Laura was following along better than he was.

"Someone could have been buying and selling equipment on the side and keeping the profit. The equipment never arrived in the location or the facility, and the serial numbers on the equipment don't seem to match up."

"Right," Laura said. "But where's the money?"

"Right there," Tavon said, pointing at the short list of foreign accounts.

"That's not enough."

"Forget about the exchange rate."

Frank watched her do the calculation in her head. "Wait, those numbers are in dollars? Not Thai bhat?"

"Thai what?" Frank asked.

"It's the Thai dollar, Dad," Laura said, annoyed. "No, that's too—it can't be."

He tapped at the laptop. "Here, the current exchange rate is almost 200 to one," Tavon said. "No idea what it was when this purchase was made. But it makes sense that the accountants seeing those numbers would assume they're in the currency of the foreign country. Not in American dollars."

"No," Frank said. "Someone would notice the extra money, either in country or on the books back here."

"Not if they were using the conversion rate to hide money," Tavon said.

Laura looked at Tavon, then over at Frank. "Hm."

Frank shook his head. "You guys need to start speaking English."

They dug into the books, going back and tracking expenses historically and then watching the foreign accounts. It happened over and over—money was used to buy products and inventory, then money was moved back into the accounts. There was no way to track if the money was converted into the local currency or not—that information wasn't in Frank's files.

"There's no way to know, not from this end," Tavon said after another hour. The room was getting sweaty, and Mrs. Havers had been in twice to check on them. Her face had started out interested, but during the last visit, Frank had noticed she looked concerned. They were nearly four hours into their conversation, and Laura was looking exhausted.

"If someone were buying equipment and then reselling it, wouldn't they have to at least take possession of the equipment?" Frank asked.

"Yes, normally," Laura added. She looked spent. "But with these foreign parts companies, they put it on the boat and that's all they care. They check the inventory at the dock, take payment, and brush their hands of it."

"So, it never arrives at Anderson?"

"Or it does but then gets diverted," Tavon said. "Or it comes off the boat and is already sold to someone else and never even comes to Ohio."

Frank shook his head. "So, you're both on board with this? These three purchasing managers or CFOs or whatever have been running some kind of foreign currency exchange scheme for eight years," he said. "I gotta get this straight in my head. Say it again."

Tavon sighed. "Boss, I'm getting burnt. Okay, yes, you got it right. They buy stuff, pay for it with the money from the foreign accounts. Stuff gets loaded on the boat and the foreign company gets paid. Boat leaves, but the stuff never arrives."

"Over and over?" Frank asked, shaking his head. "It would never work."

"But it does," Laura said, glancing at Tavon. "The equipment order is canceled, and the money paid back, but into the foreign accounts in American dollars. No exchange rate."

"Or the product arrives, gets checked in, then is sold off the floor at some later date," Tavon said. "Inventories assume the parts numbers are wrong because they're off by one digit."

"There are probably other ways, too," Laura added, sitting back. She looked sweaty. "These are just the methods we've found. They have been working together, doing this for a while. They probably have lots of ways to skim and then cover their tracks." She stopped talking, seeming to remember something. She grabbed her laptop and started looking something up.

Tavon continued her train of thought. "Yes, we're just seeing these transaction and inventory numbers for the first time. And it makes sense to me."

Laura pointed at her computer. "It looks like the last one to go through is still in progress."

Frank sat up. "What?"

She nodded at the foreign accounts list. "That's $800,000 in that account in Thailand," she said. "For aluminum sheets and other raw materials that were bought two months ago. Now, if that's American money, that's a lot. If it's in Thai Baht, it's not a lot. So, there is literally no way to tell unless you call the bank in Thailand and ask. We assume it's in bhat because that's how banks normally report holdings."

"But this bank may have been instructed to report in American dollars," Tavon added, finishing her sentence.

"By the current CFO," Frank said. "Right?"

Tavon shrugged. "No way to know. And there are accounts in... eighteen different countries. All with different exchange rates. If the CFO, or others, were working with the banks to move money around, it would be hard to track."

"And these other people, what are they doing?" Frank asked.

Laura sat up and dug through her files, finding a particular sheet of paper. "Here, this accountant firm set this up back in 1997. A double signed agreement."

"Yeah, I saw that too," Tavon said.

Laura handed it to Frank, but it made no sense. "What am I looking at?"

"Two people have to sign to move money out of accounts," she said. "I just looked. Several people signed those double sign agreements, but these three also signed several. Sometimes it was two of them, other times one of them and someone else."

"If they were working together, then the agreements they both signed could be fraudulent."

"Or not even exist at all," Tavon added. "They sign and file an agreement for the Anderson books, then call the bank and cancel it. Anderson has no idea but doesn't care because a CFO signed off on it—AND it was doublechecked by a third party. But if they're working together..." he trailed off, shrugging.

"Right," Frank said. "I get it. People expect people to steal money. Checks and balances only really work on individuals."

"But not when people work together to steal it. It could just be these three managers, or them and other people."

Frank sat back. "Wow."

"And here's another clue," Laura said, turning her laptop around. She'd been quiet for a minute while Tavon and Frank talked. She had pulled up a Google map of a town in Florida and projected it up on the screen.

"Naples? Florida?" Frank was confused.

She nodded and zoomed in. "Not their primary residences, but these three managers all have houses here. Marco Island, a swanky area south of Naples. I didn't think to cross-check all the properties owned by all the people who worked at Anderson." She moved the screen around and then showed them a town south of Naples with interconnected waterways. It reminded Frank of Venice, but it was all mansions and condo buildings lining the water. To the west, a series of huge hotels and other buildings towered over the beaches that lined the sea.

"Nice place," Tavon said.

"Expensive," Laura added. "And these three homes are all on the same small peninsula!" she said, pointing.

Frank could see as she zoomed in on a little cul-de-sac of eight or nine homes. "So, wait. Hang on. You're saying three of those homes right there in that little area are owned by people working for Anderson Tool & Die, located in Cooper's Mill, Ohio? What are the chances?"

"Zero," she said. "And others in the area might be owned by Anderson employees, as well—bookkeepers or accountants who are in on the plan."

"They're working together," Tavon said quietly, rubbing his eyes. "It's the only way this works."

Frank was relieved to find that Jill Anderson was not a proud owner of one of the Florida McMansions. That would have been just the capper this crazy case needed to push him over the top.

There was a quiet knock at the conference room door, and Mrs. Havers poked her head in again. "Mr. Harper, I have to leave soon. The library is shutting for the night."

He looked at his watch and it was nearly seven p.m. "What time does it close?"

"Six p.m. Well, everyone else left just after 6," she said. "I thought you were wrapping things up, so I stayed."

"Oh, we're so sorry," Frank said. He started gathering his things and Laura and Tavon followed suit. "We'll be out of here in three minutes."

They kept talking as they packed, but Frank had enough to go on. Now, he just needed to involve the police.

Mrs. Havers let them out the back door of the library, and they walked over to Frank's car. It was already getting dark outside, and he pulled the doors open and started loading. The animated conversation continued, with Laura stating and restating how Frank would present this to the police, and Tavon trying to shoot holes in her suggestions. They finally agreed to work together over email to come up with a simple document to walk him through their findings. Frank was relieved, as he was having trouble following the complexities of their solution to this frustrating case.

The three of them stood by his car in the secret parking lot behind the library and continued talking for a few minutes. Frank saw light flurries falling from the sky around them. They were so caught up in the investigation and trying to make their arguments easier to understand that none of them, even Laura, had noticed how cold it was.

Finally, he put up his hands.

"Okay, guys, that's it," he said. "We can't go any further tonight. I have enough to go to the cops, but they'll have to take it from there."

Laura nodded. "Not just the cops, maybe. It might involve the FBI too."

"Or the SEC?" Frank asked.

"No, it's not a publicly traded company," Laura said. "Chief King will know who they have to talk to. If that money in Thailand is in American dollars..."

"Yeah, I know," Frank said. "That means it's happening right now."

"Maybe you spooked them," Tavon said. "Background checks, right? People get alerts on that kind of thing?"

"Maybe, if they're paying someone to watch for them. And I've been doing the personal interviews..." Frank added, nodding. "Maybe they're making a big play right now. Get some money before anyone figures it out?"

"Well, it would make them easier to catch," Laura said, holding her box of papers. "If it's happening right now."

Frank nodded. "Thank you both. If you can, work on that document you were talking about. Can it get done tonight?"

Tavon and Laura both looked at each other and nodded. "Yup, we'll get it done, boss," Tavon said, speaking for them both.

"Good. If so, I can go see the chief in the morning."

"Will do," Tavon said, then looked at Laura. "Nice meeting you, ma'am." He turned and started off, walking through the alley and heading in the direction of his car.

"You want a ride?" Frank called after him.

"No boss, I'm good. Talk soon."

Frank nodded and then turned to his daughter.

"Thank you for your help in there," he said. "You were amazing."

She smiled. "Thanks. Now I gotta go get Jackson and pick up something to eat," she said. "Too tired to make anything tonight."

He nodded again. "Seriously, thanks. I'll call you tomorrow, as soon as I know something."

"You better."

They hugged and he watched to make sure she got to her car okay. Laura put her box in the passenger seat and then climbed in, driving off with a wave.

For a minute, Frank stood alone in the secret parking lot behind the library, watching the snowflakes falling slowly through the streetlights.

Could it really be solved? He didn't understand some of the details, but Laura and Tavon seemed happy. And the fact that it would take a court order to find out what was really happening with that inventory? That was actually a great piece of news—that meant a regular person would have a very difficult time double-checking the current CFO's actions to make sure they were on the up and up.

Shaking his head, he took out his phone and texted Chief King, asking for a meeting in the morning. The chief wrote back almost immediately, surprising Frank. Maybe he was finally off the chief's shit list.

King asked in his response if it was an emergency, and Frank answered, assuring him that it wasn't.

"Possible break in Anderson case, need your guys," Frank texted.

"OK, see you at 9," the chief replied.

CHAPTER 44
Report

Sunday night, after their marathon meeting, Frank stayed up late and typed up what he assumed would be a short report on his findings so he would have something to present to Chief King and the detectives of the Cooper's Mill Police Department in the morning. About half-way through, he got the document written collaboratively by Tavon and Laura, and he worked for another hour to incorporate what they had sent.

The only actual workspace he had in his new place was the smallish dining table, which sat awkwardly off to one side of the apartment's very small kitchen. He had it pushed up against the wall—otherwise there was no room to walk all the way around it—and was using it for a desk.

He heard a noise outside and looked out the sliding doors, which opened onto a small yard surrounded by a chain-link fence. Not that he would be out enjoying the back yard anytime soon—at least four inches of snow had fallen in the last twenty-four hours, and Frank was happy to stay bundled up and warm in his apartment.

Beyond the snowy yard and the chain-link fence, Frank saw the back of the adjacent strip mall, which featured a Domino's, a nail salon and the town's biggest liquor store. Frank looked at the back loading dock of the liquor place, his mouth feeling dry. He'd been thinking about the shop a lot, visiting it on occasion. A guy was standing out behind the strip mall again, smoking and talking loudly to another man who was sipping a beer.

The wind outside rattled a loose board on the back of the apartment. It was convenient, having a liquor store so close. And, although he'd been trying to cut back on his consumption over the last year and a half, it wouldn't kill him to have a beer or 24 stored away in his apartment.

Some part of him warned his conscious mind that any drinking was dangerous, a slippery slope that had gotten him into a lot of trouble in the past. But things were looking up in his life.

Laura had asked if being located so close to the liquor store was going to be a problem, but he'd assured her it would not. Now, standing alone in his apartment, all he could think about was pulling on his coat, trudging through the snow that separated his apartment building from the strip mall, and making yet another purchase at the liquor store. He was becoming quite the regular. You knew you were buying too much alcohol when the store proprietor—and their employees—called you by name.

Frank shook his head and went back to the dining room table, sitting down to finish the report. In the end, after reviewing everything and streamlining the report, he had about eight pages of notes and information to pass along. At this point, he had done everything he could from his end. If they wanted to, the cops would need to run with the ball.

CHAPTER 45
Interview

The next morning, he arrived at the police station at 9 a.m. He waited in the lobby and said "Hi" to Lola, the receptionist and dispatcher who worked the front window of the police department. Neither one of them mentioned the fact that Frank had seen her and Chief King together at the HarvestFest. Frank had no idea how many people knew that King and Lola were dating, and he wasn't about to get involved. He'd just earned back Chief King's trust—there was no way he was going to do anything to torpedo their fragile relationship.

Frank waited until 9:20 before Lola let him back into the police station proper. It was a ring of offices with a large, open "bullpen" in the middle, a dozen cubicles for the street cops to work on reports and make phone calls. The higher ups, including Chief King and his two detectives, had actual offices around the perimeter of the large room. To the north, the entire glass wall was taken up by two large conference rooms, with windows that looked out onto the back of a nearby shopping center. Lola showed him to one of the conference rooms and asked him to wait.

"Not the chief's office?"

She shook her head. "No, he's dealing with something. It's why he's had you cooling your heels in the lobby. Sorry about that. I figured you'd rather wait in here," she said with a smile. "And there's coffee there," she said, pointing at the nearby galley. "Make yourself at home, and I'll let him know. Again."

"No problem," he said. Once she was gone, he took out his journal, which was full of notes, and the three copies of his report that he had printed. He wished he'd brought Laura or Tavon along to explain the more complicated financial parts of his findings, but there would be time for that. And their notes and explanations were part of his report. If he was right, there would be many more meetings with whoever Chief King brought in to assist with the complicated case.

He sat and waited for another ten minutes, then left the conference room to make himself a cup of coffee. Frank knew his way around the station—he'd worked here for a time with Deputy Peters when they had been fielding calls and field reports related to the abduction of Laura and Jackson. The maniac Joe Hathaway—Frank would always think of the guy as an evil maniac—had arranged to kidnap them, and then used them as bait to get Frank to chase Joe to a location that had some memories for Frank. It had been a tragic series of events—Frank had recovered Laura and Jackson, thank God, but Deputy Peters was killed in the process. And Joe had escaped.

In the kitchen, Frank was waiting on the Keurig to finish making his cup of coffee when a cop walked in.

"Hey, Harper," the man said. "Good to see you again." Frank recognized him but didn't remember the guy's name and glanced at his badge for the reminder.

"Hey, Officer Grant," Frank said. He'd met Grant during Laura's abduction investigation.

"Things going okay?"

Frank nodded. "Yeah, just meeting with the chief."

"Oh, he should be done soon," Grant said, pouring his own cup from the pot. "They've got something going on with Columbus today, something hush-hush, related to the election last week."

"I'm happy to wait."

Frank took his leave and headed back to the conference room and opened his journal, making more notes on the Masterson case to pass the time. He found the folded stack of cemetery photos and printouts that Mrs. Havers had given him several days ago, and flipped through them, looking for anything familiar. Frank realized that he'd neglected to say anything about it to her last night at the library. He hoped she didn't think he was being rude. It was just that all of his attention was on the Anderson case last night. Frank was jotting down some ideas and a note to talk to her when Chief King walked into the room.

"Sorry about that, Frank," King said, shaking Frank's hand before sitting. "You got a coffee? Good," the chief said.

"Yeah, hope you don't mind."

"Nah, you're good. You know your way around."

"Yup. Everything okay? Officer Grant was getting a coffee same time I was. He said it was Columbus, an election thing?"

Chief King sighed. "Yeah, someone's up in arms about a protest last week, saying it was too close to one of the polling locations. I don't think the Attorney General is going to move forward on it. Just some guy in Cleveland rattling cages. But they wanted to do an all-hands call of everyone in the Dayton area to see if there were any other reports like that one."

"Nothing?"

"No, we're good. AG's just making sure nothing comes back on us later. So, what you got for me?"

Frank nodded. "The Anderson case."

"Yup, you said."

"I think we might have made a breakthrough. It's complicated, and all financial. But if I'm right, your guys will have to take it from here."

Chief King frowned. "Hmm, I'm not good with money, but Detective Smith is."

"Does he know the case?"

"Yeah, I had him read up on it when you took the case."

Frank smiled. "Thought I might make some progress?"

"I've learned not to bet against you."

King went to get Detective Smith, a large fellow who joined them in the conference room.

Frank handed out his report and started at square one, explaining how he'd been brought on to investigate the thefts, first and foremost. He got to use a little bit of his prepared statement that Tavon and Laura hadn't been interested in hearing—or too anxious to get started.

Once he got past the introduction and started to dig deep into the money transfers and foreign exchange, Detective Smith started asking questions, most of which Frank could only answer because he'd been paying close attention to what Laura and Tavon had been talking about the night before. Smith started taking notes in the margins of Frank's report. And Frank kept waiting for them to start shaking their heads, but they never did.

Forty-five minutes in, Smith was nodding along, and Chief King was leaning forward.

"Based on this stuff, I need to make a few calls," Smith told the chief, tapping his copy of the report. "I have a guy at the Cinci office who would know more about exchange rates."

"FBI?" King asked.

Smith nodded. "I don't remember anyone talking about this in the files, but any wire transactions should be recorded on both ends. Including the exchange rates. But I'd need a warrant for that, I think."

"Jill Anderson will agree to anything you want," Frank offered. "She wants to make progress, wherever it goes."

Chief King nodded and then looked at Detective Smith. "Make your calls."

Smith got up and left, taking the report with him.

King turned to Frank. "Send me this electronically," he said, holding up the report. "And no need for you to stay. It's gonna take him a while. I'll text you as soon as I hear anything."

Frank nodded. "Will do. Should I talk to Jill? Sounds like she's going to be getting some calls."

"Yeah, give her a heads up we're involved again," King said, standing. He took his copy of the report. "Judge might want to talk to her before authorizing the warrant for her accounts. Or might not. I don't know. But don't get her hopes up."

Frank stood as well and gathered his things. "I won't."

"I'll get a couple of other people on this to help Smith," King said. "Assuming they find something, can you come back at say...1 p.m.? That gives them a few hours."

"No problem."

King walked Frank out, and Frank got in his car and headed to his "office," the diner, for a late breakfast. He didn't feel like going home—somehow, going home seemed like an admission of failure. Like going home meant the cops hadn't found anything of value in his investigation, but staying out, ready to respond to their calls, kept it alive.

CHAPTER 46
Trapper

"Anything?"

Trapper shook his head even though he was on the phone. He was sitting in his car in the parking lot of a Mexican restaurant across from the Cooper's Mill Police Department. "No, he's leaving the police station now."

"Probably going to that gross diner he loves so much," Joe said, his voice staticky. Even through the slight distortion—the cell service out on the compound sucked—Trapper could tell he was nervous. All of their planning, all the threads set up as bait, and now a bunch of things were happening that they had absolutely no control over.

Apparently, there was some break in one of Harper's cases, based on the very long meeting he'd had at the library the night before and the flurry of emails he'd been sending out.

Trapper had managed to place a virus into Harper's computer— the man had horrible firewall protection, so when he'd visited the "Ohio's Unsolved Mysteries" website, the computer had downloaded in the background a small program. Now, Trapper and Joe were in Frank's computer, monitoring all of his email and web searches. The Church of Xavier's web development team had proved to be very skilled, especially in the area of hacking individual computers.

"I've been through the report he wrote," Joe said on the other end of the phone. "He had a break in that theft case. Anderson something. I went back through his files he's been working this for months."

Trapper nodded. "They were at the library yesterday for a long time. His, his daughter, and some black guy. Maybe cracked it?"

"Maybe," Joe said. "It could affect our timeline, but...wait. Hang on."

Trapper could tell he was reading something else. "Ah, he just emailed the report to Chief King."

"Okay, gotcha," Trapper said. "Stay on him?"

"Follow him, see what you can find out. DO NOT BE SEEN," Joe said, then hung up.

Trapper smiled. Like he needed to be reminded.

CHAPTER 47
Sting

After settling in at the Tip Top Diner and putting in his order, Frank put his phone on the table and called Jill.

"And the police are involved again?" she asked, once he explained the bare minimum to her.

"Yes, but don't get your hopes up, Mrs. Anderson," Frank said. The waitress set his omelet and toast down in front of him, and he nodded his thanks. "They are looking into some financial transactions, ones I can't get access to."

"Okay. That sounds like progress. And Jill, for the love of God, Frank."

"Okay. And yes, maybe. A little bit. They're working with the FBI to reach out—"

"The FBI?"

"Yes. But it happens a lot."

"Who is it? Who from my company is involved. Do you know?"

"No, nothing yet," Frank lied. There was no reason to get her hopes up, or to get her mind racing down roads that led to her calling other people or confronting them. They were a long way from something like that. "I'll let you know. But you will probably be hearing from Chief King or the county prosecutor on the warrant. Kevin Whitlowe is his name. It's probably going to be a warrant to seek more information about funds held by your company in foreign institutions."

"Okay, absolutely. Anything they need," she replied instantly. With that, any hesitation he might have had, or any doubts he might have had about her innocence, melted away.

"I'll call you as soon as I hear anything," he said, hanging up and digging into his breakfast, which had silently arrived while he was on the phone. There was no point in telling her that he was heading back to the police station at 1 pm, or that King had put at least three people on the case.

He ate his breakfast quietly, catching up on his emails on his phone and trying not to think about Jill Anderson and her financial managers and a bank in Thailand that may or may not hold a bunch of her missing money. He couldn't do anything about it right now, so stressing about it did no good. When he was caught up, he read the stack of papers from the front counter—here, people often read their newspapers and left them in a pile near the register for others to share. He read the *Dayton Daily News* and someone had left a copy of the *Wall Street Journal*, which had a huge writeup on the results of the presidential election and a bunch of state-level races and initiatives.

When he was done, Frank got back in his car and ran errands. He didn't want to jinx the case by going home. Instead, he ran to the post office up on North Hyatt, then grabbed the stack of cemetery photos and used Google Maps to find some nearby.

He spent the next two hours driving west and south of Cooper's Mill, locating three of the cemeteries closest to Trotwood, the location of the Salem Mall and the 1997 abduction. The cemeteries he found were small and crowded in between newer buildings and in neighborhoods that had seen better days. None of them seemed right to him. Frank had pictured small cemeteries out in the middle of nowhere, far away from prying eyes. He passed the Salem Mall and shook his head—it looked like it was closed for good, now, after the gang had been run off. Would the local government reopen it or tear the place down?

Heading back to Cooper's Mill, he checked his phone for the twentieth time, but there were no messages from anyone, so he assumed the meeting was still on. After a few minutes on the I-75, heading north, Frank arrived back in town and parked in front of the police station. He got out and headed inside, taking his journal just in case.

"Oh, there you are," Lola said once he entered the station. She stood and disappeared, going around to open the door for him into the station. "Chief said to walk you back as soon as you got here."

Frank nodded and followed her back to the conference room, which was now abuzz with activity. Detective Smith was in there with two other cops, and King was on the speaker phone with someone. King waved Frank into an empty chair.

"And that's a confirmation?" Detective Smith was saying into his own cell phone. Frank sat and flipped open his journal, grabbing the rest of the cemetery photos and flipping through them. There were at least thirty more to check out, and he had no idea where to start. He'd need to chat with Mrs. Havers again, find out if any in the area were connected to the Masterson family.

"Okay, thanks," Smith said and hung up. "Mr. Harper, good."

"Any luck?" Frank asked.

"Actually, yes," Smith said. "The FBI verified that the funds are there in Thailand and that they're not in Bhat—they're in American dollars."

"Is that...good?"

Smith nodded. "Yes, based on your accounting. We got the warrant, and now they've got an electronic tag now on the money—if someone moves it or withdraws it, the tag will follow, and we'll know."

"And we'll know where it's going," King said, ending his own call. "Okay, our people are ready at the location. Now, Frank, we need your help."

"Name it."

"Call Jill and tell her to reach out to her current CFO. I've got people outside his place now. He lives down in Oakwood, so we're coordinating with their officers. Tell Jill Anderson that the cops have had a break in the case. Tell her to tell him—hang on, let me get the words right," Smith said, reading from his notes. "Here. Tell her to say 'the cops are looking into foreign transactions in Europe right now and will be expanding globally in the next 24 hours.'"

Frank smiled. "Gotcha," he said, grabbing his phone.

A few minutes later, Jill texted Frank and confirmed that she'd reached out to her current CFO. Frank shared the text with the other men in the room, and then they waited. They had people from the FBI on speaker, and the agents in the Cincinnati office were giving them a play-by-play of their monitoring software. Eight minutes later, they got a ping.

"Okay, a transfer request just came through," the FBI on the other end of the line said, reading off a string of digits that made no sense to Frank. "Okay, now waiting for the transaction header to come through." There were no sounds for a full minute on the line, and Frank was starting to think they got disconnected when the voice came back on. "Okay, we got it. $800,000 from the Thailand institution. Not converted. Moved to a bank in Grand Cayman. We have the account numbers. Verifying—yes, that account is registered to a dummy corporation we've been monitoring for the past two hours. It's owned through a shell company by the Anderson CFO."

Chief King nodded and then placed his own call. "Okay, you're a go."

Frank assumed they were breaking down the door of the CFO, and waited as Chief King waited, the phone up to his ear. A minute later, he nodded. "Good. Okay, bring him in. And leave the computer *in situ* until the FBI arrives. Lock down the house and leave two men outside. I'll get the other two picked up."

King ended the call and looked up at everyone in the room. "Good collar. So far. Let's not get cocky—there's more work here. I've got people on the other two—we'll have all three in custody in the next half hour. Call Jill and have her come in."

Ten minutes later, Frank met Jill Anderson in the lobby.

"You're kidding me."

"Nope not kidding," Frank said. He directed her over to a bench in the lobby and they sat down. "Not in the slightest." Frank showed her the list of names while keeping one eye on the doors to the outside.

"No, this can't be right," Jill Anderson said, looking at the page from his journal that he was showing her. "These are...these are my CFOs. Three of them. Or they have been, over time. And held other positions."

"It is," Frank said.

"Not the last three, but close," Jill said, pointing at the list. She looked up at him. "What are you saying? They were all stealing?"

He nodded. "Yup. Working together. They had a plan and executed it over the last eight years. They've been shaving money off the side, moving it around and covering it up through bogus purchases and foreign accounts. It looks like they worked closely together over time. Any losses were covered up."

"I don't...why wouldn't that come up in an audit?"

"Not sure," Frank said. "But that's why they were so hard to catch. One was moving money around and the other two were helping cover their tracks. They also had help, we think, from some of the bookkeepers and accounting staff. Not sure about that, yet, but the FBI is looking into it. We caught Wilson, your current CFO, moving money this morning from a monitored account in Thailand."

"Wait, you said they were doing stuff in Europe, not Thailand," she said, then looked up at him sharply. "You knew the money in Thailand was sitting there. Me telling him about the European investigation got him to move it, right? That's how you caught him?"

"Yeah, sorry about that," Frank said. "I couldn't tell you anything. We needed to scare him into action so the FBI could track the money moving and get the account numbers."

She looked at the list again, shaking her head. "I just...I can't believe it. Three of them, working together? And maybe others?"

"That's our theory. Might turn out to be off by a little, but it's a start."

She looked up at him, her eyes suddenly sad. "What about my father?"

"Nothing on that, yet," Frank said. "We're pursuing the fraud and theft investigations first. That is ongoing and easier to prove. But the CMPD and FBI are working on it now, and they are very aware of your father's passing. And his investigation into the missing money. If there is any connection to these three men, or any of their accomplices, they will find it."

"They'll check their vehicles?"

"They'll check everything."

"When did you figure all of this out?"

"Late last night, after a meeting with my people. We finally figured out the flow of the money in and out, and how they might have covered it up by purchasing bogus equipment that never arrived. It took a while to guess that three people were working together—in most cases, thefts are carried out by one person. That these people could steal together and not turn on each other? That's rare."

"You found some of the money?"

"Maybe," he said, hedging his bets. There was no reason to get her hopes up yet. "Or it could be phantom money, stuff that exists only on the books. They're looking into it now. But they're also bringing in Wilson and the others for questioning," he said, glancing at the door.

"Ah, okay," she said. "That's why we're in the lobby."

"I just wanted you to see them first. You can usually tell by how they are reacting to the cops bringing them in."

"Well, over the past eight years, I've estimated that nearly $4,000,000 has evaporated. It would be nice to get some of that back."

"We'll see."

Just then, a police SUV pulled up in front and two cops got out, opening the rear door. They pulled Anderson Tool & Die CFO Wilson out of the back of the car and walked him inside. The man was older, with thinning white hair and a white beard.

"You son of a bitch," Jill Anderson said to him as soon as he was inside. Frank went to restrain her as she lunged at the man in cuffs. "Did you kill my father? DID YOU?"

Wilson looked at her and Frank could see in his eyes that he had stolen the money. The old man looked relieved. Frank had seen that look before on the faces of a hundred people. Now they could relax. Sometimes, going to jail was better. Most people hated keeping secrets.

Frank was surprised at Jill's anger. He didn't say anything but held her back as she tried to get loose. The cops walked CFO Wilson past the receptionist window and into the police station proper.

Jill shrugged his hands off and turned to Frank. "Did he do it?"

"The money? Yes, I think so," Frank said, nodding slowly. "He looked relieved, almost. I've seen that look before. But I don't think he had anything to do with your father's death."

"Oh, I'm so angry, my hands are shaking," Jill shouted, sitting down and steadying herself. "The others?"

"On their way. Chief King's men were waiting to pick them up."

They sat in the lobby and waited, Frank putting an arm around the woman. She seemed like she was teetering right on the edge of losing it. When the other two ex-employees came in at the same time, Frank stood and put himself between them and Jill.

She stayed seated, crying and glaring at them. "If you guys were involved—"

"Involved in what?" one of them asked before getting elbowed by the other.

"Shut up," he said. "Keep your trap shut."

The cops took the two of them into the back, and Frank knelt down in front of Jill.

"That's it for now, I'm afraid," he said. "Nothing else either of us can do. I'm going to leave and let the cops do their jobs."

"But what if they need answers from me, or you get another lead?"

"Then I will call you," Frank said quietly. "They need time to work. And you need to relax, get some rest, and go home. Have a meal and cross your fingers. Watch some T.V. and soon we'll have more information."

CHAPTER 48
Wilson

"Okay, now he's leaving," Trapper said, scrunched down in his car so no one would spot him. There had been a lot of cars in and out of the police station parking lot in the last half hour. "I have no idea who the three guys were who they took inside. I got pictures and sent those over. The Anderson woman just left—she was crying, upset. Harper's leaving in his car."

"Okay," Joe said on the other end. "And the cemeteries?"

Trapper looked down at his notes and read off the locations. "Three of them, down by Trotwood. So, he's interested, at least."

"Too interested—we're not ready yet."

"But we are, boss," Trapper said, reassuring the man. "We are. If Harper heads out there today, we could scramble the men. But the Board is set," Trapper said, using his boss's word for Donnelly Forest. He could hear his boss tapping away at a computer, back in their little pair of bedrooms at the Church of Xavier compound. Trapper had to be the one out in the world, keeping an eye on Harper.

"This first photo you sent me is of some guy named Wilson," Joe said on the other end of the phone. "He's the current CFO at Anderson Tool & Die, according to their website. That's the case Harper is working on."

"I'm guessing that's progress, if they're bringing people in for questioning."

"Yup," Joe said. "We can't see Harper's texts, but he just emailed his daughter that the case is 'moving forward.'" Trapper could almost hear the man's mind racing, calculating possible outcomes and surging ahead to figure out the most probable solution. "And if this case of his is wrapping up, Harper might concentrate on the Masterson women. Should we staff up the Board today?"

Trapper nodded, watching Harper leave. "I'll follow him, see where he goes. But yes, we should get ready. I'll call in to the church and get everyone headed out."

CHAPTER 49
Party Time

Over the next twenty-four hours, the Anderson case came together nicely.

Frank was on the phone regularly with Chief King and Detective Smith, getting updated on the latest. His report had formed the basis of their new case, which was coming together quickly, and the FBI had sent two men up from Cincinnati to assist. The CMPD offices were now so busy that he tried to stay out of the way when he was there.

Wilson and the other two men hadn't confessed, but King was able to hold them for questioning. If Frank had anything to say about it, one of them would break and turn on the others. That was the problem with working with other people—your group was only as strong as the weakest person. One of them would give up the others in exchange for "leniency," whatever that meant in a financial case where the facts were dizzyingly complex.

Frank emailed both Laura and Tavon and let them know that things were moving. "Don't be surprised if you see something on the local news about arrests," he told Laura. She sounded thrilled. Tavon wrote back, sounding surprised. "I didn't think anyone would take anything we said seriously."

By late Monday evening, Frank was tired of waiting for more news and went to bed early. He'd had a couple of drinks to celebrate, and the vodka and beer weren't cooperating. His stomach rumbled for half the night.

Tuesday morning, he had voicemails waiting from King and Detective Smith—arrests had been made. And Jill was ecstatic to hear the case was progressing so quickly.

"Thank you so much, Frank. Seriously. I'm heading to the police station now—Chief King has some stuff he wants me to clarify. Should I have you tag along?"

"No, no, you're good," Frank said. He didn't need to be there, and his head was killing him anyway. Hangovers sucked. "Call me when you're done or if you need anything. King probably just wants your full statement."

Frank returned all the calls he'd gotten, then went back to bed. His head was killing him, and the Advil wasn't helping. Later on Tuesday, he figured out why—while cleaning up, he discovered he'd put away nearly a quarter of the bottle of vodka. You couldn't just jump back in the pool with both feet, he told himself. You gotta take it easier.

Jill called with the good news about the arrests, and Frank pretended to hear it for the first time from her. It was good news, to be certain, but his head was killing him. When he finished the call with her, he called Laura.

"Arrested? Seriously?"

"Yup. Good work," he said, holding his head. He wondered; how long did it take for four Advil to kick in?

"We should celebrate. Yes! Let's go out. Mexican food. Please?"

He was agreeing before he even knew what he was doing.

"And we should invite Tavon," Laura added, excited. "And that kid you have working for you. Do it!!!"

Three hours later, Frank was meeting Laura and Trevon and Travis for dinner at a Mexican restaurant she liked in downtown Troy, about ten minutes north of Cooper's Mill. He realized he was near the square and the County Prosecutors Office and the courtroom where he'd testified against Joe Hathaway. No matter where he went, Frank couldn't get away from the guy and his memories.

Getting out of the car, his phone rang. It read "Cooper's Mill Public Library." Frank rolled his eyes and answered.

"Hello?"

"Oh, good, I caught you, Mr. Harper."

"Hi, Mrs. Havers. Call me Frank."

"Oh, okay. And I'm Edith."

"Hi, Edith. What can I do for you?"

"I got another call from that author today."

"Oh, really?" Frank leaned against the side of the Camaro and wondered how long he was going to have this headache. "What did he say?"

"Oh, just a lot of questions, really. Said that he thought the cemeteries I had searched up were a good idea and asked me to pass along my list. Said he was going to visit. Were you going to find at them?"

He rubbed his temples. "Yes, I am. In fact, I visited three yesterday."

"Oh, which ones?"

"Not sure," he said. "I'll have to look and text them to you."

"Oh, please email me. I don't do text. Or drop by. I can't figure out the little buttons and such. You know, my granddaughter is so good at the texting—she uses her thumbs and just types away like a little dynamo."

Frank felt like chucking his phone into the street and watching it get run over by the passing cars. Instead, he listened to Edith Havers rattle on about her granddaughter, making his head hurt even more. When there was finally a break, he jumped in.

"The three I visited were down in Trotwood. Anything else?"

"Oh, yes. Sorry, I tend to ramble. He asked if I knew the name Donnelly?"

It sounded familiar, but he couldn't place it. "Maybe."

"The author said it had something to do with the Masterson family, like it was an old family name or something. Ancestry.com, I think he said."

"Not sure," he said. "Mrs. Havers, I have to run. I'm meeting some people—"

"Edith."

"Edith. Yes. But I will email you that list."

"Thank you. And anytime you want to talk—"

"I will," he said, already in the process of hanging up. "I promise."

He pushed END and put the phone in his pocket. His eyes hurt, his face hurt, everything hurt. He needed to take it easy on the vodka—for some reason, it was kicking his ass. Or maybe he should just stick to beer. He grabbed his journal and headed inside, quickly finding Laura and Tavon at a table on the left side of the restaurant.

"Hey everyone," he said weakly, passing the greeter stand and weaving between the tables to get to theirs. Tavon shook his hand and Laura stood, hugging him.

"Congratulations," she said as they sat back down. "This is a big deal."

"So, they arrested 'em?" Tavon asked. He was digging into the chips and salsa and seemed happier than at any time Frank had ever seen.

"Yup, and the FBI is adding additional counts," Frank said. He saw Travis walk in and look around and Frank waved him over, making room. "Travis, this is Tavon and my daughter, Laura."

"Hi, hi, nice to meet you," Travis said. Frank got the impression that Travis didn't get out a lot. "So, what happened?"

"Travis doesn't know yet," Frank said to the table. "Laura, tell him."

Laura launched into the news about the arrests, and Travis looked at Frank, his eyes wide. "Wait, what? Are you guys serious?"

Tavon nodded. "Deadly, man. Arrested by the FBI. Damn."

The three of them chattered excitedly as Frank squinted at the menu. He hadn't been here before, but it had the standard menu of any Mexican restaurant worth its salt—fifteen pages of ten thousand different combinations of the same ten ingredients. One whole page of different kinds of fajitas, and another page that listed every conceivable combination of tacos and burritos and tostadas and flautas.

He got to the drinks page and stared greedily at the large, full-color photos of Mojitos and Tequilas and Margaritas. All of his friends, all together again. They looked wonderful. Maybe just one. Or two. But then he glanced up and saw Laura, talking to Tavon and Travis, and decided against it. No need to start that fight again. It was going to be a nice night, and he didn't want to ruin it.

The meal went well—everyone was excited to hear that Frank was buying, and Travis got the table laughing by threatening to order "steak and lobster and four desserts to go."

"Go ahead," Frank dared him.

The group enjoyed their food as Laura and Tavon explained to Travis all about overseas financial transactions, and Tavon went into depth on tracking inventory levels and equipment purchases at the Anderson facility. Travis, in turn, finally relaxed enough to talk about working at the facility itself, and both Tavon and Laura were fascinated to learn that Frank had Travis working "undercover" at the facility.

"Undercover?" Laura asked. "That's so exciting!"

Travis started telling them about how he'd gone around and gathered some of the inventory numbers off the factory equipment, trying to do it without attracting too much attention.

"Well, that really helped, man," Tavon said, tipping his glass at Travis. "Seriously, it mighta broke the case for us. Those numbers were part of a—"

Donnelly.

Frank finally remembered where he'd heard that name. Taking out his journal, he flipped through it until he got to the page of the Masterson case where he'd been writing down his thoughts and the results of his internet searches. Listed under the Ancestry.com area, he found it.

DONNELLY.

"I'll be damned," Frank said.

Laura looked over and saw his journal. "You're working? We're eating fajitas and having fun and you're working?"

"No, not really," Frank said, putting it away and going back to his chimichanga.

The party wrapped up and Frank paid and then walked everyone out to the parking lot. They said their goodbyes and departed, with Laura being the last to leave.

"Thank you for including me in this," she said. "It was fun, and it was nice to be part of something you were working on. Are they all like this?"

"What?"

"When you solve a case. Are they all this exciting? I can see why you do it."

"No, they don't all end this way," he thought. Suddenly he was thinking about Ben Stone, dead in an alley in Coral Gables, Florida. He'd been a better shot than Frank, almost as good as Joe Hathaway.

"No, they don't all end well."

"Well, this one did," she said, taking his arm and hugging it. "You do good work."

"No, not on this one," he said, pulling her into a real hug. "You and Tavon broke the case. I was just along for the ride. Seriously, without you two? We would never have found the money."

She pulled away so she could see his face.

"Okay, I'll take the win. And I'm serious: that was fun. ANY TIME you have anything like this you want help with, you let me know. It was the most exciting thing to happen to me in a while. Probably since Jackson and I got kidnapped—and this was much more fun."

Frank nodded, not saying anything. She and Jackson had been taken by Joe Hathaway as a ploy to get to Frank. Joe had used her as bait to trap Frank. Never again. He'd never let anyone get to her like that again. And if that meant keeping her at arm's length from his cases, then that's what would happen.

"Okay, gotta go," she said. "Thanks again!"

"No problem. Love you," he said, and he meant every word of it.

Watching her drive away, he pondered the idea of checking out the Donnelly cemetery tonight. But it was already dark, and they were predicting snow overnight. Knowing the twisty country roads, he'd probably never find it in the dark.

Instead, Frank Harper thought about the beer and vodka he had at his apartment and decided to head for home.

CHAPTER 50
South

"Nope, south," Trapper said, watching the Camaro. "Back to Cooper's Mill."

"Okay, follow him," Joe said on the other end of the phone. He sounded relieved.

"Will do."

"Make sure he gets home, then sit on his place all night," Joe said. "I'll cancel the men for tonight. Keep me in the loop tonight and in the morning. I'd rather we do this during daytime."

"Agreed."

They passed the McDonalds on their left and moved up the long slope that led over the highway. He stayed back, not wanting to be spotted, then followed Harper as he turned his old Camaro onto the I-75 and headed south, leaving Troy. They merged with traffic and Travis let Harper get a quarter mile ahead before speeding up to match. Trapper didn't want to lose him.

"Okay, on the highway."

"I'd prefer the morning anyway. It's just easier."

Trapper nodded. "Will do, boss. I'll call you in the morning, as soon as he heads out. You think it will be tomorrow morning?"

"There was an 10% chance he would go tonight, even in the dark. Snow incoming, so that helped. I thought he'd wait till tomorrow. Unless he gets called back into the Anderson situation, there's an 85% chance he'll go in the morning. I'll rally the troops at be out on the Board by 7."

"That early?"

"He's old, like me. A morning person. Likes to get an early start, 'before anyone has a chance to screw up the day,' he once said to me. Stay on him. He might get an early start, or he might sleep in. It depends."

"Depends on what?"

Joe laughed over the phone. "How much he drinks tonight."

PART 3
Fire

CHAPTER 51
Heading Out

It was Wednesday morning, November 14, and Frank slept in. He'd come home after the Mexican dinner/celebration with his team and decided to keep the celebration going. That involved several beers while watching television, flipping between the local news and reruns of Forensic Files.

Some part of him was hoping to see a mention of the Anderson case on the TV, but it was far too soon for that. They were still doing interviews and arresting people and talking to bankers in Thailand. It would be weeks before they had indictments and grand juries and press conferences.

Frank smiled, thinking about a press conference he'd run with Chief King only weeks after he'd arrived in town the very first time. They had been working together on a kidnapping case, and Frank had used the press conference to try and "rattle" the kidnappers into making a move.

King hadn't liked that.

Frank made himself some coffee and downed four Advil, then gathered up his journal and his cemetery printouts and his thermos of coffee and headed out. It was a cold, crisp mid-November day, and the sky was achingly clear. He squinted at it and wondered if it would cloud up and snow again.

Driving north, he headed in the general direction of Troy, Ohio, before exiting the highway between Troy and Cooper's Mill and heading west into the country. He was looking for the Donnelly cemetery, one of the ones in the stack of photos that Mrs. Havers had given him. Last night, after he got home, he'd dug through the photos and then a quick Google search had given him the exact location. It was somewhere south of a town he'd never heard of called Mt. Pleasant. He wondered how pleasant the place really was.

Driving the back roads, he was surprised to see that there was still a lot of corn to be harvested. He passed three combines, out and shaving the green and brown and golden corn shocks from the ground. It seemed late to be harvesting, but what did he know? All he knew was that saying, "knee high by the Fourth of July," and they were well past Independence Day.

His phone rang, and he answered the call without looking at the name.

"Hello?"

"Frank, it's Jill. You got a second?"

"Yeah, just driving. What's up."

"They found some of the money."

"What? Already?"

"Yes, yes," she said. "It's still tied up in the investigation, of course, but they told me I'm getting at least $800,000 back. They have to hold it until the case is settled, but it's mine."

"That's great, Jill."

"And you remember what I said at our first meeting, right? What's mine is yours, money-wise. I want you to have some of it."

He wasn't sure he heard her right.

"What do you mean?"

"A reward."

He shook his head, watching the road. There was a turn somewhere up here. "I don't remember you saying anything about splitting it with me. If you did, I would have assumed you were joking. You paid me plenty already—"

"I'm keeping most of it," she said with a laugh. "The factory is getting an upgrade. I mentioned it at our first meeting. A finder's fee. Eight percent. It's what I said."

"No, I can't take that. It's too much."

"Might be more, depending on what they find," she said. "The FBI thinks there's another $400k in Qatar. There might be more. Who the hell knows. But I need to give some part of it to you, okay? It just feels right."

"You've got to be kidding me," he said, repeating the same words she had said when he had told her the case had likely been solved.

"I am not kidding", Jill said. "You're helping me recover this money, sure, but you're also putting a stop to future thefts by these idiots. And, more important, the cops are investigating my father's death. If they can solve his murder, and these three people are involved, not only do I get some of my money back, but I can also see these three assholes go to jail."

Frank smiled. Jill never cursed, so it was funny to hear.

"Well, I can't take your money," Frank said. "You already paid me to research the case and look for the—"

"Don't even talk about that," Jill said. "Don't piss me off, Frank. You're taking the money."

Frank was curious. "Why?"

"Call it...I don't know. Call it good karma. I'll be happy to have the money back, that's for sure, but I really want to know what happened to my father. And you're the first person to help me, really. The first person to listen to me. To believe me."

"Um, okay."

"I owe you. And it's just money. I've got plenty. So, when they release it to me, I'll release it to you. 8% of whatever they recover. The missing money, seized assets, whatever. Share it with your team, go on vacation, buy a boat. I don't care. Really, I don't."

He didn't know what to say. "Well, okay. Thank you."

"Well, don't get all choked up on me there, big fella," Jill said with a laugh. She sounded happier than he'd ever heard her.

He said goodbye and thanked her again and hung up.

"Well, damn. Isn't that something," he said to the empty car.

Frank smiled to himself and drove through the pretty morning sunlight, searching for the turn. He listened as Waze directed him onto a series of smaller and smaller country roads, including several that had not been plowed since it snowed yesterday.

As he listened to Waze on his phone, talking out loud and giving him directions, he thought it was pretty cool that he could unlock his phone with just his thumbprint. And that his phone was talking to him, calmly telling him where to turn.

He took the roads carefully, slowing down where needed so he didn't get bogged down in the deep layer of snow that covered portions of the road. While he drove, he pondered his hangover. Lately, Frank had been feeling good about his ability to control his alcohol intake. It wasn't such a big deal anymore, and he felt like he had a really good handle on it. Drinking was in his blood, and he'd learned to control it. Even though he still felt a little woozy this morning, Frank knew he could control his liquor. He just needed to take things slow, and not let it run his life.

His new place was great. It was going to be great, at least. And having a liquor store right next-door to his apartment also made it very convenient for him to pop over and get alcohol whenever he needed. It was like having an infinite store of alcohol right next door.

It was good that he didn't have to keep much alcohol in the house, especially if Laura and Jackson were over a lot. She did not need to see him stockpiling vodka, or looking under the kitchen sink and finding three spare cases of beer.

There was no need—the liquor store was literally a stone's throw away.

After getting straight at his "gangster rehab clinic" last year, as Laura liked to call it, Frank was now able to master his ability to handle his alcohol. It was clear that he could still get all the work done he needed to while drinking what he wanted when he wanted. Hell, he'd just broken the biggest financial case of his life.

Finally, the Waze app on his phone spoke up, telling him to slow down. He turned onto a small, unmarked farm road. There was no sign, so he had to trust Waze.

The wind was picking up a little, and through the blowing snow, he could see the road was narrow, unpaved. It didn't have a center line down the middle or edge lines to mark the shoulders. He followed it through several turns, moving away from the main road, and then up a small rise that ended in a snowy, flat area surrounded by trees.

From the crunch his tires made, he assumed it was a gravel parking lot, the snow hiding the gravel. Beyond, he saw trees curving around the small parking lot and, just inside the tree line, a small, fenced cemetery. Even from here, Frank could see the humps of white snow marking where the headstones and grave markers stood, as they had for decades. Forgotten.

Getting out, the first thing Frank noticed was just how absolutely silent it was.

He could hear the wind, of course, and the trees moving in the wind, cracking and creaking like a pirate ship. He could also hear the hissing of the snow, moving over itself like sand on a beach. He would only be gone for a minute, so Frank left his journal and the maps in the car and gun in the car, locking them up. He brought his keys and his phone to take pictures of the headstones.

He walked away from the Camaro, the snow starting to slide across the cooling hood. Frank marveled at the silence, then stopped. It was quiet out here, so quiet that he couldn't hear any car noise or the distant road or anything else. For some reason, the isolation gave him pause, and he turned and went back and retrieved his weapon. Standing by his Camaro, Frank checked to make sure it was loaded, then applied the safety and tucked the gun away in the holster under his left arm.

Ever since getting jumped in the parking lot a year ago, Frank had taken to carrying his weapon everywhere he went. You just never knew, did you?

Frank turned and worked his way along the edge of the snowy patch, a rectangular area that he assumed was the small parking lot for visitors to the cemetery. He glanced around, suddenly worried. Frank was in the middle of nowhere, alone, and no one knew he was out here. He was pulling a Ben Stone.

Shaking his head, he sent a text to his daughter, sharing his location like she'd shown him how and explaining why he was out here in the middle of nowhere all alone. Just sending the text made him feel better—and he needed to remember that he didn't need to be a lone wolf. That's part of what Trudy had hated, and part of what had ended their marriage. He needed to make sure he tried harder with Laura.

Crossing the snow, he could see what looked like the outline of a foundation. Probably a house had once stood here, and now all that was left was the graveyard and the parking area.

A snow-covered gravel path wound from the parking area to the clutch of gravestones, huddling under the trees. His feet crunched on the gravel and snow, and when he blew out his breath, he could see a cloud.

The cemetery was ringed with fence, twisted and broken in places. He could see at least a dozen headstones, each dusted with snow, and a large sign that arched over the graves: "DONNELLY."

Frank glanced back at his car, but there was no one around. It felt odd to be out in the middle of nowhere. Stepping over the fence, he searched the headstones, brushing off the snow on each one and reading off the names. None of them sounded familiar, but he took photos of each. And none of them seemed any more "fresh" than the others. If the Masterson woman or her daughter were buried out here in what could be their family plot, then their graves would surely be the most recent, right?

Off to one side he saw two headstones, these newer than the others. The edges of the stone were sharp. The headstones sat at an angle so the fronts, where the names were carved, were covered with a thick layer of snow.

Frank stepped over a stump and reached for the headstone and felt a shock run through his body the moment he stepped down onto the ground. Electricity coursed through him, but some part of his brain registered there was some kind of plastic pad or something under the layer of snow in front of the headstones. His entire body seized up, as if he'd been tased, and Frank fell sideways, the whole world around him going black.

CHAPTER 52
Awake

Frank heard someone talking.

"No, wait until he's awake."

Frank shook his head—he was groggy, like after a hard night of drinking. He tried to open his eyes, but they didn't want to open, and it took all of his strength. Finally, he could see.

He was in a forest, or at least an area with a bunch of trees. There was a clearing, the ground covered with a thin layer of snow. In the middle of the clearing, a low campfire burned, putting out a degree of warmth that he could feel even fifteen feet away.

There was a group of people standing around him. Frank could see their feet, their boots dusted with snow. He hadn't looked up yet—it hurt too much to move his head. Finally, he tried sitting up and realized his hands were tied behind his back. Tied together. And his feet were tied together.

Whoever these guys were, they had taken his shoes and socks. Now he was in his bare feet.

"Wake up, Frank," a voice said. Groggy, Frank lifted his head and listened.

"Are you comfortable?" someone said from behind him.

"Not particularly," Frank said. "Who are you?"

Frank heard footsteps of a man as he walked around in front of him and crossed his arms. It was a man he didn't recognize.

"You remember me?"

Frank started to shake his head and it hurt so much he stopped.

"No. Do I owe you money or something?"

"No, not me," the man said with a laugh. He took out a large, angry-looking knife. "You remember this?"

Frank looked at it. "No."

"I took it off that dead cop. At that farmhouse north of Troy. Remember that day?"

Frank looked at him, but the guy's face wasn't familiar. But Frank remembered that day very clearly.

"Oh, I'm sure Mr. Harper remembers that day, Trapper," another voice spoke up.

That voice Frank recognized immediately. It came from behind him, a thin, raspy voice he had heard in his sleep. Too many times.

Joe Hathaway stepped into Franks' line of sight. The man looked older, thinner. Drained, maybe from his months on the run. Assuming he'd been hiding, or running, trying to stay ahead of the law.

Joe was holding Frank's gun, moving it around slowly in his hands. Frank felt the blood drain out of his face.

"Frank remembers me, at least," Joe said with a smile. "Right, Frank? Big reunion, all of that."

"Hathaway," Frank said through gritted teeth.

Joe smiled, then pointed at the man with the knife. "You might not remember Trapper, but your daughter would. He was following her in his truck, the night he kidnapped her and Jackson." Joe spoke slowly, watching Frank's eyes. Eager for a reaction, Frank thought. "Trapper here brought them to that farm where I was hiding. You know that house, right? You got shot there. That dumb deputy died there."

Frank struggled to move, ignoring Joe. This was not how he'd imagined his reunion with the crazed killer. Trussed up like next week's Thanksgiving turkey —

"Oh, you can tug on those ropes all day, Frank," Joe said dismissively, as if he were already getting bored of the conversation. "I learned my lesson and outsourced it. Someone else tied you up. He's an expert in ropes and knots, and you'll never get free, not until I want you free. See, I learned."

"Learned what, Hathaway? How to hide?"

"You can't predict my behavior if I have someone else do it," Joe said with a laugh. "You can't extrapolate data you don't have."

Frank didn't know what to say, so he said nothing.

Joe shook his head and looked down at Frank's gun. "Is this what you carry? What a piece of crap," he said, unloading the gun and pocketing all of the rounds before tucking the gun in his pants.

"Hathaway, what are you doing out here?"

"Me? Doing here? Oh, Frank, I've been out here for weeks. Getting things ready for you. Setting the Board."

"What?"

"And I have to say, you were so easy to manipulate," Joe said, laughing. "So predictable. Dangle an old cold case in front of you and you come running."

"Like a fish to bait," Trapper added, still moving the knife in his hand.

"Yes, Trapper," Joe nodded, agreeing. "Like a fish to bait. Wave a couple of missing women in front of you and you dash right on over."

"What do you want, Joe?" Frank said, his voice tired. All of him felt tired. "I'm tired." He couldn't lift his head much, and whatever they had used to knock him out had seemingly sucked all the energy out of his body.

"You like that little shock, Frank? I had no idea that was going to happen. What was that, Trapper?"

"Oh, it's called a shock mat," the man said to Joe and Frank and the other four men that stood around Frank in a half-circle. He hadn't looked at any of their faces yet—it hurt too much to move his head. "They use it on cows to neutralize them. Don't have to get too close—you just wait for them to step on it. They use it on troublesome animals."

"Very clever," Joe said. "Good job." He turned to Frank. "See, Frank. You're troublesome, aren't you, so it makes sense."

Trapper looked pleased with himself.

"Now, boss?"

"No, not yet," Joe said, shaking his head. "I need to talk to Frank. Give us a second, okay, boys? Two of you, move his car."

Frank saw the other sets of boots move away, some of them moving to the other end of the clearing and others moving out of his range of vision. Joe walked over and knelt in front of Frank, close enough so that their knees were touching.

"I'm tired, too. Tired of running. Tired of hiding," Joe said. "But mostly, I'm just tired of you. Been tired since you interviewed me and the rest of the coffee klatch. Now it's time to take you off the board. For good."

Frank looked up at him and tried to smile. "Good one. You practice that one? Waiting to see me so you could give me some speech about how tired you are? Screw you, Joe."

Joe smiled. "Yeah, I might have practiced. I've been getting ready for our little game for a while."

"Game? What game?"

"Oh, the ultimate game," Joe said. "I'm the ultimate hunter, and you're my prey."

"What?"

"You. I've been waiting for us to chat again in person. And I've been planning this since the river. You will die today. But first, you're going to run. I'm going to hunt you. Like you hunted me. And, in the end, you'll fall. And then I can get on with my life."

Frank shook his head. "Oh, that's tired. Seriously. You're going to hunt me in the woods. Wow, so original. It's been done a thousand times." He looked up at Joe. "You're supposed to be the smartest person on the planet, and that's the best you could come up with? I read this in a book when I was a kid. Sherlock Holmes, I think. 'The most dangerous game' or something like that."

Joe looked at him. "Yes, I know. It's been done before. But we're going to replay it now, here, in this forest. I've set things up for us. The Board is set."

"I don't even know how to play chess," Frank said with a smile. "It's a dumb game, pieces with weird moves jumping around the board."

Joe didn't answer. Instead, he stood and backed away and waved someone over. "Oh, you're going to play, Frank. You'll play my game, and the way I want."

"Did Tom Mercato play your game?" Frank asked, spitting out the words.

The man named Trapper walked around into Frank's range of vision and kicked Frank, knocking him over onto his back. Two other men grabbed Frank and held him as flat as they could on the ground. Trapper stood over him, brandishing the knife.

"I took this off that dead lady cop. Hispanic lady, I think. Big girl, good fighter, but not good enough. Remember her?"

"No," Frank said as he struggled. He looked at Joe. "You gonna have him cut me? How's that a fair fight?"

Joe smiled. "It's not. I don't fight fair," he said. "I learned that from you."

"What do you mean?" Frank asked. Just keep the crazy guy talking while you figure a way out of this whole mess.

Joe didn't take the bait. He turned. "Okay, Trapper. Do it."

Trapper lifted the knife and plunged it into Frank's stomach.

The pain exploded through him. Frank gritted his teeth and felt the pain washing over him.

"More," Joe said. "Sideways. Two inches to the left. No more."

Frank couldn't see it, but he felt Trapper slide the knife sideways, slicing through Frank's belly like he was cutting a watermelon. It burned like lava, his blood leaking out of him.

"Good," Joe said, watching eagerly. "Good. Okay, that's enough."

Trapper stood and backed away and Frank could see blood dripping from the knife. His blood. The men let him go, and Frank rolled to the side, screaming in pain. The blood dripped from the knife and painted the snowy ground around him, a splash of scarlet on a field of white. The pain roared through him like an animal freed from a cage. Frank struggled weakly against the ropes, but they did not even budge.

"Okay, that's enough," Joe said. "Frank, we're moving on to the next phase. That's where you run and I shoot at you. It will be over soon—but not too soon, I hope. And don't think of running away—we're in the middle of nowhere. I picked this land for just that reason. No one will hear us, or the guns. There is nothing you can do now but run, though I hazard to say that might be difficult for you," Joe said, nodding at Frank's belly. "Do you have any questions for me?"

Frank stared at the ground, trying to push the pain away. He wished he could go back to just having a hangover. He wished he could go back to when his biggest problem was some old woman calling him in the parking lot of a Mexican restaurant.

He looked up slowly. "Yeah, I do have a question," he said through gritted teeth. "Did you enjoy killing that young woman over in Indiana?"

The others looked at Joe, who only smiled.

"Did you know she was pregnant?" Frank asked, panting. "She had a baby inside of her when you caused the car accident that killed her."

Trapper started to say something, but Joe put his hand up.

"She was an idiot, Frank. Of course I knew. And she was way too young for Tom Mercato. He was cheating on his wife. He and his girl both deserved to die."

Frank nodded and it made his head hurt so he stopped. "And you're the...you're the one who decides who lives and who dies?"

"Sure. Someone has to."

Frank looked slowly around at the other men. There were six total, including Joe. "You guys are all cool with that? Just so I know up front."

None of the other men said anything. They all just stared back at him until Trapper stepped closer.

"No, don't get close," Joe said, waving Trapper back. "He's taunting you. Probably trying a headbutt or something."

Trapper stepped back but then nodded at Frank. "Joe's a good guy,

Harper, and a good boss. You, on the other hand, are a drunk who falls ass-backwards into success."

"Maybe," Frank said weakly, looking down. "But I don't kidnap kids, champ."

Trapper started to reply but then held his tongue. Frank wanted him to keep talking, keep interacting with him, but then Frank suddenly felt very tired. Blood was oozing from this stomach and painting the front of his jeans, his energy literally draining from his body.

"Okay, that's enough," Joe said, but not to him. He was talking to Trapper, apparently, who stepped around Frank and approached him from behind.

"Night, night," Frank heard from behind him. Before he could move or even react, he felt the two hard points of a handheld Taser on his back. Trapper flipped the switch and Frank felt the energy course through him and he blacked out again.

CHAPTER 53
Phase 6

Joe smiled and waited, then walked around behind Harper, who was passed out on the ground at his feet. "Good job, everyone," Joe said. "Trapper, nice work with the knife. How long do we have?"

"Eleven minutes at that voltage," he said, waving the Taser around. He nodded at a bag on the ground. "I have three other Tasers in my bag, and they're all fully charged."

"Good," Joe said. He pulled out the laminated sheet of paper from his jacket. It had his Plan, typed up on both sides in large numbers and letters. "Okay, you two head to Bishop, the other two to Knight. Where is his car?"

One of them spoke up. "We moved it behind the trees just north of Rook 1, as planned."

"Okay," Joe said, looking at his list. "Phase 7 is a go. Oh, phones?"

The men all shook their heads, including Trapper. "No sir, everyone left them back at the Church compound."

"Good," Joe said. "If he could get a phone, this would all be over. Everyone know where they're supposed to be next, right?"

Everyone nodded in unison. They had practiced this over and over. Trapper had been doing rehearsals of the Game for days, running them through the steps like they were putting on a production of Hamlet.

"Any questions? No? Good. Go."

The men hurried off into the woods. Joe turned to Trapper.

"Let's do his phone."

Trapper pulled a phone from his pocket—Harpers. Trapper tapped to wake the iPhone and then leaned over, using Harper's thumbprint to unlock it.

"I'm in."

"Good. Set it so it doesn't lock again and remove the password."

Trapper tapped at the screen, going into the settings. "Okay, I removed his thumbprint, and the new password is 7878."

Joe nodded. "Now turn on the airplane mode and mute it so it doesn't get texts or ping the cell towers."

Trapper nodded, then handed it over. "Done.

Joe took it gingerly—Harper's whole life was in this phone. Joe could send texts as him, emails, whatever. He scrolled through the texts, finding the one he'd sent to Laura. Joe had time, but that one might be a problem. After he killed Harper, Joe planned to also ruin his reputation. He'd have months to do it, making it seem as if Harper had gone on the run. Maybe Joe should kill someone and make it look like Harper had done it.

Maybe the daughter and her brat kid.

It was something to think about. Joe dropped the phone in his pocket.

"Okay, I'm heading to Rook 2. Bind his wound and leave him here, tied up. Do it fast. Where is that glass?"

Trapper looked at him. "What?"

Joe was looking around at the snow on the ground. Some of it was spattered with Frank's blood, red on white. "The glass. The piece he needs to find to cut his ropes and get free. It was supposed to be here where he could see it, but the snow covered it up. Get started on him."

Trapper rolled Frank over and started binding the large wound in his stomach, wrapping it to slow the bleeding. Once he knew Trapper was doing it right, Joe dropped to his knees and searched the snow with his gloved hands until he found the piece of glass. He set it in a place where Frank could find it.

"Okay, we're good. Hurry up and get out of here," Joe said, glancing around to make sure the clearing was ready." He waved the walkie talkie he'd taken from his pocket. "I'm heading to Rook 2. I will call you."

"Sure thing, boss," Trapper said as he finished wrapping the thick gauze around Frank's midsection.

CHAPTER 54
Gutted

Frank came to, and his stomach was burning. For a second he thought he'd passed out from the pain before remembering that the Trapper guy, Joe's henchman, had zapped him with a Taser.

Frank figured he'd been out for a while. Someone had wrapped his belly with gauze and medical tape. The wound would eventually bleed through the covering, depending on how much he moved, but it looked like someone had made an effort to slow the bleeding. Why would someone stab him, then immediately get to work repairing the damage? It didn't make any sense.

Of course, this was Joe Hathaway. Everything made sense, if you knew what to look for.

He looked around at the clearing, expecting to see Joe standing there with a gun, but Frank was alone. There was nothing here but the remains of the small fire, sending up a few wisps of black smoke. All the people, including Joe, were gone.

Gingerly sitting up, Frank looked around the clearing. He couldn't tell where he was in proximity to the old graveyard, but through the trees, he could see patches of clear sky overhead. It looked like the snow had stopped and it was still early morning, so not much time had passed. He was tied up and barefoot, left alone in the snowy clearing.

"Great," he said to himself out loud.

He shook his head slowly and tried to stand, but his legs were tied together. With no shoes, he was able to shimmy the rope down to his feet and over his ankles and finally kick the rope free. He got his feet underneath him and painfully pivoted himself up onto his knees, going slowly so as to not disturb the wrapped gauze around his midsection. Frank turned slowly on his knees, searching the clearing.

Several sets of footprints moved off in different directions, so it was impossible to tell where Joe and Trapper and the other men had gone. They sounded like they had a plan, so likely they'd all moved off to their next locations. Joe was having fun, moving people around like pieces on one of his chess boards.

And Frank was one of the pieces.

Assuming he was being watched, Frank started to struggle to his feet but saw a piece of glass shimmer off to his right. It looked like part of a Coke bottle or something, sticking part-way out of the snow. It was small enough for him to grab but large enough to cut through the ropes that bound his hands. Getting himself free would be a good first step in figuring out how to get out of here.

Frank shuffled on his knees over to it and then turned around, backing up and feeling around in the snow until he found the glass with his hands. He got to work on the ropes that bound his hands. It took a few minutes, but he slowly sawed his way through them until they fell away, and his hands were free.

"Finally," he said, grasping his arms and rubbing them to get the circulation going. Grabbing the rope, he started to chuck it and the piece of glass into the woods and stopped.

This was Joe Hathaway.

He was the smartest person in the room, all the time, always. He left nothing to chance. In Frank's experience, the guy was always reminding people of that "fact," either through the way he talked or through his actions. And yes, the man was smart. But often he was too smart for his own good.

Frank held up the piece of glass and looked at it. Had Joe left it there where Frank could find it? Had Joe tied him up—or more likely had him tied up—just so Frank could get himself free?

Joe liked mind games. Frank needed to take his time, be smart, go slow and be deliberate. Think out each step, taking nothing for granted. Joe liked to set up these elaborate games, like the clues he'd sent Frank to figure out where Joe and his people had been holding Laura and Jackson.

The piece of glass had been left there on purpose.

So, that was the way this was going to go, Frank thought. Anything like that, anything that's easy, it's probably been left on purpose.

Frank glanced around the clearing. The fire, the glass, the way the footprints left the clearing—it was all planned. Joe had worked all this out ahead of time.

And so, Frank was going to need to be rash, unpredictable. He needed to whoop and holler and do all the crazy things that Joe wouldn't or couldn't anticipate.

And, most importantly, Frank was going to have to think his way out of this mess.

Before moving, Frank did a quick assessment of what he had on him. He turned out his pockets but found nothing there. His phone and keys were gone, along with the small pocketknife he usually carried. And his gun, obviously. Standing, his hands now free, he pocketed the piece of glass and the rope. You never knew when they would come in handy. Of course, maybe Joe was counting on him taking them, and the glass or the rope would figure into the game somewhere later.

Just the idea of trying to outthink or outplan Joe Hathaway made Frank's brain hurt.

And Joe was relying on Frank to try to outthink him, right? The best thing Frank could do would be to try to be unpredictable.

Frank checked the bandage around him. The wrapping was thick, stretching from his nipples down to the top of his waist. The thick fabric went around him at least four times, and you could see from the square outline that there were some bandages under the wrapping. At the ends, Trapper had used surgical tape to hold down the edges. Frank touched the bandage gingerly and felt the pain spear through him.

Again, he had the feeling he was being watched. He turned and glanced around but saw no one within eyesight. Joe was probably watching from far away, some elevated position. And hidden—Joe had taken the time to create a "blind" in the trunk of his car when he'd taken shots at Frank and Peters on the lake. He hadn't accounted for the enclosed space, though, and temporarily deafened himself.

But Joe liked to hide. It was built into his DNA, apparently, so he would likely be hiding, watching.

Frank glanced around again, searching for hidden blinds, but saw nothing helpful. He walked the clearing, checking the ground for clues or other helpful items. He tried to walk fast but it hurt to move. He also took his time—Frank didn't want to leave this immediate vicinity until he knew more about what he was dealing with.

The fire in the clearing had gone out, and he walked over to it and used a stick to poke at the burnt logs. Nothing of interest there. The logs had cooled to the point where he was unable to use them to light anything else on fire. He tried some leaves and the rope from his pocket, but nothing worked. He was starting to get cold and would have loved a little bit of warmth. They had taken his jacket, shoes and socks, leaving him out in the snowy wilderness in just a T-shirt and jeans.

Too bad he couldn't get anything burning. For a moment, he imagined him making a torch and starting a forest fire—that would throw a wrench in Joe's "game."

Three trails led off into the woods, all in different directions. There were footprints in the snow at each trail, and it was impossible to tell who went where or how many people.

Shaking his head, Frank started down one of the trails, taking the one that felt like it would lead back west, in the general direction of the cemetery. Based on the direction of the sun, the way he was walking felt like it was west.

Of course, he could be completely wrong.

If he could get to his car, Frank might be able to get out of here. Of course, Joe had told them to move it, so maybe it was gone. He didn't have a lot of options and walked the trail, searching. There were no signs of the trees thinning or the graveyard.

Frank was following the footprints on the ground when there was a loud report, a sharp crack in the distance. A second later, a tree branch near him exploded, sending fragments of wood and dirt and snow out and all directions.

They were shooting at him.

Frank ducked instinctively, dropping to the ground and waiting, but there were no other gunshots. The sudden movement made the pain flare in his stomach again as he laid down on the snowy ground. But were they driving him or trying to kill him? Was he supposed to go forward or back?

Frank didn't think Joe would want to kill him from far away. If Joe was planning to take Frank out—and that looked like a growing certainty—Joe seemed like the kind of man who would want to watch. To see his victims die close up. If it was possible, Frank thought Joe would want to stand over his victim and watch the life drain out of him.

He waited for a few minutes, then stood, his bandage redder than before. He was losing blood even through the gauze. With no stitches, Frank thought he had an hour, maybe two, before he'd need serious medical attention.

Frank walked slowly over to the tree that had been struck by the bullet, looking at the hole. He dug around in it with his finger, hoping to see the caliber of the bullet. It was a good-sized bullet hole, with enough punch to easily kill a man. Frank guessed at the caliber and, from that, assumed Joe wasn't trying to shoot him. Not yet. And Joe rarely missed, anyway. If Joe wanted Frank dead, he'd be dead.

That only left one option—Frank was the prey, and Joe was hunting him. Toying with him, playing with him. And trying to get him to move in the correct direction.

Back to the west was bad?

Frank turned and continued in a westerly direction, back towards where he thought the cemetery might be located.

Another shot rang out, this one hitting a tree near his head.

Much closer, that time.

Frank ducked down to think. Taunt the old man, or turn back? Clearly Joe had a plan. Let it play out, or color outside the box?

Frank was the ultimate game – that was the name of the old story, written by somebody, about humans hunting humans. Frank couldn't remember who did it first—it was probably a concept that went back to ancient times. But the modern take on the story, man hunting man? He wasn't sure. It might've been an Arthur Conan Doyle story, the same guy that wrote all the Sherlock Holmes books.

Either way, Frank knew what was happening. Joe had lured him out here into the middle of nowhere, and now was going to spend a jolly afternoon hunting Frank. There would be running and hiding and finally, when Joe got tired of the game, he'd corner Frank and kill him. Likely with a gun, based on Joe's marksman ability, but not so far away that Joe couldn't approach and watch Frank die.

The guy would have planned it all out, down to the last detail.

And Joe probably expected Frank to put up a fight.

Frank remembered back to the icehouse on Trapper's Lake. Joe had put an insane amount of effort into prepping that cabin. He had gone around and used an auger and other tools to drill a series of holes around the outside of the cabin to weaken the ice. This had made it easier to use heat to warm the ice and allow the house to break through, sinking under the ice and drowning anyone inside.

This could be worse. How much time had Joe had to prepare this little "game?" Frank had no idea.

In the end, he went with his ears. He could hear running water and thought about Joe falling backwards into that river to escape. Frank felt like the river would be important to Joe, and headed back the way he'd come, in the direction of the river.

CHAPTER 55
Phase 7

Joe was splayed on the floor of the tent at Rook 2, watching Harper through his scope. The man was stumbling around the Queen clearing, looking at the footprints, Joe assumed.

Trapper called in on the walkie talkie. "You there, boss?"

Joe picked up his walkie talkie and keyed the button. "Yup, here. What's up?"

"I got two men at Knight, ready to move in. We ready?"

"Give me a sec," Joe said, then went back to the scope.

Harper had dropped to the ground when Joe had fired that scare shot. It had taken him a few minutes to get back up. Now, the man was making loops around the clearing, shuffling and looking at the ground. Trapper had fired at Harper as well, and the old cop spent a few minutes digging at a tree, trying to dislodge the bullet. Even from here, Joe could see Harper starting to shiver.

This would all be over fairly quickly. Between the cold and the blood loss...Harper headed west again, back toward the cemetery. He needed more correction, so Joe fired again, closer to Harper's head this time. The man stopped and looked around. Then, after a few more minutes of thinking, Harper turned and headed back east, moving out of Joe's visual range.

"Okay, he's on the move to King," Joe said, keying the button. "He'll pass Knight in a few. Let him pass, then send in your guys."

"Should I take another shot at him?"

"No, he's getting closer. He would triangulate your position."

"Gotcha," Trapper said. "And my men—they are supposed to try and kill him, right?"

"Yes," Joe answered. "That's why we gave them the guns and the ammunition."

"I'm not sure I like this plan, boss," Trapper said. Joe could hear over the walkie talkie the sound of Trapper moving through the woods. "You sure you disabled the pins?"

"Yes," Joe hissed. "I know what I'm doing. And don't talk so loud—they might hear you."

"Gotcha, boss," Trapper whispered. "Out."

CHAPTER 56
On the Lookout

Frank had no idea where he was going or even what direction he was moving in. He'd left the big clearing and now was struggling down a trail, heading what felt like east. He could hear a river in this direction, and there were footprints on this trail, as with the others. Frank had also heard the occasional sound of people talking and moving about the woods, so he knew he wasn't alone.

Holding his stomach, Frank continued east, or at least what he thought was east, and then moved into another clearing.

There were two men there waiting for him.

Both were armed, their guns aimed right at him. These were two of the men from the first clearing, where when he'd woken up. Both of the men were younger, probably in their twenties. Frank raised his hands and made a pained face.

"Hey, guys, you got me, okay?" Harper slowed, putting his hands up. "I need a doctor."

The two young men said nothing.

Frank slowly lowered one arm and pulled up his shirt, showing the bandage. "I'm cut, okay? I...I'm bleeding all over. I'm not gonna fight you. I can't fight you."

The two young men looked at Frank and then at each other. The taller one, who turned out to be the braver one, spoke up.

"We're just supposed to hold you here until Mr. Hathaway gets here. He said he wants to..."

Frank fell to the ground as if he were passing out, aiming for the ground between him and the pair of young men. But instead of falling, he tucked his head in and rolled forward, covering the distance between him and the two young men in a moment. It was a dangerous move, especially in his condition, and one you never, EVER did on rough terrain.

And it hurt like a son of a bitch.

The forward roll was an advanced move, one he rarely taught to his occasional Krav Maga students because it had the potential for one to really hurt oneself. And doing it on a forest floor, with rocks and leaves and snow and fallen branches? Bad idea.

Frank did it anyway and felt something tear as he finished the roll and popped up near the first gunman, the taller one. Frank ignored the pain in his gut and swept his arm upward, knocking the gun free. He used his forward momentum to push the man backward into a tree, knocking him down.

Frank turned to find the gun, but it had spun away into a mass of leaves and snow, and he looked up at the other gunman, who aimed his gun at Frank's face and pulled the trigger.

Nothing happened.

The man made a face and pulled the trigger again, four or five times, as Frank closed the distance between them and took the gun from him. The gun removed, Frank dropped his right hand back and rounded, punching the kid in the side of his face, knocking him out.

The clearing grew quiet again.

Frank moved to a tree for cover and caught his breath. The stomach wound was really hurting now, made worse by that roll maneuver. He'd been lucky he hadn't rolled over a sharp stone or something worse. He rubbed at his shirt, hoping to massage some of the pain away, but it only made things worse.

While he recovered, Frank inspected the gun, a revolver. It was loaded, and Frank could see the six bullets peeking out from the chambers. He pulled the hammer back and checked it, then test fired it into the ground.

Nothing.

There was also a small piece of white masking tape wrapped around the handle.

A decoy gun? Designed to jam?

He popped the revolver open and looked inside. The firing pin was gone.

Without it, the gun and bullets were useless.

Frank thought it could've been a mistake, and he spent the next couple of minutes searching, finally finding the other gun, the one he'd knocked free. It was in some brush near the foot of a tree. He knelt down to grab it, and stayed down, checking the gun itself. Again, it was fully loaded but refused to fire. Frank confirmed the firing pin was missing from this weapon as well.

Frank stood, checking on the fallen young men. Both had been knocked out cold. He checked to make sure they were alive and breathing. No one had fallen backwards onto a pointy stick like they did in the movies. People were always dying in stupid ways in the movies. Neither had wallets or radios or phones or anything on them other than the guns.

When he was done, he stood to continue east when a thought occurred to him. Were these two men sacrifices? Was Joe playing chess and sending Frank people to take out? Was he trying to build up Frank's confidence? Or get him guns that Frank would rely upon, only to find out too late that they had been disabled?

Frank shook his head. There was no way to outthink this guy. It was pointless to try.

Heading east again, Frank shook his head and pocketed both of the useless guns. It didn't make a lot of sense, sending sacrificial men out here to fight him and not give them working guns. That probably meant the unconscious men didn't understand that they were only pawns in this game.

Literally.

Maybe he could take the bullets out and throw them at someone. He remembered seeing that on TV show sometime. The good guy had knocked a bad guy down, then dropped a bullet on him, telling him to get out of town. And he had a warning about future bullets: "The next one's coming faster."

Not sure what else to do, Frank continued toward the sounds of rushing water.

CHAPTER 57
Missing

Joe watched from his blind. Of course, Harper disarmed the two kids and took their weapons. He'd used a rolling attack that Joe had not anticipated. Now Joe was down two pieces with nothing to show for it.

While Harper was hiding behind a tree, inspecting the two revolvers with white tape on their handles, Joe pulled out his phone and quickly researched Krav Maga rolling attacks. It seems that they were not a standard part of Krav training, but not because they didn't work well. The literature said they were very effective but rarely taught because the instructors found them hard to master.

Joe smiled. Of course, Harper was an expert. Boring. Joe had read that Harper even taught classes and trained people in Krav Maga techniques. If this weren't all going to be over in the next half-hour, Joe would've thought he needed to do more research. In the end, none of Harper's fancy moves would matter. Joe would shoot him from a fifth of a mile away and Harper would die.

Joe heard his radio click and picked it up. "Yes?"

"Okay, boss, he's moving east again, toward the river. He picked up both guns and pocketed them."

"I saw," Joe said. "Phase 8 is over, moving on to Phase 9. I'll take a few more shots and then relocate to Rook 3. After that, take a couple of shots from behind him. Drive him to the next location."

"Gotcha. Confuse him. Then can I check on my men?"

Joe thought about it. His inclination was to leave them be until this was over, even if they were badly hurt. It could wait. But Trapper obviously was worried.

"Sure, but not until Harper's at King."

"Roger that."

Joe nodded and laid his gun aside. He started backing out of the blind, taking his binoculars and the radio with him. Once he'd gotten out, he stood and clipped the radio to his waist.

The blind was arranged on the top of a small hill that overlooked the forest to the south. Joe walked north, down the hill and away from the forest behind him, careful of the wet spots. The snow had come in earlier and dropped a couple of inches overnight, messing up some of his plans but ultimately not complicating anything important.

Walking down the narrow mud path between two wide patches of snow, he got to the Gator and climbed in, starting it up. It was a straight shot through the edge of a field of corn to the north, skirting trees to get to Rook 3, which stood on a rise above a turn in the creek that ran south along the eastern edge of the property. Stands of trees populated the water's edge, but the blind afforded a great view of the creek and the large eastern clearing he'd dubbed King.

Harper would be there soon, and Joe would finally put an end to all of this.

Joe put the Gator in gear and started down the slope, heading north.

CHAPTER 58
Pieces on a Board

Frank stopped.

That was an engine.

Someone started up an engine off to his north, through the trees and in the general direction from which some of the bullets had traveled. He leaned against a tree. Frank needed to think.

Okay, so Joe had this all planned out. He had a bunch of people working for him, including Trapper and those two kids back at the last clearing. And Joe had been shooting at Frank, not to kill him but to keep him moving. If Joe had wanted Frank dead, Frank would be dead.

Then Joe had those young men attack Frank. But Joe had set them up to fail, giving them guns that didn't work. Frank was supposed to beat them, like he was supposed to find that piece of glass and cut his bindings.

And, out here, they must be using radios or something to communicate, but Frank had found nothing on either of the young men.

Now, someone was on the move, starting up an engine. It didn't sound like a car. Maybe a golf cart or ATV? Joe had had a lot of time to plan, so he'd obviously been out here in these woods for a time, prepping. He probably knew the forest better than Frank would have time to learn.

But that didn't mean Frank had to be predictable.

Frank thought about the young men back in the clearing. He'd checked them for other weapons and radios, but there was one thing they had that he couldn't steal—their knowledge of this forest. Would someone come to check on them? Joe wouldn't care—clearly, he'd sent them to be defeated by Frank—but maybe they had recovered? He could follow them, or follow whoever came in to help them. Would Joe send in aid or let them suffer?

It could be worth the risk.

After pondering it while walking, he stopped and waited. No shots rang out. Frank ducked down behind the line of bushes and trees and started working his way back the way he'd come. He felt like an idiot, of course, bent over and walking while holding his belly. But if Joe was watching, he'd fire a warning shot, right?

Nothing happened.

Frank continued west, thinking and watching the trees. If Joe had been watching him but was now on the move, using that vehicle Frank had heard, then Frank had a momentary advantage. Maybe Joe was changing locations or someone else was moving in behind Frank to keep him moving east?

There was no way to tell.

And if someone was watching him, they'd have trouble seeing him. Frank made it thirty feet back down the path, heading back the way he'd come.

He passed over a snowy patch and saw more blood on the ground. Assuming it was his, Frank stopped and checked his bandage. It was soaked through. He tried to squeeze blood out of it, splashing the ground. Frank knew time was growing short. He didn't have time for this whole production that Joe was putting on. It might be a great play, but Frank felt like he was destined to miss out on at least the ending minutes.

Joe was planning to kill him, and it was Frank's job to frustrate those plans. Even if Frank was the special guest star, and Joe was the main character, they had forgotten to give Frank his lines.

But Frank was happy to make things up as he went.

He continued through the forest, holding his stomach and cursing under his breath. When he approached the clearing with the two fallen men, he ducked down behind some bushes off the main path and waited.

What he wouldn't have given for his phone. Or a working gun.

- - - - -

Trapper walked quietly through the forest, his head on a swivel. He had his gun out and was carrying his small black leather duffle bag, the one with the tasers. Trapper's boots crunched on the fallen snow and the layer of wet leaves beneath. The path he was on ran between two clearings and had been tracked up with footprints.

And blood. Frank Harper's blood, easy to spot on the snow.

Trapper did not like this.

He loved working for Joe, loved helping the old man out and acting as his assistant. Trapper had even gotten a thrill out of kidnapping various people, and occasionally causing a little mayhem.

But this whole situation? This was crazy.

Setting up a the "Board," as the old man liked to call it, that had been fun. Getting it all planned out, setting up the various locations—it had all felt like they were setting up for a movie shoot or something.

And the other part, where Trapper played the part of a book author, calling his "tips" into the local library and whetting that old woman's appetite? Calling the police with more information? Working with the Church of Xavier folks to build the fake "Ohio's Unsolved Mysteries" website and populating it with a bunch of made-up and copied stories to make it look real? Using a black-market website to purchase that virus that had uploaded to Frank Harper's computer, giving them access to all of his emails and documents?

Yeah, that had all been fun. Not only that, but hundreds of other people had also visited the same website, and the virus had installed itself into the systems of over forty visitors that surfed the web without adequate antivirus protection. Now, Trapper was looking forward to cracking open those users' computers to see what he could discover—and steal—from those people. When this whole operation was over, he'd steal a few identities or figure out a way to make those hijacked computers turn a profit.

But this part? Chasing this injured man through the woods, treating him like game? It felt wrong, somehow. Off. And Joe wasn't getting his hands dirty, either. They had all worked together to lure the old cop out here into the middle of nowhere, but Joe was happy to sit safe way up in his blinds, far from danger, while other men, including Trapper, skulked around in the forest, chasing Frank Harper.

Moving through the forest made Trapper nervous.

As he walked, Trapper checked his gun and reloaded from the bullets he had in his pocket. He was carrying a Glock 733, which held ten rounds in the slide magazine and one in the chamber. Trapper had used the same gun for as long as he'd worked for Joe, who had given it to him a year ago. Joe had a way of asking you questions and figuring out which gun was perfect for each person. He would've made a great shooting instructor if he'd had more patience with people.

As it was, Trapper loved this gun. Walking in the woods, reloading, he wasn't sure how this was all going to turn out. He was certain Joe would kill the old cop—that was not even in question. But Trapper wondered how many other people would die. Joe didn't care about the church people, certainly, but would Joe sacrifice Trapper to kill the old cop?

Trapper didn't want to think about that. He was pretty sure he already knew the answer.

Joe Hathaway was obsessed with Frank Harper. And even though the old cop was hurt, bleeding out, and didn't have any weapons, he was still an ex-cop. Harper knew martial arts. People could get hurt, or die.

Trapper hoped to stay on this side of the dirt.

He flipped on the gun's safety and then tucked the gun back into the back of his waistband. It was getting colder. Snow started to fall from the sky again, and Trapper pulled his white coat tighter around him.

Before he got to the Knight clearing—God, these names were so over the top—Trapper stopped and waited, watching. He could see into the clearing and one of the young men on the ground, not moving. Was he dead? Had Harper killed him with his bare hands?

He stopped, waiting and listening. While he waited, he unzipped his little bag and found the walkie talkie, turn it off. He didn't need it squawking while he was sneaking around. The bag held his four tasers as well, one dead and three charged.

Waiting another minute and not seeing anything, Trapper moved in. Joe had told him to wait, but Trapper didn't think it was necessary. Joe had said the old cop was moving to the east—he'd be near the river by now. Trapper wanted to check on these guys—and Joe was probably already lining up his final shot.

- - - - -

Frank saw the guy in the white jacket approaching.

It was Trapper, the man who had cut Frank in the belly. Frank saw the white jacket first, blending into the snow-covered trees around it. But then he'd found the face and body that went along with the jacket and watched. Trapper waited on the edge of the clearing for at least two minutes, watching silently. At least the guy wasn't a complete idiot.

But he'd never have Frank's level of patience. Frank could stand here, silent, up until the moment he passed out. It was how he conducted his interviews. Stay quiet, stay present, and eventually, people started talking.

People hated silence. He wondered if they hated stillness as much. Finally, Trapper nodded and walked slowly into the clearing.

Frank waited, gripping one of the guns in his hand. It was getting cold, and his legs were starting to shiver, standing still for as long as he had. At least the cold numbed some of the surging pain in his gut.

Trapper walked slowly into the clearing and stopped again, listening before moving over to one of the fallen young men.

"Toby," he said quietly. "Toby, wake up."

It was now or never.

Tensing his legs, Frank leapt out of the trees and rushed at the man in the white coat.

- - - - -

Joe drove the Gator to Rook 3 and got out, climbing a muddy track similar to that at Rook 2. When he was settled, he used his binoculars to survey the land below. He had a good view of Queen clearing and the river beyond.

Calculating on the ride over, he'd figured there was a 55% chance Harper was in Queen, hunkered down and working on his stomach wound. There was also a 35% chance he had moved through Queen already to investigate the river beyond. It had been one reason he'd had the men build up those bushes and wilderness area to screen Queen from the river. If Harper knew how close he was to the water, he might try to use the river to escape.

He searched Queen and the river and saw nothing.

That was okay. There had been a 10% chance he had fallen on the trail between Knight and Queen, or that he doubled back.

It didn't really matter. Even if Harper backtracked all the way to the Knight clearing, Trapper was there. Or Joe could take him out on the trail between. If not, Joe could return to Rook 2 and finish the job.

Moving the binoculars sideways, Joe couldn't see anything. No sign of Frank, not on the trail, not in Queen, and not in the river. Unless he had fallen somewhere, the man had disappeared.

- - - - -

Frank took Trapper to the ground quickly, knocking a black duffle out of his hands. In the scuffle, Trapper reached around and pulled a gun from his waistband, but Frank knocked the Glock away. Rolling over, he pressed Trapper flat and laid awkwardly on top of him, using his body weight to stop Trapper from moving. Frank held down the man's hands with his own.

"Hey, stop moving," Frank said to Trapper, his face inches away from the man he was lying on top of. "Stop it."

"Get off me!" Trapper screamed in Frank's face.

"Hey, quiet," Frank said. It was super weird and awkward, lying on top of the struggling man. An outside observer might have thought these two men were about to kiss. His lips were only inches from Trapper's.

Trapper got quiet, his eyes huge.

"What are you doing, man. Get off me!"

"Shut up, Trapper. You stabbed me, and now I'm trying to decide if I want to kill you or not," Frank said, his tone conversational.

Trapper started to say something and then stopped. He went back to struggling, trying to break free, but Frank held him down tight. As a police officer, they taught you how to control other people's bodies, for their own safety as well as your own. And it was something Frank had never forgotten.

Trapper stopped struggling and looked down. "Man, get off."

"No, I gotta stay low so your boss can't see me."

Trapper looked around, then back at Frank. "Okay, what?"

"Tell me about the plan."

"Screw you," Trapper said. "And you're bleeding all over me."

"Yeah, sorry about your white jacket," Frank said. "You're going to need to get that dry cleaned when this is all done. Blood is hard to get out. Where's Joe?"

Trapper looked away and said nothing.

Frank moved suddenly, pushing Trapper's left hand behind Trapper's head and grabbing it with his own left hand. Frank rolled a little to his left side and was able to hold down both of Trapper's arms with one hand and arm, although the position was very awkward and wouldn't last.

It wouldn't have to.

Frank reached over and grabbed the Glock from the snow and, using one hand, flipped off the safety before pressing the gun into Trapper's side.

"From here, this shot might kill me, too," Frank said. "Of course, I'm bleeding out anyway, so it probably won't matter."

"Dude, stop it, seriously. Get OFF!"

"The shot will kill you. Where's Joe?"

Trapper struggled and Frank pressed the gun in harder, digging into the soft part of the armpit. Frank didn't have a good hold on Trapper's arms, so this little wrestling match was going to be over soon, either way.

"Okay, stop it," Trapper said. "That hurts."

"Like where you stabbed me? I think I win that contest. Where is he?"

Trapper looked at him. "He's north of here," nodding.

"That's north? I was right. What's he doing?"

Trapper didn't answer and Frank pushed the gun in a little more. He could feel it grinding against bone.

"Arrr....Jesus. He's waiting for you to appear at Queen. Or the river."

Frank looked over his shoulder. "Queen?"

"Clearings. He named the clearings after—"

"Chess pieces. Gotcha. Okay, the one with the fire?"

"King."

"And Queen is to the east? And there's a river, right?"

"Uh huh."

"Where's my car?"

"There is a line of blinds to the north. He calls them Rooks. 1, 2 and 3, west to east. He's at Rook 3 now. Your car's near Rook 1, but you'll never get that far. Joe's watching and—"

"Joe can't see me if I crawl. And thanks," Frank said, then pulled the gun out and hit Trapper in the side of the head with the pistol, knocking him out.

Finally, Frank rolled off him. He'd nearly passed out from the pain. Putting all his weight on his stomach—and the cut—had him seeing stars. He leaned up on his back and looked around at the other two men, but they were still out.

Now the clearing held three of Joe's men, all out cold. And Frank had a gun. No way to test it, no way to be sure it wasn't yet another fake out, but he'd have to take that chance.

Frank gave himself thirty seconds to rest, breathing in and slowly, his breath forming little clouds. He stared up at the sky above the clearing, where there were breaks in the trees. It had started to snow again, lightly, gingerly. The sky had gone back to being a scuddy gray. Looking up into the falling snow, it looked like driving on a snowy night and watching the flakes approach the headlights and then drift away above or below or to the sides.

Grunting, Frank sat up slowly and began checking Trapper's pockets. The front of Trapper's jacket was a dark red patch of Frank's blood. The pockets held ten or twenty more rounds for the Glock, his wallet, and some pocket change.

Frank crawled over to the black leather duffle the man had been carrying. It was lying upside down in a small snowbank. He pulled it over and unzipped the top, finding four yellow tasers, some keys marked "John Deere," a map—

and a walkie talkie.

Nice.

Frank smiled and zipped it all back up. He needed to mosey.

Standing, he stayed ducked down and walked over to one of the young men. He checked him again, more thoroughly this time, and pulled the man's shoes and jacket off. The young kid might freeze out here, but Frank needed his coat. Sorry. The shoes were a little tight, but would definitely help him make better time—

The young man groaned and started to move.

Frank pulled on the second shoe quickly and then grabbed the duffle, digging out the tasers. Each had a "charge" light on the front—three were green, and one was yellow. Likely the one Trapper had used on Frank earlier.

Frank grabbed one of the green ones and tased the young man, who shook and bucked for the three seconds that Frank depressed the "ACTIVATE" button on the front of the taser. When he let up on the button, the charge stopped, and the kid fell silent.

Nodding, Frank pulled on the kid's jacket, feeling warmer. He put the map in one pocket and a fully charged taser in the other, then stood and zipped up the bag, slinging it over his shoulder. He tucked the Glock into the waistband in the small of his back. He'd wished there was something he could do about his injury, which had gone from screaming to throbbing, but there was nothing he could do other than get out of this situation alive. His best bet? Get out of the forest, back to the cemetery and the road beyond. This forest was Joe's domain. Flag someone down, call 911.

Or, barring rescue, he could at least expend the rest of his energy—and the last few minutes of his life—tracking down and killing Joe Hathaway.

At least that case would be solved, he thought with a laugh.

Of course, Frank would have to be clever about it. Joe knew guns better than anyone Frank had ever met, even Ben Stone. So, guns were out. And Joe was a crack shot from any distance, so it would have to up close.

Personal.

Frank was pretty sure he could take out the old man in one-to-one combat. But Joe was too clever to ever let that happen.

Frowning, Frank stood again and slowly duckwalked out of the clearing, feeling like an idiot. But keeping his head down was the only option. Frank headed northwest, in the general direction where Trapper had come from.

- - - - -

Joe had no plan.

Well, of course he had a plan, but Frank Harper wasn't cooperating. And neither were his people – no one was answering their walkie talkies, and Trapper was nowhere to be found.

This was Harper, making trouble.

Joe was still in Rook 3, searching the forest below for any signs of Harper or Trapper or the two other men who were supposed to be waiting at the clearing that Joe had named "Bishop." The plan was that Trapper was supposed to shoot, driving Harper east to Queen, and then the other two men would attack. Hector was not among their group—Trapper had specifically asked for young men, knowing they might be injured. And Hector was pretty close to Xavier Castillo. There was no way Joe was going to let Hector or anyone important get killed by Harper and spoil Joe's relationship with the Church of Xavier.

But Joe could see nothing down in the forest. He had a great view of Queen, but the clearing was empty. And he could see through to the riverbank, where he and the others had added brush to screen off the river view from the small clearing at the water's edge. There was no one there.

Joe tried the walkie talkie again. "Any read?"

Finally, a voice came back. It was Tyler, one of the two young men at Bishop.

"Tyler here, boss. Waiting on Trapper."

Joe gritted his teeth. He'd told them over and over again, no names over the radio.

"Copy that," Joe said. "Eagle has overwatch. No sign of Dude. Hold your position," he said, using their code names. He felt like an idiot.

"Roger," the young kid came back. At least he didn't say "Roger, Mr. Joe Hathaway."

Joe put the walkie talkie down and looked at the map again, scanning it. Trapper had been north of Knight, and those two kids were down at the same location. Harper had been moving east and then probably doubled back, catching Trapper by surprise. Took his gun, walkie talkie—and his map.

Dammit.

Okay, just adjust the plan. Roll with it, create permutations for the variables, calculate the odds...

1. *Harper now has a working weapon and a map with the clearing locations and Rooks marked.*

2. *Harper is bleeding and will want to resolve this quickly OR get away and call for medical attention and backup.*

3. *Harper will likely torture Trapper and now knows Joe's location at Rook 3.*

4. *Joe needed to move.*

Joe nodded. Harper would head to Rook 3 to get the drop on Joe, so Joe would relocate.

He rolled over on his side and started gathering his things. Knowing that Harper was coming here, Joe removed anything that could be helpful. He packed up and left, crawling out and taking the sniper rifle with him. Outside, Joe stood and looked around, assessing the situation. There was no way Harper could already be here, but Joe was a careful man. Thoughtful.

When he'd assessed that there were no people around, especially no bleeding ex-cops, Joe started down the muddy hill to the Gator. It was snowing again, and the path was even more treacherous than before, but he made it to the Gator in one piece. Starting it up, he drove it east, down around the trees and onto the small beach that ran along the river. He turned south, driving partly in the creek and partly on the bank, making his way south.

Joe had a new plan.

- - - - -

"What do we do now?"

Tyler looked over at Brandon. They were hiding in "Bishop," the old man's silly name for this clearing. They had been assigned to this mission by Hector, one of Brother Xavier's top men, and Tyler was certain it meant big things for him.

He was desperate to move up in the organization and had been putting in lots of hours working in the tunnels, digging and expanding their underground location. Among the people of the church, the underground complex was known as "the Garden," a strange name for a dark maze of tunnels and unlit rooms. But Brother Xavier called it "the Garden" because it represented a refuge, a sanctuary against the coming troubles. The Tragedy approached, relentless, like the tide. For people like Tyler, any plan to ride out those horrible days in relative safety was a plan to be followed. Ruthlessly.

And if that meant volunteering for some weird "hunt" in the woods, that's what you did.

Hector said the old man and his assistant were trying to trap and kill a dangerous cop that had broken the law on numerous occasions. The old cop had even planted false evidence and framed the old man for several murders, including that of a young pregnant woman.

"What do we do?" Brandon hissed, and Tyler put up his hands.

"Not sure," he whispered, waving the radio. "His man Trapper was supposed to be here by now, and the old cop was supposed to be moving to the river. Hathaway—sorry, 'overwatch'—was going to shoot him from Rook 3." Tyler thought about it. "But now he's saying to hold here. That probably means Trapper is hurt or out of the picture."

"We were supposed to fight him, shoot him with these guns," Brandon said, tapping his pocket. He had one of the guns with the white handles, and Tyler had the other. "Do we move out or stay?"

Tyler shook his head. "Not sure," he whispered. "For now, we stay."

Brandon made a face and shook his head, but remained on the ground with Tyler, hiding under a low set of bushes. They had a good view of Bishop and the trail beyond that ran from King to Queen. So far, they hadn't seen anyone.

"For now, we stay."

CHAPTER 59
Endgame

Frank made his way along the trail back to the clearing with the campfire, stopping frequently and holding his stomach. The tape had gotten wet again and come loose, and now there was no pressure on his wound other than what he placed there with his hands. Subsequently, it had started bleeding again.

He tried to ignore it as best he could. Based on the map, the clearing he was headed to, marked "King" wasn't too far from the cemetery and was due south of "Rook 1," which looked like an elevated blind with views of the cemetery and "King," the clearing where Frank had been awakened and stabbed.

Joe had a plan, that much was for certain, Frank thought as he continued west. But how would he roll with some changes?

Frank emerged back into "King," carefully scouting the clearing before moving fully into it. The map said Rooks 1 and 2 had good views of this clearing, so he stuck to the tree line on the north side and stayed down as much as he could.

He skirted the clearing and continued on a thin trail marked on the map that led through the woods. Minutes later, he emerged from the trees and saw the cemetery to his left. He turned right, skirting the trees and looking for an area to the north that hopefully held his Camaro and led to Rook 1.

- - - - -

Joe drove the Gator to the clearing near the river and parked, getting off. He should have given this clearing a name—all the other important ones had names, and this was supposed to be the one where Harper would die. Why had Joe neglected to give it a name? "Pawn" didn't sound right, but all the other names were taken. He didn't want to name it something else, or change the naming convention this late in the game, so, as he unloaded the Gator, he decided to just call it "the river."

He pulled his items free and then walked them over to the south side of the clearing, near the place where Hector and Trapper and the others had piled up all the loose branches and trees they had removed from other areas. Joe went around behind it and set his rifle on top of it. He pushed some of the branches away to create a small, round area where he could hide and still see to the north and west, the north being Rook 3 and the west being the place where the trail to King came out. Joe found a thick tree stump and rolled it over into the small blind he'd created, then stood it up on its end to make a stool for him to use as a seat.

Nodding, Joe took out his binoculars and searched. No one was on the trail coming from King. He turned and looked up and saw Rook 3—even without the traffic cone to mark it now, he could easily find it. It looked like a dark shadow on the hill to the north, an innocent place between some trees and a bush, but even from here he could spot the camouflage outline of the tent. It was much easier to see if you knew what you were looking for.

He scanned the inside of the blind but saw no movement.

Joe set the binoculars down on the branches next to his rifle, then walked back down to the creek and started covering the Gator with branches and sticks. He tried to conceal it as best he could.

- - - - -

Trapper woke, feeling the side of his head. It throbbed, and his fingers were bloody when he pulled them away. He sat up slowly and looked around. Harper was gone and it was snowing again, the flakes falling lightly around him. He saw the other two young men were still out, and it looked like one of them was missing their shoes and coat.

The Glock was gone. Trapper felt in his jacket, but the bullets and his wallet were gone too. He also didn't see the black satchel, which meant Harper had his tasers and the map. And the walkie talkie. Trapper couldn't call for help or warn Joe about what had happened.

That was okay. Joe was smart—he'd roll with it. But how pissed off would he be with Trapper? No, Trapper needed to find Joe and warn him, even if Joe already knew. Trapper needed to stay helpful, and loyal, or Joe would toss him aside.

Trapper had seen it happen.

He slowly stood, his head ringing. Trapper guessed that Harper would try to escape, which meant getting back to his car at Rook 1. Sadly, that wouldn't work too well for him: Joe had the keys to the Camaro, so all Frank would find would be a locked car.

- - - - -

Frank rounded the edge of the forest and saw his Camaro parked next to a Gator, a John Deere vehicle that looked like a cross between an ATV and a fancy golf cart. He had never been happier to see his car.

Walking over to it, he tried the doors, but they were locked. He checked the ATV, but there were no keys there either. What had they done with his keys and his phone? Joe Hathaway probably had them, but now Frank regretted knocking Trapper out so quickly. One more question would have helped this situation immensely.

He turned and, following the map, slowly made his way up the hill to the camouflaged blind known as Rook 1. Getting gingerly down on his stomach, Frank crawled inside. The place was cozy, and the southern end opened up with a great view of the cemetery and the forest below.

Frank also found a sniper rifle and rounds, along with food, water, and a first aid kit. He smiled at the last thing found and rolled over onto his back. He pulled off the coat he'd taken from the young man, balled it up, and put it behind his head. Next, Frank opened up the first aid kit and got to work.

- - - - -

Joe was all set up in his new little blind, waiting. Snow was drifting down around him, falling a little harder than it had only a few minutes ago. Joe kept checking his view of Rook 3, waiting for Harper's head to pop into view, but, so far, nothing.

The river was off to his right and the sounds were constant, water rushing and gurgling around him. It made it hard to hear the other sounds of the forest around him. He strained to listen, hoping to hear something. But it felt like he was alone in the forest, just him and his gun and the river.

- - - - -

After a few minutes, Frank's stomach was feeling better.

He'd removed the old, blood-soaked gauze, then rewrapped it with fresh gauze and tape. He used up all the medical tape on the edges of the bandages, but found some other yellow masking tape and used that to securely tighten down the whole situation. He could hardly breathe, but the bleeding had stopped.

He also downed four Advil from the medicine kit, then stuffed the rest of the kit in the black duffel bag he'd taken from Trapper.

He knew he needed to be moving, but Frank instead rested for a few minutes, giving the Advil time to kick in. He drank some water and ate one of Joe's granola bars. While he rested, his eyes closed, he made a plan. The way he saw it, Frank had two choices. Find his keys, or find Joe. If Joe had his keys, then both options became just one option. Frank's keys could be at one of the other blinds, Rook 2 or Rook 3. Frank could keep searching for his keys, maybe finding them. He could come back to his car and drive to safety.

Or he could find Joe.

It was a risky move, but then it would be done. One way or another, Frank would be done looking over his shoulder. If Joe escaped again, as he had before, Frank would never know peace.

Frank had a decision to make.

- - - - -

Tyler and Brandon remained on the ground under their bush, waiting.

"How long are we waiting?"

Tyler looked at him. "I have no idea, man. What do you think, I'm psychic?"

"We shoulda kept our phones."

"No, Hathaway was checking for that."

"Man, I'm getting cold," Brandon said. "We need to get out of here. This whole thing looks like it's going to shit. You really want to get caught up in this mess?"

Tyler didn't know what to say.

- - - - -

Joe's legs were starting to cramp up, so he sat down on the wooden stump he'd rolled into the new blind. It was a little too short, and he couldn't see over the stack of branches and sticks they had piled up.

He didn't like the idea of disturbing the pile of sticks—he had gone to great lengths the other day to make them look as natural as possible, so he left them alone. Instead, every few minutes he would stand, leaning over the side of the blind, and use the binoculars to check Rook 3. But, so far, it was just Joe and his gun and the river.

- - - - -

Trapper walked through the forest. He was heading east, toward the river.

He had no idea where anyone was without his walkie talkie, so he walked slowly, trying to keep his head on a swivel. Harper was missing, and with that, all of Joe's plans were out the window. The old man's brain was probably calculating, coming up with new plans and permutations and ways of bending reality to his will.

Trapper just hoped that he would still have a place in that future. Joe could be vindictive. He held grudges, sometimes for years, and made plans for elaborate and exhaustive plans for revenge. Just look at this whole "game" for Frank Harper—Trapper got the feeling that the plans for this little festival of sadness had been percolating in the back of Joe's mind for ages.

He walked on, rubbing at the red stain on the front of his jacket. Harper had lain on top of him, getting his blood all over Trapper's white jacket. Payback, to be sure, for stabbing Harper and sliding the knife sideways to increase the size of the wound.

- - - - -

Tyler saw movement on the trail and shushed Brandon.

"There. Someone."

It was hard to see who it was through the trees, but someone was walking along the trail that connected King with Queen, passing south of Bishop, the clearing Tyler and Brandon were hiding in. Tyler could see it was a man, and he had a large bloody stain on his shirt. They ducked down as he passed well south of the clearing.

"It's the hurt guy, the old cop," Brandon said. "His shirt."

"No, I don't think so," Tyler said, shaking his head. "He was walking fast, like he wasn't injured." Tyler waited a moment, then started to climb from beneath the bushes. "Either way, I'm going to follow him. It's better than staying here, waiting for the cold to get us."

Tyler stood and brushed off his clothes. He heard Brandon climbing out as well. Together, they started off after the figure.

- - - - -

Joe was watching Rook 3 through his binoculars. There was no movement, nothing. More time had passed, and now visibility was less clear. Joe cursed under his breath. If Harper knew where Joe was, why didn't he make his move? He'd had plenty of time to circle around and get to the blind. Hell, Joe had had time to relocate down here to the river, where he'd been for nearly ten minutes.

Off to his left, Joe detected movement. It was a long way away, down the path to Queen. He set the binocs aside and got his rifle, using the scope.

A figure was walking toward the river, making good speed. Joe couldn't make out anything about the person at this distance, but he was moving too fast and with too much confidence to be the old cop. Of course, Harper might be feeling better. The figure had a cut across the stomach—

Ah, there. The front of his shirt was a bloody red mess, the blood covering most of his stomach.

Joe smiled and flipped off the safety. He lined up the shot, ignoring the rest of Harper's body and aiming for the gut. Joe would shoot him there to make it hurt even more.

He placed his finger on the trigger and, after a moment, gently squeezed.

The crack of the rifle surprised Joe. It was louder than he'd expected, probably because he'd been surrounded by the sounds of nature for several days and his ears had adjusted.

Through the scope, he saw the figure fall. He looked for the fake guns falling out of Harper's hands, but it was too far away.

Now, Harper rolled around slowly on the trail floor, holding his stomach again. The pain must be excruciating.

Joe smiled.

He stood, gathering up his gun and the binocs and getting out of his blind. He didn't want to get too close, but he needed to see the look on Harper's face as he died.

- - - - -

"What was that?"

"Somebody shooting," Tyler said. "Come on."

They hurried down the path behind the figure, who was now lying on the ground and writhing around in pain.

"See, I told you it was the old cop," Brandon said as they approached. Tyler couldn't see the man's face, but the stomach wound was obvious. There was blood everywhere and a hole in the man's stomach. But hadn't he already been bleeding before the gunshot?

Tyler slowed and approached, and it took him a second to realize it was Trapper.

"Oh, shit," Brandon said.

They went to him. Trapper's stomach was blown open, and you could see inside. Wet pipes and tubes that weren't meant to be seen. Trapper was holding it all in and doing a poor job of it.

"Help me, man...help me," the man said weakly. "Joe...made a mistake."

Tyler pulled Trapper's jacket off and stuffed it into the wound. "Stay with me, Trapper," Tyler said. He looked at Brandon. "Joe's down that way. Go tell him he shot Trapper and we need an ambulance. Hathaway's the only one out here with a phone."

Brandon nodded and took off running, heading east.

- - - - -

Joe stopped and knelt down on the trail and pointed his rifle. From here, he should be able to get a good look at Harper on the ground, rolling around in pain.

The first thing he saw was a young man running full speed down the path towards him. One of Xavier's kids. He was still a fair distance away, so Joe ignored him and focused beyond him, looking for Harper. He found a man on the ground and another person, one of the kids from Bishop clearing, leaning over him. It looked like he was trying to help Harper. Why would he be helping the man they were all out here to kill—

The kid moved and Joe saw that the man on the ground was Trapper.

Trapper? He'd been running down the path, his gut covered in blood. How? How had that happened?

It felt like part of Joe's brain seized up, and for a second, Joe didn't know what to do. Trapper was hurt, maybe dying. Gut shots were the worst. Even if you stopped the bleeding, the internal damage and infection were difficult to manage.

Trapper was down, and Harper was missing. And these other two kids were witnesses.

Joe slowly backed off the magnification and found the kid running down the path at him. He would arrive first and was therefore the first target. Joe could say that Harper killed him. Joe lined up the shot, waited for a moment in the kid's stride when he was closest to the ground, and fired.

- - - - -

Tyler heard the second shot and turned. Brandon fell to the ground, skidding and rolling.

It looked like he was dead before he hit the snowy dirt.

Tyler knew. In an instant, Tyler knew.

Joe was cleaning up.

Tyler rolled away to his right, into the trees and off the path. He knew Joe knew these woods like the back of his hand, but Tyler hoped he'd be distracted. Trapper was dying, Brandon was probably dead, and the old cop was out there somewhere.

Would Joe care about Tyler enough to chase him?

Tyler ran through the thick woods, staying off the path between King and Queen but moving parallel to it. He heard no more shots and wended his way around trees and gullies and thick patches of bushes, running for his life.

- - - - -

Frank knew that sound.

Five shots, fired within four minutes of each other. Down in the forest. One shot, then four more a few minutes later.

He'd made it to Rook 2 but found nothing of interest there either. He was feeling better—the wound was bound tight, making it harder to breathe, but Frank wasn't losing any more blood. The food and water had helped. Who knew that snacks would be provided?

He'd been walking down the short trail from Rook 2 to the Gator when he heard the shots. They were well off to the south. It was a sniper rifle, so it had to be Joe. But who was he shooting at?

- - - - -

Joe fired a few more shots at the kid who was escaping into the woods. He hadn't bothered learning any of their names. He'd assumed Harper would kill them all or, in the end, the young men would return to the safety of the Church of Xavier.

Now, one of them lay dead, half-way between here and Trapper. And the other was gone.

Joe stood, picking up his rifle and moving down the trail, heading west. If he were Frank Harper, this is when he would've struck, while Joe was distracted by all this activity.

But Frank did not appear.

The first body Joe reached was the running kid. He was dead, eyes open, staring at the sky. Half of his neck was gone, blown away. The head was barely still attached.

That was bad. Joe had been aiming for the forehead, missing by at least eight inches.

Joe checked the kid's pockets but only found one of the fake guns marked with a white piece of tape on the handle. In frustration, he screamed and threw it away into the woods.

He got to Trapper a few minutes later, but the man was dead. His only friend in the world, really, and Joe had shot him in the gut and let him bleed out. Joe wondered if Trapper had known in the end who had killed him. Had he seen it as a betrayal?

Making a face, Joe checked Trapper's pockets. He found nothing. That confirmed what Joe had suspected: Harper likely had a map of the area—and a working gun.

Joe started to stand and then thought better of it. Harper could be at one of the blinds. Now, Harper was at an elevated position. And there had been guns left at Rook 1 and 2—it was possible, even likely, that Harper had a sniper rifle as well.

Joe stayed low to the ground and crawled away to put some distance between him and Trapper's body. Now what? Let's calculate:

1. *Harper has a weapon, cover, and the high ground.*

2. *Joe is the better shot, even with the advantage of an elevated position.*

3. *Harper wasn't a sniper and was not used to long-distance shooting. He was a dumb cop, used to shooting fleeing thugs in the back.*

4. *Joe was running out of helpers—but he didn't care.*

5. *They were in the endgame now.*

After running more calculations in his head, Joe determined that the safety course of action was to return to the river. Harper would either go to Rook 3 and try to shoot Joe, or he'd circle around and come down the river. Once Harper found Joe's hidden Gator, he would know Joe was in the area. And Joe couldn't afford to try and fight the man one-on-one. The Krav Maga made it an unfair fight.

No, Joe was going to make sure this fight was decided by firepower.

- - - - -

After running through the woods, Tyler curved back towards the larger trail and came out near the entrance to King. He found the campfire, still smoking, and two of the other men from his church sitting next to it. As he appeared, they both stood and hurried over.

"What is happening?" one of them asked. "We were waiting for Trapper."

"He's dead," Tyler said. "Hathaway killed Brandon, too. We need to move. I'm heading back out to the cemetery and the road beyond. I think we need to get out of here."

They both nodded and the three of them took off running. They had all been in these woods long enough to know exactly where to go. Moments later, they were ducking through the forest, following the thin game trail in the direction of the Donnelly Cemetery.

- - - - -

Frank followed the map and found Rook 3 with ease. He hoped his keys would be there. That would allow him an easy out—he could take his car and go. If he could get to a phone fast enough, the cops might be able to get out here and capture Joe.

Frank walked up the hill, watching for the Rook. There was a very good possibility that Joe was down there by the river, waiting for Frank to pop into the rook. Frank had brought Joe's sniper rifle and the attached scope, but he didn't want to use it unless he had to. It would instantly give away his position.

He found the top of the hill and the camouflaged tent. It was just like the others. He dropped down to this chest and started crawling, getting to the tent. He didn't pull back the flap but simply crawled slowly under it, pushing the rifle ahead of him. Frank didn't want any movement in the tent. Joe could be watching for that.

Slowly, he crawled inside and up to the front open window

that looked out over the forest and river below. Moving slowly, he unhooked the scope from the rifle and lifted it up to his eye.

Below, he could see the clearings. Queen was there, or what he guessed was Queen. It looked different from this angle. He slid his scope to the left, following what he could see of the trail, and ended up at a riverbank. He could see a sandy beach area, now littered with branches and leaves and snow. Beyond that, a thin creek flowed away to the south.

He scanned the riverbank area, going over the shadowed areas and the trees and the bushes, expecting at any second to see an eye staring back at him, followed by the distant puff of a gun being fired.

So far, so good.

Harper finished scanning the entire clearing next to the river but didn't see anything.

He turned over onto his side, giving his stomach a break while he had a good think. What to do next? He could stay here, or he could go.

That reminded him and, after checking the clearing below again, he sat up and rummaged through the interior of the blind. He found nothing of interest other than food and bottled water. No phones, no keys to any Camaros. Nothing that could be helpful.

- - - - -

Joe returned to his blind by the river, moving slowly and carefully once he was out of cover. He sat up on the stump and trained his binocs on the blind.

There. Movement.

Someone was definitely in the blind. Joe switched out the binocs for his rifle and aimed, following the movement. The blind had been moving, slightly, as if someone was inside of it, but now it was still. But there was something sticking out of the front of the blind.

The barrel of the sniper rifle.

He had him.

Joe lifted his gun to fire.

- - - - -

Frank backed the rest of the way out of the blind and then slid to the side. He'd kept the scope and left the rifle, sticking it out of the front of the blind. Frank used the scope to look back down at the river one more time before he left—

There was Joe.

Right there, near the river.

And he was aiming his rifle up the hill.

Frank did what he did next by instinct. When someone was aiming a gun at you, even from a quarter mile away, you rolled and ducked. Frank moved, ducking and turning away just as he heard the distant gunfire. Once, twice, three times, bullets sailed through the blind, ripping it to shreds and throwing equipment and food in all directions. All three bullets passed through the center of the camouflaged blind, and one hit the barrel of the sniper rifle pointing from the front of the tent. It flopped to the side, bent and ruined.

Frank rolled away and moved, jogging down the hill and getting to the Gator as quickly as he could. What would Joe do next? Stay down there, or keep firing up the hill? Or come up the river to find out if Frank was dead?

Come up the river. And before he did that, Frank had to hide. Which meant leaving the Gator. He turned and ran for the creek to his right, splashing into the water.

- - - - -

The blind exploded from the force of Joe's bullets, with food and equipment being thrown free. Joe fired again, pumping new bullets into the rifle's chamber. He twisted the gun, firing in an arc around the tent to make sure he got the old cop.

Joe waited for quiet and scanned the edge of the hill and the remains of the blind and the broken gun barrel. Nothing moved.

If Harper had been in the blind, or near that weapon, he was dead.

And Joe was holding the rifle from Rook 3 in his hands. That meant the other rifle had to have been brought there by someone else, likely Harper. Everyone else was accounted for or dead.

Joe waited. He could be patient. After five minutes of no movement, he lifted a stick into the air, half expecting Frank to take a shot at it. Harper might not be as good with a sniper rifle as Joe, but he was a cop. And there was a THIRD rifle, the one from Rook 1.

But the stick in the air remained untouched. He waved it around, just to be sure, but nothing happened. Joe took a breath and stood, expecting a shot to ring out.

Nothing.

He needed to go up to Rook 3 and make sure. The man was up there dying. Joe hurried to gather his things and started for the Gator, but then changed his mind. He would walk up the riverbank and circle around to Rook 3. The Gator was too loud, and there wasn't time to uncover it from all the branches.

- - - - -

Frank watched.

Joe came around the corner, his rifle out. He was pointing it ahead of him, looking upriver and up at Rook 3, watching to see someone come around the corner.

Frank was already here. He was on the other side of the creek, ducked down by a fallen tree. He'd been there for a few minutes, running ahead and crossing the creek and finding a place with good cover. He would only get one shot at this, and he had to get Joe before the man could turn and fire.

Joe slowed—there was a sharp turn here, and a blind corner. It was why Frank had picked it.

Frank was hidden, the Glock out and loaded and propped on a tree stump, barely visible. Even if Joe looked right at him, he'd never spot him. Frank just hoped the Glock worked. Maybe it was all another part of the game.

He pointed it at Joe anyway.

"JOE HATHAWAY! DROP YOUR WEAPON!"

Joe froze and stopped. He turned slowly, facing the river.

"HARPER? YOU'RE ALIVE?"

"DROP THE WEAPON OR I WILL OPEN FIRE!"

Frank could see Joe's eyes, scanning the river and the fallen trees and snow on the other side. Frank could hit him from here, to be sure, but Joe was the better shot.

The only way to be sure was to get the drop on him.

Joe took two steps towards the river.

"THAT'S FAR ENOUGH. DROP YOUR WEAPON."

Joe laughed. "Ah, always the policeman. Right Harper? You going to arrest me?"

Frank knew what he was doing. Joe's eyes were ranging, searching, calculating. He knew Frank was over here in the flotsam of the creek. He was trying to figure out which patch of shadow was large enough to hold Frank. He was trying to get Frank to talk—and each time he did, Joe had more information about where Frank was hiding.

Okay, last chance.

"DROP IT OR I WILL FIRE!"

Joe found him. He spotted him in the trees, somehow, either by following his voice or by figuring out the dark patch to the left of the large fallen tree had to be Frank.

Joe suddenly lifted his weapon and Frank fired.

The gun spat out a bullet, but it went wide, missing Joe.

Frank moved the gun slightly and fired again, the sound loud in his ears. He was stretched out flat on the ground, the gun three feet away from his head. The second bullet knocked Joe back. The rifle slipped from his hands.

A hit.

Joe gritted his teeth and blood bloomed from the man's shoulder. He swore and bent to pick up his weapon.

"DO NOT LIFT YOUR—"

The gun came up and Frank fired as Joe fired. Frank's shot missed—something must be off with the Glock—as did Joe's shot, which Frank heard splinter a tree trunk off to his left.

Frank fired again, taking his time, and hit Joe in the chest. It knocked him back but Joe held onto the gun and lifted and fired. Frank felt and heard the bullet pass through the area over his head. Joe had only missed him by inches. He dropped the front of his weapon and dug more rounds out of his pocket.

He was reloading. Joe had two bullets in him already and he was reloading.

Frank fired again, once, twice, three times. That was the magic of a magazine-fed handgun instead of a breech-loading rifle. Frank had more shots between reloads.

He took them all.

Bullets whizzed across the narrow creek and hit Joe and the gun and the sand at his feet and the trees behind him. Frank lost count, squeezing the trigger even after it was empty.

Joe fell back and collapsed onto the ground.

Frank didn't move, other than to turn on his side and reload with bullets from his pocket. Trapper had carried extras, and Frank was glad for it.

Joe struggled on the ground, still moving. The sniper rifle at his feet, a massive dent in the barrel likely rendering it useless. The old man rolled onto his side, feeling at the holes in his body. Chest, shoulder, and one in the leg, at least, Frank saw as he reloaded without looking.

When the magazine was full, he chambered a bullet and finally stood from behind the fallen trees and branches where he had been hiding.

"STAY WHERE YOU ARE!"

Joe looked at him, his face twisted in a grimace of pain.

"You got me, Harper. You got me." Joe sat up on one arm, then rolled onto his side again and up onto all fours. "You have me, Harper. You win." He slowly worked his way to his feet, standing awkwardly.

Frank walked to the edge of the water.

"Hathaway. Put your hands behind your back."

"What are you going to do, cuff me? You don't have any cuffs," Joe said, suddenly sounding old, tired. He took a step toward Frank, eyeing the river.

Frank had an idea of Joe's latest plan. His mind was always working, always calculating.

Could he get away?

Frank shook his head.

"DO NOT MOVE OR I WILL FIRE!"

"Shoot me? An unarmed man?" Joe looked at him and shook his head and Frank could see the bone in his shoulder, shining in the wound. "You have to arrest me. You have to arrest me," Joe said. His eyes looked wild. "You have to arrest me."

He stumbled forward, grabbing for the gun at his feet. Or maybe he was trying to get to the river. To fall into the water, to float away and escape.

"Not this time," Frank said quietly, and fired.

A red hole bloomed in the center of Joe's forehead, and blood and bone from the back of his head sprayed the trees and snow beyond. The force of the bullet stopped Joe in his tracks, and he looked at Frank confused. After a second, he fell backwards and landed on the snowy beach.

Frank waded across the shallow creek, the Glock pointed at Joe. The guy was a phoenix. Frank walked out of the water and walked over slowly, ignoring the pain in his stomach and the falling snow and the water dripping off of his body.

His eyes were on Joe Hathaway.

Frank walked up to him and kicked the sniper rifle away. He nudged the old man with his toe, then gave the man a light kick in the ribs.

Nothing.

Keeping his gun trained on Joe, Frank bent next to him, feeling for a pulse. There was a thready heartbeat, weak, fading. Frank did a sternum rub, the kind of hard rub with your knuckle down the sternum that hurt so much it brought people out of delirious states or convinced young punks to stop pretending to be asleep.

Joe did not move.

There were splashes of scarlet and bone on the snow around and behind Joe. Between the head shot and the other two shots to the chest, Frank was pretty sure he was a goner. But he stayed with him anyway, feeling until there was no pulse. Even then, he knelt next to Hathaway for another minute, making sure.

Frank tucked the gun in his pants and then began feeling around on Joe's person, looking for anything he could find. And he found a lot: Frank's gun, Frank's car keys and phone, Joe's own wallet, the keys to a Gator.

And something else he hadn't expected to find: a gold wedding ring.

He pocketed the items, then stood, wondering what to do next. He could drive the Gator back to his car, or call for help and wait here with the body. He didn't feel like leaving Joe here. For some reason, even though he was dead, Frank was sure the body would stand up and wander off just as soon as Frank moved out of visual range.

Call it superstition. But then, it wasn't every day you were hunted by a madman and then managed to turn the tables on him.

In the end, he decided to call in for help. But the phone was locked, and his thumbprint didn't work. It had a new passcode he didn't know. Everyone who knew it was probably dead. All he could do was call 911. They were able to connect him to his daughter.

"Laura? I need help."

A few minutes later, he was on the phone with King and the cops were on their way. He gave them directions. "I'm deep in the woods."

"And Joe Hathaway?"

Frank looked over at the body, half expecting to see it slinking away. "He's dead."

"Good," Chief King said. Frank could hear the relief in his voice.

While he waited, Frank looked at the golden ring. It looked like a wedding or promise ring, thin and gold. He had no idea who it belonged to. Could it have been Tom Mercato's? Or the young pregnant woman? Or another victim no one even knew about?

Frank couldn't remember. Just another mystery.

But this one?

Frank couldn't care less.

CHAPTER 60
Dinner Out

They sat across from each other at the Mexican restaurant near the prosecutor's office in downtown Troy. Whitlowe was nursing a margarita, and Bridget wondered how long he'd be able to make it last. He'd had a rough few months, of course, with the loss of his father. Now, with this whole Joe Hathaway business, she needed to keep an eye on him.

"You doin' okay?"

He looked up at her. "It's just crazy. Joe Hathaway is dead."

"I know," she repeated. He'd said it three times just since they'd sat down. Joe Hathaway had turned up, alive and well and back in Ohio. No one had seen him, and Joe had tricked that old cop, Frank Harper, into coming out into the middle of nowhere. Hathaway had somehow found the time and resources to prepare a stretch of forest and proceeded to hunt Harper, stabbing him and then chasing him around the woods with the intent to kill him.

Harper had gotten the better of him, and now Joe Hathaway was dead. At least there was one good thing to come out of it.

A lot had happened in the last twenty-four hours. The investigation was ongoing, of course. Soon, all the details would come out.

But Kevin only had one question for the investigators—how long had Joe Hathaway been back in Ohio?

"I just can't believe he was here. Right here in Ohio!" He slammed his hand down on the wooden table, making their drinks rattle. Bridget didn't need to look around to know people were looking at them. She could feel their eyes.

"Look, it's over now," Bridget said quietly. "He was convicted, and now that he's dead. It'll show as a completed case. You won."

"But I didn't win," Whitlowe said, shaking his head. "It was the last case my father saw. We talked about it every day. You weren't there, Bridget. You didn't see him at the end. He was so disappointed that Hathaway got away."

"Well, it was only temporary," she said. "Now he's dead. Can't get much more definitive than that."

"I know, I know."

She sat back and looked around at the restaurant. They'd been in here, Whitlowe and her and the rest of the crew from the District Attorney's office, when they'd heard that the jury in the Joe Hathaway case was done deliberating. She remembered the look of unadulterated joy on Whitlowe's face when he'd heard. They had all assumed the jury would take their time and deliberate for hours. No one had expected them to come back so fast.

It usually meant only one thing—a clear conviction.

And that had turned out to be the case. Not that it mattered that much—Hathaway had bolted, sneaking out of the hospital and disappearing with the help of his cult-like followers.

"Someone had to see him," Kevin said, looking at his plate. "Right? You can't just live and work in the area and no one sees you, right?"

"I guess he was hiding out somewhere," Bridget said. "Maybe some of the Keepers of Truth were hiding him," she said, mentioning Hathaway's crowdfunded cult.

"Maybe," he answered. "I just can't believe he came back. I figured he had run off to Bolivia or something."

She started to say something else when a group of waiters and greeters filed past the table. They gathered around a nearby table and one of them produced a large sombrero. As a group, the waitresses and greeters and kitchen staff launched into a hearty version of some Mexican version of *Happy Birthday*, though the melody had been changed just enough to keep them from getting sued.

Bridget waited until the song was over—and the cake had been presented and the applause died down—before answering him.

"Bolivia would be nice," she said, "or someplace that doesn't extradite."

He nodded. "I wish I'd known. This week, last week. Anytime would've helped."

"Well, I'm glad you didn't know. It might've postponed or canceled our meeting last week."

He looked up at her and smiled. "I don't know—that meeting went off the rails. We started out talking about your cases, but things took a crazy turn."

"How could I forget?" she said, leaning forward and smiling at him. "And I liked that crazy turn. Thank Christ you finally told me how you felt about me. I was getting tired of waiting on you."

"Waiting on me? You were the one dragging your feet. Plus, I'm your boss—technically, you should have to hit on me first."

She smiled and laughed. "Oh, is that what HR said?"

"No, not talking to them about this," he said. "I don't even want to think about what they'll say. We're co-workers and I'm your boss and we work on sensitive cases. Cases where people could attempt to blackmail us if they got some dirt on us. No, this whole thing is going to be a huge mess."

"Oh, don't complain," she said, smiling. "You love it. You love complications, and at least this is a fun one. And don't worry, we'll work it out. We're both adults, and we're happy. Or I'm happy and I think you're happy."

"I'm happy," he said, and then he got a strange look on his face and sat back, looking around the room. His moods could be mercurial, she knew, but this was different—he went from being happy and mollified over their situation to one of dark sadness.

She didn't say anything and went back to working on the plate of fajitas they were sharing. The food here was excellent and very fresh. Almost too fresh—one of the lime slices in her margarita still had part of a sticker on it. But she could do with a little "realness" after the last few days.

This whole situation with Joe Hathaway was almost too much to believe. And the way the whole thing had come together, with Hathaway luring Harper out by planting a fake clue about a missing person's case from the 1990s. Who thought up this kind of stuff? Who had the time to just sit around, spinning webs of intrigue, hoping to catch your nemesis in a trap? It was bizarre.

As was the "death hunt." That's what the reporters were calling it, and that's how the media was portraying it on the evening news. It was straight out of the movies. Hathaway hated Frank Harper, the same local PI who'd been involved in protecting that Hollywood starlet last month. Hathaway blamed Harper for his conviction in the previous murder case, and after he escaped, Hathaway had apparently set about planning his revenge.

And it wasn't just any revenge. Hathaway, an avid shooter and award-winning marksman, wanted to hunt Frank Harper. Like, actually 'hunt' the guy the way people hunted elk and deer. The whole thing was set up ahead of time, and Hathaway hunted the "world's most dangerous game." One of the cops investigating the scene had mentioned the name of an old book in his report, a book from the

1800s that described big game hunters out chasing the ultimate prey—humans.

It was all too crazy to believe.

She waited for him to talk, and ate her food in silence. Sometimes you just needed to give people time to talk—and the space in which to decide for themselves when they would speak up.

I just can't believe he's gone," Whitlowe said from across the table. His voice was so low, Bridget could barely hear him.

"Joe Hathaway?"

"No," he said, looking up at her. "My father. I mean, he was there for me all the way through law school, and some bad years right after. I can't imagine going on without him. You know?"

She didn't know, but she wasn't going to say that. Not here, and not now.

"I was happy, there for a second," Whitlowe said. "Happy with us, happy with the case. And then I suddenly remembered that he'd dead. Rotting in the ground. I'm sitting here, drinking and eating and enjoying my life." He looked at her. "And he's dead. Winter is coming, and there will be snow on his grave. He'll be cold and alone."

He looked down at his plate.

Bridget didn't know what to say. What she did do was reach over and put her hand on his hand. They were dating now, finally, and even though they were in public, she thought the gamble was worth it. Someone might see.

But he was hurting. And she could help.

- - - - -

He let go of her hand and went back to eating, not really hungry anymore. Kevin picked at his food, but now he only wanted to leave. He felt like an idiot, tearing up in public. If anyone saw, they'd think he was a weak man. They were only a half-mile from his office. People knew him.

The two of them ate in silence, and he wasn't sure what else to say. They were together, so they had that going, at least. But they still needed to figure out where they were going, and when and how to involve HR. It was a complicated mess, and he wasn't sure if he had enough bandwidth to deal with it.

"You okay?"

He looked up at her and smiled. "Yeah. I just miss him."

She reached for the little bottle of green hot sauce. She smiled at him and nodded. "Okay, I know how to make it better. When we get out of here, we're going to your place. We can talk about it, talk about your father. But he would be proud of you, and you know that. Hathaway is dead, and the case is closed. You won."

He looked up at her. "I guess you're right."

"I am right," she said with a smile. "And don't you even think about arguing with me. Plus, if you play your cards right, you might get some quiet time with me. And not in public," she looked around. "You know what I mean?"

He suddenly felt like being serious. "You're crazy."

She nodded. "I think it's been long enough. And I don't really care about the rules."

"Are you going to announce our engagement at the Christmas party? Like your friend?"

Bridget smiled and looked at him again, holding his eyes for a long moment. "I would be so lucky."

He looked down and chuckled and went back to his food, thinking about his father. He had liked Bridget, liked her spirit. What would his father have said about dating her? Was it worth it to gamble his whole career on her? What if she changed her mind and he got charged with harassment? It was a lot to risk.

His father had reminded him, over and over again: do the work. Get good grades. Don't get distracted, and you'll go far. What if Bridget ruined his career? And his life?

Was it worth the risk?

"You thinking about him again?"

Whitlowe looked up. She had a genuine, caring look on her face.

"Yeah. And remembering all the things he said to me. I miss...I miss being able to ask him questions, really. And every day I'm in his office, it feels weird."

"It's your office now."

"Is it? It still doesn't feel like it. Not to me."

She looked around at the hubbub of the restaurant. The place was loud, one of the reasons he loved it. You could be singing at the top of your lungs in here most nights, and no one would pay any attention. Unless it was your birthday, and then they would bring you either cake or a shot of Rumchata, depending on your age. He preferred the Rumchata.

"You're going to be okay," she said quietly. "Maybe not soon, but you'll be okay."

They went back to eating, and he went back to thinking about their future together. Did they have one? Was it worth it? Or would it all blow up in their faces? What if she was playing him? If they had a relationship and then she ended things, she could claim that she was pressured into having sex. He'd be out, and she was next in line for the job.

That's one way to get a promotion.

She got a text, and he took the opportunity to run to the restroom. It was nice to be out with her, in public, and not feel weird about it. They were just two colleagues, having dinner and talking shop. Finishing his business, he went to the sink and washed his hands, looking at himself in the mirror. It felt good, being with her. It felt right.

When he got back to the table, she was beaming. Something had happened, and she was holding up her phone for him to see a screen full of messages.

"Good news?" he asked, sliding into the booth across from her.

"Oh yeah. That whole thing with Frank Harper? Joe's 'game' and the chase and the shootout and one dead Joe Hathaway?"

"Hard to forget."

"Well, we knew Joe was staying somewhere. But look," she said, waggling the phone. He followed her finger on the phone screen, reading. He finally got to what she was pointing at—

"Wait, what? No."

"Yes."

"They knew Joe?"

"Yes, it looks like it. He'd been staying out there with them.

"You didn't see him when you were out there visiting the place?"

"No, I didn't," she repeated. "But it's a huge compound. But you're missing the point. If they helped him, there might be forensic evidence on the compound. Look, the equipment found at the crime scene—now we know it belongs to the church. The two Gator vehicles and a truck found at the location. Guns too."

"When's Harper going to be interviewed?"

Bridget shook her head. "Dunno. He's still in the hospital."

"Oh, didn't know that."

"But this gives us a search warrant to look for evidence that Joe was there. On the compound. I mean, could you think of a better place for Joe to hide out? No one and I mean no one knows who's out there at that compound. They could have Amelia Earhart for all we know, her body all preserved and propped up in the corner," she said.

Whitlowe nodded, following her logic.

"It would be a good place to hide out. I wonder how they hooked up? But if they were harboring a known fugitive..."

"Conspiracy to commit murder, harboring a fugitive, RICO, all kinds of possibilities." She sat back, her face a beacon of happiness and satisfaction, shaded with a tinge of triumph. "I've got them."

Whitlowe looked at her and smiled.

"No, Bridget. We've got them."

CHAPTER 61
Laura

Laura was still pissed.

It had been a week since Frank's frantic phone call. "Laura, stay calm. I need help. Call Chief King. Have him get here. And bring an ambulance or two."

She'd been standing in the salon, in the middle of cutting a woman's hair. It was all she could do to not stab the woman in the side of her head. She excused herself and stepped away, then made him repeat what he'd said. And, while he was talking, it was obvious he was hurting. He didn't sound like himself.

"Are you hurt? Who is hurt?"

"I am—I got stabbed, honey. It's okay, though. I bandaged it up."

"Stabbed?"

"Yes, but it's okay. Just hang up and call Chief King," he said, giving Laura the direct number. "Their dispatcher Lola will get him. It would be faster than calling 911. Just tell him that Joe Hathaway is dead."

"Joe...Joe Hathaway? He's back?"

"Well, not anymore," her father said, and then he started laughing and the laughing changed into a weird coughing sound. "Oh, can't do that," he said, not to her but just out loud, like he was talking to himself.

"Okay, okay," she said, her voice too loud. Other people in the salon were looking at her. "I'll do it. And where is that location?"

"Pleasant Hill, or someplace with a name like that. Don't come— the cops will be all over this place."

"So what do you want me to do?"

"Just keep working."

"You're an idiot, dad," Laura said. "I'll meet you at the hospital."

"Okay, meet me at the hospital. I'll have King call you and tell you where to go."

She'd hung up, then called the number Frank had given her. She talked to a nice sounding woman named Lola, and then to Chief King, and he'd given her his cell phone number and she'd forwarded the text with Frank's location.

And then she'd tried to go back to work, but the salon with abuzz with questions.

Her customer didn't even seem interested in having her hair finished—all she wanted to know was what was happening and to whom and was Frank okay and who was dead? Laura went through all of what she knew, which wasn't exactly much, and held back Joe Hathaway's name. You never knew who was listening.

Obviously, Laura had trouble concentrating, so she finished up her appointment and then rescheduled the rest of her clients for the day. And she'd ended up ignoring Frank's instructions and, putting the texted location into her phone, driven out to the location.

He'd been right—there were cop cars from five different towns. Dropping her father's name got her past four roadblocks and she finally made it up to where his car was parked along with three ambulances and three police cars from the Cooper's Mill Police Department. She parked off to the side and checked on his car first—the passenger side window was shattered, glass all over the seat.

Finally, one of the CMPD directed her to where Chief King and Frank were, and she was headed in that direction when her father came out on a stretcher being pushed by two EMTs.

"Dad!"

Frank saw her and made a face. "I told you not to come."

She looked at his stomach, a patchwork of gauze and bloody bandages and tape. The front of his jeans was bloody and red all the way to the shoes, which she did not recognize.

"You should see the other guy," Frank said, making a joke.

"That's not funny."

"No, it's not," Frank answered. "But he is dead."

"Joe?"

Frank nodded, smiling weirdly. "He set this whole thing up, a big hunt to catch me. I guess I was a little too clever."

She shook her head. "What were you thinking, coming all the way out here alone?"

"It's no big deal, really," he said, and she went to slap him on the shoulder when she saw blood there as well.

"Oh, that's not mine."

She walked him over to the ambulance and they loaded him inside.

"Want to ride with him?" one of the EMTs asked, and she locked her car and climbed in.

The ambulance pulled away, and she sat next to Frank's head. He seemed like he was drifting in and out of it.

"You guy medicated him already?"

The EMT nodded. "He was in a lot of pain when we got here. Sweaty, shaking. We gave him Proximid for the pain, and they'll give him more when we arrive."

She looked at his wound, which the woman was checking. It looked like a nasty cut, almost surgical, several inches across.

"Someone did this on purpose," the woman said, examining the wound even though the ambulance was bouncing around on the back roads as if she and Laura and Frank were all in a fun house. "Cut is perfectly flat."

Laura nodded, trying not to look. "Stitches?"

"When we get there. He'll need...I'd guess ten. But they'll need to check inside first before sewing him up. He might have internal injuries."

She went back to covering the wound, swapping out new gauze and compresses for the old, which were soaked in wet, fresh-looking blood. Laura looked away and turned to face his head. He was saying something, and she leaned closer.

"I'm sorry," he said, over and over.

"What?"

"I'm sorry."

She could guess why he was apologizing. "You heading out here to investigate this mystery clue of yours? That was a dumb idea."

"I know."

"How much did you drink last night?"

"Not a lot," he said, his eyes closed. "Okay, some."

"Were you still drunk this morning when you left?"

He shook his head, his eyes still closed. The EMT did something and he grimaced. "No, just hungover. Nothing this morning."

She sat back, relieved.

Now, it was a week later, and she was visiting him in his new place. He was laid up on the couch, watching television and scooting around the place in a wheelchair. He wasn't supposed to be walking anywhere except to get food, go to the bathroom, and get into bed, so he'd been sleeping on the couch to save trouble.

"And you're not drinking?"

"No, Laura, I'm not," he said, his face tight. "I told you, nothing since I got stabbed in the gut."

"Doesn't mean you need to be mean to me," she said, looking him in the eyes. "You were drinking the night before. After our celebration. And that affected your judgment. Nobody in their right mind goes out into the middle of nowhere alone."

"Actually, it happens all the time," Frank said. He made one of those faces that tells you the person thinks they've pulled the wool over your eyes.

But Laura wasn't her mother. She wasn't Trudy and she wouldn't be fooled.

"Bullshit," she said. "Mom might have believed you, but I don't. You've been drinking more and more since you moved up to Ohio. You think I'm an idiot? You think I can't tell when you're out 'looking for clues' or whatever you want to call it? Drinking is bad. And worse for you in particular. You can't control it. I've seen it happen a lot, more than you would know."

He looked at her but didn't answer.

"I can't...I can't have you drinking around Jackson."

She saw his expression change when she mentioned her son. Something shifted in his face from defiance to embarrassment. It was a subtle change, but a change, nonetheless.

"Okay," he said. "I promise."

"And you need to start going to meetings," she added. Laura dug in her purse and pulled out a flyer, setting it on the coffee table for him to see. "Alcoholics Anonymous."

She looked at him. "You can't control your drinking. There's nothing wrong with you, or wrong with that. But if you want to keep leading a productive life, you'll have to get it under control."

"I know."

She stood to go. "I like your place, dad. And call me if you need anything—I can run over and help."

Turning for the door, she made a point of not giving him a hug or a kiss. He was pretty smart and would figure it out. She walked but then turned before entering the hallway and out of his sight. Laura turned back and looked him dead in the eyes.

"Are you gonna be sober for Thanksgiving next week?"

His face clouded, as if he were getting mad again. Good. She was mad, so it was only fair. Instead, she could see him making a point of calming himself, and then he looked at her and said one word: "Yes."

"Okay," she said, nodding. "Good. If you're sober, you're invited to our place for dinner. If not, feed yourself. I don't want that around Jackson."

She left, pulling the door shut behind her. It felt harsh, but just the right amount of harsh. And Laura felt proud. She had stood up for herself and Jackson.

She loved her dad, but the drinking was getting bad again. If she had to blackmail him into getting better, that didn't bother her in the least.

She started for her car, shaking her head and pulling her coat tighter around her. A cold wind was kicking up, blowing snow across her path as she walked to her car.

"It's going to be a cold winter," she said to no one in particular.

AUTHOR'S NOTE

Thanks for reading this far, dear readers. Hope you enjoyed another fun adventure with that wacko named Joe Hathaway. He's a piece of work, right?

It took many iterations to get this story right, but I was happy to revisit Frank and his nemesis and see if they could work things out in an interesting way. I'm convinced that Joe was the kind of guy who would be obsessing about his vengeance, so it made sense that the man would go to "insane" (ha ha) lengths to plot some kind of elaborate scenario in which to get his revenge on the guy he blames for all of his problems.

Locations

As usual, Cooper's Mill is the setting for much of this Frank Harper book, and the town is based on Tipp City, Ohio, where I live. My wife and I moved to Tipp in 2005, looking for a small town after living in the frenetic suburbs of Washington D.C. It ended up being a very good decision—Tipp is a great place to live and a great place to raise our three children. We live near the downtown area and can walk to the bank, several restaurants, churches and a plethora of shops and activities.

Frank's "Cooper's Mill" is a fictionalized version of Tipp, with much of the city preserved and reflected in the stories. Public locations, like the parks, schools, and street names, all retain their "actual" names, so if you're keeping track, there is a real Kyle Park and a real Broadway Elementary.

In the time since I wrote the last book in this series, I actually purchased the local newspaper, the *Tippecanoe Gazette*, the basis for the *Cooper's Mill Gazette*. But the lady editor of the real paper is completely different from the Cooper's Mill version. They did used to have an office on the second floor of the Monroe Township building, highlighted in *Green with Envy*. In another strange coincidence, we recently opened an office for the Tippecanoe Gazette—and it's in the same building. Our new office is actually on the same floor and NEXT DOOR to the office from the books, which was the old Tipp Gazette office.

Portions of this story take place in Tipp City's beautiful downtown shopping district, of course, and at the Tipp City Library. There really is a "secret" parking lot behind the library, and yes, there's a great conference room downstairs anyone can reserve. Next time you're in town, ask to see it and maybe reserve some time to solve a complicated financial mystery.

Another location is Courthouse Plaza and the Miami County Safety Building next door. Courthouse Plaza features a beautiful fountain out front, and there's a great view from the fictional offices of Kevin Whitlowe on the second floor of the Safety Building next door. While you're there, check out the new Ramen place next door, Speakeasy Miso, or the Mayflower, an indoor performance venue that used to be a movie theater.

The Church of Xavier and their impressive compound don't exist, unfortunately, but I would guess their farms would be located somewhere near the Milton Mills quarry in Ludlow Falls, Ohio.

If you're looking for "Tips and Tails," the Walker's dog grooming place over on Salem Avenue, you won't find it, but if you're in the area, check out George's for a great meal. And alas the Salem Mall was torn down years ago—in my reality, it still exists.

There are, in fact, many small cemeteries dotted around the entire Midwest, and Ohio has its share of them. You might not even notice them as you drive around, but they're there. And be careful—one of the headstones might be booby trapped.

And a little plug—I own the local newspaper here in Tipp, so grab a copy of the ***Tippecanoe Gazette*** if you're ever in town. And I run a website dedicated to Tipp City, which lists all our awesome shops, restaurants, and area activities. It's at www.visittippcity.org. I've added a whole page to that website that's dedicated to Frank Harper tourists, listing lots of the locations featured in the books. Hope you enjoy it.

Until then, drop by our great little town, visit the coffee shop and the soap store and Coldwater Café, which in fact does feature a bank vault. Sugdens Furniture does, in fact, have an underground parking lot. And yes, there's a Freeman Prairie, and yes, they burn it regularly, or they used to.

I often get complements on how "real" my fictional town of Cooper's Mills feels—and I have to confess, sometimes I'm just describing the real-life setting here in town. I don't know if I'm clever enough to come up with Freeman's Prairie, a real place east of town that gets burned every year. And stay tuned for more "secret" locations in upcoming Frank Harper books.

Well, that's it for this time. Until next time, thank you for reading. Talk soon!

— Greg

About The Author

Greg Enslen is an Ohio author of thirty-six books, including nine fiction novels and a series of "Game of Thrones" and "Mr. Robot" Binge Guides. All of his books are available on Amazon and via Kindle, and several are available from his publisher, Gypsy Publications.

To receive updates, visit his website at www.gregenslen.com, follow him on Facebook or use subscribe to the "A Murder of Crows" Newsletter.

BOOKS BY GREG ENSLEN

All titles are available on Kindle:

Fiction
Black Bird
The Ghost of Blackwood Lane
The 9/11 Machine

Frank Harper Mysteries
A Field of Red
Black Ice
White Lines
Yellow Jacket
Green with Envy
A Splash of Scarlet
Welcome to Cooper's Mill (companion book)

Guide Series
A Field Guide to Facebook
A Viewer's Guide to Suits for Season 1
A Viewer's Guide to Suits for Season 2
A Viewer's Guide to Suits for Season 3
Game of Thrones: A Binge Guide for Season 1
Game of Thrones: A Binge Guide for Season 2
Game of Thrones: A Binge Guide for Season 3
Game of Thrones: A Binge Guide for Season 4
Game of Thrones: A Binge Guide for Season 5
Game of Thrones: A Binge Guide for Season 6
Game of Thrones: A Binge Guide for Season 7
Game of Thrones: A Binge Guide for Season 8
Game of Thrones: A Binge Guide to the Full Series
Mr. Robot: A Binge Guide to Season 1
Mr. Robot: A Binge Guide to Season 2
Mr. Robot: A Binge Guide to Season 3
Mr. Robot: A Binge Guide to Season 4
Mr. Robot: A Binge Guide to the Full Series
Back to the Future: A Binge Guide to the Trilogy
Emergency!: A Binge Guide to the Classic Series

Newspaper Column Collections
"Tipp Talk" Newspaper Column Collections: Years 2010-2013

Anthologies
Women Who Shaped America, an anthology of American Heroines